Playing God

Playing God

THE BIBLE ON THE BROADWAY STAGE

Henry Bial

UNIVERSITY OF MICHIGAN PRESS
ANN ARBOR

Published in the United States of America by
The University of Michigan Press
Manufactured in the United States of America
⊚ Printed on acid-free paper

2018   2017   2016   2015   4   3   2   1

A CIP catalog record for this book is available from the British Library.

ISBN 978-0-472-07292-7 (hardcover : alk. paper)

ISBN 978-0-472-05292-9 (pbk. : alk. paper)

ISBN 978-0-472-12151-9 (ebook)

For Jane Barnette

Acknowledgments

Without counsel, plans go wrong, but with many advisers
they succeed.

   —Proverbs 15:22

Woe to him that is alone when he falleth, for he hath not
another to help him up.

   —Ecclesiastes 4:10

There are many institutions and individuals without whom this book could not have been completed. The University of Kansas provided a sabbatical leave that allowed me to initiate the archival research for this project, as well as additional support for research assistance, travel, and photo permissions. In particular, I benefited from the university's General Research Fund, the College of Liberal Arts and Sciences Faculty Travel Fund, and the Kimbell Faculty Enrichment Fund, as well as additional support from the Department of Theatre and the College of Liberal Arts and Sciences.

Over my ten years at Kansas, I have been blessed by a vibrant community of faculty and students who have stimulated my thinking while themselves modeling the highest standard of scholarship. Those colleagues who have been most supportive of this book and its author include (alphabetically) Danny J. Anderson, Michael Baskett, Marta Caminero-Santangelo, Darren Canady, Stuart Day, Ben Eggleston, Iris Smith Fischer, John Gronbeck-Tedesco, Michelle Heffner Hayes, Nicole Hodges Persley, Randal Jelks, David Katzman, Paul Laird, Mechele Leon, Cheryl Lester, Eve Levin, Paul Lim, Tim Miller, Rebecca Rovit, Misty Schieberle, Ann Schofield, John Staniunas, Sherrie Tucker, Jack Winerock, Peter Zazzali, and Stephanie Zelnick.

While I draw energy and inspiration from all my students, special thanks are due to two Kansas graduates, Jean Bosch and Seokhun Choi, who helped me to shape my thoughts on biblical theater through a semester-long seminar, and whose deep knowledge of and commitment to Christian theology challenged me to confront some of my own assumptions about the performance of religion. Another former student, Scott Cox, provided research assistance in the early stages of the project. As an administrator, I have also depended on staff members Amanda Burghart, Karen Hummel, and Terri Rockhold to keep me organized enough to have time for research and writing.

LeAnn Fields at the University of Michigan Press has been a friend and supporter of my work for more than a decade. She never stopped believing in this project, even when I had doubts myself. Between LeAnn's keen editorial counsel and the outstandingly detailed and constructive advice provided by the Press's two anonymous readers, the process of revising this manuscript for publication has been a genuine pleasure. I am grateful as well to Christopher Dreyer, Marcia LaBrenz, and the rest of the Michigan team for their work on the copyediting, design, and production of the book you now hold. Of course, any errors that may remain within these pages are the exclusive responsibility of the author.

Most of the primary research for this book was conducted at the New York Public Library for the Performing Arts. I commend director Jackie Davis and the entire staff of the Billy Rose Theatre Division for their professionalism, and thank them for their unfailingly cheerful assistance in accessing the library's archival holdings. Additional assistance came from Deborah Dandridge of the Spencer Research Library at the University of Kansas. Among those who helped me secure reprint permissions for the photos in this book are Thomas Lisanti of the New York Public Library, Michael Schulman of Magnum Photo, and Richard Valente of Long Island University.

I was fortunate to have multiple opportunities to share portions of this research as I developed the book. For their invitations to speak and for their helpful feedback I thank the faculty and students of the University of Missouri at Columbia, Muhlenberg College, and Bowling Green State University. At Brigham Young University, Megan Sanborn Jones, Wade Hollingshaus, Rodger Sorensen, and the students in the Department of Theatre and Media Arts helped ensure that *The Book of Mormon* would not go unnoticed in my analysis. I am grateful as well to the members of the American Society for Theatre Research (ASTR) and the Association for Theatre in Higher Education (ATHE), most particularly my fellow scholars of religion and theater, including but not limited to Peter Civetta, Donalee Dox, Harley Erdman, John Fletcher, Lance Gharavi, Barbara Grossman, Ted Merwin, Carolyn Roark, Jill Stevenson, and Kevin Wetmore.

During the writing of this book, I have been humbled by the generosity and personal support of many friends and colleagues. Many times I fell, and each time one of these people was there to help me up: Josh Abrams, Jeffrey Anbinder, Christine Bial, Sara Brady, Adam Burnett, Lizzie Czerner, Bill Doan, Jill Dolan, Christin Essin, Carrie Fleider, Dan Gerstein, Brian Herrera, Amy Hughes, Jeffrey Eric Jenkins, Stephanie Anne Landers, Jill Lane, Scott Magelssen, Rose Malague, Deb Margolin, Carol Martin, Heather Nathans, Jennifer Parker-Starbuck, Jim Peck, Richard Schechner, Judith Sebesta, Artie Shaw, and Stacy Wolf.

In addition to being a dear friend, Cynthia Bates has been my "first reader" since our days as graduate students in the 1990s. Cindy read the entire first draft of the manuscript and offered valuable feedback, especially on chapters 2, 3, and 5. At a time when I most needed to hear it, Cindy assured me that there was, in fact, a book here.

My father, Ernest Bial, gave me my first copy of the Bible, a King James Version he had been issued in the U.S. Navy. My mother, Martha Bial, took me to my first Broadway play, and to countless more throughout the 1980s, including *Joseph and the Amazing Technicolor Dreamcoat*. Together with my sister, Amy Bial Heavenrich, they have supported and encouraged my adventures in theater, religion, and academia without reservation or judgment. I can't imagine a better family in which to grow up.

Finally, I thank my partner Jane Barnette, to whom this book is dedicated, and my daughters Anna and Emily for their boundless love and patience.

Henry Bial
Lawrence, Kansas

Contents

v   Acknowledgments

CHAPTER 1
1   Faith-Based Initiatives

CHAPTER 2
35   *Ben-Hur*, Biblical Fan Fiction

CHAPTER 3
62   In the Beginning: Theatrical Creations

CHAPTER 4
91   These Are the Generations of Noah

CHAPTER 5
116   Why Do the Righteous Suffer?

CHAPTER 6
141   Jesus Christ, Broadway Star

CHAPTER 7
174   Hard Job Being God

187   Notes

221   Bibliography

239   Index

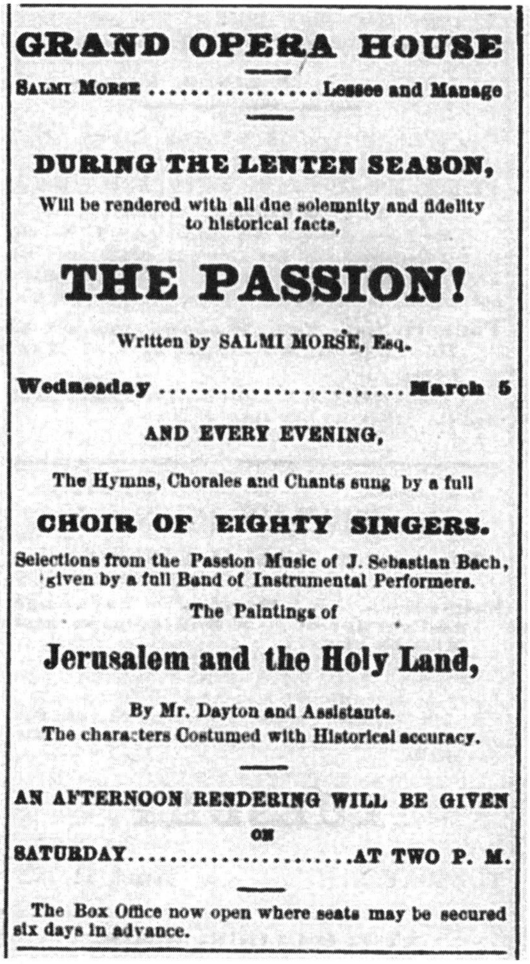

GRAND OPERA HOUSE

SALMI MORSE .... Lessee and Manage

DURING THE LENTEN SEASON,

Will be rendered with all due solemnity and fidelity to historical facts,

THE PASSION!

Written by SALMI MORSE, Esq.

Wednesday .... March 5

AND EVERY EVENING,

The Hymns, Chorales and Chants sung by a full

CHOIR OF EIGHTY SINGERS.

Selections from the Passion Music of J. Sebastian Bach, given by a full Band of Instrumental Performers.

The Paintings of

Jerusalem and the Holy Land,

By Mr. Dayton and Assistants.

The characters Costumed with Historical accuracy.

AN AFTERNOON RENDERING WILL BE GIVEN

ON

SATURDAY..................... AT TWO P. M.

The Box Office now open where seats may be secured six days in advance.

Figure 1. Newspaper advertisement for *The Passion,* 1879. *Daily Alta California,* March 1879. (Image courtesy of California Digital Newspaper Collection, a project of the Center for Bibliographic Studies and Research, University of California–Riverside.)

CHAPTER ONE

Faith-Based Initiatives

Probably few very devout persons ever go to the theatre.
—*New York Times* review of *Ben-Hur*, 1899

On April 16, 1879, three days after Easter Sunday, the actor James O'Neill was arrested in San Francisco for impersonating Jesus Christ. O'Neill, best remembered today as the father of playwright Eugene O'Neill, played the savior in *The Passion* by Salmi Morse.[1] Though the controversial production had its supporters, including theatrical impresario David Belasco (who helped stage the production) and the Most Reverend Joseph S. Alemany, the Catholic archbishop of California, the piece faced strong opposition and protests by two groups of Protestant ministers who eventually persuaded the city government to force the play's closure.[2] Following an unsuccessful appeal in municipal court on April 21, O'Neill, Morse, and other members of the company were convicted and fined, after which the show formally closed.[3]

Morse—whom Belasco later described as "an apostate Hebrew"[4]—then took his script to New York, where he tried unsuccessfully for three years to secure a production. Though he initially contracted with Henry E. Abbey for a run at Booth's Theatre, the announcement of the production drew protests not only from religious groups but also from the theatrical press. As Charles Musser details in his essay "Passions and the Passion Play," the effort to prevent the production found an unlikely leader in Harrison Grey Fiske, editor of the *New York Dramatic Mirror*.[5] Fiske, writes Musser, "was convinced that the anti-theatrical prejudice that remained strongly rooted in Protestant thought and doctrine would be reenergized around this issue."[6]

In other words, Fiske sought to preemptively condemn a project that he feared would damage the theater's attempts to achieve respectability. In addition to advocating against *The Passion* in the pages of the *Dramatic Mirror*, Fiske rallied theatrical and religious leaders to lobby the Board of Aldermen to ban any "play, performance, or representation displaying or tending to display, the life and death of Jesus Christ, or any play, or performance or representation calculated or tending to profane or degrade religion."[7]

Though the aldermen did not adopt quite such a sweeping ordinance, they nevertheless passed a resolution on November 23, 1880, that directed the corporation counsel (the city's attorney) to investigate "whether any of the laws now in force would be sufficient to prevent [*The Passion's*] introduction, and if none exist, whether the Common Council have the power to pass an ordinance prohibiting the introduction and exhibition of this play before the public."[8] Facing such intense public pressure, Abbey canceled the production days before its scheduled opening.

Morse did not give up so easily, arranging a staged reading for an invited audience on December 3. This reading received a detailed account from the *New York Times*, in a piece headlined "The Passion Play Read: Listened to in Cooper Union by a Small Audience. No One of Prominence Attends."[9] The article itself began, "If Mr. Abbey had been present at the Cooper Institute last evening, when Mr. Salmi Morse read his play of 'The Passion,' he would have come to the conclusion that he had acted the part of a shrewd manager in withdrawing from all contracts for the production of this sacrilegious spectacle."[10] Unsurprisingly after such a public judgment, Morse was unable to find another producer willing to back *The Passion*, and it appeared that the play would never have a New York opening. Yet the persistent playwright managed to secure a lease for a building on Twenty-Third Street. This he outfitted as a theater (which he called a "temple"), and in December 1882, he petitioned Mayor Edward Grace for a license. After not one but two public hearings wherein testimony was offered both for and against *The Passion*, Grace ultimately refused to issue Morse a theatrical license on the grounds that "it appears from your statement that the hall is to be used for the exclusive purpose of producing the Passion Play [*sic*], and I am satisfied of the impropriety of licensing a place to be used for such a purpose."[11]

As Morse continued to litigate his case, (unsuccessfully) petitioning the Superior Court for a writ of mandamus to compel the mayor to issue a license, he also continued with preparations for his production.[12] Most provocatively, in February he began to hold open rehearsals of the play—with the actors in street clothes—at his "temple" on Twenty-Third Street. When he proceeded to dress rehearsals, the police department intervened, preventing *The Passion* from continuing. In a last-ditch effort to save his production, on which he had apparently staked his life savings, Morse sought an injunction against the police department on the grounds that his "temple" was a private residence, not a theater, and therefore beyond the jurisdiction of the city. After this request was denied, Morse announced that he would give an open dress rehearsal in defiance of the ruling. A standing-room-only crowd (estimated by the *Times* at two thousand) heard the orchestra begin to play as the curtain rose on the first scene. No more than a few lines were spoken before Morse was arrested and the performance halted.

On March 13, the Court of Special Sessions ruled that *The Passion* was in fact a play, but that the open dress rehearsal did not constitute a public performance under the statute.[13] This proved to be a pyrrhic victory for Morse. He was cleared of the misdemeanor charge, but the determination meant that he would be unable to open the play to general audiences without the license that he had repeatedly been denied by the city. The company played a single performance unmolested by police to an invited audience on the evening of March 30, and Morse announced plans to stage additional performances where admission would be charged, with the proceeds benefiting the Salle D'Asile Francaise, a charitable organization.[14] This last gambit failed, however, and the benefits were scuttled. After some additional legal wrangling, Morse, exhausted and out of money, withdrew his remaining appeals and shuttered the production in April 1883.[15]

The Passion was the first attempt to mount a Broadway production of a play based on the Bible. It would hardly be the last.

In the Beginning Was the Word

This book is about Broadway adaptations of the Bible. As a communal activity, one that seeks to give spectators a transcendent experience, theater, we might say, aspires to the condition of church. Conversely, church, if not exactly aspiring to the condition of theater, recognizes its value in reaching, preaching, and teaching the masses. In the West, and especially in the United States, the Bible is understood to be the source of nearly all religious discourse. *In the Beginning was the Word. The People of the Book. Jesus loves me, this I know / For the Bible tells me so.* Broadway, meanwhile, represents both the highest and lowest aspirations of the American stage, the pinnacle of theatrical excellence and excess. What happens when a culture's most sacred text enters its most commercial performance venue?

Regardless of whether we regard the text as divinely authored, divinely inspired, or simply a human invention, the "Good Book" may be understood as a sacred performance text, a framework for an instructional theater that enacts the shared moral, ethical, and spiritual values of a community. As Israeli theater scholar Shimon Levy writes, "It should be borne in mind that the Old Testament was not intended only for silent reading, but also to be read aloud in public. In this respect, it can easily be regarded as 'dramatic,' or 'theatrical,' and certainly performative."[16] Indeed, dramatic adaptations of biblical texts have long been a standard means of delivering the Word to the masses, from medieval mystery plays to early modern *Purimshpielim* (Purim plays) to contemporary adaptations targeted for use in Sunday schools to epic pageants like Gerald L. K. Smith's *The Great Passion Play*, put on every summer in a four-thousand-seat amphitheater in Eureka Springs, Arkansas (and which claims to have played to more than seven million spectators since its opening in 1968).[17]

Such instructional dramas are rich and fertile ground for analysis for theater critics and historians. Dorothy Chansky, for example, in a 2006 article on contemporary Passion plays, argues that such religious dramas can be seen as a significant example of theater for social change, activism, and community formation. Depending on the denomination producing the play, we could even regard them as "minority theater." Similarly, John Fletcher's *Preaching to Convert: Evangelical Outreach and Performance Activism in a Secular Age* (2013)[18] explores how religious performances productively challenge scholars who advocate for socially efficacious theater to confront their own biases and assumptions. Medievalist Claire Sponsler's *Ritual Imports: Performing Medieval Drama in America* (2004) demonstrates how communities in the United States have used biblical dramas to reimagine their ethnic, religious, and national identities in relation to an imagined European past.[19]

While indebted to these and other prior studies, this book tackles a slightly different question. I am less concerned with how faith groups employ theatrical means in the service of religion than with how secular theater artists use religious texts—specifically the Bible—in the service of the theatrical endeavor. For a half-century or more, theater practitioners have searched, in one way or another, for what director Peter Brook, writing in 1968, called "The Holy Theatre." Though Brook did not refer to scriptural theater per se, his notion of "The Theatre of the Invisible-Made-Visible," of the stage as "a place where the invisible can appear,"[20] clearly seeks to bring the apparatus of the stage closer to the realm of ritual. Or as avant-garde director Lee Breuer, writing in the 1980s, put it, "Theatre's language comes up from the street and down from the church and meets."[21] It should therefore be neither surprising nor insignificant when a theater artist chooses to adapt the Bible for the stage.

Moreover, just as modern literary study has strong genealogical ties to the tradition of biblical exegesis, biblical theater criticism might offer a model that can be applied to all of theater studies. After all, some of the central tensions of theatrical representation—reality and illusion, fate and free will, originality and representation—are brought forward and heightened in the biblical play. Or to put it another way, the Bible-based drama doesn't have the luxury of shying away from two of contemporary theater's greatest problems: the crisis of representation and the impossibility of transcendence. It must confront them.

Take off your shoes, for the ground on which you stand is holy.[22]

The Biblical Play as Profitable Feature of Theatrical Enterprise: A Brief Historical Overview

For the purposes of this study, the biblical play is defined as a drama—musical or nonmusical—that takes its central plotline from the Bible (Old or New Testament). This includes plays such as *Noah* (1935) and *The Flowering Peach* (1954) that explicitly dramatize biblical stories, as well as traditional miracle plays given Broadway productions (e.g., David Belasco's 1929 production of *The Freiburg Passion Play*). It also includes plays that we might call Bible "fan fiction"—works that borrow from or refer to the imaginative universe of the Bible to tell new stories about its characters. The scriptures, after all, are not comprehensive biographies. For example, Exodus 2:10 states, "When the child grew older, she took him to Pharaoh's daughter and he became her son. She named him Moses, saying, 'I drew him out of the water.'" Exodus 2:11 begins, "One day, after Moses had grown up . . ."[23] What happens in between the verses? There is a long tradition in both religion and the arts that attempts to imagine the answer, often in the hope that such exegesis will enhance our understanding of the original text. In the realm of Broadway productions, Mary Magdalene comes in most often for this expanded treatment, as in Paul Heyse's *Mary of Magdala* (1902) and Robert McLaughlin's *The Eternal Magdalene* (1915). Judas is also a popular choice, featuring prominently in both of the previously mentioned works, as well as plays such as John DeKay's *Judas* (1910) or Walter Ferris and Basil Rathbone's *Judas* (1929). There is a second-order of "fan fiction": plays that use the Bible's setting to tell stories that are religious in nature but centered around characters not mentioned in the scriptures. In this category I place Wilson Barrett's *The Sign of the Cross* (1896), William Young's *Ben-Hur* (1899), and two different stage adaptations of Henry Sienkiewicz's 1895 best seller *Quo Vadis*.

Not included in this study are plays in which the Bible is merely quoted, invoked, or evoked in a manner incidental to the play's central action. Hence I do not here consider a show such as Jerome K. Jerome's *The Passing of the Third Floor Back* (1909; revived 1913), a drama in which a mysterious character who may or may not be Jesus Christ (but whom most critics would call a "Christ figure") helps the residents of a contemporary boardinghouse find redemption for their sins. Nor do I consider a play simply because one brother finds himself pitted against another, even if the text refers to them as similar to Cain and Abel. Slightly further afield, it has occasionally (e.g., during the height of the *Ben-Hur* vogue at the turn of the twentieth century) been fashionable for playwrights and producers to attach biblical titles (e.g., *A Coat of Many Colors*) to shows with minimal biblical content, perhaps as a way to "class up" an otherwise undistinguished production.[24] Such works are obviously beyond the scope of this study, though the frequent recurrence of the practice points to the powerful hold that the Bible has on the public imagination.

A trickier proposition is the play in which the narrative outline of the Bible is followed loosely, and in which the characters and settings have been updated to the present day. Examples include Thornton Wilder's *The Skin of Our Teeth* (1942; revived 1955 and 1975), in which the story of Mr. and Mrs. George Antrobus bears a strong and not accidental resemblance to that of Adam and Eve, and Neil Simon's *God's Favorite* (1974), a retelling of the Job story set on contemporary Long Island. For purposes of this book, I have chosen to exclude *The Skin of Our Teeth* while including *God's Favorite*. Wilder invokes the Adam and Eve narrative not as an exploration of the book of Genesis but as a convenient way to illustrate that the Antrobus family stands in for all humanity. The latter part of the play diverges sharply from the Bible's narrative. By contrast, Simon's adaptation, though it takes a number of aesthetic liberties with the book of Job (most notably, moving the action to contemporary Long Island), seems clearly intended as an exploration of the biblical narrative as such.

If we use this definition of the biblical play, there have been (as of this writing) 121 theatrical productions of such plays since the dawn of Broadway's modern era in the 1890s.[25] This figure represents ninety-one new-to-Broadway plays and thirty revivals. As noted above, the catalog begins in 1896 with Wilson Barrett's *The Sign of the Cross*, "a four-act drama the scene of which is laid in Rome at the time of the persecution of Christians under Nero,"[26] which apparently holds the distinction of being the first biblical drama to be produced on Broadway. After a successful run at the Lyric Theatre in London, the play transferred to New York's Knickerbocker Theatre in 1896, where it was produced by Charles Frohman and Frank W. Sanger. Though Frohman and Sanger were almost certainly aware of Morse's catastrophic failure with *Passion Play*, it appears that Barrett's success in London earned *The Sign of the Cross* a chance. It no doubt helped that it was not, in fact, a passion play and did not include Jesus as an onstage character. Rather, the play depicts the conversion to Christianity and eventual martyrdom of a Roman noble, Marcus Superbus (played by Charles Dalton). *The Sign of the Cross* received lukewarm notices, and closed in less than three weeks, though it evidently enjoyed a long life "on the road." As a 1906 *New*

York Times article notes, "'The Sign of the Cross' is known practically wherever English-speaking theatrical companies have traveled."[27] This same *Times* article credits 1899's *Ben-Hur* with starting "what may be called the revival of religious drama" on the New York stage.[28] Dramatized by William Young from Lew Wallace's famous 1880 novel and featuring original music by Edgar Stillman Kelley, *Ben-Hur* opened in November 1899 with a reported budget of $100,000, a remarkable figure for the time. It ran 194 performances and was revived twice, in 1900 and in 1911. Perhaps in an attempt to capitalize on the success of *Ben-Hur*, producers offered not one but two adaptations of Henry Sienkiewicz's novel *Quo Vadis*, based on the apocryphal Acts of Peter, in 1900. Neither was very successful. Of the first, authorized, adaptation the *New York Times* noted, "Not very much . . . need be said now or at any other time about Miss Gilder's dramatization of 'Quo Vadis,'"[29] and the show closed after only thirty-two performances. The second, unauthorized adaptation of *Quo Vadis* also ran only thirty-two performances, but as it opened at the end of December, it did ensure that the Bible would be represented on Broadway in 1901 as well. By the end of 1906, the biblical play had been recognized as a genre, as evidenced in an unsigned feature headlined "Religious Subjects as Matter for Dramatic Treatment" in the *New York Times* that bore the secondary headline, "The Biblical Play a Profitable Feature of Theatrical Enterprise."[30] Citing the "immense vogue of 'Ben-Hur,'"[31] the author focused especially on the opportunities the biblical milieu provided for spectacular stagecraft. "The age of the Old Testament," noted the newspaper, "with its barbaric splendor, affords a wonderful field for the ambitious producer. The era of the dawn of Christianity . . . is no less picturesque."[32]

Indeed the first decade of the twentieth century would prove a boom-time for biblical plays, featuring more than two dozen productions, including DeKay's *Judas*, which starred Sarah Bernhardt in the title role. The flow of Bible stories to Broadway continued at a steady but unspectacular pace—roughly one per year—through the beginning of World War II, but there were only a handful of commercial successes, most notably Marc Connelly's *The Green Pastures*, which ran 640 performances from 1930 to 1931. After the war, the pickings get noticeably slimmer, even when considered as a percentage of Broadway offerings. The 1950s saw only three Bible shows, all from the Old Testament—Clifford Odets's *The Flowering Peach* (1954, Genesis), Archibald Macleish's *J.B.* (1958, Job), and Christopher Fry's *The Firstborn* (1958, Exodus), featuring original songs by Leonard Bernstein and produced as a limited engagement under the auspices of the America-Israel Cultural Foundation in honor of the tenth anniversary of Israeli independence. The 1960s saw two hits, Paddy Chayefsky's *Gideon* (1961) and the Bock and Harnick musical *The Apple Tree* (1966); and two flops, the musicals *I'm Solomon* (1968) and *Trumpets of the Lord* (1969, adapted from James Weldon Johnson's 1927 book of sermons, *God's Trombones*). The 1970s saw a slight resurgence (eight shows), led by 1970's *Two by Two* (a musical adaptation of Odets's *The Flowering Peach*) and the cultural phenomenon that was *Jesus Christ Superstar* (1971). Since 1980, the Bible has been even rarer on Broadway, with only four original productions, including three musicals: *Joseph and the Amazing Technicolor Dreamcoat* (1982), *Don't Get God Started* (1987), and *King David* (1997), and a handful of revivals, including *Joseph* (1993) and *Superstar* (1977, 2000, 2012), as well as a limited-engagement staged reading of Oscar Wilde's *Salome* featuring Al Pacino and Marisa Tomei (1992). There was a short-lived revival of *The Apple Tree* at Roundabout / Studio 54 in 2006, and a revival of *Godspell* that opened at the Circle in the Square in October 2011, under the direction of Daniel Goldstein, briefly overlapping with the 2012 revival of *Jesus Christ Superstar*. Colm Tóibín's monologic adaptation of his own novel *The Testament of Mary*—about Mary, the mother of Jesus—played a limited engagement in spring 2013, with Fiona Shaw in the title role.

While this book does not provide an exhaustive catalog of all Broadway's biblical adaptations, some brief quantitative observations may be of interest: Overall, the New Testament is slightly more common as a source than is the Old Testament (though several shows draw on both). Since World War II, however, the Old Testament has the edge. Perhaps in the aftermath of the Holocaust, Jewish producers were more reluctant to stage the Passion narratives that were popular earlier in the century.[33] Within the Old Testament, the book of Genesis is the most common source text, but Broadway shows have also been adapted from Exodus, Joshua, Judges, 1 Samuel, 1 Kings, Job, and Esther, as well as books some consider Apocrypha (Judith and Tobit). Due to narrative overlap among the four gospels, it is often difficult to identify whether a New Testament–based play is based primarily on, say, the book of Mark as opposed to the book of John. It is worth noting, however, that several plays, particularly those early epics such as *Ben-Hur* and *Quo Vadis*, have their origins in apocryphal texts such as the Acts of Peter (*Quo Vadis*) or modern historical fiction inspired by the Pauline epistles (*Ben-Hur*).

Approximately two dozen, or about one-quarter, of the biblical plays in Broadway history are musicals, with the proportion of musicals to straight plays growing noticeably higher in recent years. The most successful shows at the box office (based on length of initial run) are the Tim Rice / Andrew Lloyd Webber hits, *Superstar* and *Joseph*, at over seven hundred performances each, followed closely by *The Green Pastures* at 640. The longest running nonmusical biblical play is *J.B.* (364 performances), followed by *Gideon* (238).

This book focuses on a selection of eleven works that achieved significant commercial success or critical recognition or both, as well as a handful of notable "flops" that highlight the difficulties in adapting the Bible for the Broadway stage. While commercial success—as measured in length of run, subsequent national tours, and so on—is not a measure of quality in the literary or aesthetic sense, it indicates the degree to which a given production captured the attention and imagination of audiences in its era. Moreover, because Broadway theater is first and foremost a commercial enterprise, ticket sales and the like are measures that producers themselves use to evaluate whether a particular production achieved its ends. As David Savran reminds us, "Any history of production is inextricably linked to modes of consumption, which are especially important . . . [when] patronized (at different times in different venues) by fractions of the working, lower-middle, upper-middle, and even upper classes."[34] Further, to the degree that Broadway has always been a business in which success encourages imitation, knowing which shows "did business" is helpful in understanding choices made by subsequent productions. Finally, it is axiomatic that a production that enjoyed a long run reached more audience members—and therefore presumably had more cultural influence—than one that closed quickly.

At the same time, critical attention serves as a rough proxy for "prestige" or "importance." In particular, critical recognition in the form of Tony Awards or Pulitzer Prizes grants a production a kind of canonical status that ensures it will be remembered within the annals of theater history. Whatever one thinks of *The Green Pastures*, for example, its status as the winner of the 1930 Pulitzer Prize for Drama means that it "deserves" to be mentioned in the same breath as such essential works as *Death of a Salesman* (1949) and *Angels in America* (1993).

Ways of Seeing

Each of these biblical dramas invites inquiry and response along several intersecting axes. Like any theatrical performance, there is an aesthetic element, in terms of both audience response and critical reflection. Similarly, as the play does not exist in a social vacuum, there are questions of context that are informed by ideology, representation, and so on. This is to say that the history and criticism of the biblical play is to some degree simply an exercise in theater history and criticism as those fields are currently practiced. In examining the biblical play as a distinct genre, however, we bring several other issues into play, demonstrating that a thematically oriented study provides a strong platform for intersectional and interdisciplinary analysis.

Perhaps the most urgent question is whether the biblical drama is understood to be primarily a religious exercise or a theatrical one. There is a tradition in both Judaism and Christianity (as well as other faiths that are not Bible-based) that allows—in limited and carefully prescribed ways—for the theatrical presentation of sacred narratives as a religious practice. In the Western tradition, some of our earliest examples of the drama include medieval dramatizations of the Easter liturgy (the so-called *Quem quaeritis* trope) and other biblical stories. These plays were intended in part as instructional dramas, sharing the biblical narrative with those who might not choose (or might not be able) to read it themselves.[35] This is also true of Jewish *Purimshpilim* that retell the story of the book of Esther.[36] In the Catholic tradition, the annual recitation of the stations of the cross can be read (and has oft been expanded to) a processional Passion play.[37] Meanwhile the children's nativity pageant has become a ritualized part of many churches' Christmas celebrations. As Megan Sanborn Jones and others have demonstrated,[38] the Church of Jesus Christ of Latter-day Saints (the Mormon Church) has long used reenactments of its religious history as a means of communicating the community's spiritual values to the next generation.

In the more recent context of the United States during the period of this study (1896–2014), the acceptance of such religious dramas by traditional faith-based communities has tended to be understood as a special exemption. That is to say, the drama is ordinarily understood as a secular genre, the theater as a secular space. *Probably few very devout persons ever go to the theater.* In part this is because American theater—especially in urban areas—enjoyed its largest growth during a period of maximum integration and so became co-opted (or positioned itself) as a vehicle for intercultural encounter and "melting pot" assimilation. This worked both at the level of the immigrant audience, for whom the theater provided lessons in how to be American, and at the level of the immigrant artists, many of whom used the theater as a way of escaping the ethnic and religious ghettos.[39]

In fact, the American theater has long made a virtue of its secularism. That is to say that the U.S. theater industry, originally the province of religious minorities (first Irish Catholic, then Jewish) has historically valorized religious neutrality if not always tolerance.[40] This is strategic. Touring is critical to the economics of theater, and the United States is a religiously diverse market; so it makes sense to keep religion out of the conversation as much as possible. Yet it is also representative of a genuine aspiration of theater people toward tolerance and religious freedom. The theater has often been a vehicle for nation-building.[41] As a result, even people of faith who are drawn to it have tended to emphasize similarities over differences, as evidenced in the plays of (inter alia) Jewish playwright M. M. Noah (*She Would Be a Soldier*) and Protestant playwright Anne Nichols (*Abie's Irish Rose*).[42]

Nevertheless, the world of aesthetic performance is frequently positioned as antithetical to the religious tradition. Even as the industry sees itself as *secular* (positive), many faith-based communities see the theater as *profane*, a site of sin and iniquity. This is partly due to business practices (most urban theaters were open on the Sabbath),[43] partly due to a perception about who participated in the theater (Jews, homosexuals, women of questionable virtue), and partly due to ontological objections (the display of the body, the frivolousness of subject matter). Hence there is a long antitheatrical tradition among U.S. religions. In some Jewish communities, theater other than Purim plays (which are presented in a strictly carnivalesque context) was forbidden (or at least forbidden for women). In many Protestant communities, theater was banned by local ordinance or relegated (as an undesirable activity) to marginal spaces such as tents on the edge of town. In 1884, Josiah W. Leeds, a historian and reformer associated with the Society of Friends (Quakers) published an eighty-five-page pamphlet titled *The Theatre: An Essay Upon the Non-Accordancy of Stage-Plays with the Christian Profession*, a volume representative of the broad trend of antitheatrical reform efforts that peaked in the late nineteenth century. Leeds writes:

> It will be the scope of this essay to show the adverse estimation in which stage-plays have been held by the best of men of ancient and modern times, and how local communities and States have, in very self-defense, forbidden them; that many actors themselves, conceding the demoralizing character of their occupation, have united in condemning the plays, whilst others of them—apologists for the stage—have been unable successfully to defend, as they have likewise repeatedly failed in the effort to reform, it, seeing that it "exists only under a law of degeneracy"; that an invariable accompaniment of stage-plays, and that which establishes the constant trend to degeneracy, is the dissimulation and violation of truth involved in the acting.[44]

Leeds's essay was widely praised by clergy of multiple denominations. It would go through several printings between 1884 and 1896 and was translated into German and French.

This perceived conflict between theater and religion long predates Leeds, however, and has long outlasted him. At different times and different places, organized religions have sought to ban theater activity outright, or else to place strict limits on who is allowed to participate, who is allowed to observe, and what subjects may or may not be dramatized. This history has fascinated many scholars, including but by no means limited to Margot Heinemann (*Puritanism and Theatre*),[45] John Houchin (*Censorship of the American Theatre in the Twentieth Century*),[46] and most notably Jonas Barish in the influential *The Antitheatrical Prejudice* (1981). Barish's concept of the antitheatrical prejudice gets a reformulation in Martin Puchner's *Stage Fright: Modernism Anti-theatricality and Drama* (2002).[47] More recent scholarship in this area includes *The Idea of the Theater in Latin Christian Thought* (2009) by Donalee Dox and *Catholic The-*

atre and Drama: Critical Essays (2010), edited by Kevin Wetmore.[48] By looking at biblical adaptations on the Broadway stage, my study builds on that scholarly tradition to explore the many ways the tensions between theater and religion manifest in a popular commercial environment.

For those who regard the theater as not merely a secular space but a profane one, the biblical play takes on a heightened significance. It is perhaps no exaggeration to suggest that the encounter between the Bible and the stage can become an encounter between good and evil, or between the Word and the Infidel. When it goes well (in this view) the biblical play represents the just barely tolerated exception, the Good Play that brings into relief the moral bankruptcy of the rest of the theater industry. Even here, however, the commercial nature of the production can be difficult to rationalize, as the explicitness of the profit motive colors many people's interpretation. The irony of paying a top ticket price for the privilege of watching Jesus bless the poor is hard to miss, and when asked to buy a T-shirt with the Savior's face in the lobby it is difficult not to think of the moneylenders in the temple. When it goes badly (again in this view), it represents *a shanda fur die goyim*,[49] a debasement of the sacred text, a despoiling of the temple, sacrilege. It is for this reason that many religious groups have resisted the idea of the biblical play altogether, regardless of execution.

Conversely, many nonreligious or minimally religious people in the theater world also see the biblical play as the site of an apocalyptic struggle, but in the opposite direction. That is, the biblical drama may be seen as an unwelcome intrusion of a repressive or divisive set of ideas and beliefs into a space (the theater) that they imagine as a secular utopia.[50] We should also bear in mind that the assertion of secularism is rarely (though it frequently claims to be) neutral toward organized religion. As Janet R. Jakobsen and Ann Pellegrini note in the introduction to their edited collection *Secularisms*, the dominant understanding of secularism is central to a narrative of the Englightenment that "poses religion as a regressive force in the world, one that in its dogmatism is not amenable to change, dialogue, or nonviolent conflict resolution."[51] Such a perspective, in partnership with a modernist sensibility that is tied to the twentieth-century professionalization of literary and dramatic study and criticism, ensures that moments of spirituality in the theater are often dismissed as sentimental, naive, or juvenile. "Religion," wrote one reviewer of *Ben-Hur*, "like patriotism, like a political bias, is never more than a cheap means of effectiveness in a drama."[52] Charles Isherwood's review of the 2011 *Godspell* similarly opined that the production "brings to mind a somewhat less venerable but also popular dispenser of moral lessons to its happy flock of followers: 'Sesame Street.'"[53]

To the degree that theater and religion come into conflict over the biblical play, "victory" in terms of critical reception, box office success, or even whether a play gets produced in the first place is likely to hinge on which side sets the terms of evaluation. If the terms are religious or doctrinaire in nature, the theater is always at a disadvantage. Its partisans frequently lack the credentials or knowledge to hold their position in a theological argument. Furthermore, in a discussion of adherence to biblical teachings, a discourse that historically emphasizes the primacy of the original text, the adaptation of the Bible is by definition inferior to the scriptural source. Finally, as the theater is understood in this formulation to be an *immoral* space, theater partisans must defend their practice on moral grounds rather than aesthetic ones. So producers who wish to entertain, to make art, or simply to sell tickets find themselves forced into reimagining (at least for public relations purposes) their mission as educational and humanitarian. Such rhetoric appeals to the tradition of ritual drama to legitimate commercial productions: *We hope to use our play to bring this story to the masses, just as the medieval pageant wagons did. We hope to share the uplifting message of this Passion play— which had heretofore been available only to a select few religionists— with everybody who can afford a ticket.*[54] *We are excited to demonstrate that the theater can be uplifting as well as entertaining.* There is a rich history of biblical shows taking just this tack in marketing and public relations. While often effective, this strategy invites criticism from both ends of the spectrum. The religionists smell snake oil, while the secular wonder, Why Are We Pandering to the Ignorant? Moreover, if the theater is a sector of U.S. culture in which marginalized people—Jews, homosexuals, communists—have found themselves welcomed (largely) without hesitation, then the introduction of the Bible into that space may feel like an infringement on their personal liberty.

Such infringement is most often policed by the critical establishment, who insist on evaluating (and, usually, dismissing) the biblical play on aesthetic grounds. One early review of *The Sign of the Cross*, for example, declares, "The moral and ethical aspects of the production of 'The Sign of the Cross' may well be left for discussion another day, with the mere statement that the spirit of the thing seems to be sufficiently reverential to suit ordinary playgoers."[55] While at the opposite end of the chronological spectrum, critic Charles Isherwood remarks archly, "The agonies of Jesus are terrible to behold, of course, but on a far more trivial level one of the agonies of 'Jesus Christ Superstar' is the unhappy combination of Mr. Lloyd Webber's stick-in-your-head melodies and the often flat-footed lyrics they are wedded to."[56] By bracketing off the biblical narrative as outside the realm of criticism, the critic asserts that such concerns are not properly the province of theater at all, and that only aesthetic criteria should apply.

The theater is therefore free to do what the theater does best, and this focus on the aesthetic not only justifies the existence of *some* Bible plays, but also justifies any departure from doctrine by citing aesthetic necessity. A bit of collateral damage from this practice is that the biblical narrative is often positioned as Just Another Source text. From such a perspective, the biblical adaptation is not significantly different from, say, the adaptation of classical Greek mythology, or of a novel to the stage. As we shall see, however, this view significantly overestimates the ability of audiences to set aside their prior associations with the Bible.

Sharper Than Any Two-Edged Sword

The New Testament book of Hebrews warns of the consequences of disobeying Christ's teachings: "The word of God is living and active, sharper than any two-edged sword, piercing until it divides soul from spirit, joints from marrow; it is able to judge the thoughts and intentions of the heart."[57] This passage has been subject to a wide range of theological interpretations, but for our purposes it serves to illustrate the stakes involved (from a believer's perspective) in any attempt to stage the Bible: these words are not ordinary words. These words have a life of their own ("living and active") and may be interpreted in contradictory ways ("two-edged sword"). The way a reader (or adapter) interprets these words is a critical shibboleth or litmus test for one's faith and piety ("able to judge the thoughts and intentions of the heart"), and may even determine whether one is ultimately redeemed ("it divides soul from spirit").

Even for those who do not believe that the Bible represents the word of God (or that there is a word of God at all), the cultural weight such words carry is readily apparent. Secular theater artists may not fear God's judgment, but the judgment of public opinion is a powerful motivator, and as newspaper critic James Huneker once wrote, "Blasphemy—alleged or real—does not rhyme with box office."[58] In the case of the commercial theater, this necessitates at least some deference to religion. Or to put it more cynically: on Broadway, one must pay lip service to God in order to serve mammon.[59]

Hence, though they may not be asked explicitly, certain questions present themselves any time religious concerns are brought to the dramatic stage: To what degree, if any, do religious imperatives constrain (and inspire) the playwright's dramatic choices? To what degree, if any, do religious concerns motivate the way a given production then stages the playwright's work? Conversely, when do aesthetic considerations such as plot, character, language, or spectacle trump theological or spiritual ones? The answers to these questions will be unique for each given production. In fact, as the case studies in the subsequent chapters will demonstrate, it is not uncommon for a biblical play to be a site of conflict along just these lines, with fault lines springing up between members of the company, or between the company and the critics, the critics and the public. In the case of Broadway, because of its high cultural profile *and* high focus on commercial viability relative to other U.S. theatrical enterprises, the stakes of such conflicts are high indeed, whether measured in souls or dollars.

Some of these details can be considered at the literary level, including but not limited to questions such as: Is God a character? Is Jesus? Who is the protagonist? Has the playwright changed the sequence of events from that described in the Bible? Has the playwright invented new events, characters, or dialogue not described in the Bible? Has the playwright taken dialogue directly from the Bible, and if so, which version (e.g. the King James or the Revised Standard)? Does the playwright's interpretation of the Bible seem to betray an allegiance to any particular sect or denomination (or an antireligious stance)? We must focus equal or greater attention, however, on the questions that arise from the circumstances of theatrical production, a partial list of which might include: Will God be played by an onstage actor or an offstage voice? If onstage, what race should that actor be? What gender? What age? How historically accurate do the costumes and settings need to be? Such performance elements are essential to any study of theater, but even more so in the case of biblical dramas because many of the most critical and sensitive issues involve the presence or absence of the divine, something not easily gleaned from reading the play-script.

Performance-based analysis is also crucial because audience response is frequently shaped by the circumstances of production. *The word of God is living and active.* Dramas performed in a ritual context (e.g., the stereotypical nativity pageant) can be safely assumed to be motivated by the playwright's desire to spread "The Good News." Yet the more religiously observant spectator may be reluctant to even venture into the "sinful" theater district, while the religious playwright or director may have qualms about subjecting the divine presence to the profane stage. Salmi Morse's *Passion* drew objections not because it was anti-Christian in content or intent, but simply because it dared to represent the Savior and the Crucifixion. Making a similar point in a vastly different context, Levy cites the Second Commandment—thou shalt not make unto thee any graven image, nor any manner of likeness—to argue that, for some, "the closer we get to the core of 'The Holy,' the more impossible it is to theatricalize it, at least in biblical terms."[60]

Yet if moving too close to the divine risks blasphemy, moving too far from the Word is equally perilous. Believers regard adherence to the original as a demonstration of both spiritual commitment and religious understanding. So the further a play moves from the Bible in tone or content, the more doubts may be raised about the artist's good will toward the source material. Nor should it escape our notice that many theater artists, critics, and audiences feel this way about adaptations in general: that adherence to the source text is a sacred (or quasi-sacred) obligation. But the biblical play, wherein the source text is literally sacred, offers an intriguing limit case.

Faithful Adaptation

Linda Hutcheon's seminal *Theory of Adaptation* notes, "For a long time, 'fidelity criticism,' as it came to be known, was the critical orthodoxy in adaptation studies."[61] Hutcheon questions the "morally loaded discourse of fidelity," arguing instead for a three-part definition of adaptation.[62] The first part of Hutcheon's definition is "an announced and extensive transposition of a particular work or works."[63] This transposition can involve a change in medium (a novel adapted into a film), in context (moving the narrative from one historical period to another), or even in relationship to reality (the adaptation of a historical event into a fictional play). Noting that adaptation is a process as well as a product, Hutcheon also theorizes adaptation as a creative activity, one that necessarily requires the adapter to both (re)interpret and (re)create the source text. Finally, Hutcheon argues that adaptation is itself a process of reception, by which she means that the spectator or reader participates in creating the meaning of the adaptation through her intertextual association with the source. By acknowledging the importance of both creation and reception to the meaning of an adaptation, Hutcheon moves us away from an original-versus-copy understanding and toward a critical discourse that focuses on two key interactions: between the source text and the adapter, and between the adaptation and the audience.

Despite Hutcheon's theorization, the specter of the Original always (or almost always) seems to return to haunt the theatrical adaptation. Perhaps this is because when it comes to theatrical production, the play that is adapted from another medium (or another play) is always already a double adaptation. That is to say, there are (at least) two transformations/transpositions that happen to the story. First, the playwright takes the original story and adapts it into a dramatic text. Second, the director, actors, designers, and other creative personnel take the dramatic text and bring it to life on the stage, a process that we in the theater often call "interpretation." For example, we might speak of Peter Brook's *interpretation* of Shakespeare's *A Midsummer Night's Dream*. Sometimes, a director or theater company's interpretation moves far enough afield from the original drama that critics, audiences, or the artists themselves may regard the piece as an adaptation, rather than an interpretation.[64] Other plays—often based on classic works no longer under copyright (so that neither the playwrights nor their estates can intervene legally)—traverse a gray area between "adaptation" and "another play."

As we can see from figure 2, theater critics and practitioners tend to use differing terms to talk about the transformation/transposition

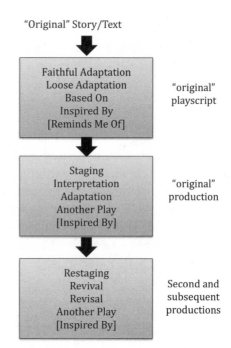

"Original" Story/Text

Faithful Adaptation
Loose Adaptation
Based On
Inspired By
[Reminds Me Of]

"original"
playscript

Staging
Interpretation
Adaptation
Another Play
[Inspired By]

"original"
production

Restaging
Revival
Revisal
Another Play
[Inspired By]

Second and
subsequent
productions

Figure 2. Multiple sites of adaptation. At each site, perceived fidelity to the original may range from high to low.

of the narrative, depending on the stage of the creative/production process to which they are referring. So in considering a play-script as a literary work of a solo playwright, it is common to speak of the "faithful adaptation" as opposed to the "loose adaptation": the former adhering most closely to the source text, the latter taking greater liberties.[65] The "based on" or "inspired by" subgenres tend to overlap the "loose adaptation category." The distinction between one or the other usage seems to vary based on the genre of the source text and the way in which the playwright (or the producer) wishes to position the work. Overall, the range from faithful to loose adaptation or "inspired by" should be regarded as a fluid spectrum rather than a rigid classification scheme. There does, however, seem to be general agreement that at a certain point there is a shift in kind, not merely in degree; at some point the work is no longer considered an adaptation at all, but is considered Another Play. This may be in the eye of the beholder, which is to say that the playwright may feel she has created an adaptation, while critics and audiences may feel it is an entirely different story.[66]

It is also the case that sometimes adaptations supersede and outshine their originals, to the point where the source texts are largely effaced, and where audiences and historians (at least, historians of theater) reposition the original as a kind of "pre-text" for the theatrical adaptation. This is especially true in the realm of musical theater, perhaps because the introduction of a musical score represents a creative contribution that rivals or exceeds the plot in presumed importance to the integrity of the work. Lynn Riggs's *Green Grow the Lilacs* (1930), for example, is today considered (if it is considered at all) primarily as the play on which Rodgers and Hammerstein's *Oklahoma!* is based. Such "original adaptations" also occur with nonmusicals. The history of celebrated playwrights—Brecht, Shakespeare, etc.— who borrowed plotlines, characters, and even lines of dialogue from previously existing texts or stories suggests that there is some level of creative genius that, when applied to the adaptive process, can make the adaptation into a New Work, which is different from Another Play in that it gains a kind of independence from its source while avoiding the charge of infidelity. The biblical play, however, does not have this option available to it, for regardless of the adapter's artistic innovation, the Bible is too powerful a symbol to be so effaced.[67]

The term "faithful adaptation" is a telling one—it speaks to the quasi-sacred status of the source text, and by extension its author. We might trace this sacralization of the source to a kind of genealogy: since the origins of theater lie (at least in part) in the performance of sacred narrative, the very nature of dramatic adaptation is bound up in the sacred. So even when the source is clearly *not* sacred, the structural primacy granted the original carries a certain power. Or perhaps it is a more basic philosophic premise dating back to Plato that always measures the copy by its presumed fidelity to the original. In this latter sense, the question of "faithful" is more like being faithful to one's spouse; it denotes a powerful, even sacred bond, but not necessarily an act of faith.

A more radical reading, however, might go something like this: any notion of originality—in art or in life—is susceptible to the problem of infinite regression, either the "chicken-egg" variety or the "turtles all the way down" variation. *Yes, but before that, what?* The

Western monotheistic faiths solve this problem (or forestall it) by introducing a God who stands outside of time and space, the Prime Mover. *In the Beginning God created the heaven and the earth.* Hence all subsequent references to fixity, to absolute values moral or physical, can be understood as appeals to Divine Authority, a fact that is more evident when we work the problem in reverse. Attempts to contradict the "truth" are seen, rightly, as an attack on the fundamental cosmological order of the universe, which is to say they are heresy.

If the original seems like a sacred text and the original author seems like God, then the attempt to first intuit and then execute the Author's Intent is neither more nor less than the Golden Rule—or, more appropriately, the "WWJD"—of the adapter. Consider that in the second-order adaptation, which is to say the move from dramatic script to theatrical production, the mainstream of Western theater in the last century has tended exactly in this direction. Even today, nearly four decades after Roland Barthes first declared the Death of the Author,[68] it is not at all uncommon for theater practitioners to identify their work as subject to authorial intent even when the author is quite literally dead. Michael Bloom, for example, writes in a recent directing textbook, "Producing a play in its afterlife requires significant interpretation because of the difficulty of divining a deceased author's intention."[69] Though the phrasing is ironic, the sentiment represents the common understanding: the director, actors, and designers contribute to the creative process through "interpretation," while the "author's intention" represents a kind of Platonic ideal against which all interpretations must inevitably fall short.[70]

Yet if we reject the primacy of the author, fully embracing the postmodern *weltanshauung,* then we lack a fixed point against which to measure our efforts. In poststructuralist terms, we've lost the "transcendental signifier" that fixes the stars in the heavens. *In the Beginning was the Word.* But if the Word cannot be trusted, whither then? Or what if the original does not beget the copy, but the copy (as theorist Walter Benjamin suggested) calls into being the Original?[71] We know that the copy is not the original, that the dramatic adaptation cannot perfectly reproduce the aesthetic, emotional, or cultural impact of the story from which it is drawn. This is theater's crisis of representation. To overcome this crisis, to go on making theater with full understanding of its limitations, requires an act of faith: the "as if" that is so integral to all theatrical performance. Or perhaps the true act of faith is the designation of any single original as a starting place, as a fixed point that resists turtles-all-the-way-down deconstruction. That the biblical play deploys such an act of faith in service of, perhaps, an act of faith, is a coincidence that bears further investigation.

Blasphemy, Heresy, and Reverence

The Bible both is and is not a stable original. Whether one can treat it as a fixed point is partly a matter of dogma, as some sects and denominations advocate belief in the text as the literal (and infallible) word of God, while others do not. Even among the denominations that believe in the Bible's divine authorship and inerrancy there are disputes as to whether the entire text is to be taken as a literal historical record or whether certain portions should be understood as metaphoric in nature. Denominations may splinter further over precisely which sections of the Bible are literal truth and which are metaphor. Further complicating matters are the many competing translations, and the fact that Catholics, Protestants, Jews, Muslims, and Mormons all claim the Bible as an authoritative text, while differing significantly on which "Books" are part of the scriptural canon.[72] In other words, the Bible is simultaneously an authoritative source for millions of people who treat it as a fixed and stable original *and* what philosophers call an essentially contested concept. As defined by Scottish philosopher W. B. Gallie, the essentially contested concept is *not* simply a point of irresolvable dispute, but a concept that causes disputes "which, although not resolvable by argument of any kind, are nevertheless sustained by perfectly respectable arguments and evidence."[73] Most notably, for Gallie, a defining feature of the essentially contested concept is "the derivation of any such concept from an original exemplar whose authority is acknowledged by all the contestant users of the concept."[74]

Hence the Bible-based play presents a peculiar problem when considering the relative social power of the "author" and the adapter(s). As noted, for a certain segment of the population, the author of the book of Genesis is a religious question. Judeo-Christian tradition has held that the Bible's first five books (the Torah or Pentateuch) were written by Moses (hence the oft-heard phrase "Five

Books of Moses"). Though there is wide variation in doctrine, the "mainstream" version is that Moses was merely a recorder, and that the true "author" was God, who dictated the text to Moses on Mt. Sinai. This origin narrative is preferred by those theologians who believe in the Bible as literally true. However, some scholars (including scholars of faith) believe instead that Moses did not directly receive the text from God, but simply compiled existing accounts that had been written by others. Sometimes called the "tablet theory," this theory suggests that the earliest books of the Bible were initially generated as eyewitness accounts by its characters: Noah, Abraham, and so on. In this narrative, Moses functions as a kind of dramaturg or editor (but not, significantly, an adapter). Still others believe that the Bible (as indicated earlier) represents a codification of an earlier oral tradition, and that the written form of the Old Testament can be traced to anonymous scribes in the eighth or ninth century BCE. All of these groups can be subdivided by religion (Jewish, Christian, Muslim, Mormon) or denomination (Orthodox, Reform, Catholic, Lutheran, Baptist), but this last group can also be subdivided into what we might call "believers" and "nonbelievers." That is, among those who regard the biblical text as stemming from an oral tradition, some nevertheless regard the text as sacred, while others do not. Where one falls on this spectrum of belief is likely a determining factor in how one chooses to regard plays adapted from the Bible.

For believers, the text is sacred, and any adaptation therefore runs the risk of blasphemy (giving offense to God) or heresy (contradicting church dogma). The adapter therefore is always already suspect, and the adaptation is likely to be seen as an unauthorized appropriation unless it is carried out by ritually consecrated persons in an appropriate religious context. Adaptations that explicitly represent God are the most prone to charges of blasphemy. It is here that theater's crisis of representation is most acute: if the best we can hope for is an imperfect copy, how can we appropriately represent the perfection of the Almighty? Plays that do not attempt to represent the divine presence are less likely to be regarded as blasphemic, but just as with translations of the Bible from one language to another, the transposition of the Word into the medium of theater carries significant risk of heresy.

For spectators of faith, heresy may be tolerable if the tone of the play is otherwise sufficiently respectful to God and to the faith. If the audience is composed of children or nonbelievers, for example, the expectation of fidelity to the Word may take second place to the outreach mission of the play. That is, if a play encourages its audience to engage with the Bible, then it may be regarded as positive despite its theological shortcomings. Responses by clergy members to *The Green Pastures*, for example, tended to praise the play's uplifting pro-religious message while skating over the play's loose approach to religious doctrine. On the other hand, if the play seems intended as a serious engagement with theological questions, then stricter scrutiny may be applied to the playwright's dramaturgical choices, as in the case of *J.B.*, which provoked so much debate among religious leaders that *Life* magazine invited three prominent theologians to write exegetical responses.[75] Of course, from a religious standpoint, if audience members feel that seeing the play obviates the need to read the Bible, then the adaptation—while not blasphemous—is clearly undesirable. Thus, perhaps surprisingly, those whom we might most expect to be originalists, people of faith, sometimes take a highly nuanced view of adaptation that echoes Hutcheon's decentered theory, though they are rather more prescriptive in which interpretations they will countenance.

From a secular point of view, however, blasphemy and heresy are meaningless concepts. One cannot fear offending a God in whom one does not believe. One cannot fear contradicting a religious authority one does not recognize. But one can seek to forestall the objections of the religious. *Blasphemy does not rhyme with box office.* As noted above, however, forestalling those objections requires shifting the terms of evaluation. Instead of religious terms such as blasphemy and heresy (which are also subject to denominationally specific variation), secular artists and critics speak instead of reverence. In this context, "reverence" indicates respect for, but not necessarily belief in, religion. By adopting a generalized respect for the beliefs of others, by performing reverence, the biblical play can sidestep the two-edged nature of "the word of God." Not only is such a culture of respect for others' religion deeply ingrained in Broadway history,[76] this attitude toward the Bible is common (though not universal) in American culture more generally. That is to say that even among those who doubt the Bible's divine authorship, the text itself is frequently revered beyond the respect given to secular literature.[77]

With respect to the biblical play, reverence is especially useful because as an aesthetic criterion it can be disconnected from the actual (or perceived) beliefs of producers, playwrights, directors, and actors. That is to say that reverence (or irreverence) is something that can be sensed in the performance itself. We can recognize it without making a judgment about the correctness of the play's theology or the piety of its creators. Moreover, while critics cannot readily evaluate a production's execution of faith (an individual choice), they can (and do) judge the performance in part on how well it balances reverence for the source material with other artistic considerations.

Ultimately, it is the recognition of sufficient reverence that enables some Broadway adaptations of the Bible to elide or ameliorate objections from religious leaders and go on to some measure of critical or commercial success. Yet too much reverence for religion may alienate secular viewers, while too much concern with performing reverence can lead theater artists to neglect other elements of stagecraft. Reverence may be a necessary condition for staging the Bible, but it is not sufficient to ensure success. The precise balance of reverence, irreverence, and entertainment value that is necessary to please both religious and secular audiences is often dependent on factors external to the performance, such as the artists' reputations, the publicity surrounding the show, and the specific social and historical conditions of its production, the zeitgeist. The case studies that comprise the remainder of this book explore some of the specific strategies by which playwrights, directors, and producers have navigated this complex terrain.

Spectacle, Authenticity, Sincerity, and Irony

Though it is tempting to historicize a production as a single gestalt, it is more accurate to think of a play as a complex constellation of choices in both production and reception, some of which shine brighter than others, but all of which are part of the performance event. Theater may aspire to a state of *communitas*, in which performers and spectators transcend their individual selves and join together in a quasi-sacred experience of collective awareness. That such moments of transcendence do occur in the theater is beyond question, but so is the fact that such moments are frustratingly brief and elusive. The live performance is an enormously dynamic and fragile system that depends in large part on the willingness of all participants to approach reality in a way other than the everyday. In the case of the biblical play, where transcendence inevitably takes on a religious dimension, the stakes are even higher, and the difficulty in achieving the necessary interplay between text, performer, and spectator is even greater.

In order to better understand the peculiar challenges of the biblical genre, I offer a model of four "performance strategies" that can, under the right conditions, overcome the crisis of representation and help performers and spectators achieve moments of transcendence: spectacle, sincerity, authenticity, and irony. These four performance strategies can interact with and blur into each other in a variety of ways, both concurrently and consecutively. Each production can be understood as a unique recombination of these concepts, its success dependent on how well that particular admixture captures the hearts and minds of audiences and critics.

Spectacle refers to those elements of a performance—lights, bodies, scenic elements—that exceed the written text, with a particular emphasis on those elements that convey magnitude or exoticism. This concept of spectacle is hardly new to the theater, yet as theater historian Amy Hughes points out, the significance of the spectacular is often elided in theater history.[78] Hughes's *Spectacles of Reform* "advocates for a consideration of spectacle as methodology: a unique system of communication, employed in myriad contexts, that rehearses and sustains conceptions of race, gender, and class in extremely powerful ways."[79] The book's robust theorization of spectacle and its association with reform activism (the abolition, women's suffrage, and temperance movements) in the nineteenth century demonstrates that the spectacular elements of a theatrical production cannot be dismissed as simply frills or amusements. Spectacle's ability to connect audiences to the performance in excess of the textual drama can significantly enhance the ability of a theatrical production to impact the popular consciousness. As scholar Henry Jenkins argues in *Wow Climax*, "Popular culture, at its best, makes us think by making us feel."[80]

As applied to the biblical Broadway play, a production's use of spectacle is similar to what Jill Stevenson, studying contemporary performances aimed at Christian spectators, calls "evangelical dramaturgy," in that it is "designed to manipulate the physical, rhythmic encounter between user and medium."[81] For Stevenson, the "evangelical emphasis on immediate, personal experience as a trust-worthy, even superior, source of religious knowledge" means that a powerful aesthetic response to a performance may well be experienced as spiritual, especially when that spectacle is deployed in association with a religious theme.[82] Thus believers may experience *Ben-Hur*, *The Green Pastures*, or other spectacular exhibition as a religious experience despite its commercial context. Furthermore, I argue, the same affective process may lead a nonbelieving spectator to a state of awe, a transcendent "wow" moment that is experienced as reverence.

Authenticity refers to an element of the performance that is perceived as real rather than representational. The horses in *Ben-Hur* (see chapter 2), for example, are not "playing the role of horse." They are, in fact, horses. As this example suggests, authenticity is often used in conjunction with spectacle. The "wow" factor of the theatrical spectacle is enhanced by the irreducible reality of one or more of its constituent parts. Put another way, an "aura of authenticity" can legitimate the use of spectacle by communicating that the stage is not necessarily a place of illusion and deception. Evangelical dramaturgy, argues Stevenson, depends on just such "devices that urge spectators to oscillate between 'presence' and 'representation.'"[83] In secular contexts, meanwhile, the presence of the authentic has frequently been used to move the experience of theater closer to that of ritual, to find something "real" that raises the stakes of theatrical representation.[84] This, too, can offer moments of transcendence and create a sense of reverence.

Authenticity is not simply about real objects and bodies, however. As folklorist Barbara Kirshenblatt-Gimblett explores in *Destination Culture*, authenticity can be located in a variety of sites within the larger performance: in the genealogy or training of the performers, for example, or in the provenance of the artifacts or methods used during the performance. The legitimating discourse can be within the performance itself ("the story you are about to hear is true") or externally in publicity, programs, and reviews ("The characters Costumed with Historical Accuracy"). Alternatively, authenticity may be inferred after the fact as a matter of reception: if the performance *feels* right, if the spectators are *moved* by the experience, then the performance is deemed sufficiently authentic. Significantly, Kirshenblatt-Gimblett notes the high political and emotional stakes involved in defining authenticity for performances that claim to represent a national, ethnic, religious, or communal group. Authenticity, then, is itself an essentially contested concept, one that fractures along many of the same axes as the biblical. Yet it is precisely because of this similarity that disputes over the biblical play can sometimes be ameliorated or elided by displacing them onto questions of authenticity.

Sincerity is the freedom from hypocrisy, that is, consistency between one's professed beliefs and one's actual behavior. Where authenticity refers to an inherent and unchanging quality, sincerity refers to behavior and must continually be reasserted. In the theater, where the characters and events exist only in the alternate reality of the play, sincerity is closely intertwined with authenticity, to the point that some critics seem to use the terms interchangeably. However, when the audience believes that the characters and events have some reality external to the play—common in the case of all adaptations and especially true in the biblical play—then sincerity and authenticity may diverge. The character of Mary Magdalene in *Jesus Christ Superstar* (see chapter 6) may be played sincerely, but may nevertheless be judged as inauthentic if her beliefs or actions are inconsistent with the "real" Mary described in the Gospels.

Like authenticity, sincerity is often associated with reverence. This may be because we associate sincerity with the social contract of respect for others. In his influential *Sincerity and Authenticity*, the late literary critic Lionel Trilling argues that sincerity is a preferable basis for interpersonal relations because in its insistence on "the congruence between avowal and actual feeling,"[85] sincerity prioritizes the needs of the larger society.[86] At the same time, to those who see human beings as fundamentally flawed or corrupt, sincerity often carries with it connotations of simplicity and innocence. Such innocence (sometimes referred to as "earnestness") can be disarming, as in André Obey's *Noah* (see chapter 4). It can also seem naive or saccharine, especially to those who prefer theater that takes a more "realistically" cynical view of human nature.

Irony is often the preferred strategy for the "sophisticated" theatergoer. Where authenticity and sincerity value consistency, irony prizes contradiction. Irony at its most basic can mean saying one thing and doing another, often as a form of humor or critique. It requires the audience to hold two competing ideas in mind at the same time: the thought being expressed verbally and the counter-point being enacted. At the level of the plot, we may speak of tragic irony, in which a character's well-intentioned action brings about negative consequences. We also use the term *dramatic irony* to refer to a situation in which the audience knows more than the characters; this superior knowledge both creates comedy and allows spectators to feel superior to the characters depicted. Indeed, when we step back to a critical distance, it would appear that all theater has a level of irony, for it depends in part on the recognition that the actors are pretending. This kind of irony can undermine theatrical representation, separating the spectator from the performers. Yet under the right conditions, irony can be a contributing factor in a transcendent experience.

"Wrestling irony within its muddling definitional field," notes literary critic Matthew Stratton, "presents many challenges to clarity, and the difficulties multiply exponentially with the addition of equally contentions terms like 'aesthetics' and 'politics.'"[87] Irony, in other words, is yet another essentially contested concept. Nevertheless, Stratton argues, irony does have a particular genealogy relative to American aesthetic and political discourse, and therefore cannot be ignored as an aesthetic component of the twentieth-century drama, biblical or otherwise.[88] For our purposes, let us note that irony is a moving target that shares affinities with our other key terms even as it appears opposed to them. If we postulate an opposition between intellect and emotion, then irony (thought) is opposed to spectacle (feeling). Yet if we reframe the debate along the lines of truth-value, we may find that irony and spectacle, both of which depend on dissimulation, are allied against authenticity and sincerity. Yet to the degree that both irony and authenticity depend in part on the artist or spectator's ability to stand momentarily outside of the reality of the play, both therefore stand opposed to (innocent) sincerity and (all-absorbing) spectacle.

Of course, all such binary oppositions are artificial. I introduce these terms—spectacle, authenticity, sincerity, irony—because, as this book will demonstrate, they offer a way to crystalize concepts that repeatedly come to the fore when examining the myriad attempts to stage the Bible as a commercial theatrical venture. The capacity of these terms to hold multiple valences also allows us to think about the concept of the faithful adaptation without reinscribing preexisting assumptions about either religious or theatrical fidelity. The complexity of their relationships to one another highlights the enormity of the challenge involved in "playing God." While this schematization may be applied to other types of performances, I offer it here as a way to momentarily apprehend, and therefore comprehend, the multitude of dynamic forces—religious, aesthetic, cultural, and historical—that shape the production and reception of the Bible on the Broadway stage. There is not, however, a magic formula that determines which plays succeed and which do not, which plays engender protest from religious leaders and which plays win their praise. While the following chapters identify some general trends and recurring phenomena, each successful adaptation of the Bible, and each failure, is best understood as a unique and complex assemblage drawn from multiple sources, speaking to multiple audiences, and advancing multiple agendas . . . not unlike the Bible itself.

And It Shall Come to Pass . . .

Chapter 2, "*Ben-Hur*: Biblical Fan Fiction" focuses on the earliest examples of biblical adaptation to reach the Great White Way. I have chosen to focus on *Ben-Hur* because the play's spectacular treatment of biblical subject matter in many ways represents the birth of the modern Broadway experience. Critics, audiences, and theater artists celebrated *Ben-Hur*'s use of a large cast, electric light, and innovative stagecraft even more than they took note of its religious source material (an issue that the chapter explores). In addition to *Ben-Hur*, this chapter considers an important precursor, *The Sign of the Cross* (1896), and one of the subsequent productions that appeared to attempt to cash in on the new vogue for biblical epics, *Mary of Magdala* (1902). What is striking about all three examples is that they are "inspired by" the Bible without being true adaptations. Nevertheless, they were each perceived as sufficiently reverent to satisfy most religious authorities. To explore this, I use the anachronistic concept of fan fiction to describe the dramaturgical strategy by which these plays negotiate the thorny problem of how to stage the divine presence without committing blasphemy.

If *Ben-Hur* represents the genesis, as it were, of Broadway's on-again, off-again fascination with the Bible, chapter 3 considers two productions that stage the literal (in both senses of the word) Genesis. Marc Connelly's *The Green Pastures* earned both critical acclaim and unprecedented commercial success with its epic retelling of the Bible as a Louisiana folktale, featuring an all-black cast and a large gospel choir. In addition to considering the social and political import of a Broadway production wherein the role of God is played by an African American performer, I also consider the ways in which music can create an experience that audiences may (or may not) perceive as spiritual. The remarkable success of *The Green Pastures* is brought into relief by comparison to a later, less successful retelling of the Creation and Garden of Eden narratives: Arthur Miller's *The Creation of the World and Other Business* (1972). Taken together, these works shed light on the relationship between divine creation and its artistic double, as well as the issues involved in having a human actor portray the God of the Old Testament.

The narrative counterpoint to the Creation story (Genesis 1–4) is that of Noah and the Flood (Genesis 6–9). Though Noah's story is also depicted in *The Green Pastures*, chapter 4, "These Are the Generations of Noah,"[89] focuses on four productions that take Genesis 6–9 as their central plotline. French playwright Andre Obey's *Noah* was presented to New York audiences twice in consecutive seasons (1935 and 1936), once with an all-white cast and the second time with an all-black cast. The comparison of the two productions, which came on the heels of *The Green Pastures*, further demonstrates how racial and national identity inform popular and critical understandings of sincerity and authenticity. The second part of the chapter considers Clifford Odets's *The Flowering Peach* (1954, revived 1994) and its musical adaptation *Two by Two* (1970), offering another chance to consider how music functions in regard to the task of biblical adaptation. We also see how audience perceptions of Jewishness (*The Flowering Peach*) and celebrity (*Two by Two*) can shift the delicate balance of spectacle, sincerity, authenticity, and irony.

This delicate balance is further explored in chapter 5, "Why Do the Righteous Suffer?"[90] which focuses on the book of Job, perhaps the single narrative in the Bible that most lends itself to dramatic interpretation. The Walker Portmanteau Company's presentation of *The Book of Job* (1919) briefly captured the public imagination with a production that was "dramatic, but not theatrical." Archibald

MacLeish's *J.B.* (1958) stands as a landmark of dark humor, and its critical and commercial success belies the retrospective characterization of the 1950s as period of innocence. Neil Simon's *God's Favorite* (1974) is offered as an example of what happens when ironic treatment goes too far, alienating critics and audiences alike.

Chapter 6, "Jesus Christ, Broadway Star," is devoted to the two biblical adaptations that stand head and shoulders above the rest in terms of commercial success and penetration of both the critical and popular consciousness: *Jesus Christ Superstar* (1971, revivals 1977, 2000, 2012) and *Godspell* (1971 off-Broadway, 1976 Broadway, revival 2011). *Superstar*, I argue, succeeds by combining irony and spectacle with a rock-and-roll score in order to frame the traditional passion narrative in terms of late twentieth-century celebrity culture. *Godspell*, by contrast, performs the same narrative in a mode of sincerity and authenticity as an explicit rebuttal to that same sociohistorical moment. The chapter recounts the process of adaptation that produced each musical, and notes some of the reasons for their differing levels of post-Broadway success: *Superstar* has proven more enduring as a commercial box-office draw, while *Godspell* has remained more beloved of amateur companies and actual religious organizations. This chapter also briefly considers the composers' Old Testament "encores" to their New Testament hits, Rice and Lloyd Webber's *Joseph and the Amazing Technicolor Dreamcoat* (1968 cantata, 1969 concept album, 1973 West End, 1982 Broadway) and Schwartz's *Children of Eden* (never performed on Broadway).

The concluding chapter, "Hard Job Being God," takes its title from a short-lived musical by Tom Martel. This 1972 rock-and-roll retelling of the book of Genesis clearly hoped to cash in on the success of *Superstar* but instead closed after just thirteen performances. This chapter considers *Hard Job Being God* along with another failed Broadway adaptation of the Bible, *I'm Solomon* (1968), as a way of revisiting the remarkable difficulty of balancing the artistic and the religious, the secular and the sacred, the ironic and the sincere in the context of biblical adaptation. When we only look at the successes, we might wonder why more playwrights and producers have *not* tried to build on the foundation laid by *Ben-Hur*, *The Green Pastures*, and *Jesus Christ Superstar*. An examination of some of the failures reminds us that any successful adaptation of the Bible is—like all successful theater—nothing short of a miracle.

Postscript

On February 22, 1884, ten months after he finally abandoned his attempt to open *The Passion* in New York, Salmi Morse's body was found floating in the Hudson River. Despite widespread speculation that a despondent Morse had taken his own life—or, alternatively, that he had been murdered—a formal inquest eventually ruled his death to be an accident. One month after Morse's death, his theater at 141 West Twenty-Third Street was leased by the Congregation of the Gospel Tabernacle to be their new house of worship.

Ben-Hur, Biblical Fan Fiction

Nobody will find any sort of offense in the stage version of
"Ben-Hur," unless he believes that sacred subjects should never
be treated in the theatre.

—*New York Times*, December 3, 1899

In 1879, Salmi Morse's *The Passion* was closed by police in San Francisco. In 1883, following three years of lawsuits, petitions, and public
outcry, Morse abandoned his attempt to produce *The Passion* commercially in New York. In 1884, Morse died, apparently by drowning
in the Hudson River, a fate that some religious figures of the day felt
was justly deserved. Nevertheless, by 1906 the biblical play was an
established fixture on the New York stage, with the *New York Times*
recognizing "The Biblical Play [as] a Profitable Feature of Theatrical
Enterprise."[1]

What happened in the ensuing years to so thoroughly change public opinion with regard to the biblical drama? The short answer is
Ben-Hur. This wildly successful 1899 adaptation of Lew Wallace's
1880 novel revolutionized the Broadway theater with its spectacular
and inventive stagecraft. While the critical and commercial success
of *Ben-Hur* may or may not be attributable to its religious content,
the play nevertheless would have a legitimizing effect on all attempts
to adapt the Bible for the stage, casting its halo over subsequent dramas and ushering in a new era of what came to be called "toga plays."
As theater historian David Mayer explains, the term was "coined in
derision . . . because these plays were viewed by late Victorian critics
and sophisticates as melodrama which articulated a simplistic mo-
rality, enacted formulaic plots detailing lurid events, and pandered to

a species of primitive and evangelical Christianity that cannot be located within the doctrines of an identifiable sect."[2] Yet despite these perceived shortcomings, plays such as *Ben-Hur*, Wilson Barrett's *The Sign of the Cross* (1899), and Paul Heyse's *Mary of Magdala* (1902) enjoyed significant success in New York and on tour, a fact that often proved vexing to mainstream critics.

For many, the true appeal of the toga play was not the celebration of early Christianity but the lavish spectacle of the Roman Empire. From this point of view, the biblical or historical themes of such plays served primarily as fig leaves, giving theater and film producers license to appeal to the audience's baser desires for sex, violence, and other forms of dramatic mayhem. This does not mean, however, that the "toga plays" lacked social or cultural importance. In fact, as Mayer illustrates, these spectacles can be read as reflective of American and British attitudes about a host of issues, including immigration, imperialism, and changing gender roles. Considering *Ben-Hur* as a "toga play" acknowledges the production's emphasis on spectacular imagery while simultaneously recognizing it as a descendant of early nineteenth-century dramas such as Robert Montgomery Bird's *The Gladiator* (1831) and Louis Medina's *The Last Days of Pompeii* (1835) and as a forerunner of the influential Italian *peplum* or "sword and sandal" films, most of which made no pretense of religious content.

I argue, however, that *Ben-Hur's* sensational impact on American stagecraft (and, later, filmmaking) cannot be so easily divorced from its religious subject matter. As this chapter will show, the original New York stage version of *Ben-Hur* was shaped specifically to address the challenges of adapting the Bible for the stage. The strategies employed by its producers set a template that would influence the biblical drama on Broadway for nearly a half century.

The novel *Ben-Hur: A Tale of the Christ* was written by Lew Wallace and published by Harper & Brothers in November 1880, the same month that the New York City Board of Aldermen passed their resolution against Morse's *Passion*. Called by one contemporary historian "the most influential Christian book written in the nineteenth century,"[3] Wallace's novel was unquestionably the most successful American novel of the 1880s. It would eventually become the best-selling American novel of all time, surpassing Harriet Beecher Stowe's *Uncle Tom's Cabin* (1852). By 1900, the book had been published in thirty-six English editions and translated into twenty other languages.[4] Until the 1936 publication of *Gone with the Wind*, the only English-language book that sold more copies than *Ben-Hur* was . . . the Bible.

Given the vast commercial success of *Ben-Hur*, Wallace was besieged with offers to license the novel for theatrical adaptation. Yet for almost twenty years, the author refused to allow it. Wallace felt it would be sacrilegious for an actor to impersonate Jesus Christ on the stage. Ultimately, the theatrical producing team of Klaw and Erlanger[5] came up with an ingenious solution: Instead of a human actor, the presence of the Christ would be represented by a tightly focused spotlight. Wallace agreed, and the stage version of *Ben-Hur*, adapted by William Young and featuring original music by Edgar Stillman Kelley, opened at the Broadway Theatre November 28, 1899, with a reported budget of $100,000, a remarkable figure for the time. The process by which the show reached the stage was the subject of multiple news reports, aided in part by the producers themselves, who no doubt saw such features both as free publicity and as an opportunity to preempt protest from religious groups. Klaw and Erlanger were, like Morse before them, children of Jewish immigrants and no doubt wished to keep their own religious origins from becoming a focal point for criticism. Three and half weeks before the New York opening, for example, the *New York Herald* reported a story under the headline, "How General Lew Wallace's Famous Novel Was Turned Into a Religio-Historic Spectacle":

> And no sooner was the announcement made in the HERALD that General Wallace's objections had been overcome than there were numerous inquiries on all sides as to how the book was to be treated. What scenes were to be utilized, was asked, and which were to be eliminated? Was it to be a Passion Play or not, and how were the stupendous mechanical difficulties to be overcome in such scenes as those of the galleon sea fight and shipwreck and the famous chariot race? And, it was asked, *How is the religious atmosphere of the book to be preserved without introducing characters and touching upon events the stage representation of which would offend the feelings of devout Christians?*[6]

It is noteworthy that the question of whether *Ben-Hur* would be a "Passion Play" is asked in the same breath as the question of how the stage effects would be accomplished, followed immediately by the question of whether the play could preserve a "religious atmosphere" without "stage representation" that "would offend the feelings of devout Christians." These three questions are closely linked to any attempt to stage the Bible, and the way that *Ben-Hur* navigates them is instructive. Young's adaptation is *not* a Passion play in the sense that it does not directly stage the traditional Passion narrative and is not focused on the character of Jesus. *Ben-Hur* is not authentic to the Bible, in the sense that it dramatizes characters and incidents not included in the Gospels, and could therefore be considered an affront to Christianity. Yet the novel avoided this charge in part by using a spectacular literary style to generate a sense of reverence. Wallace enhanced this sense of reverence by calling attention to the historical authenticity of many of the novel's details. Translating this sense of reverence to the medium of theater would require an especially creative use of spectacle, balanced by select markers of authenticity and sincerity.

Spectacle as a Theological Problem

In *Ben-Hur*, spectacle begins as a theological problem that producers must solve: How can the sacred be represented appropriately in the secular (not to say profane) space of the theater? How can human actors represent the divinity without committing blasphemy? Recall that Salmi Morse's sin, such as it was, was *not* that he had the temerity to stage the Bible. True, some religious and community leaders opposed any attempt to mix sacred narrative with the profane art of the stage, but the fact that some of the religious authorities from whom Morse sought endorsement were willing to consider his request at all suggests that the staging of scriptural narrative per se was potentially acceptable. The trouble with *The Passion* was specifically that it involved a human actor portraying Jesus Christ. Such a portrayal runs up against several distinct religious objections. The most obvious is that a fully realized human manifestation of the divinity may be considered a violation of the Second Commandment, which reads in part, "You shall not make for yourself an image in the form of anything in heaven above or on the earth beneath or in the waters below. You shall not bow down to them or worship them; for I, the LORD your God, am a jealous God."[7] Different faiths and denominations have interpreted this passage in a variety of ways. Some believe the prohibition to be limited specifically to idol worship (e.g., the golden calf), while others extend it to include all forms of mimetic representation regardless of subject or medium.

The veneration of religious sculpture and iconography, for example, is widespread among Catholics, and the Church has a long history of using drama for religious purpose, from medieval mystery plays to contemporary pageants representing the Nativity and the stations of the cross. Such mimetic representations of religious figures are much less common among U.S. Protestant denominations. In fact, anti-Catholic politicians and ministers have often used the charge of idolatry to support their opposition to immigration from Ireland, Italy, and other Catholic countries, especially during the period in which that immigration was most common: the mid to late nineteenth century. This explains, perhaps, why the Protestant establishment in San Francisco was unmoved by the endorsement that Morse claimed to have received from the Catholic archbishop of California. In retrospect, we also see that the attempt to justify the staging of the Passion by citing the precedent of Oberammergau's *Passionshpiel* (Passion Play) was misdirected. It seems likely that Morse and his erstwhile patron David Belasco, both Jews, underestimated the doctrinal difference between Catholics and Protestants. More cynically, nativist politicians (of which there was no shortage in either San Francisco or New York) may have seen in the censorship of the Passion an opportunity to appease their more ardent anti-Catholic supporters.

Ironically, in their resistance to the stage portrayal of Jesus, Christians found common cause with critics whose perception of theater was almost diametrically opposed. For the latter group, which included Harrison Grey Fiske of the *New York Dramatic Mirror*, a leader of the effort to prevent the New York staging of Morse's play, the problem with a human actor playing Jesus was not that he would be too deceptively Christlike, but rather that a human actor would inevitably fail to properly represent the divine aspect of the Messiah. Subject to human flaws and limitations, the actor could not help but portray Jesus as merely human. For those who believe He is the Son of God, this amounts to blasphemy. This distaste for what we might call a blasphemous failure of representation was the most commonly voiced objection to the Passion, one that Morse was never able to rebut, perhaps because he did not fully grasp the theological implications. Morse's actions, including scheduling a reading of the Passion as a benefit for a Catholic charity and attempting to have his theater relicensed as a house of worship, suggest that he was trying to demonstrate his personal piety, when what was at issue was not his belief, but his action (the blasphemous act of impersonating Christ).

The fear of blaspheming God by failing to properly represent Him was similarly on the mind of Lew Wallace, author of the novel *Ben-Hur*. Ultimately, it would be this line of thinking—not the "false God" worries of the Second Commandment—that would guide the dramatic adaptation of *Ben-Hur* for the stage and provide a model for subsequent biblical dramas on Broadway.

Biblical Fan Fiction

Though the use of the term is anachronistic, I consider Wallace's novel and the subsequent stage adaptation to be prime examples of what I call the "fan fiction" approach to the Bible. Most often associated with popular science fiction (e.g., *Star Trek*), the term *fan fiction* (or "*fanfiction*" as it is sometimes used) "refers to stories produced by fans based on plot lines and characters from either a single source text or else a 'canon' of works."[8] Such interpretive storytelling has been linked to the rabbinic tradition of midrash, oral commentary on the *Tanakh* (Hebrew Bible).[9] As Daniel Boyarin explains in *Intertextuality and the Meaning of Midrash* (1990), the Bible "is notorious for the paucity of detail of certain sorts within its narrative. . . . The gaps are those silences in the text which call for interpretation if the reader is to 'make sense' of what happened, to fill out the plot and the characters in a meaningful way. This is precisely what midrash does by means of its explicit narrative expansions."[10] For example, the book of Genesis makes no reference to Abraham's youth. The genealogy of the great patriarch of the Jewish faith is mentioned at the end of Genesis 11, and Genesis 12 begins with God calling to Abraham to leave his father's home in Harram and travel Canaan, where "I will make of you a great nation."[11] But why was Abraham chosen for this honor, and why did he follow God's call? One third-century CE midrash attempts to explain this by offering a story of Abraham's formative years, suggesting that his father Terah was an idol-maker, and that young Abraham rebelled against the practice of idolatry even before being called by the Lord.

In their introduction to the edited collection *Rabbinic Fantasies: Imaginative Narratives from Classical Hebrew Literature*, David Stern and Mark Mirsky write, "It is worth recalling that before the twelfth century the Hebrew language had no word for the imagination . . . the authors of most of the narratives in [midrash] probably would not have considered their works as being primarily imaginative or fictional.[12] In this respect, it is important to recognize that even in the modern era, different faiths may have different relationships to the facticity of the Bible. Some believe that the Bible is a historical record *and* one that has continuity through to today. *This is what the Lord did for me when I came out of Egypt.* Some believe that the Bible is literal truth but that humanity has suffered a fall from grace since that time. For these audiences, the men and women of the Bible, from Adam and Eve through Jesus and the Apostles, are larger-than-life figures. In either case, stories that dilate the narrative, allowing us to see the patriarchs and matriarchs as relatable human figures, are perhaps comparable to historical fiction and dramas from time immemorial. And even for a less religiously certain audience, the idea of filling in gaps in the biblical narrative has a certain appeal to a modern audience, for whom the rise of the novel has created a greater expectation for detail and character development. As Arthur Miller writes, "The [Bible] stories are told with the spareness of electrical diagrams, perhaps that's part of the fascination—you are left to fill things in, to create what has been omitted."[13]

It may be argued that the link between fan fiction and midrash is strained. After all, midrash is meant to explicate thorny questions of law or ethics, while fan fiction is primarily used for entertainment and community-building. And while midrash arises from a culture that encourages dissent and learned disagreement, its goal is ultimately to reach a consensus agreement on the validity of a sacred text.[14] Its attitude is reverent. Fan fiction on the other hand involves what Henry Jenkins calls "textual poaching"—taking existing narratives and changing or repurposing them for individual or subcultural desires—which may seem oppositional.[15] Yet fan fiction can also be motivated by fierce devotion to the original.[16] Conversely, Bible-inspired narratives such as *Ben-Hur*, *The Sign of the Cross*, and *Mary of Magdala* serve as entertainments, even when grounded in doctrinaire theology.

In this light, it is significant that fan fiction seems most common in the genres of science fiction and fantasy, where narratives tend to be utopian, always already invested in wish-fulfillment as a trope. The Bible is also a space of "impossible" stories—miracles, prophets, characters living hundreds of years. We might say, then, that the tradition of midrashic commentary (as well as other forms of biblical exegesis) offers a legitimating discourse for what I am anachronistically calling the fan fictional approach to staging the Bible, in which the structural similarity between secular fan fiction and religious exegesis gives the adapter of the Bible a certain kind of artistic license.

Ben-Hur: A Tale of the Christ

Lew Wallace would certainly have rejected the term "fan fiction," and "midrash" would have been a stretch, too. Writing from a position of Christian faith that included a belief in the Bible as a work of true history, he approached the task as a historian, meticulously researching the Middle East. As journalist Amy Lifson reports, Wallace "traveled to multiple libraries across the country to ensure he had the exact measurements for the workings of a Roman trireme. He provided detail after detail on the design of Persian versus Greek versus Roman chariots. He did everything short of going to Jerusalem himself."[17] In interviews, lectures, and his own memoirs, Wallace frequently used the depth and accuracy of his research as evidence of his faith. Only a true believer, he intimated, would rehearse the history and geography of the Holy Land in such detail. This kind of authenticity, in other words helped demonstrate Wallace's own sincerity. He did not just pay lip service to truth of the Bible; he treated it with genuine reverence. As we will see, this approach would be mirrored in the stage adaptation of *Ben-Hur.*

Nevertheless, there is a certain point at which faith cannot be adequately represented by recourse to history, and for Wallace, this point was the representation of "the Christ" himself. As David Mayer writes, "Wallace had already grasped that he could not fictionalize the birth and boyhood of Jesus nor venture without offence beyond what was stated in the Gospels."[18] Instead, he would have to describe the Son of God through "an intermediary character whose identity and potential for action had not been compromised by scriptural narrative."[19] Hence, instead of directly retelling the story of the Gospels, *Ben-Hur* (Subtitled "a novel of the time of Christ") uses as its protagonist a Jew named Judah Ben-Hur who is a contemporary of Jesus. The fan fiction aspect of the novel allows *Ben-Hur* to explore and expand upon the biblical narrative in some interesting ways, while remaining deferent to its central characters (Jesus, John the Baptist). Wallace created a set of characters (Judah Ben-Hur, Messala, etc.) who do not appear in the Bible, but who occupy the same narrative universe. They interact with scriptural characters, several of whom (notably the magi) are fleshed out significantly from the brief sketches provided by the scriptures.

In particular, Wallace's novel emphasizes the spectacular aspects of the "time of Christ." The desert landscape, the bodies of galley slaves, the sights and sounds of the arena, and other vivid images are described with a level of detail that is found nowhere in the Bible but is actually a common feature of nineteenth-century American literature. As Amy Hughes explains, using the Greek word for spectacle, "The *opsis*-centricity of US culture during this time reveals that Americans were tuned to images, to spectacle—to seeing sensation."[20] So, for example, the novel opens with a description of one of the magi, whom the Bible describes only as "wise men from the East":[21]

Judged by his appearance, he was quite forty-five years old. His beard, once of the deepest black, flowing broadly over his breast, was streaked with white. His face was brown as a parched coffee-berry, and so hidden by a red *kufiyeh* (as the kerchief of the head is at this day called by the children of the desert) as to be but in part visible. Now and then he raised his eyes, and they were large and dark. He was clad in the flowing garments so universal in the East; but their style may not be described more particularly, for he sat under a miniature tent, and rode a great white dromedary.[22]

This thick description is supplemented by another, longer paragraph in the following chapter, dwelling on the appearance of the man's face after he removes his headscarf. These descriptive passages are typical of the literary approach to spectacle that Hughes identifies, in that "they are presented proscenium style, focusing the reader's attention on the central characters; and they are rendered realistically, with an acute attention to detail."[23] For Hughes, this level of detail in literary description is an indication that nineteenth-century print culture tended toward the theatrical, and therefore generated a powerful affective response, priming the audience to be moved by staged spectacles. "The intense and cumulative character of the spectacle," she writes, "demands the viewer's attention and calls forth his affective response."[24] Thus before we can fully grasp the level of spectacle on display in the stage version of *Ben-Hur*, we need first recognize the spectacular scope of the novel.

The narrative is organized into eight "books"—not an uncommon device in nineteenth-century novels, but in this context impossible to read as anything other than a conscious imitation of the Bible. The first book, which describes the Holy Nativity as seen from the vantage point of the three wise men, or magi, is the closest in spirit to midrash. It takes the comparatively brief nativity scene sketched out in Matthew 2, and dilates the narrative, meditating in particular on the motivations of Balthasar, the Egyptian wise man. He is joined by Gaspar (Greek) and Melchior (Hindu). This speculation is enhanced by what Wallace believed was a faithful portrait of the political climate in Jerusalem, offering a fair amount of exposition about the Sanhedrin (Jewish religious authority), King Herod, and the Roman occupying government.

The second book introduces the title character, Judah Ben-Hur, a "prince" of Jerusalem (i.e., the scion of a prominent Jewish family), and Messala, his boyhood friend who is not Jewish but Roman. When the Roman procurate is accidentally harmed while passing in front of Ben-Hur's house, Messala refuses to defend his friend, and young Judah is sentenced to serve as a galley slave in a Roman ship. While the Romans are marching him to Jerusalem with a group of other slaves, Judah passes through Nazareth, where he first encounters Jesus Christ, a mysterious figure who offers him water: "And so, for the first time, Judah and the son of Mary met and parted."[25]

In book 3, Judah's ship is wrecked, but he is rescued by a Roman *duumvir* (admiral) who adopts him as a son and protégé. The young man rises through the ranks of Roman colonial society, becoming a prosperous merchant. Eventually he returns to Judea (book 4), where he reconnects with his father's old major domo, Simonides, and is able to recover part of his inheritance, but learns that his mother and sister have been imprisoned. The fourth book also reintroduces Messala, now clearly established as the villain of the novel, and Balthasar the magus (wise man), who tells Judah of his experience at the Bethlehem nativity, and explains that Jesus of Nazareth has begun to build a following among the occupied people of Judea. Judah's decision to renounce his adopted Roman citizenship and publicly claim his Jewish identity is motivated by this story of the Christ, but also by his desire to take vengeance on Messala, which he hopes to do by defeating the latter in a chariot race.

The fifth book frames the race as a turning point for Judah Ben-Hur, his first public act as a Jew since returning from exile. The race is described in extensive detail, spanning (from start to finish) nearly fourteen pages.[26] The chariot race, with its spectacular imagery and pulse-pounding suspense, would become for many a synecdoche of *Ben-Hur* and (as we shall see) a key to its dramatic representation. Even before the novel was adapted for the stage, public readings of this section (sometimes given by Wallace himself) were a fixture on the Chautauqua circuits. Though he wins the chariot race, Judah falls victim to a deceitful plot by Messala. Presumed dead, Judah goes into voluntarily exile in the desert, while his mother and sister are arrested.

Book 6 introduces the character of Pontius Pilate, now the Roman prefect in Judea. Through Pilate's intervention, Judah's mother and sister are released from prison, but they have contracted leprosy during their imprisonment and flee to live among the unclean beyond the walls of Jerusalem. Angered and radicalized by the fate of his family, Judah goes to Galilee to help build a Jewish insurgent militia to raise arms against the Romans. It is there, in book 7, that Judah's path crosses with "the Nazarite" (John the Baptist) and, eventually, with "the Nazarene" (Jesus).

In the concluding section of the book, Jesus returns to Jerusalem with Judah, and Judah's mother and sister are among the lepers healed by the Christ on Mt. Olivet. Jesus proceeds into Jerusalem, and the events of the traditional Passion narrative are retold from Judah's outsider point of view. Hence the reader does not see the Last Supper, but reports of Judas's betrayal reach Judah, and he is ultimately a witness to Jesus's crucifixion. Bearing witness is the final piece of Judah's spiritual journey. He realizes then that he should not fight God's divine plan, and resolves to spread the Gospel of Jesus. In the novel's final chapter, Judah is a wealthy Christian (or proto-Christian) who before he dies wills his fortune to build the catacombs in Rome that would later save Christianity during the Dark Ages.

Using Hughes's definition of spectacle, it is clear that the most sensational and affective scenes in the novel are the same ones identified by the *Herald* as those most difficult to stage: "the galleon sea fight and shipwreck and the famous chariot race." These scenes are the most spectacular because they combine epic scale and chaotic action with mortal danger. Though "visual effects, the cacophony of crisis, and the chaos of movement all contribute to the scale and intensity of the spectacular instant," argues Hughes, "to be unequivocally sensational, a scene requires a virtual/actual body experiencing fictional/factual peril."[27] In the novel, however, the peril that Judah experiences is always understood as an index of the even more significant, more extreme suffering of the Christ, which itself is described in excruciating detail:

> Then came the NAZARENE!
>
> He was nearly dead. Every few steps he staggered as if he would fall. A stained gown badly torn hung from his shoulders over a seamless under-tunic. His bare feet left red splotches upon the stones. An inscription on a board was tied to his neck. A crown of thorns had been crushed hard down upon his head, making cruel wounds from which streams of blood, now dry and blackened, had run over his face and neck. The long hair, tangled in the thorns, was clotted thick. The skin, where it could be seen, was ghastly white. His hands were tied before him. Back somewhere in the city he had fallen exhausted under the transverse beam of his cross, which, as a condemned person, custom required him to bear to the place of execution; now a countryman carried the burden in his stead. Four soldiers went with him as a guard against the mob, who sometimes, nevertheless, broke through, and struck him with sticks, and spit upon him. Yet no sound escaped him, neither remonstrance nor groan; nor did he look up until he was nearly in front of the house sheltering Ben-Hur and his friends, all of whom were moved with quick compassion. Esther clung to her father; and he, strong of will as he was, trembled. Balthasar fell down speechless. Even Ben-Hur cried out, "O my God! my God!" Then, as if he divined their feelings or heard the exclamation, the Nazarene turned his wan face towards the party, and looked at them each one, so they carried the look in memory through life. They could see he was thinking of them, not himself, and the dying eyes gave them the blessing he was not permitted to speak.[28]

This passage is just one of several that fill in the gaps—in fan fictional style—of the Gospels' account of the Passion. But this climactic portion of the novel could not be staged without running afoul of the representational dilemma of impersonating the Christ.

Staging *Ben-Hur*

The *Ben-Hur* production team ultimately solved the "problem of the spectacular"—that is, the potential for blasphemy in representing the divine—by making the production even *more* spectacular, but doing so through the use of authentic production elements that offset the play's overt theatricality. The use of a beam of light to represent the Christ was the first and most critical of the production's many scenographic innovations, which included elaborately detailed scenic drops, a choir of over one hundred voices, large crowd scenes, and most indelibly, a chariot race featuring three scrolling panoramas and eight live horses. The staging of the chariot race, in particular, was an unprecedented spectacle that required a treadmill for each individual horse.[29] The treadmills were yoked together in banks of four, one for each chariot, so that Judah's chariot could pull ahead of Messala's or vice versa as needed. From beneath the stage, large electric fans ensured that dust would billow out from the chariots. Behind them, three scrolling panoramas (one on each side, one across the back) supported the illusion that the chariots passed around a circular track in front of a teeming crowd. The stagecraft was so innovative that it warranted a lengthy feature story in *Scientific American* (see figure 3).

Critics (and, later, historians) lavished great attention on *Ben-Hur*'s stagecraft. The *Dramatic News* called *Ben-Hur* "the most stupendous production ever given in America," and the *New York Globe-Democrat* reported that it took 350 people to perform and operate the show, including forty "stage machinists, electricians, carpenters and property men."[30] Yet even as they praised the production's spectacular elements, reviewers largely downplayed (or dismissed) its treatment of religion as a dramatic theme. As Edward A. Dithmar wrote in the *New York Times Saturday Review*, "'Ben-Hur' on the stage is panoramic, pictorial, musical, terpsichorean, religious (in as reverent a way, probably, as a stage play can be reli-

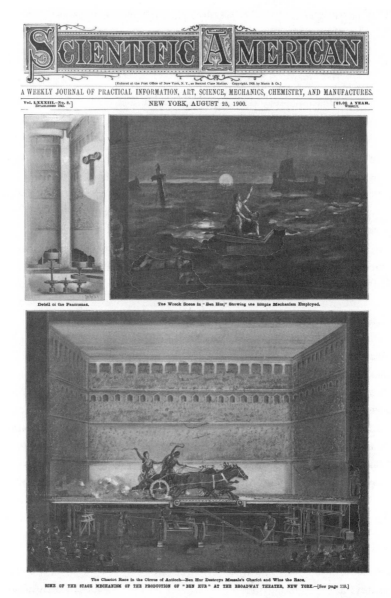

Figure 3. Cover of *Scientific American,* featuring "Some of the Stage Mechanisms of the Production of 'Ben Hur' at the Broadway Theater, New York." (Image courtesy of *Scientific American.*)

gious), and only fitfully dramatic."[31] Similarly, Clement Scott of the *New York Herald* called the show "A gorgeous pageant, more than a play, as such triumphs of stage management must necessarily be."[32] This may be because the play—a self-described melodrama in six acts—lacks literary merit, but it is also because the spectacular performance, when placed in the service of a religious theme, resists critical interpretation. The critic, trained to evaluate the effectiveness of a fictional representation against a quasi-objective standard of aesthetic achievement, is frustrated by a lack of vocabulary with which to assess spiritual impact, an impact that is in any case individual and subjective. It is much easier, then, to dismiss the religious dimension of the play on the grounds that its success (when it succeeds) is attributable not to artistry but to the source material. As the *Boston Herald* explained when the play opened at the Colonial in 1900, "Religion is never more than a cheap means of effectiveness in a drama. In relying upon these springs of emotion, the author can securely count upon a ready-made sympathy; he does not need to work upon the sympathies of the audience, he need be at no pains to make his dramaturgic art appeal to them, for the whole appeal can come from the very nature of his subject."[33] To put it another way: if the audience is moved when Jesus heals the lepers, this reflects no merit on the part of the play or the players, because the incident itself is inherently moving.

But exactly what the critic sees as an artistic limitation, the audience member (particularly the spectator of faith) may see as evidence that *Ben-Hur* is not simply "entertainment" but something more. As Hughes argues, the theater artists and reformers of the nineteenth century "knew that spectacle is effective because it is *affective*."[34] Spectacular scenography and other nontextual elements such as sound effects and music can lead audiences to a different, less intellectual, more visceral and deeply felt engagement with a performance. When spectators are conditioned by the play's subject matter to expect a religious experience, this embodied response may be experienced as a distinctly spiritual moment of transcendence, wherein spectators feel connected to the divine, a phenomenon Stevenson calls "affective piety."[35] Even spectators who do not believe in the play's particular theology may nonetheless experience the spectacle as an embodied experience, and this in turn may translate unconsciously into reverence for the religious narrative.[36] Such affective engagement is often dismissed by secular critics who privilege the intellectual pleasures of theater, in part because, as Stevenson notes, "secular discourse has largely ceded the language of affect to religion."[37] Unable or unwilling to grant credence to the notion that a commercial theater production can produce genuine religious feeling, critics sidestep "ready-made sympathy" in order to focus on aesthetic considerations.

Yet if this "ready-made sympathy" is what moves the spectator, it only goes so far. If the spectacle is perceived as overly false or illusionistic, the specter of blasphemy returns. *Ben-Hur* avoids this fate by balancing spectacle with authenticity. The most revealing example of the authentic in *Ben-Hur* was the aforementioned chariot race. The real horses and chariots, real dust and wind and noise, conveyed an aura of authenticity on the entire production. Writing about contemporary Civil War reenactments, performance theorist Rebecca Schneider notes that such real elements of production can exceed the theatrical frame of a performance event. In Schneider's terms, the real act, object, or body is "not, or not only, mimetic."[38] Judah Ben-Hur's horses may be, in some sense, playing the role of "horse" but they are also and simultaneously living breathing running horses. "Both are true," writes Schneider, "real *and* faux—action *and* representation—and this both/and is the beloved and often discussed conundrum of theatricality in which the represented bumps uncomfortably (and ultimately undecidably) against the affective, bodily instrument of the real."[39] This affect, felt by the audience, resists critical analysis. It is hard to put into words, and it seems, at least by the terms of a secular modernist sensibility, other than artistic.

Yet evangelical dramaturgy, as Stevenson notes, depends precisely on such "devices that urge spectators to oscillate between 'presence' and 'representation.'"[40] The tension between the real and the representational contributes to, rather than detracts from, moments of affective engagement that may be experienced as piety (for the faithful) or reverence (for the secular). As noted evangelist Billy Sunday would put it some years later:

> "Ben-Hur" with its powerful effects, its galloping horses in the chariot race, typical of man's mad race for happiness, its slaves, its lepers and its beautiful "light" that irradiates the world is like a plow digging deep into men's thoughts and stirring their consciences. I'd like nothing better than to talk to 50,000 men and women just after they had seen "Ben-Hur."[41]

To put it another way, if the horses and chariots representing horses and chariots really *are* horses and chariots, then perhaps by some alchemy that beam of light that represents the divine presence really *is* the Divine Presence, or at least close enough to produce a "wow" moment that opens the spectator to the possibility of transcendence.

The Sign of the Cross

In its spectacular, fan fictional approach to the Bible, *Ben-Hur* followed a model set forth four years earlier by British actor and playwright Wilson Barrett, whose *The Sign of the Cross* made its U.S. debut at the Grand Opera House in St. Louis in March 1895 with Barrett himself playing the leading role. The production toured several U.S. cities that spring, including a stop in Brooklyn in May, but closed without reaching Broadway. A brief examination of *The Sign of the Cross* and its decidedly mixed critical and commercial reception offers an interesting counterpoint to *Ben-Hur* and helps explain why the latter quickly eclipsed the former in popularity.

Wallace's novel had gotten around the problem of representing the divine in "A Tale of the Christ" by shifting the narrative focus to Judah Ben-Hur. *The Sign of the Cross* avoids the problem of how to represent Christ by shifting the narrative forward in time to approximately thirty years after the Crucifixion. The play depicts a series of events in the life of Marcus Superbus, a fictional Roman prefect in AD 64. Initially complicit in the empire's persecution of early Christians, Marcus falls in love with a Christian woman, Mercia, and subsequently attempts, unsuccessfully, to advocate for Christians with Emperor Nero. At the play's climax, Mercia is sentenced to die in the arena, but is given the chance to recant her Christianity and marry Marcus. She chooses to die rather than renounce Christ. Moved by her passion and motivated by both love for Mercia and a newfound faith, Marcus tells the guards, "Return to Caesar—Tell him Chrystos hath triumphed—Marcus, too, is a Christian."[42] The couple exit to their presumed deaths as the curtain falls.

Critics did not miss the parallels to *Ben-Hur* in Barrett's treatment of the Bible as source text. One *New York Times* writer called *The Sign of the Cross* "a sort of theatrical 'Ben-Hur,'"[43] while the *Memphis Commercial Appeal* declared, "Wilson Barrett has attempted to do for the drama that which Lew Wallace has done for the novel—to strike the highest possible note by bringing the hearer or the reader into close touch with the life and times of the Savior."[44] The focus on the early Christian martyrs, as opposed to on Jesus or any of the apostles, allows *The Sign of the Cross* to represent a variety of profane and sensational events, including "luxurious revels worthy of 'The Last Days of Pompeii,' flower-crowned guests, bacchanalian orgies," and the torture of a young boy (actually an adult actress) on the rack.[45] Despite this, Barrett insisted that his work was evidence of "the potency of the stage as a moral force."[46]

Though the initial American run of *The Sign of the Cross* had mixed success, Barrett followed it with a successful London run later that year, and in November 1896 a new production, now featuring Charles Dalton as Marcus Superbus and staged by Priestly Morrison, opened at the Knickerbocker Theatre in New York, where it won praise for its lavish scenography, but was generally dismissed as a minor work. The reviewer for *The Illustrated American*, for example, wrote, "There was no lack of beautiful scenery or magnificent costume, while everything that could in any way contribute to the *ensemble* has been given by a generous management. From a religious standpoint, however, the lesson of the play is one of mild importance."[47] The *New York Times* review concluded, "The scenery was showy and the pictorial representation of life in ancient Rome was as good as we have the right to expect in a play. The moral and ethical aspects of the production . . . may well be left for discussion another day, with the mere statement that the spirit of the thing seems to be sufficiently reverential to suit ordinary playgoers."[48] The use of the phrase "sufficiently reverential" is telling here. *The Sign of the Cross*, the critic implies, is respectful enough that "ordinary playgoers" will not take offense. Yet the description of the stagecraft as "showy" and "as good *as we have the right to expect in a play*" indicates that the entire spectacle lacked authenticity, remaining on the level of the representational.

This may explain why most critics were disinclined to comment on the religious content of *The Sign of the Cross*, which they seemed to regard as little more than a novelty. One writer compared it favorably to Henry Arthur Jones's contemporary (nonbiblical) *Michael and His Lost Angel* (1896), "the only other attempt we have had here to stage religion in any form."[49] Jones's play had lasted a mere thirteen performances at the Empire Theatre the previous January, and *The Sign of the Cross* did not do much better. After three weeks of mostly disappointing ticket sales, the company decamped for Boston, and continued on an extended national tour that lasted for much of 1897 before returning for three more weeks in New York at the 14th Street Theatre in early 1898. Reviews from the road also emphasized the production's use of spectacle, though they acknowledged that the piece could occasion powerful feelings. The *Boston Transcript*, for example, wrote, "In spite of its tawdriness, its clap-trap, its obvious theatricality, and its wonderfully absurd misuse of the English language, its scenes still have a vital power to move even the most unimpressionable non-religionist."[50]

What did *The Sign of the Cross* lack that made it only a modest success in comparison to *Ben-Hur?* Certainly, the latter had greater name recognition due to the bestselling novel, and a larger production budget. But it may also be that the authenticity of the production elements (the horses, the music, the light, etc.) allowed *Ben-Hur*'s use of spectacle to provoke a stronger affective response. Such authentic touches, perhaps, bridged the gap between presence and representation, allowing the play to transcend "obvious theatricality," and give spectators an experience that went beyond "sufficiently reverential."

Ben-Hur also directly invoked the divine (albeit in the form of a beam of light) while *The Sign of the Cross* did not. In this sense, we might see Barrett's play as John the Baptist to *Ben-Hur*'s Jesus, preparing the way for the Son of God to make His Broadway debut. Extending the metaphor, the success of *Ben-Hur* gave rise to a number of plays that attempted—with varying degrees of success—to walk in its footsteps. The first decade of the twentieth century saw nearly two dozen biblical adaptations on Broadway. Of these, none were more provocative or celebrated than *Mary of Magdala*.

Mary of Magdala

To this point, the biblical dramas on Broadway had focused on invented characters: Judah Ben-Hur, Messala, Marcus Superbus. That would change in November 1902, when Minnie Maddern Fiske, known colloquially as "Mrs. Fiske," opened at the Manhattan The-

Figure 4. Mrs. Fiske as Mary of Magdala, 1902. (Image courtesy of Billy Rose Theatre Division, The New York Public Library for the Performing Arts, Astor, Lenox and Tilden Foundations.)

atre in the title role of Paul Heyse's *Mary of Magdala* (Mary Magdalene). Mrs. Fiske also directed, and one sign of how much *Ben-Hur* had changed the theatrical landscape is that the play was produced by her husband Harrison Grey Fiske, the same Harrison Grey Fiske who as editor of the *Dramatic Mirror* had led the New York opposition to Salmi Morse's *The Passion* twenty years earlier.[51]

Paul Johann Ludwig von Heyse (1830–1914), a celebrated German writer who would go on to win the 1910 Nobel Prize for Literature, wrote *Maria von Magdala: Drama in Fünf Akten* in 1901, and the play had its public premiere in Bremen, after which the German government's attempts to ban further productions on religious grounds made it something of a cause célèbre.[52] As a result, the Fiskes' production of William Winter's English version, billed as "the original in German prose by Paul Heyse, the translation freely adapted and written in English verse,"[53] arrived in New York (following previews in Milwaukee and Chicago, cities with large German populations) as the subject of considerable scrutiny. "Before the play opened," write theater historians Anne L. Fliotsos and Wendy Vierow, "it was examined by New York clergy members—including ministers, priests, and rabbis—to avoid any religious objections."[54] The Fiskes, well aware of the fate that had befallen Morse, actively sought such clerical endorsements and referred to them frequently in promoting the production.

The play depicts the events of the traditional passion narrative from the point of view of Mary Magdalene. Placing a female character at the center of the story was itself something of a radical act; there are only a handful of such heroine-driven dramas in the ranks of Broadway's biblical adaptations, and *Mary of Magdala* was the first, anticipating works such as Thomas Broadhurst's *The Holy City* (1905) and Maurice Maeterlinck's *Mary Magdalene* (1910).[55] The choice to foreground Mary Magdalene echoes a particular kind of fan fictional strategy: taking a supporting character and retelling the events of the narrative from her point of view. Yet doing so with the character of Mary Magdalene carries particular risks of offending religious spectators. As the most prominent of Jesus's female followers, her presence may introduce heterosexual desire into the passion narrative. Edgar Saltus's 1891 novel *Mary Magdalen* generated significant controversy for suggesting that Mary Magdalene was in love with Jesus, and further that Judas was in love with Mary, suggesting that Judas's betrayal of Christ was driven by sexual jealousy. Though

Saltus's love triangle was not complete—he did not suggest that Mary's romantic feelings for Jesus were reciprocated—the addition of sexual intrigue to the Passion narrative did not sit well with religious leaders, a fact that almost certainly shaped the way the Fiskes would present their production of Heyse's play to the New York audience.

In promoting the production, the Fiskes were careful to publicize the degree to which *Mary of Magdala* would be sufficiently reverential in its treatment of the religious subject matter. Shortly before the play opened in New York, feature stories appeared in a number of papers emphasizing the degree to which this production would *not* be sacrilegious. The *Brooklyn Daily Eagle*, for example, wrote:

> The very wide popularity of "Ben-Hur" has shown that the time and scenes of the life of Jesus will be regarded as reverently in the theater as elsewhere, and the revival of "Every Man" has shown that the stage and the church may still be allies rather than enemies. But "Mary of Magdala" draws more largely upon the persons and incidents of the New Testament than any other drama, save the Passion Play, and in its treatment judgment and taste were large factors.[56]

Thus while noting that it is possible to treat the subject of the Bible "as reverently in the theater as elsewhere," the author also implies that by moving closer to the original biblical narrative, the playwright has a greater risk of giving offense and thus a greater responsibility to exercise "judgment and taste." The article goes on to cite the extensive research undertaken by Mrs. Fiske in preparing the production, as well as the lengths to which the company went to ensure that all production elements were as authentic as possible, based (allegedly) on Mrs. Fiske's own extensive researches.

The Fiskes encouraged such stories and freely provided the press with a formal statement to accompany the news feature. Co-written, in all likelihood, by Harrison Fiske, and appearing under the banner, "Mrs. Fiske Promises a Dignified Production," the sidebar to the *Eagle* feature is worth quoting in its entirety:

> At our first reading of Paul Heyse's powerful and poetic drama, "Mary of Magdala," it seemed to me to be a commendable ambition to represent it on the stage in a manner befitting the universal interest in, and the nobility of the subject, as well as in a way that would do justice, as nearly possible, to the dramatic force and dignity of the work.

If there ever was a time when such a drama could be regarded as opportune that time is now, in view of the lack of nobility and inspiration in many stage subjects.

In placing "Mary of Magdala" in the theater we have been guided by every available suggestion of art, and whatever shortcomings may be seen in this production no earnest observer of it can fail to note that infinite care and pains have been bestowed upon it. During the two years that the subject has been under treatment skilled hands and learned minds in this country and abroad have been concerned in it. Scenically, in costumes and in all accessory details the effort has been made to present pictures of the time and the place that archaeology could not question when we remember that in all things human achievement falls short of human aim, and that of all places the theater, perhaps, from the very nature of its work, is so often fallible, because it deals with semblances rather than with realities.[57]

This statement is noteworthy for its claims of authenticity, its promise of spectacular entertainment, and its assurances of reverence. In short, without saying it in so many words, the statement signals the Fiskes' promise that *Mary of Magdala* will follow the *Ben-Hur* model.

Critics generally felt that the production offered an adaptation of the source text that was faithful in both senses of the word. "The sacred narrative is but slightly varied even in matters of detail," wrote one reviewer, adding, "The Saviour is nowhere made to appear bodily, and every allusion to him is of the tenderest and solemnest sort."[58] This absent presence of Jesus is a theme repeated in several reviews. The *Eagle* declared, "Heyse has accomplished the difficult problem of making a play out of the betrayal and crucifixion of Christ without offending religious sensibilities. He has done this by skillful construction which makes the spirit and sayings of Christ pervade the whole play, while the chief personage is omitted from the scene."[59] Clayton Hamilton declared, "No symbol of light or voice is used to suggest the Savior. But His spirit is made immanent in the action of all the characters."[60] Hamilton was so impressed that a decade later in his influential text *The Theory of the Theatre*, he would cite the play as an example of the phenomenon wherein characters' importance can be heightened by their absence from the stage.[61]

In *Dark Matter: Invisibility in Drama, Theater, and Performance*, scholar Andrew Sofer traces the dramatic power of such an absence to the *Quem quaeritis* ("Whom do you seek?") trope of medieval drama. These performances demonstrated the Resurrection of Christ by enacting the moment when the three Marys (Mary the mother of Jesus, Mary Magdalene, and Mary the sister of Lazarus) visit Christ's tomb on Easter morning. At the climactic moment of the performance, the sepulcher is opened and revealed to be empty. Describing this moment in the *Play of the Resurrection of the Lord*, a mystery play from the late Middle Ages, Sofer writes, "The true proof of Christ's divinity is the . . . *absence* of his physical body," adding, "The real presence of Christ is paradoxically guaranteed by his felt absence—an absence designed to move the crowd from theatrical wonder to reaffirmed faith."[62] For Sofer, this demonstrates the power of theater's "dark matter . . . the invisible dimension of theater that escapes visual detection, even though its effects are felt everywhere in performance."[63] Such invisible presences are by no means limited to plays with religious themes. In fact, argues Sofer, all theater relies on such felt absences, though some exert greater force on the dramatic action than others.[64] According to this logic, *Mary of Magdala*'s ability to make palpable the invisible presence of Christ is not strictly a product of the biblical narrative, but neither can it be divorced from it. By building a drama in which the central characters are directly and explicitly motivated by love for Jesus, Heyse ensured that Jesus's influence would be felt by the audience, regardless of faith. But for those audience members conditioned by the Easter liturgy to experience Christ through his absence, an absence that in fact proves his divinity, *Mary of Magdala*'s structural similarity to the *Quem quaeritis* may have given the play a level of authenticity that surpassed even *Ben-Hur*'s steeds. That is, for believers, the play's invocation of Christ's absence transformed *Mary of Magdala* from a representation of religious drama to a real religious drama, in which the experience of transcendence comes not from the *implied presence* of Christ, but from his *real and palpable absence*.

This may be why the *New York Times* explicitly pronounced *Mary of Magdala* superior to *Ben-Hur*, *The Sign of the Cross*, and other religious dramas, declaring, "It is as truly religious and truly dramatic as these are falsely religious and falsely dramatic."[65] Further evidence can be found in the testimony of the Reverend Percy Stickney Grant, Episcopal minister of New York's Church of the Ascension, who wrote in the *Critic*:

I was astonished as the play went on to see that the stage was capable of touching Christianity in a way that no other art, or even the pulpit, could rival. No one can intelligently see the play without knowing as he never knew before, why Christianity conquered the ancient world and why today there is nothing superior to its teaching.[66]

Despite Reverend Grant's assertion, of course, not all spectators were predisposed to accept the truth-value of Christianity. For those secular or Jewish spectators, however, the absent presence may yet have stirred a reverent aesthetic response, juxtaposed as it was with the spectacular elements of production: the grand scale of the sets, the lavishness of the costumes, the realism of the stage effects, the swelling of the music, the depiction of the human body in extremis, and the thrill of mortal peril facing the protagonist.

It is critical to note, however, that these propositions are not mutually exclusive. As Stevenson and others have demonstrated, the spiritual experience is itself affective, and it is in no way unusual for it to be accompanied by spectacle, from the rousing church revival to the literal miracle (real or perceived). But one condition is essential: that the spectacle not be perceived as (merely) theatrical, but as authentic. The fan fictional approach to staging the Bible demonstrates that this feat is significantly easier to accomplish when the divinity is not visibly manifest on stage. This is due in part to the fact that in both Christian and Jewish tradition, it is often God's physical *absence*—the empty tomb, the burning bush—that authenticates God's divinity. As we shall see in the next chapter, it is also the case that when a human actor is asked to play God, the gap between representation and reality raises the risk of blasphemy or irreverence.

Ben-Hur's Legacy

The two decades following the premiere of *Ben-Hur* would prove a boom-time for biblical plays, featuring more than two dozen productions, including Hall Caine's *The Prodigal Son* (1905), Louis N. Parker's *Joseph and His Brethren* (1913)—in which James O'Neill, once jailed for playing Jesus, earned good notices in the challenging paired roles of Jacob and Pharaoh—and the Broadway premiere of Oscar Wilde's *Salome* (1917). The success of these biblical dramas of the early twentieth century was due in part to the fact that they were not, strictly speaking, *adaptations* of the Bible so much as they were *inspired by* the Bible. The playwrights typically did not attempt to represent the holy scripture, nor did they frame their attempts as such. Rather, the plays followed a fan fictional approach, creating scenes, storylines, and characters that ran parallel to and occasionally intertwined with those of the sacred text.

Significantly, the majority of these plays are explicitly Christian in orientation though many of the producers were not. Given that these performances occur at the peak of Jewish migration to the United States, and the growing perception of the New York theater as a Jewish-dominated industry, as well as the sorry fate of Salmi Morse, the apostate Hebrew, it is tempting to suggest that the focus on the New Testament in *Ben-Hur, The Sign of the Cross, Mary of Magdala*, and others represents a strategic attempt to make the stage a welcoming space for religious Christian audiences. One *New York Times* writer suggested as much, referring cynically to *The Sign of the Cross* as part of "the strenuous efforts of various interested persons to indicate the growth of a purely imaginary union between Church and Stage."[67] It seems more likely, however, that in an era when Broadway was still establishing itself as an industry, producers of all creeds were simply seeking to imitate the successes of others.

Over the first quarter of the twentieth century, in fact, the biblical drama became so well established as a genre that George Bernard Shaw would parody it not once but twice for his own political purposes: *Androcles and the Lion* (1915; revived in 1925, 1938, and 1946) and *Back to Methuselah* (1922; revived 1958). Charles Rann Kennedy's one-act, *The Terrible Meek* (1912), ended with a tableau of the Crucifixion, but the audience saw only a brief silhouette of the aftermath (stage direction: "*Above them rise three gaunt crosses bearing three dead men gibbeted like thieves*") before the curtain fell.[68] It was not until 1929 that an actor was asked to visibly play the part of Jesus—in David Belasco's presentation of the *Freiburg Passion Play*—and not until 1930's *The Green Pastures* that God the Father would appear in human form, as opposed to a light, a disembodied voice, or a suffusing presence on a Broadway stage.

The *Freiburg Passion Play* was a special case. Presented in German, with the exception of a brief prologue, the production was offered to the New York audience as an anthropological artifact: a seven-hundred-year-old traditional pageant reenacted at the Hippo-drome, then New York's largest indoor performance venue, best known in the late 1920s as a site for circus and sporting events. The production played a limited engagement of seven weeks to generally mediocre reviews.[69] It would be another four decades before the role of Jesus was again assayed on Broadway, in 1971's *Jesus Christ Super-star* (see chapter 6). But *The Green Pastures* demonstrated that audi-ences and critics could, under certain circumstances, accept a human actor in the role of God. As we shall see in the next chapter, such representations are typically linked to the book of Genesis, and to God's role as the Creator of the world.

CHAPTER THREE

In the Beginning:
Theatrical Creations

No weird light on the stage can ever signify or
communicate holiness.

—Marc Connelly

Rabbi Joseph Soloveitchik, one of the most noted Jewish theologians
of the twentieth century, writes in *The Lonely Man of Faith* that the
biblical figure of Adam can be understood as having two distinct incarnations, each representing a type of human relationship to the
world. In Genesis 1, God creates humankind in his own image. *In the
image of God created he him; male and female created he them.*[1]
This "Adam the first," as Soloveitchik calls him, "engages in creative
work, trying to imitate his Maker (*imitatio Dei*) . . . a creative aes-
thete. He fashions ideas with his mind, and beauty with his heart."[2]
For Soloveitchik, this type of human is represented by the scientist or
theoretician, concerned primarily with the functional workings of the
universe so as best to exercise the responsibility that God has bestowed upon him. *And God said, Let us make man in our image, after our likeness: and let them have dominion over the fish of the sea,
and over the fowl of the air, and over the cattle, and over all the
earth, and over every creeping thing that creepeth upon the earth.*[3]

Soloveitchik contrasts this first version of humankind with that
implied by the second iteration of the creation narrative, expressed in
Genesis 2: *And the LORD God formed man of the dust of the ground,
and breathed into his nostrils the breath of life; and man became a
living soul.*[4] Adam the second is placed in the Garden, not to rule but

"to dress it and keep it."[5] He represents the second type of human, more concerned with the metaphysical. "He does not," writes Soloveitchik, "ask a single functional question. Instead . . . he wonders: 'Why did the world in its totality come into existence? Why is man confronted by this stupendous and indifferent order of things and events?'"[6] The true man of faith, Soloveitchik argues, must combine both of these aspects of humanity: the creative and the questioning, the confident ruler and the humble seeker. Both dimensions of humanity are accounted for in the opening chapters of Genesis.

It should not be surprising, then, that the creation of the world has a particular fascination for some playwrights and directors. Who, after all, emulates Adam the first (*imitatio Dei*) more than the theater artist? Who, like the Creator, calls forth a world, furnishes it with an environment, and peoples it with living beings solely through the power of words. *And God said, Let there be light: and there was light.*[7] At the same time, the world the theater artist creates can itself be a device for wrestling with the existential questions that fascinate Adam the second. But the playwright or director doesn't work the question from the inside, as Adam does. Rather, he or she sets the parameters in which the characters search for answers. The theater, we might say, offers the opportunity to return to Eden, but this time we get to play both roles: God and Adam.

This chapter juxtaposes two examples of actors "playing God": first, the phenomenally successful *The Green Pastures* (1930), written by white playwright Marc Connelly and featuring an all-black cast; second, the comparatively infelicitous *The Creation of the World and Other Business* (1972) by Arthur Miller. Both of these plays were written by mature, oft-produced playwrights, and both, significantly, dramatize God's disappointment with His creation, calling our attention to the metaphysical connection between theatrical creation and divine creation. The playwright, like God, summons forth a world through the utterance of a few words. *Let there be light.* The playwright, like God, creates the characters that inhabit this world. *It is not good that man should be alone; I will make him an help meet for him.*[8] And in the conception of both Connelly and Miller, God, like the playwright, has what we might call "second act trouble." His characters don't perform as expected. He is tempted to destroy the whole world and start over. Considering *Creation*'s troubled history and reception in juxtaposition to the critical and commercial success of *The Green Pastures* helps to illustrate some of the issues at work in the representation of God and His Creation on the Broadway stage. Along the way, brief notice will be taken of another Garden of Eden play, *The Apple Tree* (1966), a one-act musical that makes no attempt to plumb the depths of the biblical narrative, choosing instead to use a lay version of Adam and Eve's story as a pretext for frivolity.

The biblical fan fiction plays discussed in the previous chapter emphasized spectacle and authenticity to invoke a feeling of reverence. The visible elements generated an affective response that at least some spectators experienced as spiritual, while the strategic invisibility of the divine presence allowed those plays to elide concerns of blasphemous representation. The creation plays discussed here function in a different way, emphasizing the qualities of sincerity (*The Green Pastures*) and irony (*Creation*). In fact, however, a closer analysis of *The Green Pastures* reveals that the success of its claim to sincerity rested strongly on both spectacle and authenticity. Despite its rejection of the "toga play" approach and its transposition of the biblical narrative from the ancient world to the American South, Connelly's play in many ways borrows from and elaborates on the staging techniques of the early twentieth-century epics, with the result that it was generally perceived as a sincere and reverent treatment of the Bible. *The Green Pastures* also stands as a landmark moment for African American performers on Broadway, a fact not easily disentangled from the play's perceived sincerity. Conversely, the failure of *Creation*—a play that comes to the Garden with a less reverent, more ironic approach to staging the Bible—to capture either the critical or popular imagination may be attributed in part to its own unique circumstances of production, and in part to the difficulty of balancing irony with spectacle, authenticity, and sincerity in the context of God's creation.

Despite their divergent strategies, both plays attempt to consider larger metaphysical questions about faith, family, and responsibility to one's fellow human being. *Am I my brother's keeper?* Significantly, both put God onstage as a character, played by an unmasked actor. This rare strategy flies in the face of the model set by *Ben-Hur*, and in fact turns the tables: the playwright creates God and tells Him what to say.

The Green Pastures

"I am not a religionist," Marc Connelly (1890–1980) wrote in his 1968 memoir *Voices Offstage*. "To me, any creed that has lasted more than five hundred years has merit in it somewhere, but I have never been able to accept insistences by hierarchies or sectarian policing."[9] Nevertheless, no American playwright has ever had his career more closely associated with the Bible before or since. At 640 Broadway performances, plus two revivals and a successful national tour that spanned four years and more than one hundred cities, *The Green Pastures* was the longest-running Bible-based Broadway production until 1971's *Jesus Christ Superstar*. It remains in third place on that list behind only *Superstar* and *Joseph and the Amazing Technicolor Dreamcoat* (1982). The play was also a critical success, earning Connelly the 1930 Pulitzer Prize for Drama. A film version directed by Connelly and William Keighley was released by Warner Brothers in 1936. More than a hit show, however, *The Green Pastures* was widely hailed as a major cultural event. Even before it was awarded the 1930 Pulitzer Prize for Drama in May, newspapers and magazines devoted significant column space to assessing the show's significance to theater, religion, and race relations. The *New York World*, for example, ran an editorial by Yale University folklorist Mary Austin that proclaimed Connelly's play to be the vanguard of a new wave of religious drama long overdue on the American stage. "In witnessing 'Green Pastures,'" writes Austin, "it becomes plain that the treasures of Bible story are about to be released to the use of dramatists in a degree never before possible, because finally for the majority of American audiences they are now capable of being treated at their full human values without controversy."[10] Austin's somewhat rosy assessment reflects a growing understanding among modernist artists and critics of the Bible as a work of literature rather than the inerrant Word of God. In such a view, the Bible still holds pride of place as a foundational text for Western civilization, but its particulars are not sacrosanct.[11] It may even be desirable to reimagine the Bible in contemporary terms as a means of making its wisdom more immediate and relevant to contemporary society.

Such was the motivation behind a book called *Ol' Man Adam an' His Chillun': Being the Tales They Tell About the Time When the*

Lord Walked the Earth Like a Natural Man (1928) by Roark Bradford.[12] Bradford, a white journalist based in New Orleans, had published a series of stories in which events from the Old Testament
were retold in "Negro" vernacular, as if they had taken place in rural
Louisiana. After murdering Abel, for instance, Cain flees to "Nod
Parish," while the prodigal son is one who has overindulged in New
Orleans nightlife. In *Voices Offstage*, Connelly reports that he read
the book in one evening, and that the very next day he began seeking
the stage rights. *The Green Pastures*, however, is only loosely based
on *Ol' Man Adam*. Though inspired by Bradford's device of transposing biblical narratives into a contemporary black idiom, Connelly, a
journeyman playwright and member of the Algonquin Round Table
who had collaborated with George S. Kaufman on such hits as *Dulcy*
(1921), *Merton of the Movies* (1922), and *Beggar on Horseback* (1924),
knew that for a dramatization to succeed as anything other than a
curiosity, he would need to impose a stronger narrative through-line
than existed in his source text (or, arguably, in the Bible itself). With
the willing assent of Bradford, Connelly set out to write "a religious
drama for which [Bradford's] sketches would be a loose framework."[13]

In determining the play's structure, Connelly used the character
of God as his unifying element. This represented a sharp departure
from earlier Broadway adaptations of the Bible, which had focused on
the scriptures' human characters. As discussed in the previous chapter, the highly successful *Ben-Hur* had established a model for biblical adaptation that avoided the potentially blasphemous representation of God by a human actor. This fan fictional approach to the Bible
was distinguished by the absence of the deity in physical form
(though He would sometimes be indicated via a beam of light or a
disembodied voice), relying instead on awe-inspiring spectacle con-
taining authentic production elements to create a sense of transcendence in the audience. Though often dismissed by critics as a lesser
dramaturgical achievement, such adaptations proved remarkably
successful in attracting a wide audience, while for the most part pla-
cating those who were frankly skeptical of the theater's ability to do
justice to the Holy Book. Though *The Green Pastures* (sometimes
referred to as "the Black *Ben-Hur*")[14] would in many ways rely on
spectacular stage effects and an aura of authenticity to accomplish its
dramatic purpose, Connelly's play also sets forth a new model for the

biblical drama, one in which the playwright fashions God in the image of man.

Connelly's reasons for making God a leading character were more dramaturgical than theological: most of the characters in the Old Testament are sketched thinly, and appear in only a handful of episodes, whereupon the narrative moves to a subsequent generation. This is not a problem when the entire play stays within a single episode (e.g., Abraham and Isaac); but if a playwright chooses to work on a more epic scale, as in the case of *The Green Pastures*, which spans from Genesis to Joshua (with a hint of the Gospels thrown in), then God is the only character who persists throughout the source text. Thus while Bradford, as his title implies, was primarily interested in the human characters of the biblical narrative, Connelly writes, "I did not immediately see what was to become the backbone of the play, but that God, a fundamentalist God, should be a dominating character was in my mind from the beginning."[15] Yet Connelly was also motivated by a desire to make what he saw as the wisdom of the Bible relevant to contemporary audiences. Thus his "fundamentalist God" would not be the abstract Trinitarian deity that Connelly learned about as a choirboy in St. Stephen's Episcopal Church of McKeesport, Pennsylvania,[16] but an anthropomorphic God, one whose motivations are human emotions such as pleasure, disappointment, wrath, and jealousy.

The Green Pastures opens with a prologue in which a preacher, Mr. Deshee, reads from the Bible to a group of children in a rural Sunday school. The children find it difficult to understand the Bible, because it seems so remote, and Mr. Deshee tries to reframe the narrative in a way that they will understand. So, for example, when a child asks whether the angels, before the Creation, ever had picnics, Deshee answers "Sho, dey had the nicest kind of picnics. Dey probably had fish frys, wid b'iled custard and ten cent seegars for de adults."[17] This Sunday school lesson becomes the framing device for the entire play, and though the scene never returns to the Sunday school, Mr. Deshee or the children's voices are occasionally heard as voiceovers at other moments during the action. The next scene depicts the promised fish fry in heaven, a picnic that culminates in the creation of the earth and God's announcement that "I'm goin' down dere."[18] A series of vignettes then tells the story, in abbreviated form, of Genesis 2–5 (Adam and Eve, Cain and Abel, and the enumeration of their descendants). Genesis 6–7, which describes God's displeasure with the wickedness of humans, is presented as a meeting between God and the angel Gabriel in "God's private office in heaven,"[19] and the latter half of the first act is given over to the story of Noah and the Flood. The second act follows a similarly episodic structure, with vignettes based on Genesis 12 (God's covenant with Abraham) and the book of Exodus from chapter 3 (the burning bush) through chapter 15 (the escape across the Red Sea), as well as an episode depicting the sins of Babylon (which resembles a New Orleans nightclub), and an episode based on the book of Hosea, one of the Old Testament prophets.[20] In total, there are eighteen scenes, some as brief as two or three minutes. Inspired by the use of music he had observed in black churches in New Orleans, Connelly decided that each scene change would be accompanied (and covered) by a song, and planned for a full choir in addition to a large company of actors.

Connelly spent much of the first half of 1929 trying, unsuccessfully, to find a producer for *The Green Pastures*. Given that Connelly was hardly an unknown playwright, he had little trouble getting the script read, but few producers wanted to take a chance on a show with an all-black cast. Moreover, Connelly reports that several producers found the script blasphemous, not simply because it dared depict God, but because it represented God as an African American. Even those producers who had no objection to the play's racial or religious content were concerned about giving offense to others, not to mention the difficulty and expense of staging a biblical epic that called for a cast of more than sixty (including several juveniles), a choir, and as many as twenty scene changes. Arthur Hopkins, who had already produced numerous Broadway hits, including John Barrymore's *Hamlet* (1922), told Connelly that he liked the script and that "if I knew how it could be produced, I think I'd do it."[21] Legendary producer Jed Harris was so taken with the script that he and Connelly had a series of brainstorming meetings about how best to stage it, but ultimately the two men could not reach an agreement, and Connelly shelved the project for several months.

Finally, in November 1929, Connelly's friend and frequent collaborator George S. Kaufman introduced him to Rowland Stebbins, a former stockbroker turned theatrical producer. Though Stebbins would go on to produce many Broadway hits (several under the name of his production company, Laurence Rivers, Inc.), he was at that time a relative novice in theatrical production with only two shows under his belt, neither of which had run longer than four weeks. Perhaps because he did not appreciate the difficulties of such a production, or perhaps because he wanted to work with a well-known writer, Stebbins was eager to produce *The Green Pastures*. When Connelly conscientiously warned Stebbins about "the enormous risk of disfavor that was likely to arise over a play in which God was depicted as a Negro," Stebbins response was to forgo out-of-town tryouts in cities that might be less tolerant of the play's premise, and simply open the show directly in New York.[22] Robert Edmond Jones was engaged to design sets and costumes, and plans were made to begin rehearsals at the end of December for an opening in February 1930.

Working with a Harlem-based agency, Immense Thespians, Connelly (who would direct the production) and Stebbins began casting calls in early December. There was no shortage of talented African American actors, and the majority of the roles were cast quickly. However, writes Connelly, "Filling the role of De Lawd [God] was difficult. The actor had to be physically big, have a bearing not only dignified but noble, and a voice rich with quiet authority and capable of thunderous wrath."[23] After rejecting numerous possible choices, and with the start of rehearsals looming, Connelly began to despair of finding the right actor to take on the all-important part of God. He and Stebbins considered eschewing actors entirely and seeking out clergy members, going to far as to invite Dr. Adam Clayton Powell Sr., minister of Harlem's Abyssinian Baptist Church, to take the role (he declined). In a story that would be so oft-repeated in subsequent press accounts as to have become part of theatrical folklore, it was not until the Friday before rehearsals were set to begin that a sixty-five-year-old "unknown" named Richard B. Harrison was brought in for a reading.

The son of escaped slaves, Harrison was born in London, Ontario, in 1864, and moved with his family to Detroit at the age of sixteen.[24] Though trained as a performer at the Detroit Training School of Dramatic Art, graduating in 1887, Harrison had found it difficult to find steady work as an actor, largely because of racial discrimination. He was repeatedly denied opportunities to play serious drama, and he had little interest in the types of roles that might have been available to an AfricanAmerican actor of the period. As W. E. B. Du Bois would put it later, "If Richard Harrison had learned to dance clog and make faces in his youth, he might have riches now."[25] Instead, Harrison specialized in one-man shows, touring the country as a "reader" with various variety and Chautauqua circuits. He worked closely with poet Paul Laurence Dunbar, whose work he often recited, and supplemented his income as a performer by working for various railroads as a Pullman porter and in other capacities. In 1922, he was appointed the first Department Chair of Dramatics for the summer school at North Carolina Agricultural and Technical College, a position he would hold for seven years (until his commitment to *The Green Pastures* made it impossible to continue).[26] During the winter months, he continued to organize church plays and to tour as a lecturer, which is apparently why he was in New York in December 1929. Connelly and Stebbins were so taken by Harrison's looming physical presence, rich voice, and "dauntless inner strength" that they offered him the part of De Lawd on the spot, but Harrison was reluctant on both religious and racial grounds. In religious terms, Harrison feared it might be blasphemous to impersonate God. To counter this objection, Stebbins hurriedly arranged a meeting for Harrison with Herbert Shipman, then the Episcopal bishop for the Diocese of New York, who was apparently able to ease the actor's concerns on that score. In racial terms, Harrison, who had for years worked almost exclusively in the African American community, feared that the production might be disrespectful to the black experience, a parody rather than a celebration of black spirituality. After a weekend of reflection, however, Harrison agreed to come on board. With that, Richard Berry Harrison cemented his place in theater history as the first actor to play God on a Broadway stage.[27]

The Green Pastures opened at the Mansfield Theatre on February 26, 1930, to rave reviews, nearly all of which focused on the excellence of Harrison's performance. Brooks Atkinson, writing in the *New York Times*, complimented the production for "putting the Lord on stage in such simple terms that your imagination is stimulated into a transfigurating conception of sheer universal goodness."[28] Robert Garland, reviewing the play for the *Telegraph*, remarked (under the subhead "Humanized Deity Made Hero of Bayou Negro Tragic-comedy") that "Mr. Richard B. Harrison is dignified and human and more credible than you would think possible as the Maker of Heaven and Earth."[29] While Walter Winchell wrote in the *Daily*

Figure 5. Richard B. Harrison (*left*) as De Lawd and Alonzo Fenderson as Moses in *The Green Pastures*, 1930. (Photo by Vandamm Studio / © Billy Rose Theatre Division, The New York Public Library for the Performing Arts.)

Mirror, "Prominent in the troupe as The Lord (the first time, we think, the Deity has ever been represented on a stage) is Richard B. Harrison, a charming personality, who juggles with a heavy assignment, but he delivered it with ease and was always believable," before adding somewhat backhandedly: "Never is Mr. Harrison's delicate interpretation offensive, even if he is a colored man."[30]

Winchell's comments land with a thud on the twenty-first century ear, but they are likely indicative of the two preconceptions that most white spectators and critics brought to the Mansfield Theatre (and later, to one of dozens and dozens of venues around the country in a four-year national tour): First, God is nearly unrepresentable. Second, if God must be represented in human form, surely that form would be a white man. As it turned out, however, the representation of God in *The Green Pastures* seems to have succeeded precisely *because* of the actor who played the role. In fact, reviews and other accounts often stage a kind of mininarrative of discovery: the reviewer arrived expecting a novelty act and left amazed by Harrison's embodiment of De Lawd. Even after five years of touring, Brooks Atkinson writes, "Richard B. Harrison still draws out of us a reverence and wonder that we do not often feel toward mortal men; and as long as he walks the earth like a natural man but with a serenity that now distinguishes him from his fellows, sheer goodness will continue to seem like a miracle."[31] Harrison himself attributed the strength of his performance to divine inspiration. As *Time* magazine reported:

> With the deepest humility, he feels that God has selected him to spread the Word through the theatre. Piety prevented him from accepting the part at first. Later, he says, "when Mr. Connelly 'phoned me on that Monday night, I didn't answer, but something in my soul replied: 'I'll stick with you through thick and thin, Mr. Connelly!'"[32]

Invoking this narrative absolves Harrison of potential blasphemy. More importantly, it construes his opportunity to play God as a call to preach. This suggests that he approached *The Green Pastures* with a level of sincerity, an alignment of belief and action, more commonly associated with ritual performance than with Broadway theater. Regardless of whether we take Harrison's story of God's call (delivered, interestingly, through a literal call from the playwright) at face value, the perception of Harrison's sincerity, and that of *The Green Pastures* as a whole, was critical to the play's warm reception.

Sincerity, Spectacle, and Race

Publicly, Connelly rejected the idea that *The Green Pastures* was in any way dependent on theatrical spectacle. In a profile of Connelly for the *New York World*, William Warner Lundell notes that the playwright's eyes blaze with "scorn for cheap theatrical effects."[33] Too many plays, "in the Ben Hur tradition, *will depend on stage mechanisms for effect of holiness and thereby fail of their spiritual purpose.*"[34] In contrast, Connelly told Lundell, "No weird light on the stage can ever signify or communicate holiness," adding "and as for flowing draperies to create majesty—well, we use them for comedy."[35] This framing of *The Green Pastures* acknowledges the religious spectator's distrust of overt theatricality while explicitly claiming a "spiritual purpose" for the production.

To claim "spiritual purpose" in an adaptation of the Bible is a declaration of sincerity. In surveying the critical response to *The Green Pastures*, two things become clear: first, the apparent sincerity of the production was very much in evidence; second the primary evidence of this sincerity seems to be the play's theological (and dramaturgical) naïveté. John Mason Brown, for example, noted in his review for the *Evening Post*, "But none of [the scenes in the play] are blasphemous because they have a disarming sincerity that cannot be gainsaid. And all of them form an ingenuous and diverting chronicle which only asks you to accept them on their own naïve and unpretentious terms."[36] While the *Tribune*'s Burns Mantle wrote, "In fact, nothing half so genuine as 'The Green Pasture,' [*sic*] nor half so charming in its disarming simplicity, has been exhibited in the theater of our time."[37] Similarly, Arthur Ruhl's review for the *Herald Tribune* declared, "It is strange and impressive how much of the supernatural burden of the story—the real spiritual hunger and steadfast faith of these groping souls—is carried over the footlights by the simplest and most unaffected means."[38] In reading these responses, it is clear that concerns about the potential blasphemy of impersonating God were overcome by a perception that *The Green Pastures*, for all its entertainment value, was essentially a sincere performance of faith.

This sincerity was in turn premised on a perception of authenticity operating at all levels: Connelly was thought to have created "an authentic" depiction of black spirituality ("the real spiritual hunger and steadfast faith of these groping souls"). The black actors were thought to be playing their own culture, part of what historian of religion Curtis J. Evans calls a "continued fascination with blacks as naturally religious and exotic."[39] Consider Gilbert Seldes, writing in the *Evening Graphic*, who gave *The Green Pastures* a rave review, but complained about the last scene, which he felt was inauthentic: "The theology is too complicated for what has gone before; one doubts whether it is the work of the ignorant Negro and one suspects that the author has interjected thoughts of his own."[40] Seldes criticizes the text where it takes the greatest liberties with the biblical source: a scene where God has a conversation with an Israelite named Hezdrel (played by the same actor who played Adam) about the nature of religion. Hezdrel (a Connelly invention, no such character appears in the Bible) offers a supposition:

> Oh, dat ol' God dat walked de earth in de shape of a man. I guess he lived wid man so much dat all he seen was de sins in man. Dat's what made him de God of wrath and vengeance. Co'se he made Hosea. An' Hosea never would a found what mercy was unless dere was a little of it in God, too. Anyway, he ain't a fearsome God no mo'. Hosea showed us dat.[41]

Seldes's dismissal of what he sees as the author's "thoughts of his own" suggests that part of the aura of sincerity that arises from the use of an all-black cast is linked to the idea that the *Green Pastures* company is not engaging in art (in which originality is prized), but in ritual (in which fidelity to the original is preferred).

Such a conception is, of course, radically unfair to the many talented performers and musicians who approached this play as an aesthetic work. It betrays white assumptions that Negroes were primitive and childlike. "My own guess," wrote critic Doris B. Garey, "would be that [Connelly] was searching for what one might term a sort of idealized naivete through which to view an extremely complex subject. In the Bible itself, this blend of surface naiveté and underlying maturity is perhaps most strikingly represented by the Book of Jonah."[42] In assessing the theological appropriateness of a biblical drama, both the child and the primitive are given special dispensation. The child's need to learn outweighs the potential risk of accidental offense to propriety, while the child's presumed innocence is a counterweight to any taint of theatrical dissimulation that may trouble the religious spectator. This is the logic behind church pageants, Bible-based picture books, and Passover seders. Similarly, the primitive population's unchurched condition is understood to be no fault of their own. If the biblical reenactment can bring the "savage" closer to God, then some theatrical dissembling is a small price to pay.

The "childlike Negro"—a recognizable stereotype in American literature and theater going back to *Uncle Tom's Cabin*, *Huckleberry Finn*, and *Uncle Remus*—combines elements of both innocence and primitivism. "Through the image of naïve religious blacks," writes Evans, "[*The Green Pastures*] spoke to the needs of a generation who, in the words of journalist Walter Lippmann, were haunted with the need to believe, to those who wanted to kneel and be comforted at the 'shrine of some new god.'"[43] According to this reading, white audiences saw the worship of the childlike Negro as an antidote to the corrupt, cynical, and soulless urban life of the 1920s and the corresponding disillusionment of the Great Depression. The world of *The Green Pastures* offered a utopian—indeed, Edenic—vision of a world "before the Fall." As Richard B. Watts wrote in the *Herald Tribune*:

> It must be apparent that to find the spiritual antecedent of "The Green Pastures" one must go back not to any modern drama, but directly to those almost forgotten medieval miracle plays. Those works came, of course, out of the innermost spirit of the people who produced them; when religion and its tradition and its God were very personal and intimate matters that were always as close to them as their neighbors around the corner. From time to time in recent years there has been an attempt—by, for example, Reinhardt in "The Miracle" and perhaps more sincerely and reverently, by Paul Claudel in "The Tidings Brought to Mary"—to recapture something of this close relationship that the earlier centuries brought into their folk dramas. Yet all of the efforts have failed to secure anything of the real spirit that animated these plays because that personal relationship is not in the soul of modern, sophisticated Europeans.[44]

Lost in the fulsome praise of critics such as Watts, the white audience may perhaps be forgiven for not noticing that Bradford and Connelly's depiction of black religion was as imaginary as it was infantilizing.

The near constant use of traditional spirituals, sung by an actual Negro choir (the Harlem-based Hall Johnson Chorus, hired as a group), was a critical element in conferring authenticity on this otherwise highly romanticized vision of rural black life. As discussed in the previous chapter, music carries with it an element of the real. Here, the Hall Johnson singers were not *playing the role of a Negro choir;* they were *being a choir.* In fact, the choir's singing played such a large part in the show that many in the New York theater scene thought *The Green Pastures* should be ineligible for the Pulitzer Prize on the grounds that the songs were traditional spirituals, not original to the play. Boosters of the play also highlighted the music. "Without the Negro spirituals accenting the high points of dramatic action," wrote Mary Austin, "'Green Pastures' would have been interesting and amusing. With them it becomes significant."[45] Interestingly, black audiences also found the music authentic, even if the rest of the play's depiction of African American life was off base. As Harrison told the *Herald Tribune* in October 1930, "I say that it [the play] is genuinely negro. Of course, the spirituals which our choir sings help to keep us on the right track. The songs are so completely our songs that if we ever were in danger of wandering off into something merely theatrical the spirituals would bring us back."[46] Here again, as in the story of his acceptance of the role of God, Harrison advances the claim that *The Green Pastures* is a kind of ministry, a performance whose purpose goes beyond the "merely theatrical."

Beyond the music, the performers' African American bodies themselves provided a kind of irreducible reality that appeared to white audiences as both spectacular and authentic. As Amy Hughes has argued, audiences perceive nonnormative bodies *as* spectacle.[47] Hughes traces this phenomenon through the history of the nineteenth-century freak show, a genre that not infrequently displayed nonwhite bodies as exotic curiosities. That the African American body was considered a spectacle in this way in 1930 is evident from Langston Hughes's 1940 autobiography *The Big Sea*, where he writes of "the growing influx of whites toward Harlem after sundown, flooding the little cabarets and bars where formerly only colored people laughed and sang, and where now the strangers were given the best ringside tables to sit and stare at the Negro customers— like amusing animals in a zoo."[48] Seen from this angle, Connelly's claim to eschewing the spectacle of "weird light" and "flowing draperies" is somewhat disingenuous. For white audiences, the actors themselves were part of the spectacle.

Harrison as De Lawd may be understood as an even rarer spectacle: the dignified Negro or "noble savage." *Never is Mr. Harrison's delicate interpretation offensive, even if he is a colored man.*[49] The contrast between the dignified patriarch Harrison and the more stereotypical behavior of the rest of the company only highlights his unusual character. In this sense, while Harrison is clearly a human being representing God, he is also an other-than-human spectacle not all that different from the beam of light that represented the Divine in *Ben-Hur*.[50]

If the bodies of *The Green Pastures* company were spectacular, they were also perceived as authentic. The play's emphasis on sincerity and simplicity as a framing device, combined with preexisting stereotypes, made it difficult for white critics to accept that the actors were, in fact, just acting. Nearly all of these actors were from the urban North or had fled the rural South in search of a better existence. But for a white audience unaccustomed to making distinctions between and among subgroups of African Americans, the company members were clearly black—or at least not white. Meanwhile, in black communities, writes Evans, critics "debated the play's artistic merits and its impact on broader depictions of African Americans, though many were happy to see an all black cast employed."[51] That is to say, African Americans recognized the illusory nature of the play's representation of black life, but also the authenticity of the employment opportunity it afforded so many black actors and musicians. In retrospect, however, the economic arrangements were significantly exploitative. In 1935, the *New York Times* reported that *The Green Pastures*, from its first rehearsal for Broadway to the close of the national tour, had paid out $769,924.50 in salaries for a company of eighty (an average of $9,624 per company member). Each actor, in other words, earned about $33,000 per year in 2014 dollars, while Connelly himself collected royalties of $296,563 (equivalent to $5 million in 2014), which he divided with Bradford, the white author of *Ol Man Adam and His Chillun'*, "according to their own private arrangement."[52]

Because the theological components of *The Green Pastures* had been granted absolution from heresy by the presumed naïveté of the Negro, it was fairly easy for the play to garner the endorsements of clergy across the religious spectrum. Souvenir programs bore various testimonials from religious leaders:

It contains many valuable lessons which I hope to incorporate in the review I shall give of it to my people some Sunday morning during the sermon period. (Grover C. Walters, Tacony Baptist Church, Philadelphia)

The significant aspect of "the Green Pastures" is not what it directly portrays; what the primitive finds in the Bible, but what the child sees in the great book and which all of us enjoy. (Rabbi Dr. Jacob Katz, chaplain of Sing Sing Prison)

Both as art and as religion it was magnificent. (Charles E. Raven, Chaplain to the King of England, Canon of Liverpool Cathedral)[53]

At the same time, the very presence of such endorsements indicated a lingering insecurity on behalf of producers that the show might attract criticism on religious grounds. If anything, however, the show tapped into a previously unsuspected desire for religious-themed entertainment. The *New York Herald*, on the occasion of the show's five hundredth performance, suggested that "while the Christian churches have credited to the naïve, chaste simplicity of 'The Green Pastures' a great emotional awakening of religious consciousness, it has met with equal favor among Jewish leaders."[54] What objections the play did encounter on tour were more likely to come from white supremacists (what one Los Angeles newspaper called "certain Nordic Christians")[55] who were opposed less to a black God than to a large company of African American performers arriving in their city. Ultimately, despite Connelly's initial fears of racist backlash "out of town," only one U.S. city (Lubbock, Texas) prohibited the performance of *The Green Pastures*, by refusing to grant access to its high school auditorium.[56]

On the whole, the response from white "religionists" was so positive that Austin, the folk drama expert from Yale, suggested, "It now begins to look as though we might have to thank the Negro for mediating our spiritual experience for our own use."[57] Yet as Evans reminds us, "Even as *The Green Pastures* addressed certain psychological and spiritual needs of whites, it also masked deep fears about the movement of blacks into the urban North."[58] In other words, the play's fascination with the childlike negro also indulged a nostalgia for an era in which the "darkies" (a term used without irony by several reviews, including in New York) remained peaceful, rural, and far away.

African American audiences had, of course, a different relationship to this fantasy. Given the close links between organized religion and the nascent civil rights movement, *The Green Pastures* emerged as a singularly divisive issue. Prominent black intellectuals disagreed among themselves, Evans writes, "whether it was a sacrilegious portrayal of God or a caricature of heaven, and about how blacks were depicted religiously."[59] Evans suggests that the primary way in which *The Green Pastures* offended religious African Americans was in perpetuating the stereotype that black religion is primitive and instinctual, lacking in scholarship or reason. If we consider the play in the context of other biblical adaptations, however, it may have also been the portrayal of God by an African American that black audiences found problematic. Where the white audience could dismiss "De Lawd" as a metaphorical representation by a not-quite-human actor, the black audience would have needed to confront the potential sacrilege of a human actor imitating the divine in a more direct way.[60]

As with *Ben-Hur*, the commercial success of *The Green Pastures* led to a renewed interest by producers in bringing the Bible to Broadway. Productions of the 1930s included Charles O'Brien Kennedy's comic *The Mighty Nimrod* (1931), Andre Obey's *Noah* (1935, discussed in the following chapter), and Max Reinhardt's production of *The Eternal Road* (1937), a spectacular operatic interpretation of the Exodus based on Franz Werfel's German text, with score by Kurt Weill. Yet after *The Green Pastures*, it would be more than three decades before Broadway would return to the Garden of Eden as a setting.

Under *The Apple Tree*

Before considering our next example, *The Creation of the World and Other Business*, it is worth taking brief notice of *The Apple Tree* (1966), a collection of three one-act musicals by Sheldon Harnick (lyrics) and Jerry Bock (music), the composing team behind *Fiddler on the Roof* (1964). Of the three short plays that make up *The Apple Tree*, only the first—*The Diary of Adam and Eve*—is based on the Bible, and that is at one remove. The creators of *The Apple Tree* credit not the scriptures, but rather a pair of short stories by Mark Twain— "Extracts from Adam's Diary" (1904) and the follow-up "Eve's Diary" (1906) as their source material.[61] Alan Alda played the role of Adam opposite Barbara Harris as Eve, with Larry Blyden's Snake as the only other character. These three actors would also appear (with other members of the ensemble) in the other two plays that comprised the evening: *The Lady or the Tiger?*, based on an 1882 story by

Frank R. Stockton; and *Passionella*, based on a Cinderella spoof by humorist and cartoonist Jules Feiffer. The entire production was directed by Mike Nichols and opened October 18, 1966, at the Shubert Theater. It would eventually run 463 performances, making it the longest running biblical play on Broadway since *The Green Pastures*. A fortieth-anniversary production was given a limited run of sixteen weeks (including previews) by the Roundabout Theatre Company at Studio 54 in December 2006.[62]

Twain's version of Adam's diary retells the story of Genesis 2 and 3 as a gently satirical love story, "Translated from the original MS."[63] As an adaptation of an adaptation of the Bible, Bock and Harnick's musical was not subjected to the same critical or religious scrutiny as other biblical adaptations. God does not appear as a character in Twain's stories, and the subject of the divine creation is touched on obliquely if at all. In short, Twain has removed the story from a religious context, reframing it as a kind of innocent comic fable. Instead of pondering the wisdom or purpose of God's creation, we focus instead on the Serpent, a wily character who appears only in the first four verses of Genesis 3 as the instrument of temptation leading to the Fall. It is this fairy-tale/fable quality of *The Diary of Adam and Eve* that unifies it with *The Lady or the Tiger* and Feiffer's modern-day Cinderella story.

To put it another way, the juxtaposition of Adam and Eve's narrative with the other two parts of *The Apple Tree* clearly indicate that the audience is to understand Adam and Eve's story as a fairy tale rather than as scripture. Walter Kerr, writing in the *New York Times*, called the musical a "little fable," adding that it looked "like a telescoped version of 'The Skin of Our Teeth.'"[64] The comparison is telling, as Thornton Wilder's *The Skin of Our Teeth* (1942) draws an explicit connection between its main characters, Mr. and Mrs. Antrobus, and the biblical Adam and Eve, but otherwise is so loosely tethered to the biblical narrative that I have chosen to exclude it from the present study. For Wilder, the Bible is less a source text for adaptation than a convenient signal for the play's claim to speak to a universal human condition. Similarly, I suggest, *The Apple Tree*'s version of Twain's version of Genesis comes less from a desire to stage the Bible than from a desire to assert that the play's sentiments about love and marriage are timeless and universal.[65]

Compared to *The Green Pastures*, *The Apple Tree* is what we might call an unfaithful adaptation. It uses the storyline of the Bible as a jumping off point for a performance that makes no claim of sincerity or authenticity vis-à-vis religion. Nevertheless, it stands as an important precursor to our next example, not only because of the Garden of Eden theme, but because of its star, Barbara Harris. As we shall see, Harris *almost* became the first and only woman to play the role of Eve in two different Broadway plays.[66]

The Creation of the World and Other Business

Arthur Miller (1915–2005) wrote some of the most enduring plays in the American canon: *All My Sons* (1947), *Death of a Salesman* (1949), *The Crucible* (1953), *A View From the Bridge* (1955). He adapted Ibsen's *Enemy of the People* for Broadway (1950), won the National Medal of the Arts (1993), and was married to Marilyn Monroe (1956–1961). When it came to adapting the Bible for the stage, however, Miller was not so fortunate. His little-loved and rarely remembered *The Creation of the World and Other Business* opened November 30, 1972, at the Shubert Theater, and closed sixteen days later after playing twenty-one previews and twenty performances at an estimated loss of $250,000.[67] The critics were no kinder to the play than the ticket-buying public. "By taking on the Book of Genesis," wrote Richard Watts in the *New York Post*, "Arthur Miller has tackled quite an ambitious project for himself, and I'm sorry to say I can't believe he has carried it off successfully."[68] *Time*'s T. E. Kalem called *Creation* "a feeble, pointless play," a sentiment echoed by Douglas Watt of the *Daily News*, who declared, "Arthur Miller has wrought a play devoid of wonder, mystery, or even the satisfying caress of fancy."[69]

Though little more than a footnote in the sweeping history of Miller's career (Miller himself devotes only three paragraphs of his six-hundred-page autobiography *Timebends* to it), *Creation* stands out amongst biblical dramas on Broadway for two reasons. First, along with *The Green Pastures* and Archibald MacLeish's *J.B.* (see chapter 5), it is one of only three such plays to represent the God of the Old Testament as a physically present, visible being portrayed by a human actor (Stephen Elliott). Second, it is one of a very few plays that treat the biblical narrative as a comedy. Yet where *The Green*

Pastures did so in a way that was perceived as both reverent and sincere, Miller's play is darkly ironic. If *The Apple Tree* was an unfaithful adaptation, sidestepping the religious questions posed by the biblical source material, *Creation* might best be described as a skeptical one, digging deeper into those questions and refusing to accept simple answers.[70]

According to Miller, *Creation* began as a series of character sketches inspired by his reading of the Old Testament. "I wasn't even seriously considering writing a play," he told Associated Press reporter William Glover. "They just grew. . . . I've been fascinated with Genesis since childhood. It just became part of my mind, I guess."[71] This fascination with Genesis is especially striking given that Miller—born and raised in a Jewish family—publicly acknowledged his own atheism. In a 1964 article, for example, occasioned by his planned trip to the Soviet Union, he stated simply, "I am not religious. I do not believe in Jehovah." This is, for the most part, echoed in his dramatic works. Though Jewishness is a theme that recurs throughout his corpus—most notably in *After the Fall* (1964), *The Price* (1968), and *Broken Glass* (1994), but present as a palpable absence in other works such as *Death of a Salesman* and *Incident at Vichy* (1964)—this Jewishness is most often understood as an ethnic, rather than religious identity.[72] Where Miller's Jewish characters do engage with faith, it is usually to express their doubt, dissent, or outright disbelief. Frequently, as in *The Crucible* (1953), organized religion is depicted as directly opposed to ethical or moral behavior. Miller's interest in the book of Genesis, then, is evidence that the Bible can serve as an influential text even for nonbelievers.

This may seem like an obvious point, but it is one that frequently eludes critics and spectators of faith. As we have seen, those skeptical of any attempt to stage the Bible look for signs of reverence toward the original text, which may be interpreted from the perceived sincerity of the artists involved or the perceived authenticity of the performance itself. While outright protestations of faith such as those offered by Richard B. Harrison are rarely demanded, the American audience, even in the explicitly secular and commercial realm of Broadway, seems to expect some expression of respect for religion. *Mrs. Fiske promises a dignified production.* Miller, it seems clear, felt he could not offer such reassurance in faith-based terms, choosing instead to communicate his respect for the Bible *as a work of literature.* "It's the age-old problem of civilization," he told the *New York Times,*

> the question of the individual being able to perceive his autonomy. That's why Cain is the first character in the Bible who has any psychological life. The sentence he utters about the murder of his brother ["Am I my brother's keeper?"] is the first sentence that makes the rest of the Bible possible. It sets the fundamental problem for man.[73]

This interrogation of the individual and his or her responsibility toward others is a recurring trope in Miller's earlier work, where characters are frequently forced to choose between their own self-interest and the greater good of the community.

For Miller, then, *Creation* represents "a continuation of previous themes, whether, first, a human being can be said to have any choice in his life and, secondly, if he can accept the responsibility of having made any choice."[74] Yet where *All My Sons, A View From the Bridge,* and *The Crucible* explore these themes in a realistic setting with a tone of high moral seriousness, *Creation* presents itself (at least initially) as a light spoof. The play follows the narrative sketched out in Genesis 2–4, expanding on and dilating the narrative with additional dialogue and several imaginary conversations between God and the serpent, whom Miller, following an established Christian exegetical tradition, identifies as Lucifer, the fallen angel.[75] Many Christians also conflate Lucifer with Satan (i.e., the Devil), including John Milton in *Paradise Lost,* which may have influenced Miller.[76] Though Miller does not use the term *Satan,* it is clear that his Lucifer represents the force of Evil in both the world and the play.

The curtain rises on Adam (Bob Dishy) in the Garden of Eden. God enters and after a few minutes of banter, he creates Eve (Zoe Caldwell) from Adam's rib. God departs, first warning Adam and Eve not to eat from the Tree of Knowledge. We then see an argument between God (Stephen Elliott) and Lucifer (George Grizzard) about the worrisome fact that Adam and Eve have not yet begun "multiplying." Lucifer suggests that the couple are too innocent, and recommends allowing them to eat from the Tree of Knowledge. When Lucifer violates God's desires by encouraging Eve and then Adam to eat the forbidden fruit, God casts him out of heaven, and expels Adam and Eve from the Garden. The second act takes place, presumably, on the east of Eden, as Adam and Eve struggle to scratch out a living in the wilderness.[77] Lucifer attempts to stir discord among them. The act ends with the birth of Cain. The final act focuses on the family dynamics of Adam and Eve and their now grown sons, Cain (Barry Primus) and Abel (Mark Lamos), concluding with Cain's murder of Abel and subsequent punishment. Finally, God bids farewell to Adam and Eve, as humankind will now have to get by without direct contact from the Almighty.

Despite (or because of) Miller's adherence to the biblical plot line, critics found the story of *Creation* difficult to follow. "God Serves Scrambled Eggs" ran one headline.[78] "Confusion in Eden" ran another.[79] Some of this apparent confusion may have arisen from the troubled circumstances of the production itself. At the start of the 1972–1973 Broadway season, producer Robert Whitehead announced that the play would be directed by Harold Clurman and feature Barbara Harris (who had played Eve in 1966's *The Apple Tree*) as Eve and Hal Holbrook (who took over the role of Adam in *The Apple Tree*)[80] as Lucifer. The play had its first out-of-town try-out at the Colonial Theatre in Boston. During the Boston run, both Clurman and Harris left the show. Press reports vary on whether these departures were voluntary. Rumors circulated about Clurman's declining abilities; he was seventy-one, and had last directed for Broadway six years earlier.[81] Press coverage also noted Harris's reputation as a difficult star with whom to work. Clurman was replaced by Gerald Freedman, who had recently completed a decade-long run as artistic director of the New York Shakespeare Festival. Susan Batson, a former Clurman student and Harris's standby, went on initially in the role of Eve, playing several performances in Boston and moving with the production to Washington, D.C., where she received generally good notices from critics. With the production still floundering, however, Whitehead and Miller shook up the cast once again, announcing that Australian actress Zoe Caldwell would take over for Batson and George Grizzard would take over for Holbrook.

While the latter replacement seemed like a simple case of producers looking to prop up a troubled production with added "star power" (in 1972, Grizzard was a significantly bigger "name" than Holbrook), the dismissal of Susan Batson proved more controversial. The official story put out by the production was that Caldwell was Miller's original choice for the role of Eve, but had declined because she had recently given birth to her first child. Having decided she was ready to return to the stage, it only made sense for producers to prefer the well-known star of *The Prime of Miss Jean Brodie* (1968) over Batson, a relative unknown.[82] Two factors, however, cast doubt on this narrative. First, Caldwell happened to be the wife of producer Robert Whitehead. Clearly, this suggested an ulterior motive for casting her, but such nepotism was hardly unprecedented in the annals of show business. Second and more noteworthy was the fact that Batson was African American. "When [Harris] left," Batson would tell the *New York Times*, "The first thing I asked Mr. Whitehead was whether he had considered the implications of having a black woman play Eve. He said [and here her voice throbbed with scorn and betrayal] that it had nothing to do with race, only talent."[83]

In retrospect, it is tempting to see this moment in the creation of *Creation* as a missed opportunity to intervene in the tumultuous racial politics of the era. If Eve, the mother of all humanity, were embodied by Batson, perhaps this would chip away at the dominant ideology of normative whiteness. Unlike *The Green Pastures*, where the blackness of the cast was understood as novelty and spectacle, a mixed-race "first family" might have challenged the audience to consider their preconceived notions about race and religion. At the very least, the casting of an African American actress in a lead role of a new play by Miller would represent a positive step toward the diversification of Broadway. For these reasons, Batson's mother, noted civil rights activist Ruth Batson, encouraged her to file a complaint with Actors Equity Association, alleging racial discrimination. Batson supported this allegation in part by telling reporters that Caldwell—prior to being named as Batson's replacement—had "said I shouldn't play Eve *too black.*"[84]

Given the broad latitude producers have in casting decisions, however, there was little Batson could do about Whitehead and Miller's decision. Ultimately, Batson's appeal was denied on the grounds that her initial contract as standby for Harris specifically noted that she would go on as Eve only if neither Harris nor Caldwell was available. Nevertheless, given Ruth Batson's stature in the African American community as well as the fact that the casting change occurred in the racially polarized Washington, D.C., of 1972, the brief controversy received enough press attention to destabilize an already shaky production. By the time that *Creation* opened in New York, it was (in the words of one reviewer) "an open secret that the birth pangs of this play have been excruciating."[85] Several critics observed wryly that the heavy rains that drenched Manhattan on opening night seemed to portend divine disfavor.

What If God Was One of Us?

Critics dismissed *Creation* in part because they judged it on literary grounds, as one might expect with a new play by America's most celebrated playwright.[86] In that context, the chief complaint was that the play lacked consistency of tone. Was it a comedy or a tragedy? Miller subtitled the play "a catastrophic comedy," in part to signal a creative departure from his earlier works, but it can also be read as a comment on the play's abrupt shifts between the high language of the King James Version ("Cursed is the ground for thy sake") to contemporary colloquialisms ("No more living forever. You got it?"),[87] or the progression of the plot from a one-liner-laden first act to a (literally) murderous third act.

"Uncertain in its approach," wrote Douglas Watt, the play "tries to be both playful and serious-minded, failing in both instances."[88] Similarly, Edwin Wilson in *The Wall Street Journal* complained that Miller "succeeds neither with low comedy nor with high ideas."[89] These criticisms are echoed in most later, scholarly analyses of Miller's work. Literary scholar Terry Otten, for example, notes that Miller "only partially succeeded" in creating the fictive world of the Bible,[90] while British critic Dennis Welland suggests, "This is the first play by Miller in which taste and tone are so ambivalent—even ambiguous—as to baffle interpretation."[91] Welland explicitly contrasts this ambivalence with Connelly's more sure-handed *The Green Pastures*, noting, "Because Miller is not, as Connelly was, presenting 'aspects of a living religion in the terms of its believers,' he is less successful."[92]

Connelly, as noted, was no more religious than Miller. Yet *The Green Pastures* nonetheless was received as a sincere expression of faith, because of its use of spectacle and the perceived authenticity of its simplistic representation of black religion. By contrast, Miller dramatizes the Bible in a more complex philosophical mode. The de-bates between God and Lucifer provide, in Otten's terms, "the dialectical struggle in the play, not between good and evil but . . . between the 'Good of Evil' and the 'Good of Good,' a juxtaposition of opposites."[93] Lucifer repeatedly justifies his existence with the assertion that Evil is a necessary component of human nature ("I am God's corrective symmetry").[94] The Fall from Grace, then, is represented as both tragic and necessary. *Creation* also trades in ironic self-awareness that undercuts the Bible's claim to sacredness. God, for example, explains the divine origin of man with a sideways reference to the theory of evolution, saying, "I had just finished the chimpanzee and had some clay left over. And I, well, just played around with it, and by golly there you were."[95] When God grows frustrated with Lucifer's disobedience, he orders him to "Go to Hell!"[96] It is both a literal command and a joke that plays on the incongruity of God using a mild profanity. In the final act, when a frustrated God declares an intention to abandon his creation to Lucifer's rule, a shocked Lucifer protests, "But I can't—I can't make anything!" to which God responds, "Really? But you're such a superb critic."[97] For Miller, who had grown increasingly frustrated with critics by this point in his career, this line offers something of a rejoinder.

This sense of irony was also present in the spectacular elements of the production. To simulate Adam and Eve's nudity in the Garden, the actors wore flesh-tone body-stockings bearing cartoonish representations of sexual organs (see figure 6). God, noted Wilson, "awakens Adam by leaning toward him with an outstretched finger duplicating Michelangelo's painting in the Sistine Chapel."[98] In their first appearance, angels Azrael, Raphael, and Chemuel enter singing Handel's "Hallelujah Chorus."[99] This ironic use of spectacle was read by many as inauthentic and irreverent: a "parody" or "pastiche"[100] of faith. "One suspects it was intended as some sort of dramatic cosmic comedy," declared Kevin Sanders on WABC TV, "But it's really more like a 'Flintstones' version of the book of Genesis. Still, if you take Genesis seriously, then you'll be offended."[101]

From an aesthetic standpoint, *Creation* had been condemned as bad theater. From a theological standpoint, it was by its author's own admission bad religion. The counterexample of *The Green Pastures*, however, suggests that audiences and critics may have been more tolerant of the play's shortcomings if the performance had evidenced

Figure 6. Rehearsal photo of *The Creation of the World and Other Business*, 1972. *Left to right*: Zoe Caldwell, Bob Dishy, Arthur Miller, George Grizzard. (Photo by Inge Morath © The Inge Morath Foundation. Image courtesy of Billy Rose Theatre Division, The New York Public Library for the Performing Arts. Reprinted by permission of Magnum Photos.)

greater sincerity or greater authenticity. In this regard, we must consider the possibility that *Creation*'s greatest sin, so to speak, was in its portrayal of God.

Born Elliott Pershing Stitzel to Jewish parents in New York in 1918, veteran character actor Stephen Elliott was fifty-four years old (three years younger than Miller) when he took on the role of God in *Creation*.[102] He studied acting with Sanford Meisner at the Neighborhood Playhouse in the early 1940s, making his Broadway debut in a supporting role in *The Tempest* (1945). He worked steadily on stage and screen, though he rarely played leading roles. Prior to *Creation*, his largest Broadway role had come as Thomas Stockmann in Miller's adaptation of Ibsen's *Enemy of the People* (1971). In twenty-two Broadway productions, he was nominated for a Tony Award just once, in the featured actor category, for his performance as Mr. Coulmier in *Marat/Sade* (1967). He was, in short, an ordinary actor who played God as he would any other role.

Critics responded kindly to Elliott's performance in *Creation*, while noting the difficulty of his task. "Stephen Elliott," wrote one, "though handicapped by a kind of ethereal version of a hospital orderly's uniform, is a rich-voiced and imposing looking God with nothing of much interest to utter."[103] Another noted that the character of God in *Creation* was "disagreeable and demanding, and . . . given to making a mess of things" while still remarking that Elliott was "a really impressive Deity."[104] A third noted, "Stephen Elliott's God is a bull-roaring cosmic paterfamilias," though it is unclear from the context whether this was intended as a compliment.[105] Martin Gottfried observed wryly that Elliott "had a tough time playing God (a thankless role no matter where)," adding that he seemed "burdened with the bulk of Miller's wisdom-making . . . and troubled by occasional attempts to make God funny-Jewish."[106]

The question of God's Jewishness is related here to the problem of authentic representation. There are a handful of references scattered throughout Miller's text that hint at a claim to the Jewish specificity of the Old Testament. Both God and Lucifer drop occasional Yiddish words ("Schmuck," "*unbeschreiblich*") into their dialogue. When Eve questions whether God really meant to prohibit eating from *that* tree, Adam tells her, "He said it in plain Hebrew."[107] More obliquely, some of the play's comic routines—such as an exchange between Eve and Adam about whether she is pregnant or just ate some bad clams—seem to echo a Borscht-belt sensibility. On a related note, several critics compared the family dynamics of Adam, Eve, Cain, and Abel to Miller's most famous creation, the Loman family. "And once Eden is left behind," wrote David Richards, "don't be astounded if Ma and Pa and the kiddies sound occasionally like a New York Jewish family having problems."[108] Biblically speaking, of course, there is no reason a New York Jewish God should be regarded as any less authentic than a Louisiana "Negro" God. Yet Richard Harrison could embody Connelly's De Lawd because the role was clearly marked as metaphorical, and because a white audience may *not* have recognized themselves in his performance. Perhaps Elliott's New York Jew was too familiar a character on the Broadway stage, too burdened with other associations, to bridge the gap between representation and presence.

Elliott's portrayal of God also seemed to lack sincerity. While he doubtless did his best to embody the character as a character, he did not align his performance with a profession of belief. Unlike Harrison, he did not come from a religious tradition in which laypeople may be called to preach the Word. Even if he had, the layers of irony and doubt within Miller's script would have made this a nearly impossible task. As Richard Watts suggests, "When an actor is given the role of God to portray, he must undergo a disturbing mixture of gratification and alarm. It is a flattering assignment, but it represents difficulties."[109] It may simply be the case that the role is unplayable in the context of the kind of conventional American method acting that formed Elliott's training. If God is ultimately unknowable, the actor's performance cannot be built on research nor evaluated according to its mimetic accuracy. If God is ultimately all-powerful, the stage actor's evident mortality undermines the illusion of timeless omniscience. If God *can* be played in a realistic way, in a way that causes the audience to empathize, can he really be God?

Looking beyond *The Green Pastures* and *The Creation of the World and Other Business*, the fact that so few playwrights have even tried to portray the God of the Old Testament points to a more fundamental problem, one that rests on our conception of the stage itself. The world of a play is, generally speaking, a self-contained one. The actions of the characters are preordained, the given circumstances set by an unseen Creator. The audience, on some level, recognizes this as a basic problem of the drama, and because this is, in a metaphysical sense, also the basic problem of humanity—fate versus free will—we recognize the theater as a useful microcosm through which to wrestle with issues great and small. In such an understanding of the stage, however, a character who is all-powerful and omniscient threatens to disrupt the dramatic balance. Under extraordinary circumstances, a performer such as Richard B. Harrison may bring enough sincerity to the role to transcend these limitations. More often, it seems that in the microcosm of the stage, there is room for only one all-powerful being: the playwright.

CHAPTER FOUR

These Are the Generations of Noah

When men of the theatre discuss religion they are usually
tender-hearted.

   —J. Brooks Atkinson, 1935

The wisest of us can go wrong—and what's worse, go Biblical
for our stage entertainment.

   —Billy Rowe, 1936

The Green Pastures and *The Creation of the World and Other Business* are outliers in their approach to staging the Bible, as they represent God directly via a human actor. Building a narrative around God solves one of the dramaturgical problems of adapting the Old Testament (the story problem), but it creates another one (the representation problem). Another, more ancient strategy for tackling the Old Testament is to choose a single Bible story and expand on it. This was the strategy of the medieval mystery plays such as the Chester, Townley, and York biblical cycles. The English cycle plays, theater historians believe, were designed to communicate the entirety of the Christian Bible through a series of episodic pageants, often performed on wagons as part of sacred festivals. As one element of a communal religious celebration, the mystery plays helped to communicate and affirm the story of Christianity from one generation to the next. The plays themselves, among the earliest known examples of English drama, brought to life the biblical narrative for an audience (and performers themselves) who had no opportunity to read the text. These mystery plays have often been cited by playwrights and producers as evidence that the dramatic representation of the Bible is not inherently sacrilegious.[1]

Among the mysteries, one of the most popular and enduring has been the story of Noah and the Flood, which occupies chapters 6–9 of Genesis, totaling eighty-five verses in the King James Version. By comparison, the story of Cain and Abel occupies only seventeen verses (Genesis 4:1–17), the Tower of Babel just nine (Genesis 11:1–9). There are a number of reasons why the Noah story might capture the imagination of the dramatist. From a theological perspective, the story is nondenominational in that Noah is considered a common ancestor to Christians, Jews, and Muslims. God, having grown disenchanted with the wickedness of humankind, determines to "destroy all flesh."[2] Noah, however, "found grace in the eyes of the Lord,"[3] and so God decides to exempt him and his family from the destruction. Noah is instructed by God to build an ark, where he gathers breeding stock of all the creatures of the earth in anticipation of a great flood. *And the rain was on the earth forty days and forty nights.*[4] The flood destroys all life on earth, with the exception of Noah and company, who remain safe aboard the ark. After 150 days, the waters recede, and the ark comes to rest on Mt. Ararat. Once the ark has been unloaded, God establishes a covenant with all humanity, as betokened by the rainbow.[5] There is an epilogue, of sorts, in which a drunken Noah is observed naked in his tent by his youngest son Ham, as a result of which Ham's descendants are cursed to serve those of his brothers.

This chapter considers four incarnations of the Noah story, presented, appropriately enough, two by two. French playwright Andre Obey's *Noé* (1930) was brought to the Broadway stage in February 1935 as *Noah*, in an adaptation/translation by Arthur Wilmurt with original music by Louis Horst and choreography by Horst and Anna Sokolow, where it enjoyed a brief but critically acclaimed run of forty-five performances at the Longacre Theatre. The following year, the Negro Unit of the Federal Theatre Project (FTP) brought their all-black version of Obey's play (using Carlton Moss's adaptation of Wilmurt's English text) to Harlem's Lafayette Theatre, playing a seven-week limited engagement that would later be reproduced by FTP Negro Units around the country. Considering these two versions of Noah in juxtaposition sheds further light on the role of race in staging the Bible, while also providing a unique opportunity to consider the biblical play as part of the larger phenomenon of theatrical adaptation in general.

The latter half of the chapter takes up another matched pair of Noah stories: Clifford Odets's *The Flowering Peach* (1954; revived 1994) and its musical adaptation, *Two by Two* (1970). Odets's last original play for Broadway, *The Flowering Peach* was nominated for the 1955 Pulitzer Prize for Drama and was the jury's recommended choice for the prize, though the board ultimately decided—under pressure from chairman Joseph Pulitzer Jr.—to give the award to Tennessee Williams's *Cat on a Hot Tin Roof* instead.[6] Several years after Odets's death in 1963, composer Richard Rodgers and lyricist Martin Charnin joined book-writer Peter Stone to develop a musical based on *The Flowering Peach* as a vehicle for entertainer Danny Kaye. The result, *Two by Two*, played on Broadway for nearly a year (more than twice as many performances as the Odets original), closing in September 1971. In *The Flowering Peach*, we have an example of a notable Jewish playwright staging an Old Testament narrative in an explicitly Jewish fashion less than ten years after the Holocaust. In *Two by Two*, we have a Jewish production team adapting that play for a musical featuring a Jewish singer/comedian. The comparison of the two performances offers insight into the way that Jewish artists approach the problem of biblical adaptation, as well as the opportunities and challenges presented when adapting a straight play into a musical.

Each of the plays discussed in this chapter employs elements of the fan fictional approach described in chapter 2, dilating the narrative for dramatic effect, fleshing out characters that had previously been mere names and actions, addressing what events might have transpired "between the verses." The key difference here, however, is that despite these various techniques, the plays described in this chapter present themselves as adaptations that are faithful in both senses of the word. They are faithful adaptations in the sense that they adhere closely to the characters and sequence of events that mark the original narrative, and they are faithful in the sense that they approach the biblical subject with reverence.

With regard to our terms of analysis, the biblical story of Noah, who is defined by his righteousness and his willingness to obey God, would seem to lend itself to performance in the mode of sincerity, while the descriptions of the ark, the animals, and the Flood would seem to call for a level of spectacle. Both these elements are present in all four adaptations, but they are especially prevalent in the two 1930s examples. In the latter two examples, we see the balance shift toward irony and authenticity, though that authenticity takes a different form than we have previously seen.

Noah

In February 1935, in the midst of the Great Depression, Clifford Odets's *Awake and Sing!* had its premiere at the Belasco Theatre. *The Green Pastures* company returned from its extended national tour for an encore run at the 44th Street Theatre. And on February 13, the same day that a New Jersey jury found Richard Bruno Hauptmann guilty of kidnapping and murdering the infant son of Charles Lindbergh, *Noah* would open at the Longacre Theatre. French playwright André Obey (1892–1975) had previously been represented in New York with a comic one-act, *The Wife with the Smile*, produced by the Theatre Guild in 1921, and gained a wider reputation among New York audiences with his adaptation of *The Rape of Lucretia*, translated by Thornton Wilder as *Lucrece* (1932). *Noah* would be his last and most successful Broadway outing, in a translation by journeyman playwright Arthur Wilmurt (1906–1994). The production, according to Robert Garland of the *Herald-Tribune*, was "like nothing the Manhattan stage has seen":[7]

> There are comedy and tragedy. There are poetry and prose. There is singing, there is dancing, there is pantomime. There is the wrath of God and the pity that passes understanding. All of these are there. . . . Once in a while you are reminded of the contemporary episode in "The Green Pastures," which is coming back to town. More frequently you are reminded of a Walt Disney "Silly Symphony," a sacred "Silly Symphony," if you can imagine such a thing.[8]

Obey had written *Noah* (*Noé*) while in residence with Jacques Copeau's Compagne des Quinze in the 1920s. Designed to take advantage of the company's skill at mime, Obey's script calls for a company of seventeen, in which eight of the company members play speechless animals: the Bear, the Lion, the Cow, the Elephant, the Monkey, the Tiger, the Lamb, and the Wolf. The play begins with Noah (Pierre Fresnay) alone on stage completing construction of his famous ark. As he works, he converses with God; God remains unseen however, and the audience hears only Noah's side of the conversation, for ex-

Figure 7. Pierre Fresnay as Noah with (*left to right*) Lion, Cow, Monkey, Tiger, and Wolf in *Noah* (1935). (Photo © 1935 by Alfredo Valente. Image courtesy of Billy Rose Theatre Division, The New York Public Library for the Performing Arts. Reprinted by permission of Richard Valente.)

ample, "Now, Lord, please don't think that—Oh, but look, of course I trust you!"[9] This opening banter with God is comic in a lighthearted way ("Should I make a rudder? I say, a rudder—No, no. R as in Robert; U as in Hubert . . ."),[10] setting a tone that *Time* magazine called, "unhackneyed, humorous and at times downright noble."[11] Soon enough the animals appear, represented by human actors in elaborate costumes and masks (designed by Remo Bufano). This physicalized but nonrealistic representation of the animals, combined with Cleon Throckmorton's fanciful set,[12] prompted Brooks Atkinson and other critics to use the term "fairy tale" to describe the play's aesthetic.[13]

Once the animals have boarded the ark, Noah must convince his family to do the same. This includes his wife (Margaret Arrow), addressed only as Mama or Mrs. Noah, his three sons Shem (David Friedkin), Ham (Harry Bellaver), and Japhet (Norman Lloyd), and their respective wives-to-be, whom Obey somewhat whimsically names Norma (Fraye Gilbert), Sella (Cora Burlar), and Ada (Gertrude Flynn).[14] Though all take some convincing, the first act finds the family aboard the ark as the rain begins to fall. Act 2 consists of two scenes aboard the ark. At first, the family is thrilled to have been saved from the flood, and the conversation is jocular. Later, however, they begin to fear that the waters will never recede, that they have been abandoned at sea. Frustrated with his family's lack of belief, Noah finds solace in the company of the animals. In the third act, the waters recede, and the company is able to step off the ark onto Mount Ararat. No sooner have they debarked than Noah's three sons immediately begin a struggle over dominion of the newly revealed earth. Their racially charged exchange reflects the tradition that each will become the patriarch of a different race. Japhet and Shem address Ham as "nigger"; Ham and Japhet call Shem "chink"; Shem and Ham call Japhet "whitey."[15] In aggravation, the three sons and their wives go their separate ways, leaving Noah and his wife alone atop the mountain. Saddened and exhausted, Noah cries to the heavens for some sign that he has done the right thing. "Oh, Lord," he prays, "shed Your light upon my daily job! Let me have the impression—the *feeling—Your assurance—*that You are satisfied, Will you?"[16] In response, a rainbow appears against the backdrop, symbolizing Noah's covenant with God. "That's fine," says Noah, as the play ends.

Inevitably, observers compared *Noah* to *The Green Pastures*. The comparison was sometimes favorable, as in the case of Robert Garland, writing in the *World-Telegraph*, who professed his preference for the "pale-faced Noah of Andre Obey's play" over the "dark-hued Noah of Marc Connelly's *The Green Pastures*."[17] The comparison was sometimes unfavorable, as in the case of Arthur Ruhl, who wrote in the *Herald Tribune*, "'Noah' is a sort of French 'Green Pastures,' although much slimmer and slighter than the American play."[18] Some critics, such as Atkinson of the *Times*, highlighted the similarities: "American audiences will find in it also an occasional echo of 'The Green Pastures.' Although Noah is not black, as he was in our miracle play, he is a simple-minded, reverent old cove, and he talks now and then to God."[19] Others highlighted the differences: "*Noah* has the same sort of appeal as *The Green Pastures*. But it is clearly a product from the banks of the Seine, not the Mississippi, [and] could not possibly be taken as an imitation."[20]

Noah translator Arthur Wilmurt pushed back at the comparison in an op-ed for the *New York Times*, published March 3, 1935. While acknowledging the obvious parallels between the two plays, he insists that "these undeniable points of resemblance are much more superficial than has been suggested."[21] In *The Green Pastures*, argues Wilmurt, "God is the protagonist. He walks the earth, and behaves as people everywhere hope and pray He might behave."[22] By contrast,

> Mr. Obey offers us no such satisfaction in "Noah." Behind the Bible story related by Mr. Obey is an expression of Man's attitude toward God. The God in his play is, to the end, the Unknown God. No one who witnesses "Noah," and no one who plays a part in his experience—except himself— feels the intimate presence and companionship of Him as a human being. He is in the play as He is felt in most men's lives—a presence felt, hovering above, silent, inscrutable, incalculable. We do not hear His voice when Noah asks him question. We, unless we have Noah's faith, cannot be sure, until the end, that He "is not so far away."[23]

Because the God of *Noah* is unknown and unknowable, the audience is asked instead to empathize with Noah, a much more conventional protagonist, one who must balance his desire to please his family with his responsibility to a higher calling.

Nevertheless, the simplicity and humility with which Fresnay performed the role of Noah, combined with the vernacular language of Obey's text (and Wilmurt's translation), prompted observers to describe the play in terms of simplicity, naïveté, and sincerity. "Think of *The Green Pastures* (but not too closely)," wrote the editors of *The Stage*. "Think of impromptu parlor charades, of Barrie retelling a familiar legend, of the way your little girl might tell back to you the Bible stories."[24] The fantasy element of the play was enhanced by a modern dance number, choreographed by Anna Sokolow and performed by Noah's sons and their wives upon reaching land. Garland called the play "simply entrancing," adding, "By 'simply' I mean honestly. By 'entrancing' I mean entrancing."[25] Similarly, Atkinson declared, "Sophisticated playgoers will find it naïve. Modest people will realize that it is beautiful."[26] *Noah*, then, comes across as a sincere investigation of faith, one that utilizes spectacle in a different way than we have previously seen. The approach is nonmimetic; that is, no attempt is made to convince the audience that what they are seeing is actually happening. The fairy-tale aesthetic sets it apart from the grittier, more realistic fare that a 1930s audience expected; some press accounts even suggested (dubiously) that the play had originally been intended for children.[27] As Gilbert Seldes wrote in the *American*, "Broadway is probably going to think it an ark out of water."[28]

In this sense, *Noah* lays claim to a kind of sincerity that disarms the fear that a theatrical spectacle will be either blasphemous or heretical. There is no false representation, no misleading or sinful illusion. There is simply a traditional story, told without pretense. Classical scholar Francis Fergusson, writing in 1949, would declare, "We feel behind [*Noah*], not sentimental contemporary fiction, but a theatrical-folk tradition going back to secular Medieval plays. It has some of the ancient force of the Hassidic stories about God, which are also childishly simple narratives with a very severe meaning."[29] This evocation of the classic mystery play, this sense of sincerity and innocence ("childishly simple"), combined with the fact that *Noah* took few liberties with the text of Genesis (and was therefore plausibly authentic on the literary level), explains why the Obey/Wilmurt creation drew no apparent criticism from religious organizations or playgoers of faith.

At the same time, the concerns expressed by Atkinson, Seldes, and others that the play was out of place on Broadway proved to be prophetic. Though it fared reasonably well at the box office in a limited engagement, *Noah* did not capture the imagination of the American audience in the way that *The Green Pastures* had. There was no film adaptation, no national tour. With its recognizable title and large ensemble cast, the play lived on in university, college, and little theater productions for some years, but it remained simply a play among plays, not a cultural phenomenon. There are three likely reasons for this. First, compared to other more successful biblical adaptations, the play was perceived as insufficiently spectacular. For audiences conditioned by *Ben-Hur* and *The Green Pastures* to expect stagecraft on an epic scale, the comparatively small cast, the unit set, and the minimal special effects of *Noah* could not possibly have generated the requisite sense of awe needed to do justice to the Bible. Second, the play was perceived as insufficiently authentic. Audiences accepted the childlike simplicity of *The Green Pastures* because they believed it to be a genuine expression of faith by a childlike people (sincerity), and because the music and bodies it showcased appeared to be irreducibly real (authenticity). *Noah* was sincere but inauthentic; its fairy-tale aesthetic remained exclusively representational. Third, without the interplay of the real and the representational, the stakes of the play's encounter with the divine remained too abstract. With the exception of the appearance of the rainbow at the close of the play, in fact, God's presence is nowhere indicated in the text or the production. His invisible presence sets the drama in action, but the impact of this on the audience is mitigated by the fact that the play begins *after* Noah has already begun building the ark. As a result, *Noah* remained a drama of, in Wilmurt's own words, "the beauty of God in Man,"[30] rather than a true encounter with the divine.

Noah Redux

When Garland wrote that *Noah* was "like nothing the Manhattan stage has seen," he added, "or is likely to see again."[31] The latter proposition turned out to be incorrect. Only eighteen months later, Obey's *Noah* would return to the Manhattan stage, this time a few miles further north: at the Lafayette Theatre in Harlem. This version of *Noah* featured an all-black cast, and was produced under the auspices of the Federal Theatre Project's Negro Theatre Unit. The production billed itself as "Adapted by Carlton Moss from the English text of Arthur Wilmurt."[32] Moss (1909–1997) first gained influence in the African American theater scene with his troupe Toward a Black Theatre, formed while he was still a student at Morgan State University in Baltimore.[33] During the Harlem Renaissance, Moss was a minor celebrity: he wrote a number of radio scripts for NBC in New York and hosted a radio talk show. When the Negro Theatre was established at the Lafayette Theatre on 131st Street in 1935 under the direction of Orson Welles and John Houseman, Moss was Houseman's chief assistant, serving as a stage manager for the company's infamous "voodoo *Macbeth*" (1936). When political pressures forced a reorganization of the company with an all-black administration, Moss found himself as one of three directors of the unit (along with Harry F. V. Edward and J. A. "Gus" Smith). *Noah* would become the Negro Theatre's fifth production, and its first under this administration.[34]

As such, the production was covered as national news by the African American press. "Carlton Moss," wrote the *Norfolk Journal and Guide*, "one of the race's most promising playwrights, has adapted the original story (with the cabled permission of the author, of course) for grown-ups, at the same time preserving its simplicity."[35] The changes to Obey's play in Moss's never-published adaptation seem to have been limited to two aspects.[36] First, the dialogue was "converted into English by Arthur Wilmurt and into Harlemese by Moss."[37] Second, the play was given a new musical score by African American composer Jean Stor. Also known as William Astor Morgan, Stor had begun his career as a church organist and choirmaster, and had spent much of the 1920s collecting and arranging Negro spirituals at the Selden Institute, a church-affiliated school in rural Georgia.[38] Though Stor also worked in a classical mode—his Opus 54, a suite for strings, would be performed by the New York Philharmonic in 1942—his score for *Noah* drew more on his experience as a chorister. Manuel Essman's sets and costumes for the production, as well as the animal masks, were similar to those used on Broadway in 1935, though wardrobe mistress Hilda Farnum's hand-painted homespun cloth gave the costumes a level of authenticity that the prior production lacked.

Though widely heralded in advance, this *Noah* turned out to be something of a disappointment. Calling the play "Two Hours of Goody Goody," Ralph Matthews complained that "Carlton Moss, who has behind him a brilliant record as a radio script writer, is capable of better stuff than he put into 'Noah,' and deserves a sound spanking for wasting his talents adapting so weak a piece as Andre Obey's 'Noah,' which had already flopped on two continents."[39] Billy

Figure 8. Noah (Thomas Mosely), *center*, surrounded by his family in Carlton Moss's adaptation of Obey's *Noah*, 1936. (Image courtesy of Billy Rose Theatre Division, The New York Public Library for the Performing Arts.)

Rowe of the *Pittsburgh Courier* declared it "not very Biblical, but very much wrong."[40] "The work of Mr. Moss is skillful and satirical," opined Roi Ottley in the African American newspaper the *Amsterdam News*, "but the material is hardly the kind that lends itself easily to the Negro Theatre and its quality of acting talent."[41] While some audiences were enthusiastic, there were also numerous reports of spectators leaving at intermission, frustrated by the slow pace of the story. While Thomas Mosely as Noah received generally strong notices, one critic noted that Mosely received "the applause he deserved for carrying one of the most burdensome plays of the year along to its conclusion."[42]

The biblical theme of the play came under fire as well. "Noah," suggested Ottley, "might have been imposed upon us because of the belief in the deep religiosity of the Negro."[43] This represented, in Ottley's view, an error in judgment, because "the church is a competitor and hardly will encourage its membership to visit the theatre."[44] Matthews seemed offended by the play's preachy quality, noting wryly that "bringing sinful Harlem to a realization that there is a just and living God is a new undertaking in governmental procedure."[45]

Despite its poor reception in New York, Moss's adaptation of *Noah* would go on to several subsequent productions by other Negro units of the Federal Theatre Project. Some, whether following the lead of *The Green Pastures* or simply seeking to employ as many performers as possible, added an offstage choir to maximize the church-like experience of the play. Others moved consciously away from the religious theme. Theater historian Barry Witham, in *The Federal Theatre Project: A Case Study*, notes that in the Seattle production, "*Noah* was transformed into a kind of dance musical with lots of improvisation and some contemporary references. Although the production report asserts that they remained true to the text, it also admits that after the ark came to rest on Mt. Ararat, 'The younger members, overjoyed at being on land, go through a "truckin'" number, singing improvised words.'"[46]

Like many of the all-black productions at the Lafayette Theatre, *Noah* played to mixed audiences. Yet unlike the "voodoo *Macbeth*" or *The Case of Philip Lawrence* (1937), Moss's adaptation failed to win the interest or respect of white critics. This may have been a simple case of an ill-conceived production. It may have been that on the heels of *The Green Pastures*, the sight of black actors performing a biblical story lacked novelty value. In the end, the production may have been undermined by the same questionable authenticity that plagued the 1935 Broadway version.

Perhaps the Noah narrative is simply too flimsy to support a substantive dramatic treatment. The presence of the animals and the imaginary spectacle of the flood provide an amusing story for children, but the biblical Noah is a problematic character. He follows God's commands without hesitation, and speaks only at the very end of his story, when he curses Ham for shaming him in his drunken nakedness. Moreover, between the building of the ark and the founding of a new civilization, the story has a tedious and uneventful "second act": *And the waters prevailed upon the earth an hundred and fifty days.*[47] Perhaps this is why even the favorable responses to Obey's play focus on its simplicity, its childlike innocence. Perhaps too, this is why the most successful Broadway adaptation of Noah would come from a playwright for whom naïveté often seemed to be a virtue.

The Flowering Peach

"Old Father Noah, a protagonist in medieval miracle plays, has appeared three times in my memory on the contemporary stage," wrote Euphemia Van Rensselaer Wyatt in her review of *The Flowering Peach*. "From the French point of view in the play by Obey; as a Negro patriarch in *Green Pastures* and as the head of a turbulent Yiddish family in the current play by Clifford Odets."[48] During the mid-1930s, as *Noah* played first Broadway and then Harlem, the most celebrated playwright in New York was Clifford Odets. The years from 1935 to 1937 saw some of his greatest triumphs, including *Awake and Sing!* (1935),[49] *Waiting for Lefty* (1935), and *Golden Boy* (1937). In these plays, among others, Odets gives us protagonists who are defined by their idealism. Their belief in a higher purpose puts them into direct conflict with the pragmatic and cynical world around them. Though he would surely have resisted defining his work in religious terms, it is not too much of a stretch to characterize the classic Odets hero as a righteous man in a sinful world. So while it was not inevitable that Odets should turn to Noah as a source of inspiration, neither is it shocking that some have regarded *The Flowering Peach* as the playwright's finest creation.

Odets's play departs significantly from the 1930s approach to the Bible that characterized *The Green Pastures* and *Noah*. Instead of imagining the Bible and its people as belonging to a simpler time, Odets makes his characters as fully drawn and complex as those of contemporary drama. Instead of transporting the audience back to an imaginary biblical time, *The Flowering Peach* brings the Bible narrative forward to meet the contemporary audience where they live. In an interview with the *New York Times* on the eve of the play's premiere, Odets explained, "Noah had three sons, it was a family life. I know family life. There are children and parents, with ambitions, with disappointments, with anger and love. In the play, these people think like us, speak like us, they're a distillation of the modern and biblical."[50]

In this sense, the play's setting, which Odets's script describes simply as "Then, not now,"[51] is misleading. As producer Robert Whitehead said in a press release, "'The legend of Noah is six thousand years old—older maybe; but this wonderful myth has never been told with humor and warmth, because it's always been a fairy tale about sin and punishment.'"[52] By contrast, Whitehead continues, Odets "translates the story of the Flood into human terms, real and immediate, like going to work in the morning or arguing with your wife."[53] In so doing, Odets is able to turn the story of the Flood into a drama that reaches beyond the childlike innocence of Obey's *Noah*.

In *Noah*, the curtain rises on the nearly finished ark, a fait accompli. By contrast, *The Flowering Peach* begins in Noah's home, setting the tone for what is, more than anything else, a domestic drama. Noah (Menasha Skulnik) has just awakened from a dream in which, as he tells his wife, God has told him of the flood to come and of the need to build an ark. Noah's wife, here called Esther (Berta Gersten), is skeptical. "And all this God told you in one single dream . . . ?"[54] In the second scene, Noah encounters similar skepticism from his sons. Only when God sends a sign, in the form of a singing rodent called a *Gitka*,[55] is Noah able to persuade his family to join him in building the ark. The construction process occupies the next three scenes, serving as a backdrop to an evolving family drama. Shem, the oldest son, and his wife Leah are motivated by money; they resist Noah's plan because it means giving up their accumulated wealth. Ham, the second son, is motivated by desire and is apparently unfaithful to his wife Rachel. Japheth, the youngest son, craves his father's approval but is intimidated by his brothers. Shortly before the ark is set to depart he brings home a girl, Goldie, to be his wife, though it is clear that she has eyes for Ham.

This unstable family dynamic is exacerbated once the rains fall and the family find themselves confined in the close quarters of the ark for weeks at a time. Noah quarrels with his sons and with Esther; the sons quarrel amongst each other; Japheth falls in love with Ham's wife, Rachel; Noah has a crisis of faith and gets drunk. At the long-awaited moment when the dove returns with the olive branch, indicating that dry land has been found, Noah discovers that his wife Esther has died in her sleep. Finally, in the ninth and last scene, the sons and their wives disembark on Mount Ararat by the shade of the titular peach tree.[56] Noah, however, has grown wary and refuses to leave the ark until God shows him a sign to prove that He will never again destroy the world. Then, as in the Obey play, God's rainbow appears in the sky.[57] "Yes, I hear You, God," says Noah. "Now it's in man's hands to make or destroy the world."[58] Noah steps off the ark and continues speaking to God as the curtain falls.

The Flowering Peach opened December 28, 1954, at the Belasco Theatre—the same theater where *Awake and Sing!* premiered nearly two decades earlier—under the direction of the playwright. The part of Noah was played by Menasha Skulnik, a fifty-six-year-old Polish-born Jew. Skulnik had been an established star on the Yiddish stage and also provided the voice of Uncle David on the radio series *The Goldbergs* for nineteen years, but he was a relative newcomer to Broadway, having made his debut the prior year as dressmaker Max Pincus in Sylvia Regan's *The Fifth Season*. Another Polish-born Yiddish performer, Berta Gersten, played Noah's wife. This casting ensured that for many spectators, Noah and his family would be interpreted as Jewish. The actors' accents cemented this impression, as did Odets's use of stereotypically Jewish phrasing ("A better son than Japheth you don't have")[59] and the occasional Yiddish word ("*tuchter*").[60] Thus while the words *Jew* and *Jewish* are entirely absent from the script, it was clear to most audiences and critics that, as Thomas R. Dash wrote, "Odets has taken some liberties with the Biblical account. He has made Noah and his whole tribe Judaic."[61] This was enhanced by stage business such as Noah and Shem donning traditional yarmulkes (skullcaps) for the dinner scene, and Esther making a ritual gesture over Shabbat (Sabbath) candles (see figure 9).[62]

By representing Noah as a Jew, Odets indeed departs from the Bible, where the ark-builder precedes Abraham, the first Jew, by nine generations. While it is tempting to read this choice as a claim to Jewish ownership of the Old Testament narrative, it is far more likely that Odets was simply transposing the story of Noah into the idiom with which he himself was most familiar. As Louis Sheaffer wrote in the *Brooklyn Eagle*, "He hasn't left home really. He is writing once again of a typical Odets family, the same kind of people, affectionate, bickersome, emotional, individualistic, who used to turn up in his accounts of Jewish life in the Bronx."[63] Similarly, Brooks Atkinson noted that "Mr. Odets has modeled his characters on a middle-class Jewish family that speaks a modern vernacular."[64] Washington, D.C., critic Tom Donnelly, in a review headlined "You were expecting maybe Bernard Shaw?" characterizes the play's "Odetsian rhythms"

Figure 9. Noah (Menasha Skulnik), center, speaks to God as Esther (Berta Gersten) blesses the Shabbat candles in *The Flowering Peach*, 1954. (From the collection of the author.)

as "of the 'What kind of a house is this that it ain't got an orange?' variety."[65] As Virginia Lambert would later write, on the occasion of the play's twentieth anniversary, "In the Bible according to Clifford Odets, the ark came to rest in the Bronx not on Mt. Ararat."[66]

Most critics and audiences responded positively to the Jewish element of *The Flowering Peach*. "The representation of Noah and his family in contemporary Yiddish-American terms is a delight," wrote

Harold Stern in the *American Hebrew*.[67] Wyatt, the *Catholic World* critic, saw the Jewishness of Noah as key to the play's theology, suggesting that "Mr. Odets has incorporated from the Hebrew Midrash the tradition that it was the angels who herded the animals in patient pairs beside the Ark."[68] Similarly, Alice Hughes, writing for King Features Syndicate, offered:

> Seemingly simple, "The Flowering Peach" seems to have more profundity than "The Green Pastures." The latter is a portrayal of a simple, light-hearted child-like people. Their everyday worldly lives offer a homespun contrast to the humility of God who appears among them as an old Sunday school teacher. In the Noah play God is never seen, in accordance with Hebrew teaching. His presence is felt in the struggle for reverence, justice, and fortitude.[69]

Hughes was not the only observer to draw a comparison with *The Green Pastures*. Many, however, were less complimentary. The *New Yorker* dismissed the play as "more suitable for production in a high-school auditorium than in a Broadway theatre," adding, "It aims, I suppose, at combining with the simple faith and moral dignity of 'The Green Pastures' the surefire hilarity of Yiddish dialect comedy."[70] Richard Cooke of the *Wall Street Journal* called *The Flowering Peach* "a mixed bag. A trace of The Green Pastures [*sic*], a good deal of Jewish family squabbling, dashes of insight, some engaging comedy and a varied assortment of weather."[71] Dash laments, "Had the play come to focus, we might have had a work reminiscent of 'Green Pastures,' for the mood is similar."[72]

Ultimately, responses to the play polarized around Skulnik's performance as Noah. George Oppenheimer of *Newsday*, for example, characterized *The Flowering Peach* as "a modern parable that seems to me the finest, gentlest, and most moving play of the season," while adding, "And in Menasha Skulnik, Odets the writer and Odets the director have found the finest, gentlest and most moving actor of many seasons."[73] Similarly, Hal Eaton of the *Long Island Daily Press* praised "Menasha Skulnik in the most eloquent portrayal of his career—in fact, one of the most brilliant performances of the contemporary theater," en route to his pronouncement that "'The Flowering Peach,' unveiled last night at the Belasco, emerges as a whimsical and vigorously provocative drama."[74] Though Atkinson admits that "no one would seem less suited to the part of Noah than Mr. Skulnik," whom he calls a "music-hall comedian," he goes on to praise the actor for a "rich performance" in which he displays "meekness and a purity of submission that is touching and admirable."[75] Those who disliked the play were those who found Skulnik's "garment-district Noah" (i.e., a Jewish comic Noah) inappropriate to the weighty subject matter.[76]

Yet the Jewish specificity of Skulnik's comic portrayal of Noah is key to understanding the role that irony plays in *The Flowering Peach*. The previous biblical plays *The Green Pastures* and *Noah* had as many comic moments. They even deployed a similar form of irony, in the comic juxtaposition of high (the sacred text) and low (the vernacular dialogue). Where *The Flowering Peach* diverges from these predecessors (and from its more distant predecessors of the Townley and Chester cycles) is that its humor comes not simply from having the characters of the Bible speak like ordinary people, but from a willingness to poke fun at the underlying narrative, to point out the absurdity inherent in the source text. What kind of God would behave this way? And what kind of person would obey such a God?

Unable to answer the former question, *The Flowering Peach* does offer—by implication—an answer to the latter. What kind of person would obey such a God? A Jewish person. Finding humor in the dialectic tension between doubt and belief, between rational thought and unquestioning faith, has long been recognized by scholars as a characteristically Jewish trait. As literary historian David Daiches writes, "Jewish humor at its most authentic arose from the clash between a vocabulary geared to a life of religious observance and a deeply ironical practical skepticism."[77] Odets's Noah is recognizably Jewish because of his speech patterns, but also because of his way of being in the world. As Jewish theater scholar Ellen Schiff observes, "Unlike the Noah of Genesis but in the manner of many other Old Testament figures, Odets' protagonist questions God's choice of him."[78] And like Abraham, Moses, and other Jewish patriarchs, Odets's Noah proceeds to obey God despite his misgivings. This is not to say that *The Flowering Peach* is an exclusively Jewish drama, but rather that Odets's incorporation of Jewishness into the narrative creates a space wherein irony can be perceived as authentic. This works, to the degree that it does, because the play does not treat people of faith as "other." Instead, it allows the audience to empathize with a protagonist who is *not* perfect, who does *not* always do the right thing, but who aspires to goodness.

Two by Two

Two by Two, the musical adaptation of *The Flowering Peach*, opened November 10, 1970.[79] It arrived at the Belasco, the same theater that had housed Odets's original, freighted with high expectations. The combined drawing power of composer Richard Rodgers (*The Sound of Music, Oklahoma!*) and star Danny Kaye (movie star, talk show host, and all-around celebrity) resulted in a reported $19,000 of income on the first day of ticket sales and (eventually) the largest advance sale in Broadway history to that date.[80] Peter Stone (*1776*) wrote the book. The lyrics were by Martin Charnin, who would later direct the fortieth-anniversary revival of *The Flowering Peach*.[81] The role of Shem was played by Harry Goz,[82] who had previously been one of several actors to play Tevye during the long run of *Fiddler on the Roof.* Madeline Kahn, in one of her earliest Broadway roles, played Goldie, the heartbreaker. Rodgers, who also produced the play, was presenting his first original score for Broadway since *Do I Hear a Waltz?* (1965). Kaye was playing a Broadway role for the first time in nearly thirty years.[83] With so much pent-up star power attached to the project, the biblical content of *Two by Two* appeared to be something of an afterthought.

Rodgers apparently conceived the musical as a vehicle for Kaye. "I had no notion of coming back to Broadway at all," Kaye told the *New York Times*; "then Dick Rodgers said, 'How about a musical of *The Flowering Peach?*'"[84] Odets's play, felt Kaye, was ahead of its time, "writing about the generation gap 16 years before anybody named it."[85] Kaye also felt that the show offered a robust challenge for him as a performer. In Rodgers and Stone's reworking of the plot, Noah begins the play as an old man, but halfway through the first act his youth is magically restored by God to enable him to complete the ark. This allowed Kaye to show off his dancing ability in energetic numbers such as "[I Feel Like I'm] Ninety Again" and "When It Dries." The need to build the show around Kaye also meant that the musical became even more Noah-centered than Odets's play. Noah sings in twelve of the show's eighteen musical numbers and has most of the laugh lines. The first of those laugh lines sets the tone for the show. In lieu of an overture, the play begins with a crash of thunder, followed by Noah's rejoinder, "You want us to build a *what?*" Thunder. "It's gonna do *what?*" More thunder. "Forty days and forty *what?*" The orchestra enters with a blast of horns, and Noah sets off into his opening number "Why Me?"[86] In the context of the play, the use of the sound of thunder to represent God's side of Noah's conversations with the Almighty is a simple and effective comic device, one that is repeated during the show's final number, "The Covenant." If we compare it to *The Flowering Peach*, however, we see that giving God an audible presence in this way shifts the balance of the narrative significantly. When Odets's Noah receives his orders from God, he questions himself. But in *Two by Two*, Noah questions God directly.

Martin Gottfried, reviewing the musical for *Women's Wear Daily*, associated this shift in emphasis with another significant change from *The Flowering Peach*: an erasure of the play's Jewish sensibility. "'Two by Two,'" writes Gottfried, "has virtually no Jewishness to it. . . . Without such a motif, or any other to replace it, [the play] becomes a plain re-telling of Noah's story, which is kind of incredible coming in a professional Broadway production. They even have God speaking in thunderclaps and kettle-drums."[87] Without the "Jewishness," he seems to say, the musical is akin to an amateur Bible pageant. How much Jewishness remains in *Two by Two* is a complicated question. Other than Gottfried, the only critics who alluded to Noah's Jewishness did so dismissively. "Who really wants to hear about Noah?" asked Clive Barnes, writing in the *New York Times*. "Who hasn't heard already? We had even guessed he was Jewish; we just didn't know he was half-brother to Sholem Aleichem's Tevye."[88] It is unclear whether Barnes's invocation of *Fiddler on the Roof* refers specifically to Noah's penchant for holding conversations with God, or if he is simply noting that both musicals feature a Jewish patriarch as a leading man.

Meanwhile, John J. O'Connor of the *Wall Street Journal* noted the similarity between *Two by Two* and a show that had opened the previous month, *The Rothschilds*. "Both are about Jewish families," he wrote. "This might indicate a bit of play-it-safe pandering with the typical New York theater audience . . . but that subject is best left to

Figure 10. Noah (Danny Kaye) and his family in *Two by Two* (1970). (Photo by Friedman-Abeles © Billy Rose Theatre Division, The New York Public Library for the Performing Arts.)

some bright student's sociology dissertation."[89] Such snide comments aside, Peter Stone's book actually eliminates many of Odets's Yiddishisms, though this was likely motivated by the need to economize the dialogue in order to make space for Rodgers and Charnin's songs. As in most musicals of the era, the songs carry the weight of the plot. Neither the music nor the lyrics are explicitly Jewish, nor did Kaye or any of the other performers affect a Yiddish accent.[90] Thus there is little in the play either culturally or theologically to support a reading of Noah and family as Jews. If some observers do identify them as such, it is likely due to an expectation based on prior knowledge of the Odets play. This demonstrates the complexity involved in adaptations of adaptations. The Noah of Genesis is not Jewish; the Noah of *The Flowering Peach* is; what does that mean for *Two by Two?* But questions such as these, diverting as they may be, are abstract. In practice, I would suggest that to the degree that spectators knew through extratextual means that Kaye (born David Daniel Kaminsky) and other members of the company were Jewish in real life, they may have recognized the musical as a Jewish story.[91] It is not Jewishness, however, but the performance of Kaye that captured the popular and critical imagination.

Kaye's performance represents the artistic risk (and the commercial reward) involved in "stunt casting" a biblical play. When a biblical character is embodied by a celebrity, that celebrity's preexisting persona inevitably haunts the performance.[92] "As far as Odets's play is concerned," wrote Roderick Nordell, reviewing the Boston tryout for the *Christian Science Monitor*, "the net effect is to change the mood from folklorish Jewish immigrant (remember Menasha Skulnik's Yiddish Noah?) to rising middle-class."[93] Of course, a star performer with a well-known persona can unbalance any play, but the issue is particularly acute in the case of the biblical adaptation because the play's ability to generate a sense of reverence toward the source text frequently depends on the audience's perception of sincerity and authenticity. If we are never allowed to forget that we are seeing Danny Kaye *pretend* to be Noah, can *Two by Two* ever treat the Bible as more than a pretext? Or will it be the case that, as Nordell writes, "'Two by Two' rests uneasily somewhere between Broadway and the Bible"?[94]

Still, if Danny Kaye's performance was insufficiently sincere, we can also make the case that it was highly authentic. That is to say, the audience paid to see Danny Kaye sing, dance, and clown, and this is exactly what they got. As the *Times* reported, *Two by Two* "got enthusiastic reviews from three critics, mixed reviews from three, and unfavorable from five, although all joined in cheering Danny Kaye."[95] Barnes's review is representative: "Mr. Kaye is so warm and lovable as an entertainer, such a totally ingratiating actor, that for me at least he can do no wrong. . . . There is too much rain, but then there is also a great deal of Mr. Kaye as compensation."[96] Given the hyperbolic praise Kaye received for his antics, his performance might also qualify as spectacle. Without such a star presence, however, *Two by Two* falls short of the mark. This was evident in February 1971 when Kaye tore a ligament in his ankle during the first act and missed two weeks of performances. Ticket sales plummeted so severely that the producers rushed their star back to the stage with a cast still on his foot. As "old Noah" he appeared in a wheelchair; as "young Noah" he performed on crutches. To offset his limited mobility,

Kaye took to amusing audiences by breaking character with clown-ish mugging and ad-libbed asides. "Since I hurt my leg, and was forc-ibly immobilized," he told *Variety*, "we have been forced to change [*Two by Two*] into an entertainment."[97] But of course, that's what it was all along.[98]

Over the Rainbow

Of the four performance strategies that we have identified in the bib-lical play—sincerity, spectacle, authenticity, and irony—irony may be the hardest to pin down and the trickiest to deploy in the service of biblical adaptation. The incongruous juxtaposition of biblical characters and situations with contemporary language and attitudes frequently provokes laughter, especially in the secular space of the Broadway theater. If that laughter is perceived as innocent, as in a children's pageant, the play is likely to meet with the approval of re-ligious spectators. If, as in Obey's *Noah*, that childlike innocence is executed with aesthetic virtuosity, the play may also meet with the approval of secular critics and playgoers who see it as a respite from the world-weary cynicism of more sophisticated dramas. This effect can be enhanced by spectacular elements (e.g., a rainbow) that em-phasize the parts of the narrative that confirm the audience's basic belief in the goodness of God. If the play is technically lacking, but maintains its apparent sincerity, as in Moss's Negro Theatre adapta-tion of *Noah*, critics and sophisticates are likely to chalk it up to a poor choice of subject matter. Why trot out a tired old story that ev-eryone knows? Why not take on something more interesting? This does not necessarily indicate a lack of belief in the Bible, but rather a judgment that the Broadway stage is an inappropriate venue in which to expound on that belief.

When, however, the audience senses that the playwright or the performers are laughing *at* religion, the situation can become divisive. It is all very well to treat Noah, the patriarch of all humanity, as the protagonist in a domestic comedy, but if the audience perceives a dis-connect between what is represented and what is real, between the faith of the characters and the faith (or lack thereof) of the performers, irony may be interpreted as insincere and irreverent. Regardless of how closely the play adheres to the source text, if the audience doubts the production's sincerity and authenticity, the play is likely to be received as unfaithful—in both senses—to the sacred word.

The Flowering Peach veers close to this kind of infidelity. Odets's Noah is a tragicomic figure who despite his actions displays serious doubts about God's benevolence. At a broader level, *The Flowering Peach* is an ironic work, in that it communicates doubt even as its characters evidence faith. We might expect this doubt to come across as antireligious. That it does not is testament both to Odets's skill as a playwright and to the curious status of the Noah story within the Old Testament. For the Noah of Genesis is not simply the righteous zookeeper of children's picture books. He is a human being placed in an impossible situation, a bystander to the destruction of the world by a vengeful God. Unable to argue with an unknown and unknowable God, Odets's Noah internalizes the struggle for faith, and this struggle is manifest through a darker kind of irony: that the only people righteous enough to escape God's wrath are themselves as human and fallible as any ordinary family. If we recognize this irony as an authentic expression of Jewishness, *The Flowering Peach* may strike us as among the most sincere and profound treatments of the Bible in Broadway history. If we find such irony incompatible with faith, then the play becomes "the Jewish Green Pastures" or (worse still) a kind of antireligious parody.

Two by Two also looks for irony in the story of Noah, but finds it exclusively in the domestic comedy. This Noah has been chosen by God, but he can't get his rebellious sons to follow his orders. Deprived of the Jewish specificity that grounded *The Flowering Peach*, this Noah is first and foremost a pretext for Danny Kaye to "do Danny Kaye things." Kaye's virtuosity and charismatic presence gives the performance a kind of authenticity, but as an adaptation of the Bible, *Two by Two* is the least faithful of the Noah plays addressed in this chapter. It takes the drama of the biblical patriarch and reduces it to "an entertainment."

Darren Aronofsky, the writer and director of the controversial 2014 feature film *Noah*, calls the tale of the ark "the first apocalypse story," adding, "Even though it is a story of hope, family and second chances, it is also a story filled with great destruction and misery: For every pair that survived, there were countless other creatures on the planet that drowned during the deluge, innocent and wicked alike."[99] The question of what kind of God would allow such destruction is perhaps the fundamental theological question of the modern age, and it becomes especially pointed in the latter half of the twentieth century following the Holocaust and the invention of the atomic bomb. Yet because Noah "did all that the Lord commanded him," his story offers only a limited opportunity to explore possible answers. For an extended meditation on God's questionable benevolence, we must turn to the book of Job, which is the subject of the next chapter.

CHAPTER FIVE

Why Do the Righteous Suffer?

Listen! This is a simple scene.
I play God. You play Satan.

—Archibald MacLeish, *J.B.*, 1958

"The Book of Job is a literary treasure house!" declared the Reverend Alfred Walls in 1891. "Where can its magnificent soliloquies, its prayers, and its various descriptions be equaled?"[1] Walls, a Methodist Episcopal theologian affiliated with the Drew Theological Seminary of Madison, New Jersey, wrote these words in the introduction to his book, *The Oldest Drama in the World: The Book of Job Arranged in Dramatic Form with Elucidations.* More than a century before Shimon Levy's *The Bible as Theatre* (2000) explored "the immense theatrical potential of the Old Testament,"[2] Walls transformed the book of Job into a play-script following similar principles: he retained the dialogue, used the Bible's diegetic narration as stage directions, and reformatted the entire text into twenty-one scenes spread across five acts. So Job 1:6 ("Now there was a day when the sons of God came to present themselves before the LORD, and Satan came also among them")[3] is rendered as "Act I. Scene I. A Place of Worship: Worshipers Assembled. Enter Satan."[4] Walls is careful to stress that this reformatting is intended simply to clarify what he believes to be the unknown author's original intent, to create a drama.[5] Yet it is doubtful that Walls intended or expected his script to be staged. His text offers no suggestions or caveats to those who would try to produce, for example, his act 5, scene 1, "The Lord in a whirlwind."[6] From a director's viewpoint, the published text is rife with unplayable actions (e.g. "Job is troubled when he thinks of the prosperous wicked")[7] and heavy-laden with annotations, bibliography, and other scholarly apparatus. Moreover, there is no apparent record of the theologian's play ever being staged. It seems more likely that Walls considered the drama a literary genre, and hoped that his framing of the book of Job would enhance the reading experience for students of religion. Drew Seminary president Henry A. Buttz implies as much in his "Prefatory Note": "Some will read this work for the peculiarity of its setting; all should read it for the interest and instruction it affords."[8]

Just five years later, Richard G. Moulton, Professor of English Literature at the University of Chicago, would publish an edition of Job that, like Walls's *Oldest Drama*, arranged the biblical text as a dramatic script.[9] Moulton (1849–1924) was a pioneer in the study of the Bible as literature, having previously published *Literary Study of the Bible: An Account of the Leading Forms of Literature Represented in the Sacred Writings* (1895). His edition of Job was actually the seventh in a series, "The Modern Reader's Bible: a series of works from the sacred scriptures presented in modern literary form," that would ultimately encompass twenty-one volumes published over a three-year period. Sold by Macmillan on a subscription basis, the series was later collected in a single volume, *The Modern Reader's Bible* (1907), that remained in print until the 1950s.[10] In his introduction to *The Book of Job*, Moulton argues that because the ancient Hebrews had no theater in the traditional sense, "the lack of a theatre to specialise [*sic*] drama has caused the dramatic impulse to spread through other literary forms, until epic, lyric, discourse, are all drawn together on a common basis of dramatic presentation."[11] The book of Job, in Moulton's reading, is best understood as "a dramatic poem framed in an epic story."[12] Hence while Walls rendered the entire text in playscript format, Moulton begins with a "Story Prologue" that encompasses Job 1:1–3:2, and concludes with a "Story Epilogue" that covers Job 42:7–17. Moulton justifies this strategy based on an analysis of literary forms: the opening and closing of the book of Job are written in prose ("story") with the bulk of the book in verse ("drama"). Given Moulton's emphasis on literary morphology here and elsewhere in his corpus, it seems doubtful that he intended his edition of Job to be staged any more than did Walls.

This theological and scholarly attention paid to Job as drama in the 1890s is noteworthy because it seems to run counter to the condemnation of theater by many U.S. clergymen of the same period.[13]

Coming shortly after Salmi Morse's aborted attempt to produce *The Passion* in New York and shortly before the premiere of *Ben-Hur*, such dramatic treatments of Job could be considered a foot in the door for the cause of adapting the Bible for the stage. Yet the notion that Job was originally intended to be a drama predates Walls by at least four centuries. In his influential treatise, *Quatro dialoghi in material rappresentazioni sceniche* (Four dialogues on scenic representation), Leone di Somi (Yehuda Sommo) (1527–1592), a Jewish playwright, actor, and director in Mantua, Italy, cited the book of Job as evidence to support the claim that the Jews, not the Greeks, were the true inventors of tragedy.[14] "I believe," he wrote,

> that these Greeks might have learned the art of introducing diverse characters and of making them converse from the still more ancient books of the Hebrews. . . . I declare that, in my opinion, I am right in affirming that from the afore-mentioned poem of Job (more ancient assuredly than any of which we have record) these first poets must have derived the dramatic method.[15]

Like the story of Noah, the book of Job tells of a righteous man tested by God. But where Noah's story is brief (four chapters in the book of Genesis), Job's is extended (the book of Job includes forty-two chapters). Where Noah faces one particular challenge with a clear set of instructions, Job faces a series of trials for reasons that he cannot possibly understand. Where Noah is obedient (*And Noah did according unto all that the Lord commanded him*),[16] Job is questioning (*And why dost thou not pardon my transgression, and take away my iniquity?*).[17] Where Noah, the great patriarch of all humankind, makes a covenant with God, Job is treated as an individual who must stay in his assigned place. If the story of Noah, then, offers the dramatist a hopeful counterpoint to a world that seems bent on destruction, the story of Job becomes a site for a more existential exploration: why do bad things happen to good people?

"The first thing you need to know about the biblical book of Job," writes Rabbi Harold Kushner, "is that there are two of them."[18] Kushner calls the prose sections of the book (the parts that Moulton considers prologue and epilogue) a fable, "a very old, simple folktale of faith maintained and rewarded."[19] The longer middle section he calls "the Poem of Job, a much later, more complicated work."[20] In the fable, Job is the unwitting subject of a wager between God and

Satan. *And the Lord said unto Satan, Hast thou considered my servant Job, that there is none like him in the earth, a perfect and an upright man, one that feareth God, and escheweth evil?*[21] Satan counters that Job is righteous only because God has rewarded him with wealth; were he to lose all, Job would curse God, not praise him. *And the Lord said unto Satan, Behold, all that he hath is in thy power; only upon himself put not forth thine hand.*[22] Job's possessions, lands, and even his ten children are destroyed by calamity, but still he does not waiver in his faith. *In all this Job sinned not, nor charged God foolishly.*[23] God claims to have won the contest, but Satan insists that Job still has his health; were he to suffer physical pain, Job would surely renounce God. *And the Lord said unto Satan, Behold, he is in thine hand; but save his life.*[24] Yet even when Job's body is covered with sores and he is reduced to lying on an ash-heap, scratching himself with a potsherd, even when his wife entreats him to take the easy way out ("curse God, and die") and his friends try to convince him that his faith is misguided, he still refuses to take the Lord's name in vain.[25] In the end, God rewards Job's steadfastness by restoring to him all that he has lost and then some.

Kushner explains that the theology of this fable is straightforward but problematic. "Job may be moral and righteous," he writes, "but the God of the Fable is not."[26] The desire to believe in a more just and merciful God, suggests Kushner, is the motivating force behind the Poem, which poses questions such as "Does God care about what kind of person I am?" and "Can a religious person be angry at God, even doubt the existence of God, and still think of himself or herself as a religious person?"[27] This part of Job's story is explored through a series of argumentative dialogues (hence the identification of it as "drama") between Job and his friends Eliphaz, Bildad, and Zophar; between Job and Elihu, a young bystander; and finally between Job and God himself, who speaks to Job "out of the whirlwind." The questions themselves remain unresolved, as God's response is not to answer Job's questions but to question his right to ask them. Ultimately, Job admits that he does not fully understand God's will, and he surrenders the contest. *I abhor myself, and repent in dust and ashes.*[28]

Kushner speculates that the fable and the Poem are of different authorship, a position supported by a number of biblical scholars. Yet as the text has come down to us, the two parts of the book support each other. It is Job's supreme faith and devotion to God (evidenced in the Fable) that allows him to call God to account (the Poem). In this sense, Job is indeed a classic tragic hero, a good person attempting to maintain his moral compass in the face of forces beyond his control or comprehension. Unlike the gods of classical antiquity, however, Job's God is not supposed to be subject to the anthropomorphic failings of the Greek pantheon, nor can he be represented so easily in human form. Job therefore presents a unique staging challenge, one that calls for a particularly delicate balance of spectacle, sincerity, and irony. This may be why, despite its status as "the oldest drama in the world," the book of Job has been adapted for the Broadway stage only three times, with varying degrees of commercial and critical success.[29]

This chapter explores those three divergent approaches to staging Job on Broadway. *The Book of Job* (1918), a one-act rendering by Stuart Walker's Portmanteau Theatre Company based on Moulton's edition, offers a rare example of an attempt to stage the Bible with minimal aesthetic intervention. Conversely, Archibald MacLeish's *J.B.* (1958) frames the entire story of Job as a play within a play, as not just theater but metatheater. Finally, Neil Simon's *God's Favorite* (1974) represents an attempt to explore the mystery of God's benevolence (or lack thereof) through the comparatively mundane medium of a middle-class urban comedy.

The Book of Job

"Stuart Walker's Portmanteau Theatre," wrote Constance D'Arcy Mackay in *The Little Theatre in the United States* (1917), "is proof of the fact that if you have something original to offer people, it does not matter when or where you offer it."[30] Walker (d. 1941) had been born in Augusta, Kentucky, sometime around 1887 (he was notoriously secretive about his exact age).[31] After graduating from the University of Cincinnati in 1903, he enrolled in New York's American Academy of Dramatic Arts.[32] In 1908, Walker entered the employ of David Belasco, first as a supernumerary performer and later as a stage manager. Sometime around 1910, he became the manager of the short-lived Belasco Play Bureau, which the legendary impresario had established as a means of tracking and cataloging the thousands of unsolicited scripts his office received.[33] Walker resigned his position with Belasco in 1914 to embark upon a career as an independent producer and playwright. Taking its name from the French word for suitcase, the Stuart Walker Portmanteau Theatre was initially conceived as a temporary portable playhouse. The company specialized in minimalist productions that could be set up in virtually any auditorium or public hall in a matter of hours.[34] Utilizing a single unit set and a core company of actors, the Portmanteau company developed a repertoire of more than two dozen plays and toured around New York playing schools, settlement houses, and public parks as well as conventional theaters. The company also toured nationally, making it "the only traveling Little Theatre in the country," according to Mackay.[35]

By 1918, Walker had achieved a strong enough reputation among New York theatergoers and critics that he was able to book his Portmanteau Theatre into Broadway houses. True to its "suitcase theater" roots, however, Walker continued to produce simple, nontraditional plays as occasional off-day matinees. It was in just such a circumstance that Walker first offered *The Book of Job* to a Broadway audience. On consecutive Thursday afternoons in March 1918, in between performances of Walker's own production of Hugh Stanislaus Stange and Stannard Mears's *Seventeen*[36] at the Booth Theatre, the Portmanteau Theatre played Richard Moulton's biblical adaptation on the very same stage.[37]

To help publicize the performance, Walker published an essay in the *New York Tribune*. In an apparent reference to the ongoing world war, the director explained, "Five years ago 'The Book of Job' could not have had the significance that it has today. But now to many it seems almost a personal history."[38] What would later be known as World War I was the first instance in U.S. history of conscripted Americans sent to fight beyond the nation's borders. The Conscription Act of 1917 was impersonal, without moral judgment. The righteous young man was as likely to be drafted as his impious neighbor. Once overseas, the evolving nature of warfare, especially the use of chemical weapons and bombs dropped from aircraft, meant that soldiers were increasingly likely to be maimed or killed through no fault of their own. The war, combined with the global influenza epidemic of 1918, just beginning to receive widespread attention at this time, meant that hundreds of thousands of American lives were negatively transformed by forces they neither deserved nor understood. It is not difficult then, to see how Job's central question—why do the righteous suffer?—would have struck close to home for many theatergoers.

Walker went on to note that while other biblical stories "have been used time and again in the theatre in more or less free adaptations," the book of Job provided a ready-made drama, one that he had always wanted to see staged.[39] And yet, as he explained to a reporter:

> I want to present the book dramatically, but not theatrically, and have talked with a number of leading clergymen of all denominations, whose approval and support I have in this undertaking. No attempt will be made to delve into the accuracy of the Hebraic scene, costume, or custom, nor will the Greek or any other set method of presentation be followed. I merely want to tell its great human story in a simple and reverent way and to enlist the legitimate aids of the theatre to express its message of faith and patience.[40]

It is striking that nineteen years after *Ben-Hur*, Walker still felt a need to disavow the theatrical, and to appeal to authority ("a number of leading clergymen") for justification. This seems to reflect the director's genuine concern about religious opposition to his production. It may also be the case that Walker, ever the promoter, sought to turn a potential disadvantage—his inability to stage a large spectacle within the bounds of "suitcase theater"—into a positive. In contrasting the dramatic with the theatrical, however, Walker does more than suggest that the Bible can be staged reverently without recourse to spectacle; he also disavows the outward trappings of authenticity ("No attempt will be made to delve into the accuracy of the Hebraic scene"). Instead, he offers his own sincerity of purpose ("I merely want to tell its great human story"), demonstrated by a lack of dissimulation ("in a simple and reverent way").

Walker's promotion was apparently successful, for the first performance "was witnessed with deep interest by an audience that crowded the house to the doors."[41] For this initial offering of *The Book of Job*, the title role was essayed by George Gaul, a Portmanteau regular who was then appearing in blackface as Genesis, the "negro handyman" in *Seventeen*. Twenty-eight-year-old Walter Hampden, an established star who would go on to become the first actor of the twentieth century to play Hamlet in three different Broadway productions, played Elihu the Buzite, giving "a very lively and picturesque rendering of the part," according to the *New York*

Times.[42] Most of the other actors were drawn from the Portmanteau's core company, including Edgar Stehli, Eugene Stockdale, and Henry Buckler as Job's three friends. Judith Lowry and Margaret Mower recited Moulton's prologue and epilogue "from two niches at the side of the main scene."[43] The Voice Out of the Whirlwind (God) was played by David Bishpam, who delivered his lines from offstage, "and made them deeply sonorous and awe inspiring."[44]

Walker's commitment to presenting the book "dramatically, but not theatrically" meant that *Job* was produced with a minimum of spectacle. It did, however, "enlist the legitimate aids of the theatre," including generic Middle Eastern costumes from the company's stock and a unit set designed by Frank Zimmerer (see figure 11). The production used lighting effects (designed by Walker himself) to indicate scene changes and to create an impression of the whirlwind from which God speaks. *Variety*, reviewing a subsequent showing of the production, declared, "The [whirlwind] scene is a triumph in lighting."[45] Musical underscoring (arranged by Zimmerer and Elliott Schenck) served to heighten key moments. As in Moulton's text, Satan did not appear among the dramatis personae; his role in Job's story was simply described by the narrators of the prologue. The combination of the simple staging with the "real" words of the Bible (Moulton based his text on the English Revised Version) led some observers to wonder whether *The Book of Job* could really be considered a play at all, or simply a "reading."[46] Still, the production received generally kind notices, though some reviewers felt that the play, such as it was, would have benefited from judicious editing. The reviewer for the *New York Times* assessed the performance in the same terms used by Walker: "Excellent as the play is dramatically, it lacks the merely theatric quality; and so fails at times to hold attention."[47] Yet even those elements that failed "to hold attention" may have contributed to the production's aura of sincerity, precisely because they seemed more authentic. John Corbin suggested as much, noting, "That Stuart Walker has retained the manifest blemishes of the text as it has come down to us is creditable perhaps to his sense of formal reverence. That he has produced the play at all is a thing far more creditable. It takes a great spirit to divine the intense and momentous drama of the Book of Job, and a far greater spirit to produce it on Broadway."[48] In other words, Corbin infers the production's sincerity ("a far greater spirit") from the fact that it presents

Figure 11. Sketch by Frank Zimmerer for the setting of *The Book of Job* as produced by Stuart Walker. *Theatre Arts Magazine* 2, no. 2 (February 1918): 313. (Image courtesy of Google Books.)

the authentic Bible ("the text as it has come down to us") rather than a theatrical representation.

On the strength of its limited run at the Booth in March 1918, *The Book of Job* returned to Broadway as one of nine plays in the rotating repertory of "The Walker Portmanteau Season" at the Punch and Judy Theatre. The biblical play was presented on the same evening as Lord Dunsany's *The Tents of the Arabs*, presumably so that a single Middle Eastern setting could be used for both. The 1919 production employed most of the same players as the first incarnation, with one notable exception. In 1919, the Voice in the Whirlwind was played by Os-ke-non-ton (né Louie Deer, 1890–1950), a Canadian-born Mohawk Indian chief who had come to New York to launch a career as a singer.[49] His performance was apparently mediocre from a technical standpoint: both *Variety* and the *Times* complained that his speeches from the wings were frequently hard to hear.[50] Nevertheless, Os-ke-non-ton appears to have been the first actor of color (and the only first nations performer) to voice the role of God on Broadway, eleven years before *The Green Pastures*. This may have had little effect on the reception of *The Book of Job*; the audience, after all, would not have seen the actor playing the Voice until the curtain call. Nevertheless, given the rarity of actors of color on Broadway in general, and in Broadway's biblical plays in particular, it is worth noting Os-ke-non-ton's unique place in this history.

Like Os-ke-non-ton himself, *The Book of Job* was more of a novelty than a phenomenon. After a handful of performances in the spring of 1919, the play would never again be produced on Broadway. Yet it would become a signature part of the Portmanteau Theatre's repertoire, and continued to be performed on tour well into the 1920s. Walker's "dramatic but not theatrical" staging of *The Book of Job* demonstrates the literary potential of the source text, as well as what can happen when the adapter places as few aesthetic elements as possible between the Bible and the audience. As our next example will show, the story of Job can also be told in a no less dramatic but highly theatrical fashion.

J.B.

Few plays have arrived on Broadway with as much high-art cachet as Archibald MacLeish's *J.B.*, which opened Thursday, December 11, 1958, at the ANTA Theatre on West Fifty-Second Street. MacLeish was a two-time winner of the Pulitzer Prize for Poetry for his collections *Conquistador* (1933) and *Collected Poems, 1917–1952* (1953). His stature in the literary world meant, among other things, that the script of *J.B.* was published as a book before the play was ever produced.[51] As with other high-profile biblical adaptations, many speculated about how it would translate from page to stage. John Ciardi, reviewing the book for the *Saturday Review*, explains tellingly:

> Archibald MacLeish's "J.B." is great poetry, great drama, and—as far as my limitations permit me to sense it—great stagecraft. The distinction between drama and stagecraft is a necessary one. By drama one must intend a gathering of intellectual, spiritual, and physical forces about the lives of characters who move those forces and who move within them to a conclusion that echoes within us to the root of our values. By stagecraft one must intend the manipulation of the illusions of the stage for momentary effect.[52]

We see here an echo of Walker's distinction between the dramatic and the theatrical. While Ciardi does not consider the theatrical ("stagecraft") unworthy or inappropriate to the consideration of the

Bible, he seems to persist in the assumption that the theater is a lesser art form. Though he is giving the play a positive review, he clearly regards the literary aspect (drama) of the play as superior, reaching "to the root of our values," while the spectacular aspect (stagecraft) is illusory and has only "momentary effect."

Yet MacLeish, unlike Moulton, intended for his version of Job to be produced theatrically, and produced it was. The play received its world premiere at the Yale School of Drama under the direction of Dean F. Curtis Canfield about a month after its publication. MacLeish's literary celebrity ensured that the production was considered a significant cultural event, covered as a feature (rather than a simple review) by national magazines such as *Time* and *Life*. Elliott Norton, the influential out-of-town critic, wrote in the *Boston Record*, "The story of Job is as old as the Old Testament. But its central theme of evil imposed on a good man is still pertinent and puzzling. To put it into modern terms is to give its old truths new significance. To try this was bold, even heroic."[53] Brooks Atkinson suggested that "like Thornton Wilder's 'The Skin of Our Teeth,' which is in a lighter vein, 'J.B.' will have a long life in the theatre since it speaks to the common experience."[54] Thus, when producer Alfred De Liagre Jr. announced plans for a Broadway production to be directed by Elia Kazan, the most celebrated American director of the 1950s, and featuring stage and screen star Raymond Massey in the "God role," the expectations (and the attendant scrutiny) were high.

According to Robert Downing, the production stage manager, Kazan and the company approached the project with heightened expectations themselves:

> In early instructions to his cast, the director made it clear that unusual preparation would be required of each actor before every performance. The cast approached its task in dedicated fashion; following Kazan's suggestion, the actors spent the half hour before curtain time in their dressing rooms, quietly reflecting upon the demands of the various roles. . . . MacLeish's verse, and Kazan's evident respect for the play, dominated the actors to an uncommon extent; one was reminded a bit of the legendary deference of the actors in the Passion play at Oberammergau.[55]

Downing's remarks, especially the comparison to the Oberammergau Passion, suggest that the company approached *J.B.* as a quasi-sacred text. While it was not unusual for Kazan, the quintessential "method" director, to impose a kind of mental discipline on his actors, he seems to have taken it to another level with *J.B.* Yet if Kazan felt some kind of special responsibility, it was to his own reputation and not to MacLeish's text. As the director would later write, "*J.B.* won the Pulitzer Prize and I was happy for Archie MacLeish. I must confess that the merits of that play eluded me."[56] Claiming that he merely "staged" a play whose verse structure left him cold, Kazan also notes that he admired the ability of the actors "for their persistence and seeming faith in what they were saying. Oh, God, how they believed that stuff! But they didn't suspend my disbelief."[57] More telling, however, than what Kazan believed or what the actors believed, is that their backstage reverence, their "deference" to the subject matter, became part of the larger narrative about the production.

As we have seen before, one way that a biblical play can avoid charges of blasphemy or irreverence is to convince spectators through both textual and extratextual means that the performance is a sincere expression of faith. While this sincerity can be located in the director/producer (as with Walker), it may also be located in the performers. Sponsler, for example, describing the *Black Hills Passion Play* (1939–2008), notes how promotion for the South Dakota–based tourist attraction "underwent a degree of strategic reshaping that implicitly drew on an Oberammergau-styled medievalism to present the play as the traditional ritual of devout amateurs."[58] In a similar way, the psychological discipline imposed by Kazan and the apparent devotion of the actors to their roles became part of the extratextual narrative that *J.B.* was More Than a Play. At the same time, such disciplined attention to preparation may have directly affected the quality of the performance itself, contributing to the actors' "seeming faith in what they were saying."

Yet if the actors were faithful to MacLeish's text, it is not entirely clear whether MacLeish's text can be considered faithful to its biblical source. Written in verse, and structured as a play within a play, *J.B.* is set in a deserted circus tent, where two actors-turned-vendors, Mr. Zuss (Massey) and Nickles (Christopher Plummer), decide to "play" the drama of Job. Mr. Zuss plays the role of God, Nickles the role of Satan. At the outset, Nickles insists that Zuss wear a mask:

NICKLES: Mask, Naturally. You wouldn't play God in your Face, would
    you?
ZUSS: What's the matter with it?
NICKLES: God the Creator of the Universe?
God who hung the world in time?
You wouldn't hang the world in time
With two-inch cat hair on your cutlets![59]

By referring colloquially to Mr. Zuss's unshaven cheeks, Nickles
points metatheatrically to the first representational problem the play
must solve, one we have seen before. How can a mortal impersonate
God without making God appear too human? MacLeish's solution, a
mask, avoids this problem, while accomplishing three other objec-
tives.[60] First, the masks used in the Broadway production (Nickles,
too, wears a mask as Satan; see figure 12) were classical in style, explicitly linking Job's story to the tradition of ancient Greek tragedy.
Second, as in ancient tragedy, the masks magnify and distort the actors' voices so that *"they scarcely seem their own."*[61] This in turn
points to the third and most important use of the mask as a theatrical
device: by the simple expedient of taking the mask on and off, the
actor can indicate clearly to the audience when he is "playing God"
and when he is simply Mr. Zuss, the balloon vendor performing in
this play-within-a-play. MacLeish's commitment to this staging con-
vention is evidenced by the fact that the lines the actors speak when
masked are marked in the text as if spoken by two other characters,
"Godmask" and "Satanmask."[62]

The use of masks adds a dimension of spectacle to *J.B.*, making
the nonhuman characters appear to be larger than life. Yet the way
the masks are used—put on and taken off in full view of the
audience—also creates irony. The audience is continually made
aware that Zuss and Nickles are not, respectively, God and Satan, an
awareness that the other characters in the drama are denied.

As the two masked men act out the start of the Fable ("HAST
THOU CONSIDERED MY SERVANT JOB . . ."),[63] the center of the arena
comes to life as a playing space, and we see "J.B." (Pat Hingle) at
Thanksgiving dinner with his family. In MacLeish's own words, J.B.
"bears little relation, perhaps, to that ancient owner of camels and
oxen and sheep."[64] Instead, J.B. is a contemporary American businessman, and his story is entirely transposed into the America of
1958. Thus, for example, when Satan visits death upon J.B.'s chil-

Figure 12. Raymond Massey (*top*) as Mr. Zuss and Christopher Plummer as Nickles in Archibald MacLeish's *J.B.* (1958). (Photo by Friedman-Abeles © Billy Rose Theatre Division, The New York Public Library for the Performing Arts.)

dren, one is revealed to have died in a war overseas, two are killed by a drunk driver, and so on. The purpose of bringing the biblical narrative forward in time becomes most apparent late in the first act. As in the Bible, J.B. initially responds to his losses through prayer: "THE LORD GIVETH . . . THE LORD TAKETH AWAY . . ."[65] But before he can complete the formula ("Blessed be the name of the Lord"), the play delivers its most striking coup de théâtre, an atomic explosion. As described in the stage directions:

> Mr. Zuss brings down drumstick, hangs up mask and stick. MUSIC STARTS. LIGHTS CHANGE. SOUND. Nickles darts out U.C., down steps, and slashes at imaginary tent guy ropes with knife. Tent wall collapses. In the ring, a section of the sidewall, U.R.C., breaks upward crazily; and the sections D.R. and D.L. fall backward. . . . Trap door opens, and glow of RED LIGHT shoots up. Banners, L. fall to floor. . . . a procession of women enters slowly from U.L. and up steps into ring. They cough in the murk.[66]

J.B.'s world, as represented by the circus tent, is destroyed before the audience's eyes. In the wake of the destruction, the "procession of women" (one of whom, Mrs. Adams, was played by sixty-eight-year-old Judith Lowry, who had performed as a narrator in Walker's *Book of Job* forty years earlier) function as a kind of chorus of refugees. They describe the chaos wrought by the Bomb, how an entire section of the city (including J.B.'s home and bank) has been decimated. Civil defense officers enter bearing J.B.'s wife, Sarah (Nan Martin), who has somehow survived the catastrophe. This choice—to dramatize nuclear catastrophe—makes explicit MacLeish's belief that the horrors of the twentieth century strike the innocent and guilty alike. "Hiroshima, in its terrible aspect, appalls us," he wrote in a foreword to the play published in the *New York Times*, "And we attempt . . . to justify the inexplicable misery of the world by taking the guilt on ourselves as Job attempted to take it."[67]

Like Job, MacLeish argues, contemporary Americans also have their "comforters," those who try to talk us into accepting responsibility for the impersonal workings of the universe.[68] In the second act, which takes place amid the ruins of the first, MacLeish reimagines the three friends, Bildad (Bert Conway), Zophar (Ivor Francis), and Eliphaz (Andreas Voutsinas), as a radical activist, a priest, and a psychiatrist respectively, suggesting that these are the modern "comforters" to whom we turn in times of crisis. But as in the original book of Job, they prove of little help to the afflicted man.

During the Job scenes, Zuss and Nickles comment in Brechtian fashion on the events occurring in the play-within-the-play. Watching first from a platform above the stage (representing "the heavens"), and later from the sides of the stage, the two vendors affect a kind of ironic detachment as they offer pointed opinions about what Job should or should not do in response to his misfortune. As the play progresses, however, they become more engrossed in their roles as God and Satan, until it is clear that each character cares deeply about the outcome of their heavenly wager. Yet they themselves ultimately lose control of the proceedings to a disembodied Voice. At the play's climax, when J.B. cries out in frustration, "GOD . . . MY GOD!, ANSWER ME!" it is this offstage Voice—not Zuss or his Godmask—that delivers the reply from the whirlwind, "WHERE WAST THOU / WHEN I LAID THE FOUNDATIONS OF THE EARTH?"[69] After ninety minutes of watching Mr. Zuss play with and through the Godmask, this moment seems to offer an authentic sense of the "real" God. That is, by contrast to the visible and visibly false Godmask, the very invisibility of the Voice gives it an aura of authenticity.

After J.B. has completed his assigned role ("I ABHOR MYSELF AND REPENT"),[70] the metatheatrical frame seems to collapse: for the first time, J.B. can see and hear Zuss and Nickles as each tries to tell him what he must do next. J.B. resists both extremes:

(To Nickles)
Life is a filthy farce, you say,
And nothing but a bloody stage
Can bring the curtain down and men
Must have ironic hearts and perish
Laughing . . . Well, I will not laugh!
(He swings on Mr. Zuss)
And neither will I weep among
The obedient who lie down to die
In meek relinquishment, protesting
Nothing, questioning nothing, asking
Nothing but to rise again and bow![71]

Here we see the protagonist literally caught between irony, associated with Satan, and the sincerity of unquestioning obedience, associated with God. In the end, rejecting the all or nothing proposition of the biblical conclusion to Job's story, J.B. reunites with his wife Sarah, finding in the mortal concept of love the reason to go on. Love, the play seems to suggest, is what balances the two forces, making the paradox of faith endurable.

The response of the theater world to *J.B.* was almost overwhelmingly positive. "In every respect," wrote Brooks Atkinson, "*J.B.* is theatre on its highest level."[72] "Stunningly staged by Elia Kazan, with a splendidly imaginative setting by Boris Aronson, and notable performances by a fine cast," cheered Richard Watts, adding that the play "combines theatrical effectiveness with rueful lyric brooding on good and evil with impressive theatrical power."[73] John McClain named *J.B.* his favorite play of the season, explaining, "It seemed to me it reached heights of poetry and performance seldom attempted in the history of the American theatre."[74] The play was a box-office hit as well, running forty-six weeks (more than twice as long as *The Flowering Peach*) at a reported profit in excess of $10,000.[75] In addition to the Pulitzer Prize, the production garnered Tony Awards for Best Play and Best Director. Plummer and Nan Martin (who played J.B.'s wife Sarah) were nominated for acting awards. Basil Rathbone, who took over the role of Mr. Zuss in June 1959, would go on to headline a successful national tour, and the play would enjoy a long afterlife in regional and university theaters.[76]

Among theologians and religious leaders, however, the response to *J.B.* was decidedly more mixed. Ever since the play's opening, declared *Time* magazine in April 1959, "Viewers have been choosing up sides to attack and defend MacLeish's Biblicism or lack of it."[77] The Reverend Tom T. Driver of New York's Union Theological Seminary (UTS) wrote in the *Christian Century* that MacLeish had dwelt unnecessarily on Job's human sufferings, taking the focus away from the theological discussion between God and Satan. Another UTS professor, Samuel Terrien, felt that MacLeish's J.B. was "emasculated," calling the character "the diseased victim of fate, who hardly, if ever at all, rises above the level of intellectual stupor and spiritual impassivity."[78] In May 1959, *Life* magazine entered the fray, publishing an excerpt of the drama accompanied by commentary from religious figures: "*J.B.* has aroused so much discussion," declared the magazine, "that LIFE has invited three eminent theologians [Protestant theologian Reinhold Niebuhr, Jewish Theological Seminary chancellor

Louis Finkelstein, and Catholic publisher Thurston N. Davis, SJ] to express their views of the play."[79] Niebuhr and Finkelstein both felt that while MacLeish's text departed significantly from the biblical source, it spoke to a real and legitimate spiritual yearning. Davis, on the other hand, found *J.B.* an "arid repudiation of religion."[80]

Theater historian Bruce McConachie, writing some forty years later, argues that such extended discussions of *J.B.*'s relationship to the Bible were misguided. The play's purpose was not to translate the book of Job into the modern era; it was to explore the modern era, using the book of Job as a pretext. This reading is supported in part by MacLeish's own foreword, which begins:

> A man may be forgiven for dramatizing an incident from the Bible and even modernizing it in the process. But what I have done is not so easy to excuse. I have constructed a modern play inside the ancient majesty of the Book of Job much as the Bedouins, thirty years ago, used to build within the towering ruins of Palmyra their shacks of gasoline tins roofed with fallen stones.[81]

What then, does this "modern play" mean? In McConachie's retrospective analysis, *J.B.* epitomizes the American theater of the Cold War, when "the anxieties of nuclearism even transformed theater buildings, normally houses of entertainment, into temporary sites for religious witness, as narratives of apocalypse and jeremiad played out on Broadway stages."[82] The 1950s stage became a site in which artists and audience could commune over their mutual concerns about the immanent destruction of the world (apocalypse) and the moral corruption of contemporary society (jeremiad). Most of these plays, McConachie argues, were "nominally secular," but the Bible offered a ready-built and nearly universal allegory for the contemporary moment.[83] Biblical adaptations like *The Flowering Peach* and *J.B.* spoke to anxieties about the Bomb because, regardless of whether one considers oneself religious, "they did underline humanity's ultimate lack of control over its fate."[84]

J.B., suggests McConachie, is an example of a "Fragmented Hero, torn between the expectation of justice and strength and the fear of impotence and evil."[85] His agony does not derive from his losses or his physical pain as much as from his inability to reconcile his vision of a just God with the horrors he has experienced. *If God is God he is not Good. If God is Good he is not God.* J.B.'s fragmentation of self is given visual form as his household is literally broken into pieces and strewn about the stage. The closing scene, in which J.B.'s love for Sarah allows him to be made whole, does offer a vision of restoration, but this restoration remains overshadowed by the transcendent forces beyond human control. In this reading, MacLeish's device of a play-within-a-play "abstracts the narrative of *J.B.* and, like all modes of metatheatricality, problematizes the dramatic agency of the hero."[86] J.B. is unquestionably a tragic figure, but is he a hero, an actor, or simply an allegory, a kind of Everyman? And what relationship does he bear to his biblical namesake?

McConachie's reading is compelling and thorough, explaining many of the choices made by MacLeish and Kazan. Yet his ultimate dismissal of the "cultural and religious preconceptions that conditioned the reception of *J.B.*" is somewhat disingenuous. Even if the play *does* use the source text as an allegory for the atomic age, the theological questions remain relevant. In fact, to the degree that they understood harnessing the power of the atom as an act of godlike creativity and destruction, MacLeish's audience may have considered those questions *more* relevant than ever before.[87] McConachie equates *J.B.* with Martha Graham's *Night Journey* (1947), based on the myth of Oedipus, pairing the two in a single chapter of his *American Theater in the Culture of the Cold War* (2003). Yet the Bible— even a comparatively obscure book such as Job—is not simply another myth to be used as raw material. For an American audience, at least, the Bible is too powerful and contested a concept to be used as a flag of convenience. Once the Holy Book has been invoked, the audience's interpretation will inevitably tilt in the direction of religion. This is doubly true if, as in *J.B.*, God is summoned to the stage.

Mr. Zuss and his Godmask may evoke classical Greek mythology, but the invisible Voice from beyond the frame of the play raises the stakes significantly. This is not to say that *J.B.* did not resonate with the anxieties of a Cold War audience, but rather that its biblical source almost certainly made it *more* resonant in this regard than other dramas of its era. In its delicate balance of spectacle and authenticity, irony and sincerity, *J.B.* demonstrates that it is possible to perform reverence from a place of doubt, and does so in the context of mainstream Judeo-Christian thought. While this is a credit to the play's construction and execution, we should also note that this understanding is already present in the biblical source. Though Job is remembered as the character who stayed obedient to God through thick and thin, he is also the character who dares question God's plan. Unlike Noah, Job is defined by his doubt as well as his faith. Both are necessary to shout into the Whirlwind.

Or, as the author of our next example put it, "When you tackle God, you'd better be up for it."[88]

God's Favorite

Neil Simon's adaptation of the book of Job arrived on Broadway during a turbulent time in U.S. history, premiering in December 1974, only three months after the resignation of President Richard Nixon and less than two years after the U.S. withdrawal from Vietnam. It is tempting, therefore, to understand *God's Favorite* as a response to a national catastrophe similar to our earlier examples. However, Simon's reasons for taking on Job's story were more personal. His wife, Joan Baim Simon, had died of bone cancer the previous year at the age of forty-one. *God's Favorite*, Simon would later tell the *Paris Review*, "was written as an outcry of anger against Joan's death. My belief in God had vanished when this beautiful young girl was dying."[89] For the Jewish playwright, suggests theater historian James Fisher, it would be natural to turn to the Old Testament during such a crisis of faith, and the book of Job more than any other Judaic narrative provides an extended meditation on the dilemma of why good people suffer for no apparent reason.[90] At the same time, Simon had established a career as a purveyor of frothy comedies such as *The Odd Couple* (1965), *Barefoot in the Park* (1967), and *The Prisoner of Second Avenue* (1971). How would he tackle the heavy narrative of Job? "I wasn't Archibald MacLeish," Simon reflected. "I thought it would be pretentious for me to write something like a dramatic *J.B.* So, I wrote it as a black comedy, and it did help me get through that period."[91] Yet despite whatever therapeutic value Simon may have derived from the experience of writing *God's Favorite*, critics and audiences had difficulty accepting the play's premise.

"Making a comedy out of the Book of Job," wrote Martin Gottfried, "sounds more like a Neil Simon joke than a Neil Simon idea, but there it was. . . . 'God's Favorite' is a callow play that should be offensive to anyone seriously religious."[92] Howard Kissel concurred,

"Simon's play is, in fact, so crude a parody of The Book [of Job] that it would be obscene to dignify it with a comparison."[93] Even the positive reviews began by citing the absurdity of playing Job's story for laughs. "Is Job funny?" asked Clive Barnes. "Perhaps. Certainly it seems that Neil Simon thinks that the story of Job is the ultimate custard-pie joke."[94] Often, it seemed, critics sought to make Simon himself the butt of the joke. "Like others before him, chaps on the order of Wagner and Shakespeare," wrote Douglas Watt, "Neil Simon in his maturity has been struck with the need to deal with larger, more profound themes. So he has taken the Book of Job and schlepped it over to Oyster Bay."[95]

It is in that contemporary Long Island suburb that the play finds its protagonist, Joe Benjamin (Vincent Gardenia). Like MacLeish's J.B., Joe B. is a wealthy businessman who takes pride in his rags-to-riches biography while giving the greatest share of the credit to God. The rest of his household includes his wife Rose, children David, Sara, and Ben, and two African American servants, Mady and Morris. The play opens with the family roused from their beds by a burglar alarm, and the opening twenty minutes or so are devoted to exposition, peppered with the comic badinage that characterizes Simon's earlier work. When Joe asks his drunken son David, "You think you can find your room in your condition?," for example, David replies, "Why should my room be in my condition?"[96] When it appears that the burglar alarm was in error, the family returns to their beds and Joe, distraught over the fight with his son, prays, "Give me back my David . . . If it be Your Will, dear God, that's all I ask . . . Amen."[97] Then, like many another biblical protagonist, Joe hears a mysterious Voice cry "Amen!" But when Joe responds, "Who said that?" the Voice answers, "Don't worry. It's not who you're thinking."[98]

The Voice is revealed to be Sidney Lipton (Charles Nelson Reilly), one of God's messengers. Sidney is neither angel nor prophet, but a beleaguered working schmo from Jackson Heights ("I'm not *Here Comes Mr. Jordan*. I'm a nine-to-fiver").[99] He wears glasses. He dresses haphazardly but in contemporary style. When asked to prove that he is God's messenger, he opens his overcoat to reveal a varsity letter sweater with a large "G" embroidered on it. Sidney tells Joe explicitly that he is "God's favorite" and that furthermore Satan— who, Sidney reports, looks like Robert Redford—has wagered that if Joe's life becomes miserable enough, he'll renounce God. When Joe refuses, the plot follows a familiar arc. Joe's factory burns down; he goes bankrupt; he becomes stricken with a series of physical ailments; his house burns down and the family is reduced to shivering in its ruins. Still, Joe refuses to renounce God. As a final indignity, Joe's son David is stricken blind, prompting him to cry out to the Lord, "I AM ANGRY AT YOU, GOD! REALLY, REALLY ANGRY! . . . AND STILL I DON'T RENOUNCE YOU! HOW DO YOU LIKE THAT, GOD?"[100] No voice, however, speaks to Joe from the whirlwind. Instead, there is a brief burst of lightning and thunder, following which Joe's health, fortunes, and family are restored.

If we return to Kushner's description of the book of Job as comprising both a fable and a poem, it is clear that God's Favorite confines itself to an adaptation of the fable, the wager between God and Satan. The more complex theological conversations of the poem are nowhere to be found, while the steady diet of one-liners makes clear that the play is not interested in exploring that part of the book. "Why should I, a man who has believed in God all his life, suddenly renounce Him?" asks Joe. To which Sidney replies dryly, "I take home a hundred-thirty-seven dollars a week. If you want theological advice, call Billy Graham."[101] Playing Job's story for laughs leads Simon to make other choices that further lower the stakes of the drama. Joe's children, for example, are largely spared from divine abuse, and his physical woes are repeatedly played for laughs. His torment, such as it is, manifests itself most clearly as the thing most feared by the upwardly mobile New Yorkers who populate many of Simon's plays: he becomes poor. Yet even then, his servants do not abandon him. This creates the opportunity for some more jokes (e.g., after the house burns down, "At least we only got one floor to [clean] now"),[102] but further undercuts any pathos the play might generate.

As demonstrated by The Green Pastures and The Flowering Peach, mining the Bible for humor can find favor with audiences and critics alike. Yet God's Favorite, much like The Creation of the World and Other Business (which opened two years prior), misses the mark, a fact that even Simon admits. "God's Favorite was not [a good play]," he would later write. "Not because of its subject matter, a contemporary version through this playwright's oblique view of the Book of Job, but because it was simply not done skillfully enough."[103] This negative assessment, like those of most critics and scholars, is based on the comparison of the play to the rest of Simon's creative output. Fisher, for example, sees *God's Favorite* as a pivotal (if flawed) step in Simon's transition from comedies of manners such as *The Star Spangled Girl* (1966) to more substantive and earnest pieces such as *Brighton Beach Memoirs* (1983) and *Biloxi Blues* (1985).[104] If we compare the play to other Biblical adaptations, however, a slightly different picture emerges.

Simon's use of irony in *God's Favorite* is directed not at the cosmic absurdity of Joe/Job's situation, but at the Bible itself. Unlike, for example, Odets's Noah, Joe Benjamin has no sense of irony about his situation, and little doubt about his ability and desire to remain faithful to God. Unlike MacLeish's J.B., Joe's faith is never really in question. The effect of bringing Job's story forward in time, then, is to expose the original story to ridicule. Removed from the ancient land of Uz and placed in a modern urban context, the protagonist's behavior is laughable, not noble. Without the dialogue between Job and his "comforters," the plot offers little space to explore the alternative choice: what would it really mean to "renounce God," and why would that be attractive? Simon's primary addition to the story is the beleaguered messenger Sidney, who repeatedly belittles and complains about the God whom he serves. As a result, while *J.B.* offered a reverent meditation on its protagonist's justifiable doubt, *God's Favorite* irreverently performed Simon's own personal doubt through Joe's apparently unjustifiable faith.

In performance, *God's Favorite* also undercuts its own authenticity through its use of theatrical spectacle. Not once but twice an offstage "Voice" is revealed—Wizard of Oz style—to be Sidney. Instead of an invisible presence, Simon's God is simply absent. When God is represented via lightning and thunder, that, too, quickly becomes a joke: Sidney rushes in with his raincoat smoldering and smoking, declaring "*Never* get God angry when a person is standing under a tree."[105] Any aspirations the play may have had to moral grandeur were further undermined by the self-consciously campy performance of Charles Nelson Reilly as Sidney. As Fisher writes, Reilly's "broadly exaggerated and hysterically effeminate style . . . tended to overshadow other qualities in the play."[106] Similarly, Vincent Gardenia played Joe with, in the words of *Newsweek*'s Jack Kroll, "a comic force that could be called Mostelian but that deserves its own epithets."[107] Gardenia's performance, that is, turned Joe into a character role, which may have enlivened the proceedings, but which further called attention to the play's insincerity.

The actors were clearly acting; the scenery was clearly scenery; the jokes were clearly jokes. The playwright, though he may have been motivated by a real sense of grief, was unable to convey— through textual or extratextual means—the sincerity of purpose evidenced by Stuart Walker or the balance of irony and reverence captured by MacLeish. True, the play had its aesthetic shortcomings, including a clunky plot and hackneyed dialogue, but as we have seen in several of our earlier examples, critics and audiences are often willing to overlook such shortcomings if the production overall provides some evidence of reverence for the source text. *God's Favorite*, however, was unable to generate this sense of reverence because it lacked both authenticity and sincerity. Though it got a few positive reviews and managed to run for 119 performances, *God's Favorite* prompted no larger conversation akin to that engendered by other biblical adaptations—not because it failed to take the Bible seriously, but because it failed to take itself seriously.

Based on the three times it has come to Broadway, the value of the book of Job is that, more than any other biblical narrative, it allows the theater to come to terms with the kind of calamity and suffering that characterizes the modern American experience. The Walker Portmanteau Theatre's *Book of Job* responded to World War I and (to a lesser degree) the 1918 influenza epidemic, which between them killed over sixty million people worldwide. To theatergoers whose lives had been touched by an apparently random global catastrophe, Job's experience may have been especially relevant. MacLeish's *J.B.* responded to the Cold War threat of nuclear annihilation, and with it a fear among the American middle class that they no longer controlled their own fate. Simon's *God's Favorite* was more personal, a response to the untimely death of his wife. Considered together, these three productions also suggest some general principles about the intersection of the Bible with the Broadway stage.

The problem of playing God is complicated by the fact that the Old Testament provides so few clues to his character. As Kushner notes in his study of Job, the Bible tells us "a lot about the will of God, what God wants of us, but very little about the nature of God, what we can expect of God, how the mind of God works."[108] This is a fundamental theological problem, and one of the most important ways in which the Bible differs from the Greek myths that underlie classical tragedy. Texts like the *Iliad* provide extensive discussion of the gods' moods and motivations, but "reading the Bible, we learn little if anything about God's private life or God's thought process."[109] Though Jews, Christians, and Muslims have developed extensive theological discourse around the Old Testament, there is little theological discourse to be found within its verses.[110] On stage, this theological problem becomes a theatrical one. How can a being beyond human comprehension be rendered comprehensible to a human audience? Typically, this means that God remains offstage, the Voice from the Whirlwind visible only as a flash of lightning. When God does appear before the footlights, the performance becomes—willingly or not—a site for religious debate.

At the same time, concerns about the irreverent (if not blasphemous) nature of theatrical impersonation dictate that the closer we get to representing the divine, the more pressure there is on the performance to communicate reverence through a combination of sincerity and authenticity. These performance strategies may manifest themselves through the text or in the live performance. They may be communicated extratextually, in the discourse surrounding the production. Furthermore, sincerity and authenticity may interact with each other, with spectacle, and with irony in complex and unexpected ways. Like the story of Noah, the book of Job lends itself particularly well to ironic treatment because it is one of the few extended narratives in the Bible where irony appears to be a viable, even authentic response to the theological problem it poses. Yet as Job's history on Broadway illustrates, finding the right balance of spectacle, sincerity, authenticity, and irony is a difficult task. The challenge becomes even greater when we attempt to make the divine presence visible in human form. This explains why, despite the long history of biblical adaptations on Broadway, there have been comparably few instances of actors actually playing God. It also demonstrates that the examples in the next chapter may be even more remarkable than we previously imagined.

CHAPTER SIX

Jesus Christ, Broadway Star

The Times Square Church (TSC) stands just west of Broadway on Fifty-First Street in Manhattan. The interdenominational Christian church was founded in 1987 by Pastor David Wilkerson (1931–2011) in response to the general moral decay of the neighborhood around Forty-Second Street, which in the 1970s and 1980s was plagued by prostitution, drugs, and pornography. The once vital "Great White Way" of Broadway had deteriorated to the point that theater attendance suffered.[1] Newer theaters such as the Uris (1972), the Minskoff (1973) and the Marquis (1986) were built with driveways and large interior lobbies (the Marquis is actually inside a Marriott Hotel) so that patrons would not have to interact with the denizens of the neighborhood. "I wept and I prayed," reported Wilkerson: "God, you've got to raise up a testimony in this hellish place. . . . The answer was not what I wanted to hear: 'Well, you know the city. You've been here. You do it.'"[2]

Wilkerson's fledgling mission spent two years holding services in the Town Hall building at 123 West Forty-Third Street before moving into its current location. Over the ensuing twenty-five years, the Times Square neighborhood has been revitalized, though not without controversy. Police crackdowns on drugs and prostitution under Mayor Rudy Guiliani in the 1990s went along with an influx of private investment from Disney and other corporations. The "Disneyfication" of Times Square continued under Mayor Michael Bloomberg.[3] Today, Broadway theater constitutes a major source of tourism revenue for New York, supplemented by the many retail outlets that line Times Square and (increasingly) the surrounding blocks.[4] Portions of Seventh Avenue are closed to traffic to allow for the increased

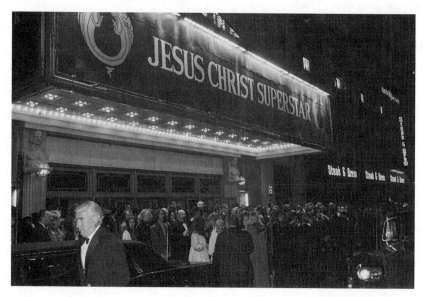

Figure 13. Opening night of *Jesus Christ Superstar* at the Mark Hellinger Theatre, 237 West Fifty-First Street, 1971. (© Bettmann/ CORBIS.)

pedestrian activity. Through all the recent changes, the Times Square Church has remained a fixture, offering prayer services, religious education, and outreach ministry.[5]

As it happens, before Wilkerson first leased his building in 1989 (the church would buy it outright in 1991), 237 West Fifty-First Street was, in fact, a theater. Built by Warner Brothers as a movie theater in 1930 and rededicated for "legit" use in 1948, the Mark Hellinger Theatre played host to several dozen shows over four decades, including the original productions of *My Fair Lady* (1956), *The Sound of Music* (1962), *A Funny Thing Happened on the Way to the Forum* (1964), and *Man of La Mancha* (1971). For devotees of the American musical, in other words, the Mark Hellinger is holy ground of a different sort. New York City, in fact, has designated the auditorium as an historical landmark, which has obliged the church as it has undergone renovations to restore as closely as possible the original architectural features. As sociologist of religion Hans Tokke describes it:

> The auditorium is centered on an extravagant original crystal chandelier, with ceiling paintings of angels gazing down on those below. The deep

Figure 14. Times Square Church at 237 West Fifty-First Street, 2015.
(Photo by Jeffrey Anbinder. Used by permission.)

cushioned theater seats are crimson velvet, with ornate wood finishes.
The platform has been reconfigured into a somewhat typical church stage
with pulpit, choir seating, space for musicians, and pastoral chairs, but
retains its theater tradition with thick curtains that are drawn to the ceil-
ing at the beginning of the service, and an array of theater lighting. Professional digital audio amplifies the music and preaching in pristine sound
quality, and large video screens project both words and live pictures of the
people on the stage. Although there are supplementary rooms in Times
Square Church, the meetings held in the main auditorium are primary to
the church's mission. The ushers wear noticeable chic gold-colored blaz-
ers to stand out from the crowd, evoking the theater theme.[6]

The opulence of the theater space is somewhat at odds with the Times
Square Church's conservative theology. Though the church is nominally interdenominational, the Pentecostal tradition in which Wilkerson was brought up generally disapproves of theater and other popular
entertainments on the grounds that they often expose spectators to

immodest and sinful behavior. At the same time, however, the Pente-costal movement in the United States has long been at the forefront in terms of using the tools of theater and performance to preach the Word of God.[7] It is therefore not altogether surprising that even though Wilkerson called on parishioners "to stand against those who would turn God's house into a theater or entertainment center for promot-ers,"[8] he saw no problem in turning a theater into a house of God.

In the larger scheme of things, the conversion of a theater to use as a church, even in Times Square, is not that unusual. Given the formal similarities between ritual and theater, the architectural needs of one are similar enough to the needs of the other that such a transformation in either direction makes practical sense.[9] Yet there is something par-ticularly appropriate about the establishment of the Times Square Church in the Mark Hellinger Theatre, for it was there, in the autumn of 1971, that Jesus Christ made his Broadway musical debut.[10]

The show was *Jesus Christ Superstar*, Andrew Lloyd Webber and Tim Rice's rock opera depicting "the last seven days in the life of Je-sus of Nazareth," and just six months earlier, another formally in-novative New Testament musical, *Godspell* had opened off-Broadway at the Cherry Lane Theatre, where it would enjoy a five-year run be-fore moving uptown to a Broadway premiere at the Broadhurst The-atre (1976). Much as *Ben-Hur* had established a new model, both for dramatic adaptations of the Bible and for Broadway spectacle, the combined success of *Superstar* and *Godspell*—both of which featured a live actor in the role of Jesus Christ—would redefine the rules for biblical plays while simultaneously ushering in a new (not to say messianic) era in Broadway musicals more generally.

This chapter compares *Superstar* and *Godspell* with an eye to-ward the differing strategies each takes toward the representation of Jesus of Nazareth. I detail the way that each show balances spectacle, sincerity, authenticity, and irony in its treatment of the Gospel nar-rative. Along the way, I also consider Lloyd Webber and Rice's other biblical adaptation, *Joseph and the Amazing Technicolor Dream-coat*, a piece that was initially developed in the late 1960s but did not find its way to Broadway until 1982.

To maintain consistency with the previous chapters, I have cho-sen to treat these examples in the order in which they premiered on Broadway. This chronological approach, however, has its limitations when confronted with the complicated paths each show took to reach the American theater's promised land. *Joseph* was the first of these projects to be conceived, but the last to be born. *Godspell* was the first to be staged in New York, but in an off-Broadway production, one that critics could not help but compare to *Superstar*, the musical "concept album" that was then topping the U.S. charts. Each show has evolved through a number of rewrites, reimaginings, recordings, and revivals spanning Broadway (*Godspell* in 2011; *Superstar* in 1977, 2000, and 2012; *Joseph* in 1993), national and world tours, film and television adaptations, and a host of productions in regional theaters, schools, and churches. Moreover, as with the Gospels themselves, sometimes two chroniclers of the same performance offer contradictory versions of the sequence of events. Therefore, while I have endeavored to provide accurate and useful dates throughout, the reader may find it helpful to understand all three examples as part of an ongoing conversation between the Bible, the Broadway stage, and other sites of performance.

Rock of Ages

With well over one thousand Broadway performances spanning four separate productions, *Jesus Christ Superstar* is the most commercially successful adaptation of the Bible in Broadway history. Yet it is for reasons other than its subject matter that *Superstar* occupies a significant place in the musical theater canon. Playfully referring to the period before October 1971 as "Broadway BC," musical theater scholar Jessica Sternfeld writes that the show "was revolutionary. It marked at once the end of what many felt was a rather weak and old-fashioned decade of musicals . . . and the beginning of a new era."[11] *Superstar*, she notes, employed several devices that would soon become standard elements of the contemporary "megamusical," including "a sung-through score with no spoken dialogue, lavish and complicated sets, and an extremely emotional, larger-than-life plot."[12] Journalist Ethan Mordden, in his six-volume history of the Broadway musical, notes that *Superstar* combined musical styles and strategies in ways never before heard in a Broadway house. "It marked a wedding of the sacred to the profane, and not only in the use of the pop idiom to narrate the last seven days in the life of Christ," Mordden writes. "The lyrics themselves mix genres, blending poetry and slang. The music sends woodwinds pirouetting over bass guitar lines, or slips difficult counts of 7/8 and 5/4 into R&B's traditional 4/4."[13] *Superstar* also broke new ground in the way that Broadway shows were marketed and sold, having been first released as a concept album. As Lloyd Webber and Rice's first Broadway production, it can be seen in retrospect as the leading edge of the so-called British invasion, ushering in such shows as *Me and My Girl* (1986), *Les Misérables* (1987), and Lloyd Webber's own *Cats* (1983) and *Phantom of the Opera* (1988).[14]

Because of its critical role in musical theater history, the origin narrative of *Jesus Christ Superstar* is familiar to many scholars and fans alike. Nevertheless, a brief rehearsal of the key points may prove useful to understanding the play in the context of biblical adaptations, especially as the artists' journey to the 1971 premiere of *Superstar* begins with the earliest version of their other well-known biblical play, *Joseph and the Amazing Technicolor Dreamcoat*.

English composer Andrew Lloyd Webber (b. 1948) and lyricist Tim Rice (b. 1944) met in 1965. After an abortive attempt to produce a musical based on the life of Victorian philanthropist Thomas John Barnardo, they achieved their first modest success writing pop songs for British chanteuse Ross Hannaman.[15] In the spring of 1968, they were asked by Lloyd Webber's younger brother's music teacher, Alan Doggett, to compose a "pop cantata" for the St. Paul's Junior School choir to perform at their annual Easter end-of-term concert. "There was no suggestion of subject matter," writes Lloyd Webber biographer Michael Walsh, "although it was understood that the work would have some quasi-religious significance."[16] Although the work was based nominally on Genesis 37–46, Rice would later claim that his true source was Logan Marshall's 1904 *Wonder Book of Bible Stories*, an illustrated collection for children.[17] The result was the earliest version of *Joseph and the Amazing Technicolor Dreamcoat*. We will return to *Joseph* in greater depth later (it would not reach Broadway for another fourteen years), but at this stage it is important because the nature of the original commission (for which the two young men split the princely sum of one hundred pounds) led the composing team to a develop a unique dramaturgical solution for one of the most common challenges in adapting the Bible for the stage: the narrative discontinuity of the source text.

Because they were asked for a cantata, not a musical, Lloyd Webber and Rice needed to tell the entirety of the story through song. They needed, moreover, to tell that story within the space of about twenty minutes time, with little to no visual staging to aid the audience's comprehension. Based on the positive audience response to *Joseph*, Lloyd Webber would later say, "We realized that it was possible to put together something continuous without a narrative line."[18] With the ability of the musical score to provide continuity, there was no need to "fill in the blanks" in the fashion of midrash or fan fiction. Instead, the story could be dramatized in a more episodic fashion and the audience would still be able to follow the plot, particularly if the original source was somewhat familiar. As Walsh writes, "Without meaning to, they had stumbled across the form, if not yet the content, of opera."[19] *Joseph* evolved from this twenty-minute song cycle for young voices into a concept album performed by "The Joseph Consortium" for Scepter Records and released in early 1969.[20] The album received generally positive reviews in the English press, and the two men decided that for their follow-up, they would take on the New Testament.

Like *Joseph*, *Jesus Christ Superstar* was initially conceived as a concert piece and record album rather than a fully staged musical. The first single to be released was "Superstar" (1969), the tune that would later become the musical's signature song, combining the now infamous choral hook ("Jesus Christ, Superstar, Do you think you're what they say you are?") with more pointed and ironic questions delivered via a rock melody ("Why'd you choose such a backward time and such a strange land?").[21] The launch of the single—perceived by some Christians as a blasphemous expression of doubt in Christ's divinity—caused some minor controversy in the United States, but it wasn't until the release of the full-length recording (a two-LP set) in the fall of 1970 that *Jesus Christ Superstar* truly became a cultural phenomenon. Buoyed in part by a growing public discourse about its treatment of religion, the album rose to number one on the American charts, ultimately earning honors from Billboard as the top-selling pop album of 1971, with more than three million copies sold.[22] The album was so popular that it spawned several unauthorized concert tours in the summer of 1971. In July, Australian producer Robert Stigwood launched an "official" concert tour featuring Jeff Fenholt as Jesus, Carl Anderson as Judas, and Yvonne Elliman as Mary Magdalene. Playing to arena-size venues for as many as eighteen thousand spectators a night, the tour earned Stigwood, Lloyd Webber, and Rice a small fortune, while further whetting the public's appetite for a theatrical staging on Broadway that autumn. Under the headline, "'Superstar' a Hit Before Opening," Mel Gussow of the *New York Times* reported that the Broadway production, capitalized at an estimated $700,000, had a million-dollar advance sale, also noting that the film rights had already been sold.[23]

Like *Joseph*, *Superstar* dramatizes the Bible as a fragmented, episodic narrative, trusting the steady beat of the score to carry the action along in the absence of spoken dialogue. The frequent use of musical leitmotifs further ties together disparate scenes to give the show a kind of coherence that the libretto itself lacks. The music also provides emotional color that helps the audience connect with characters that are otherwise rather thinly drawn. The plot consists of a series of episodes from the last seven days of Jesus's life as described by the Gospels, interspersed with scenes focusing on the viewpoints or actions of other key characters.

After an opening number in which Judas reveals his misgivings and doubts ("Heaven on Their Minds"), Jesus teaches his disciples at Bethany ("What's the Buzz? / Strange Thing Mystifying," "Everything's All Right"). Following a scene between the Jewish priests Caiaphas and Annas ("This Jesus Must Die"), Christ and his disciples enter Jerusalem amid adoring crowds ("Hosanna," "Simon Zealotes / Poor Jerusalem"). Pontius Pilate, Roman governor of Jerusalem, sings a foreshadowing solo ("Pilate's Dream"), followed by Jesus's expulsion of the money changers from the temple ("The Temple"). Mary then sings a ballad expressing her feelings for Jesus ("I Don't Know How to Love Him"), and the first act ends with Judas's decision to betray Jesus ("Damned for All Time / Blood Money"). The second act begins with the Last Supper ("The Last Supper") and Jesus's solitary prayer in the Garden of Gethsemane ("Gethsemane"). Jesus is arrested ("The Arrest"), followed by the apostles' reaction ("Peter's Denial"). Jesus is brought before Pilate ("Pilate and Christ"), who sends him to King Herod ("King Herod's Song"). While they await the outcome of Jesus's interview with Herod, Mary and the disciples sing a mournful ballad ("Could We Start Again, Please?") followed by Judas's suicide ("Judas' Death"). Jesus returns for trial ("Trial by Pilate"), is given thirty-nine lashes, and ultimately is sentenced to crucifixion. First, however, Judas appears from beyond the grave (and, traditionally, lowered to the stage from above) to sing "Superstar," backed by a chorus of angels. The play concludes with the Crucifixion ("Crucifixion") and the removal of Jesus's body ("John 19:41").

Compared to other Broadway adaptations of the Bible, *Superstar* adopts what we might call a hybrid strategy in its depiction of biblical characters and events. It is neither a "period piece" like *Ben-Hur* nor an outright modernization like *J.B.* Though explicitly set in the Jerusalem of two thousand years ago, the play uses anachronistic language ("Jesus is cool") and imagery (paparazzi following Jesus through the streets of Jerusalem) to tell the story of Jesus as a contemporary fable of celebrity culture. This is underlined by moments when ironically self-aware lyrics offer commentary on the subsequent history of the story being told. During the Last Supper scene, for example, Jesus's disciples sing:

> Always hoped that I'd be an apostle
> Knew that I could make it if I tried
> Then when we retire, we can write the gospels
> So they'll still talk about us when we die.[24]

The use of irony here is explicitly irreverent (and, for believers, potentially heretical), casting doubt on the apostles' motives. The expansion of Judas's role in the narrative echoes the fan fictional strategy of *Mary of Magdala*, but this Judas directly confronts a visibly present Jesus, criticizing him as a "superstar," someone who's "begun to matter more than the things you [Jesus] say." This comes to a head in the title song, which serves as the play's eleven o'clock number.[25] Judas questions Jesus from an explicitly contemporary perspective: "If you'd come today you could have reached the whole nation. Israel in 4 BC had no mass communication." Here, as throughout, the use of rock music offers a challenge to both Christian tradition and Broadway propriety, while the presence of both a choir of angels and a group of rhythm-and-blues backup singer-dancers offers what could be considered a grotesque parody of religious ecstasy.

Randy Barcelo's costuming of the priests and other secondary characters, as well as the elaborate sets designed by Robin Wagner, were not so much contemporary as postmodern, drawing on a variety of contemporary and classical styles in a lavish spectacle of satin, glitter, and plastic. Theater historian Elizabeth Wollman suggests that *Superstar*'s origins as a purely musical exploration left it ill suited for adaptation to the stage. Hence the director, Tom O'Horgan "decided to compensate for the rock opera's dramaturgical shortcomings and lack of narrative flow by creating a production that was as visually spectacular as he could make it."[26] In addition to large, nonrealistic, and brightly colored sets, the stagecraft included "ample use of smoke, laser beams, and wind machines."[27] In one critic's description, "Paul Ainsley plays King Herod as a drag queen, buskined, rouged, and chiffoned," while Judas "appears apotheosized high above the stage in a giant Tiffany-glass butterfly accompanied by a trio of soul singers à la the Supremes."[28] Unlike the spectacular innovations of *Ben-Hur* or *J.B.*, *Superstar*'s use of spectacle was unequivocally despised by most critics. John Simon of *New York* magazine suggested, "The entire production looks rather like a Radio City Music Hall show into whose producers' and designers' coffee cups the gofer had slipped some LSD."[29] *Newsweek* declared, "'Superstar' apparently confirms him [O'Horgan] as the Petronius of our theatrical decadence, the drag-haberdasher of the *lumpen*-avant-garde."[30] We might read in these assessments a kind of judgment of irreverence: not toward Christ, but toward a certain notion of Broadway decorum. Or as *Time* put it, "'Superstar's' vulgarity is less in the realm of religion than in theatrical taste."[31] This emphasis on the stagecraft, however, recalls critical responses to *Ben-Hur* and the other fan fictional adaptations discussed in chapter 2. By focusing on formal aesthetics, theater critics overlook or implicitly dismiss whatever affective experience the performance many generate.

In the case of *Superstar*, the affective experience was driven primarily by the use of rock music. By using rock and roll, the album invoked a genre that, by the late 1960s, had established itself as a site of authenticity in self-conscious opposition to the perceived emptiness of late capitalist social institutions including, but not limited to, organized religion. As David Chidester and others have observed, while conservative Christian groups have historically complained about the moral relativism and general debasement of American popular culture, "With particular intensity, they single out rock, rap, and other forms of popular music as being dangerously immoral, antisocial, and anti-religious."[32] In this view, rock and roll is explicitly linked to antireligious or anti-Christian practices. According to the usual argument, the lyrics advocate sin while the animalistic nature of the music encourages it.[33] Moreover, like the "theater scene" before it, the "rock-and-roll lifestyle" has been a bête noire of the Christian Right for decades.[34] *Jesus Christ Superstar*, because it employed the rock-and-roll idiom, therefore seemed to pose a threat to Christian decency.

Still, the musical contains none of the hedonistic, profane, or allegedly satanic lyrics that lead religious groups to call for warning labels. There is no "Sympathy for the Devil" in Lloyd Webber and Rice's score, nor do Jesus or any of the apostles "Rock and Roll All Night (and Party Everyday)." In fact, the score seems to anticipate (and in some corners is credited with helping to inspire) the emerging genre of Christian rock. As Chidester describes it, evangelical Christians "have created a successful commercial industry in Christian rock music—or contemporary Christian music—which is unified less by musical style, rhythm, or performance than by the explicitly religious content of the lyrics."[35] In their defining study of the genre, *Apostles of Rock: The Splintered World of Contemporary Christian Music* (1999), sociologists Jay R. Howard and John M. Streck explore the value of rock music in building alternative, antiauthoritarian identity in its audience and note the dilemma facing would be Christian rockers: while the genre may seem anathema to Christianity, it cannot be ignored by anyone who wishes to reach the American youth of the late twentieth century. Certainly much of the initial coverage of the album's success linked it to the desire among youth to develop a more personal, relevant, and immediate relationship to the Gospel narrative.

By the late 1960s the wall separating rock from religion had begun to blur. The Second Vatican Council (Vatican II, 1962–1965) had opened a space in the liturgy for vernacular music and even electric instrumentation. The Jesus People movement spread outward from California in the late 1960s, dozens if not hundreds of guitar-strumming pastors giving their implicit blessing to "God rock."[36] Several historians have linked the success of *Superstar* to the more modest successes of religiously themed pop songs such as Norman Greenbaum's "Spirit in the Sky" (1969) and Ocean's "Put Your Hand in the Hand (of the Man from Gallilee)" (1970). For those believers who had accepted rock and roll, in other words, *Superstar*'s score functioned as a source of authenticity.

For others, however, *Superstar* called attention to the evangelical fervor of the pop music industry and its potential threat to organized religion. As Chidester suggests, "Rock 'n' roll is a religion because it enacts an intense, ritualized performance—the 'collective effervescence,' as Durkheim puts it—which is generated by the interaction between ritual specialists and congregants or, in this case, between artists and audiences."[37] To put it another way, the "problem" with *Superstar* is not simply the juxtaposition between profane music and sacred text. The problem is the implicit equation between the (false) idolatry of the rock star and the true deification of the Christ. Contrary, however, to John Lennon's infamous claim that the Beatles were "more popular than Jesus,"[38] *Superstar* does not raise the rock star to the level of God. Rather, the musical reduces Jesus to the level of the rock star, and his apostles to the level of entourage or (literally) backup singers.

Visually, however, it is worth noting that the production was noticeably more conservative in its treatment of Jesus than of the other characters, a strategy that has been echoed stylistically in every Broadway production. While Judas has appeared in a variety of guises—as a countercultural African American (Ben Vereen) in 1971, as a white biker-jacket-clad rebel (Tony Vincent) in 2000, as a youthful Jewish crooner (Josh Young) in 2012—the actor playing Jesus is always cast and costumed in iconic fashion: thirtyish white male, shoulder-length hair, light-colored robe of vaguely ancient design (see figure 15). In fact, the Jesus of *Superstar* resembles nothing so much as Warner Sallman's 1940 painting, *The Head of Christ*. This image, initially distributed in a variety of formats by the Gospel Trumpet Company of Anderson, Indiana, has been so often reproduced (more than 500 million times, according to its publishers), that it is instantly recognizable. As religion scholar David Morgan notes, Sallman's painting and others like it "have served as powerful symbols in American Protestant and Catholic piety because believers have learned to regard them as illustrations, as untrammeled visualizations of what they profess."[39] Such an alignment of the representational with professed belief is a demonstration of sincerity. Visually speaking, then, *Superstar* represents the Savior in the most sincere way possible, and this may to some degree offset the blasphemous or heretical nature of the rest of the production.

Figure 15. Jeff Fenholt as Jesus and Yvonne Elliman as Mary Magdalene in *Jesus Christ Superstar*, 1971. (Photo by Friedman-Abeles © Billy Rose Theatre Division, The New York Public Library for the Performing Arts.)

Jesus, Son of Man

Some observers felt that despite the vulgar stagecraft, the original production had a kind of sincerity. John Gruen, writing in the *New York Times* magazine, for example, suggested, "For all its outrageousness, for all its gaudy theatricality, and for all its desperate striving for effects, the production bristles with life."[40] And Lloyd Webber himself told one interviewer that he and Rice didn't particularly like the Broadway staging, but "we both agree that O'Horgan's version is a very *feeling* version. We don't care how it's done, so long as it is deeply felt."[41] Though not, perhaps, an authentic expression of Christianity, Lloyd Webber seems to offer "life" and "feeling" as evidence of a sincere desire to celebrate the story of the Bible. In this sense, *Superstar* may be regarded as a form of biblical fan fiction (see chapter 2), an attempt to gain a greater appreciation for the sacred narrative by exploring its interstices. Unlike those earlier examples, however, *Superstar* eschews the felt absence of the divine for the visible presence of Jesus as a human being.

Though some critics found *Superstar* "dutifully faithful to the New Testament accounts,"[42] Rice's libretto—based largely on *The Life of Christ* (1958) by American Catholic broadcaster Bishop Fulton Sheen—takes a fair amount of dramatic license with the source text, most notably in its depiction of Mary Magdalene, who is represented as having romantic feelings toward Jesus. While there is ample precedent for such speculations, going back as far as Paul Heyse's *Mary of Magdala* (see chapter 2), Rice added another wrinkle: in order to increase the size of Mary's role, the only female principal character in the show, the character is actually a composite of three different women named in the Gospels: Mary Magdalene, Mary of Bethany, and an unnamed "woman who had been caught in adultery"[43] mentioned in John 8:1–11. As Jean L. Bosch of the Christian drama ministry Lampost Theatre points out, "There is no direct scriptural evidence to support this amalgamation, but it does have precedent in Christian tradition dating back to the works of St. Augustine of Hippo and Pope Gregory the Great."[44] But if this instance of dramatic license taken by *Superstar* seems to be justifiably authentic from a theological standpoint, the visible presence of an actor in the role of Jesus adds a problematic element: many observers of the production felt that the performances of Fenholt and Elliman gave the unspoken impression that Jesus reciprocated Mary's romantic love, or that the characters had been sexually intimate.[45] For spectators of faith, this amounted to heresy if not outright blasphemy, a problem compounded by the fact that *Superstar* does not include any overt demonstration of Christ's divinity. While the crowds in Jerusalem clearly believe he has the power to heal, for example, no acts of healing are depicted on stage. Meanwhile, Rice's transposition of Jesus's own words into the pop vernacular may have made it *too* easy for the audience to identify with the character. As Bosch points out, *Superstar* "emphasizes [Jesus's] humanity in a way that borders on the fallible. An often irritable, sometimes childish, and possibly promiscuous depiction of Jesus does not align well with the Christian doctrine that as both fully God and fully man, Jesus lived a human life yet without sin."[46] For Jewish or secular audience members who regard Jesus as an historical or fictional figure, making Jesus human rather than divine is a dramaturgical point, and one that is potentially welcome. For devout Christians, it is unacceptable.

While Christian groups complained that the play denied the divinity of Jesus and made a hero of Judas, Jewish organizations expressed concern that the play would inspire anti-Semitism by suggesting that Jews bear responsibility for the death of Christ (a suggestion that had been explicitly disavowed just a few years earlier in the Second Vatican Council).[47] In fact, though Christian groups had made up the bulk of the opposition to the concept album, it was Jewish groups who were most vocal in opposing the Broadway production. At the request of the American Jewish Committee, Presbyterian scholar Gerald S. Strober conducted a thorough study of the musical, concluding:

> In some cases, the emotional coloring is deepened to make Jewish individuals and their acts appear more sinister than the gospel record warrants. In other cases, historical facts are enlarged, modified or glossed over so as to create black-vs.-white contrasts where the record indicates only grays. These changes may have been made innocently for dramaturgic reasons, but their potential for harm remains.[48]

In particular, Strober noted, the representation of the Jewish priests Caiaphas and Annas as the characters who first decide "This Jesus must die" was both inaccurate and inflammatory. "For Jews," wrote Arnold Forster and Benjamin Epstein of the Anti-Defamation League, "the rock opera was a disaster mitigated only by the fact that the lyrics were often unintelligible and that New York theater prices might well keep many people, even those who liked rock music, away."[49] While these somewhat testy words may read, in retrospect, as an overreaction, the Jewish protests over *Superstar* indicate how high the stakes can be when adapting the Bible for the stage. One does not have to believe in the New Testament to be concerned about the way it is represented.

The multiracial casting of the Broadway production added yet another complicating factor. *Superstar* was the first biblical adaptation in Broadway's history to employ a cast that included both white and black actors. While this was generally regarded as consistent with a kind of hippie liberalism for which director O'Horgan (who had previously staged *Hair*) was known, it may have been unsettling to those spectators who unconsciously imagined all the characters in the Bible as white. Black audiences, meanwhile, expressed some dismay that Judas, of all characters, would be played by an African American actor (Ben Vereen). Interestingly, little comment was made about the casting of Yvonne Elliman, an Asian American, as Mary. Asian Americans, perhaps, were generally pleased to see Elliman cast in a role that was not explicitly marked as Asian. Conversely, white audiences may have found Mary's role consistent with existing stereotypes of Asian women as feminine and submissive.[50] However, it is also likely that as one of the few members of the Broadway cast who had played the same role on the pop album, Elliman had already gained the acceptance of the audience. Her voice, in other words, trumped her visual presence on stage.

Four decades after its premiere, *Superstar* no longer generates controversy, at least on Broadway. From the standpoint of the musical theater, Lloyd Webber and Rice have now become the Establishment against which their rock opera once seemed to rail. The business practices developed by Stigwood to exploit maximum value from *Superstar* are now standard procedure in the industry: promote the show through multiple channels; build up a strong advance sale to "critic-proof" the production; license productions around the world; and leverage merchandizing opportunities. In religious terms, the recognition and appreciation of Jesus's humanity has gradually become more acceptable among American Christians (though not to the exclusion of his divinity).[51] Furthermore, the sincerity of *Superstar* has been retrospectively established by a number of external factors, including but not limited to the Norman Jewison–directed film version (shot on location in Israel, adding an element of authenticity), subsequent better-received stage productions, and the fact that Jeff Fenholt (who originated the role of Jesus) later became a born-again Christian and an outspoken evangelist. Fenholt's website claims "over 3 million Contemporary Christian CD's sold since 2003."[52] The most intriguing element of *Superstar*'s aftermath, however, may be the one mentioned at the beginning of this chapter: the stage where Jesus first became a "superstar" is now consecrated ground.

Prepare Ye the Way of the Lord

In the fall of 1970, just around the time that the *Jesus Christ Superstar* album was released in the United States, a group of actors at Carnegie Mellon University began rehearsals for a master's thesis project created by John Michael Tebelak (1949–1985), an original play with music then called *The Godspell*.[53] Inspired by the Gospels, the performance featured ten actors in clown costumes acting out a series of vignettes based on Jesus's parables, interspersed with traditional hymns set to rock-and-roll music composed by Duane Bolick. Influenced by alternative theater groups such as the Living Theatre and Second City, the company's creative process was akin to what today is called devised theater, using improvisational exercises to construct and craft a physical score to go along with the stories drawn from the Bible. As one cast member recalled, "Everybody would take the stage and act out a story. . . . We eventually called it 'Mickey Mousing' the parables, like if you said, 'A sower sowed a seed,' you might mime someone sowing or even sewing for that matter."[54] The first act ended with a kind of nonliturgical communion, as the cast invited the audience to the stage to share wine.[55] The second act offered an abbreviated version of the passion narrative, staging—still in clown costumes—the Last Supper, Judas's betrayal, and the Crucifixion.

The Godspell enjoyed a brief December run of several performances in the university's Studio Theatre. In late February 1971, around the time that *Superstar* reached number one on the Billboard Hot 100, the production now called simply *Godspell* played a two-week run at Café La MaMa, Ellen Stewart's experimental theater in New York's East Village. Producers Edgar Lansbury and Joe Beruh liked the show enough to want to give it an open-ended run at the off-Broadway Cherry Lane Theatre, but they felt that it needed a new musical score to transform it into a full-fledged (and commercially viable) musical. For this, they contracted with a young aspiring composer named Stephen Schwartz (b. 1948).

Unlike Tebelak, a practicing Episcopalian, Schwartz had no religious connection to the Gospels. He had been raised in a "casually Jewish" household on Long Island. This, he would say later, gave him a fresh perspective on the material that turned out to be an advantage: "I didn't know these stories, these parables. I didn't have any investment in the story-telling from a proselytizing point of view, so I was just looking at it as a piece of theater, as a story on the stage."[56] The retooled *Godspell* with Schwartz's score opened May 17 at the Cherry Lane to generally strong reviews. Only Clive Barnes of the *New York Times* was negative, declaring the show too earnest in its embrace of Christianity. "It is never irreverent," Barnes wrote, "merely naïve and platitudinous in its mixture of 'Jesus Christ Superstar,' lovable circus clowns and Billy Graham."[57] Though Barnes was alone in his condemnation of *Godspell* as "rather nauseating,"[58] he was far from the only critic to draw the parallel to *Superstar* (at that point, still just a record album). Walter Kerr, for example, while praising the Schwartz-Tebelak collaboration, cautioned, "'Godspell' *isn't* 'Jesus Christ Superstar,' a much more ambitious, musically complex, in fact, superior piece of work."[59] Both Barnes and Kerr emphasized the comparative simplicity of *Godspell*, implying that it was the lesser of the two biblical musicals.

Yet by the time *Superstar* opened on Broadway in October, *Godspell* was already thriving, having transferred from the ninety-nine-seat Cherry Lane to the Promenade Theatre, a 399-seat off-Broadway house at Broadway and Seventy-Sixth Street. "Comparison of *Godspell* with *Superstar* is inevitable," wrote Princeton Theological Seminary professor Daniel L. Migliore in the October 1971 issue of *Theology Today*. "Both see Jesus as the personified focus of a radically new set of life values. In both, he is an anti-establishment hero. Both use the rock medium."[60] Migliore notes, however, significant differences between the two plays in terms of dramatic structure. *Superstar*, while episodic, is nevertheless plot-driven, organized around the same sequence of events covered by a traditional Passion play; *Godspell*, on the other hand, "depends neither on the movement of plot nor on the development of the main characters but simply on original and humorous dramatizations of the sayings and parables of Jesus performed in rapid sequence."[61] Moreover, suggested the theologian, "Whereas *Superstar* is intense and sometimes morose, *Godspell* is disarmingly light and playful."[62] These differences may help explain why, when *Superstar* closed its run at the Mark Hellinger in July 1973, *Godspell* was still going strong, en route to a remarkable 2,123 performances at the Promenade. In June 1976, *Godspell* finally had its official Broadway opening at the Broadhurst Theatre. The show would stay on Broadway for fifteen months, moving theaters twice, before closing after 527 performances. Less than two months later, *Superstar* would have its first (and least successful) Broadway revival.

Since the 1970s, the two musicals have continued to circulate within and without the Broadway theater. *Superstar*, as one might expect from a "megamusical," has remained a bigger commercial property, playing larger theaters, selling more albums, and generating greater wealth for its creators. *Godspell*, with its simple staging requirements, flexible casting requirements, and more readily singable tunes, has established a firmer foothold in the amateur repertoire. It is a rare weekend indeed that some university, school, or church somewhere is not performing *Godspell*.[63]

Feast of Fools

Like *Superstar*, *Godspell* has earned attention from musical theater historians and fans for reasons largely unrelated to its biblical content. Stacy Wolf, for example, in *Changed for Good: A Feminist History of the Broadway Musical*, considers *Godspell* among 1970s musicals such as *Company* (1970) and *A Chorus Line* (1975) that decentered traditional romantic pairings in favor of an ensemble-driven celebration of community.[64] Musical theater historian John Bush Jones cites *Godspell* as an example of the "fragmented musical," musicals that focus on character and theme at the expense of a coherent story.[65] For Jones, such musicals reflect the self-centered narcissism of the 1970s, and *Godspell* "has a fair bit of 'soul-searching' of the fragmented musical kind going on, perhaps helping to account for the show's enormous popularity throughout most of the soul-searching '70s."[66] Wollman, in her history of the rock musical, calls *Godspell* "one of the most successful rock musicals of its time," placing it in an evolutionary line between *Hair* (1968) and *Superstar*.[67] Conversely, Sternfeld, whose interest is the "megamusical," dismisses *Godspell* and *Hair* as "remote influences [that] were far less effective in paving *Jesus Christ Superstar*'s path to Broadway than the music and text of the show itself."[68] Scholars and fans of Stephen Schwartz give pride of place to *Godspell* as the composer's first successfully staged musical, a forerunner to more sophisticated works such as *Pippin* (1972) and *Wicked* (2003).[69] Musicologist Paul Laird, for example, has meticulously documented the various musical influences on Schwartz's score, which as he points out "is far better known than anything that takes place on the stage during the show."[70]

In reviewing this body of scholarship, what becomes clear is that *Godspell* is, in many ways, even more open to interpretation than *Superstar*. Its multifaceted nature, its position at a pivotal point in the chronology of the American musical, and its extensive production history combine to support a variety of critical readings. Considering *Godspell* as a biblical adaptation is, in that sense, just one more way to reframe a now-familiar work. Yet by placing the musical in the context of other biblical adaptations, by examining its unique balance of spectacle, irony, authenticity, and sincerity, we can see that *Godspell* is truly one of a kind in its capacity to unify—if only temporarily—religious ritual and the Broadway theater.[71]

Because of its origins as a low-budget, small-theater production, *Godspell* is less dependent on spectacle than most biblical adaptations. The Cherry Lane production made use of a nearly bare stage, framed by a chain-link fence located upstage. The playing space included a collection of sawhorses and wooden planks that the performers used to assemble makeshift tables and platforms for different "scenes." Occasionally, the performance spilled out into the audience space, with actors entering, exiting, or performing in the aisles. Partly for financial reasons, but mostly for aesthetic ones, this minimal set was maintained when the show transferred to the Promenade and then to Broadway. The 2011 revival at the Circle in the Square was staged in the round, eliminating the chain-link fence but otherwise keeping the "poor theater" aesthetic.[72] For a Broadway au-

Figure 16. Stephen Nathan as Jesus (*standing*) and cast in *Godspell*, 1971. (Photo by Kenn Duncan © Billy Rose Theatre Division, The New York Public Library for the Performing Arts.)

dience accustomed to musicals with large sets and multiple changes, such minimal staging may have had some novelty value, but the real spectacle of the show was the performers themselves.

Godspell's reimagining of Jesus and his disciples as a troupe of clowns was the most ironic and potentially controversial element of the musical. Tebelak had drawn his inspiration from Baptist theologian Harvey Cox's 1969 treatise *The Feast of Fools: A Theological Essay on Festivity and Fantasy*, which called for a restoration of joy and festivity to religious life. In a time of spiritual malaise, Cox argued, Christians need "Christ the harlequin: The personification of festivity and fantasy in an age that had almost lost both. Coming now in greasepaint and halo, this Christ is able to touch our jaded modern consciousness as other images of Christ cannot."[73] *Godspell*'s use of the clown motif was, at its most basic, a literalizing of Cox's metaphor. In his history of contemporary Christian music, journalist Paul Baker suggests that religious responses to *Godspell*'s treatment of the Bible were shaped by the media frenzy surrounding *Superstar*. As a result, writes Baker, "Tebelak's portrayal of Christ as a harlequin was just as offensive to the conservatives as the deluded Jesus in *Superstar*."[74] Yet if the abstract premise of Jesus in clownface seems blasphemous, the performance of the musical explicitly equates the clown costumes and makeup with sincere faith. At the start of the play, the actors wear ordinary street clothes for a prologue ("Tower of Babble") that demonstrates the lack of community in contemporary society. Then an actor representing John the Baptist calls on the company to "Prepare Ye, the Way of the Lord."[75] John baptizes each member of the cast, concluding with Jesus. After Jesus has been baptized, he takes a box of greasepaint and paints each actor's face in turn; at the same time, the company members are discovering and putting on their motley costumes. Thus the clown costumes become a sign of holiness; those who are so adorned have accepted the call of Jesus.

Here, the nontraditional staging—a product of the show's alternative theater origins—is critical in establishing a perception of sincerity. The audience first meets the actors as their "real selves," an impression enhanced by the fact that, other than Jesus and Judas / John the Baptist (the two roles are played by the same actor), the characters have no names, only the first names of the actors playing them. Because spectators see the actors' transformation from everyday clothing into clown costume, they are always aware of a level of "reality" beneath the play's theatrical surface. As Wolf writes:

> The audience watches the actor, not a character, at all times, and this direct relationship encourages a connection based not on psychological identification but rather on an affective admiration and contagious desire to play. *Godspell* makes it all look easy and invites the audience to imagine themselves as part of a similar community.[76]

As in religious ritual, the sense of shared community is further enhanced by breaking down the physical separation between actors and audience through the device of playing parts of the show in the audience space, and reaches its zenith at the conclusion of the first act, when the performers invite the audience to the stage to share wine with the company. This sharing refers to the act of Holy Communion without tempting blasphemy or heresy by irreverently mimicking it outright, while at the same time creating an authentic, nonmimetic bond between performers and spectators. Such a bond transcends the representational frame of the theater. As result, when the audience experiences the spectacle of the Crucifixion that climaxes the second act, the ontological stakes have been raised to the point where an experience of affective piety, or at least reverence, is all but ensured.

By enacting the biblical narrative within a community-oriented celebration, *Godspell* comes closer than any other Broadway biblical adaptation to crossing the line between theater and ritual. In so doing, it demonstrates a different but no less potent alchemy of irony and sincerity than earlier examples such as *The Flowering Peach* and *J.B.* Where those Old Testament adaptations used irony to explore the challenge of remaining faithful to a mysterious and unknowable God, *Godspell* uses the figure of the clown to explore the ironic possibility that walking in the footsteps of Jesus might demand resistance to contemporary social norms. As Migliore writes:

> Measured by the sophisticated standards of the wise men of this world, the gospel is near enough to childlike foolishness to be portrayed in the *Godspell* version. There is foolishness in Jesus' call to become like children and to trust completely in the fatherly love of God. And as Paul noted, there is surely foolishness in the message of the cross. At the same time the role of the clown offers a crafty vehicle of social criticism. The clown makes fun of the pretensions of the high and mighty and exposes

the absurdity of the assumptions which lead to injustice and exploitation in our relations with other men.[77]

By representing Jesus and the disciples as clowns, in other words, *Godspell* relies on the trope of the wise fool. Instead of mocking Jesus, it highlights the fact that Christianity—though we think of it as part of the Establishment—can in fact be a vehicle for social liberation. In 1971, contemporaneous with the Jesus People movement and a thriving counterculture, *Godspell*, Migliore suggested, "seems closer to the religious sensibility of many young people today who place the accent on present joy and new being."[78] Yet *Godspell* did not require audiences to be believers, or even seekers, to appreciate the "present joy," in large part thanks to the musical contributions of Schwartz, the composer.

As a Jew, Schwartz had no prior association with the material, no preexisting assumptions about the relationship between Jesus and his apostles, particularly Judas. Yet he recognized that if the show were to make sense in theatrical terms as well as spiritual terms, some way would have to be found to communicate the drama of the story for nonbelievers. As Schwartz later said, describing why he added the song "All for the Best" as a duet for Jesus and Judas:

> And so I talked to John-Michael and said, "Well, look, the major event is in the second act, that Judas betrays Jesus, so we need to set that up in the first act. There has to be something, they have to be sort of special friends. Judas has to be more of his main lieutenant, rather than just another one of the apostles." And that's what this song is for. . . . If these guys were named Rick and Joe, and it was about how Joe betrayed Rick in the second act, you would give them a duet in the first act.[79]

To the degree that we are prepared to credit *Godspell*'s endurance in the repertoire to such aesthetic—rather than religious—choices, it may seem that it can be an advantage for the adapter of the Bible *not* to be overly familiar with the source text. More likely, however, Schwartz's insistence on making the show sincere in musical theater terms helped *Godspell* connect to all audiences, both religious and secular. In addition to the pop-style musical hooks for which Schwartz would later become known, the score is filled with simple and direct melodies with minimal orchestrations, making the show's songs much easier to remember (or sing along to) to than the more elaborate *Superstar*. This, along with an emphasis on ensemble numbers where the entire cast sings together, contributes to the overall sense of community on which the play depends.[80]

Your Own Personal Jesus

Secular critics recognized the infectiousness of *Godspell*'s good humor, though they were split on whether this was a desirable state of affairs.[81] Some, like Dirk Brukenfeld of the *Village Voice*, felt that the clowning antics of the performers made "a destructive contrast with the underlying reverence."[82] Others saw simply a joyous celebration of both religion and youth culture. Tebelak's staging, wrote Walter Kerr, was "neither reverent nor irreverent, just fun."[83] Even Barnes's negative review acknowledged *Godspell*'s "manic energy and great good nature," suggesting, "It is a play that will appeal most to the religious, or the religious at heart."[84]

As with earlier biblical adaptations such as *Ben-Hur* and *The Green Pastures*, *Godspell*'s appeal to "the religious, or the religious at heart" depended in part on a heavy dose of authenticity to establish its bona fides, its sincerity of intention. *Godspell*'s initial claim to authenticity is located in the text itself. The tone is set by the second song, "Prepare Ye the Way of the Lord." As first John and then the entire company repeat that single verbatim phrase from the King James Version (Matthew 3:3 and Mark 1:3) over and over, the number announces the show's intent to be a "faithful adaptation."[85] The parables that follow are drawn directly from the Gospels themselves, with little attempt to transpose the language of the King James Version into contemporary vernacular. Instead, *Godspell* relies on the pantomime and improvisationally devised asides of the performers to clarify the meaning of the text. Further authenticity is located in the lyrics, many of which Schwartz took verbatim from an Episcopal hymnal, and simply reset to his pop score.[86] In short, a large percentage of the actual words and phrases the audience hears during a performance of *Godspell* are words and phrases they could either find in a Bible or hear at a church service.[87]

The text's reliance on parables is primarily a dramaturgical choice. Instead of trying to stage the entirety of Jesus's life (an essentially contested history), the parables provide a basis for a more episodic or "fragmented" dramatic structure that offers little in the way of narrative continuity. The show is musically fragmented as well, especially by comparison to the sung-through *Superstar* that used recitative passages and recurring leitmotifs to give coherence to its disparate episodes. Some critics have even deemed *Godspell* a "revue" rather than a true book musical. This use of the parables as an organizing principle, however, also functions as a (possibly unintentional) metacommunication that legitimizes the show itself. Unlike most other parts of the Bible, even spectators of faith recognize that the parables are not literally true: they are stories told by Jesus to illustrate particular moral principles. By invoking this tradition, *Godspell* similarly disavows that it is literally "true," while suggesting that it may nevertheless have a legitimate religious function.

The perception that the musical is a sincere expression of religious devotion grounded in an authentic reading of the Bible inoculates the play against most criticism from religious authorities. As one telling example, the Associated Press reported in 2000 that "The Church of Jesus Christ of the Latter Day Saints [the Mormon Church] takes the position that the musical 'Jesus Christ Superstar' does not recognize Christ as a deity, [but] the Church has taken no similar stand on 'Godspell.'"[88] *Godspell* even gets away with having an actor impersonate Jesus, right down to a simulated crucifixion. Other than the *Freiburg Passion Play* imported from Germany by David Belasco for a limited run at the Hippodrome in 1929, only *Superstar* had dared to do as much on Broadway. Yet the Jesus of *Godspell* is even more open to audience interpretation than the Jesus of *Superstar*. Because his clownish appearance is obviously not intended to represent the actual Jesus, his presence serves as an index to whatever each individual spectator already believes (or does not believe) about the Nazarene. For spectators who believe in Christ's divinity, the nonrealistic representation of the theatrical Jesus may in fact serve to invoke the divine absence of the real Savior as in a traditional liturgical trope. *Whom do you seek? He is not here.* In any case, several commentators have remarked that the reprise of "Prepare Ye the Way of the Lord" with which *Godspell* typically ends can be interpreted as representative of the Resurrection.

If *Godspell*'s sincerity has been a plus for spectators of faith, secular critics have sometimes considered it a negative. This was especially true when the play moved to Broadway. The show's earnestness—which some critics associate with amateurism—read differently at the Broadhurst Theatre in 1976 than it had off-Broadway in 1971. The larger house diminished the immediacy of the production (though the actors still played parts of the show in the aisles), reducing what Wolf called "affective admiration and contagious desire to play." The show's formal innovations, a novelty in 1971, seemed less inventive just five years later. Douglas Watt, for example, called the Broadway version of *Godspell* "too cute for my taste in the long run," and "a slightly dated form of theater."[89] Leonard Probst of NBC radio was less charitable, suggesting, "The show is now too young to be nostalgic and too old to be fresh."[90] For critics such as these, Jesus's moment on Broadway would seem to have passed, leaving *Godspell* as an overly sincere relic of a more naive moment in theater history. As with *Superstar*, however, the affective dimension, overlooked or undervalued by the "sophisticated" New York critics, found favor with audiences. *Godspell* outsold its reviews, running for fifteen months, longer than *The Flowering Peach*, *J.B.*, and all other previous biblical adaptations with the exception of *Superstar* and *The Green Pastures*.[91]

But What Do You Do for an Encore?

Superstar had rocketed Andrew Lloyd Webber and Tim Rice to stardom as a composing team. *Evita* (1979) would follow. *Godspell* had not exactly made Schwartz a household name in the same way, but it established him as a professional composer. His subsequent hits *Pippin* (1972) and *The Magic Show* (1974) meant that by the time *Godspell* reached Broadway in 1976, Schwartz was arguably the top young musical theater composer-lyricist on the American scene. Lloyd Webber and Rice would eventually bring the Bible back to Broadway with *Joseph and the Amazing Technicolor Dreamcoat*, a production that proved even more commercially appealing than *Superstar*. Schwartz's second attempt at staging the Bible, *Children of Eden*, appears condemned to wander in the wilderness for forty years; it has yet to receive a Broadway production. A brief examination of these two follow-up musicals—one of which achieved significant success on Broadway, and one of which has never opened there, despite expectations that it would—illustrates some of the many factors that complicate the production and reception of the Bible on Broadway, a theme to which we will also return in the next and final chapter.

Though it was, as noted earlier, the first of Tim Rice and Andrew Lloyd Webber's collaborations for the musical theater, *Joseph* was actually the last to arrive on Broadway. There had been a number of amateur productions in the United States and United Kingdom throughout the 1970s, but it wasn't until January 27, 1982, that the musical opened at the Royale Theatre. Many felt that the show, now expanded to seventy-five minutes or more, was too thin or too juvenile to support a Broadway production. This impression was compounded when the play's first professional production in New York, a limited engagement at the Brooklyn Academy of Music in 1976, received poor reviews. In 1981, however, producer Susan Rose launched a new production, featuring a reorchestrated score and a reconception of the Narrator as a female role, at Ford's Theatre in Washington, D.C., where it ran for seven months, prompting Broadway producer Zev Bufman to bring the show to New York. It opened off-Broadway at the Entermedia Theater, a former Yiddish playhouse on Second Avenue.[92] After two months of playing to near-capacity, the production was moved uptown to the Royale, where it launched a Broadway run of 747 performances, surpassing *Superstar* as the single longest running production of a biblical adaptation on Broadway.[93]

Joseph is similar to *Superstar* in a number of obvious ways. It draws loosely on the Bible for its inspiration. It is a sung-through musical with no spoken dialogue. Rice's libretto is filled with playful anachronisms, helped along by a pop musical idiom that lends itself to vernacular language. Compare, for example, Genesis 37:4, which describes Joseph's brothers' jealousy at the sight of his multicolored coat—*And when his brothers saw that their father loved him more than all his brothers, they hated him, and could not speak peaceably to him*[94]—with the parallel lines of the song "Joseph's Coat":

> And when Joseph graced the scene
> His brothers turned a shade of green
> His astounding clothing took the biscuit
> Quite the smoothest person in the district.[95]

The goal of such casual language, it appears, is to make the original text more accessible. By expressing the story in familiar, contemporary terms, the audience can understand it better. In this sense, *Joseph* also mimics *Superstar*, keeping the biblical narrative set in the ancient world while updating the language for greater accessibility.

In other ways, however, *Joseph* is more similar to *Godspell* than to *Superstar*. As Sternfeld notes, "*Joseph* was mostly a comedy, telling a potentially grand, epic story in a decidedly down-to-earth, light way. It simply does not have the scope or weight of a megamusical."[96] Critics described the 1982 production in similar terms as they had used for *Godspell*. John Simon called the show "simple . . . but not simple-minded."[97] Mel Gussow noted, "With its innocent and gently satiric attitude toward sacred material, it is decidedly a musical for young people, the sort of show that could serve as an introduction to the theater and also to Bible study."[98] While the perception of *Joseph* as a children's play may be a holdover from its origins as a school choir piece, the overall sense of innocence and joy appears to be what buoyed *Joseph* in its Broadway incarnation. "Despite the rampant silliness," suggests Sternfeld, "*Joseph* never becomes campy (although it can certainly be staged that way). It remains, more than anything, charming."[99] Like *Godspell*, *Joseph* has come a long way from a simple, experimental beginning, and while it occasionally returns to Broadway or in a star-driven touring production (David Cassidy played Joseph in a 1983 tour; Donny Osmond did the same in 1992), it remains in the repertoire primarily because of its popularity among schools, churches, and community theaters.[100]

Unlike *Godspell*, however, the religious content of *Joseph* is minimal. The story of the twelve tribes of Israel is foundational to both Jewish and Christian traditions, but the import of this is glossed over in the expository number, "Jacob and Sons":

> Jacob was the founder of a whole new nation
> Mostly on account of all the children he had
> He was also called Israel but most of the time
> His sons and his wives used to call him "Dad."[101]

Why Jacob is called Israel, why he was selected by God to be "the founder of a whole new nation," and other elements of the story that have religious significance are omitted. Instead, the story of Joseph is recast from the beginning as a domestic drama: the favorite son and his jealous brothers. Similar elisions continue throughout. One understands why, in the context of a school concert and later a commercial work, Lloyd Webber and Rice would prefer to avoid provoking the ire of religious audiences by committing to a particular interpretation of the Joseph narrative. In religious terms, then, *Joseph* is sincere without being authentic. It erases virtually all reference to God, and all but the most innocuous references to Judaism. In its joyous communal affect, *Joseph*, like *Godspell*, can occasionally envelop the audience in a moment of transcendence, but they are unlikely to experience such a moment as spiritual.

Not long after *Joseph* closed its two-year Broadway run, Stephen Schwartz was commissioned to write a piece of music for "Youth Sing Praise," a Roman Catholic youth festival in Illinois.[102] Thus began a project initially known as *Family Tree*, an attempt to dramatize the first ten chapters of the book of Genesis, from the Creation to the Flood. Following a performance at Illinois's Church of Our Lady of the Snows, Schwartz would spend the next several years trying to secure a professional production of the show, during which time he frequently reworked and rewrote the musical, first with his original collaborator Charles Lisanby, and later with director John Caird. In the late 1980s, the writing team had a falling out. After some legal wrangling, it was determined that Schwartz owned the rights to the music and lyrics, but Lisanby owned the spoken book and the title *Family Tree*. Caird and Schwartz began to write a new book for the show, now called *Children of Eden*, which opened to mixed reviews in London's West End in 1991. Despite a lavish and spectacular production, *Children of Eden* lasted only three months at the Prince Edward Theatre and took a huge financial loss. Undaunted, Schwartz and Caird continued to tweak the show for several more years. The musical had several regional theater productions in the 1990s, but the closest it came to Broadway was a well-received engagement at New Jersey's Paper Mill Playhouse in 1997. "Although it has not yet had a Broadway run," wrote Paul Laird in 2014, "*Children of Eden* is popular among school, community, and religious groups."[103]

Laird notes that of all Schwartz's musicals, *Children of Eden* is "his only show with the character of a pageant, including a chorus of Storytellers and children who play the animals that Adam and Eve name in Act I and that board the ark in Act II."[104] As Broadway producers become increasingly cost conscious, this need for a large cast is one of the factors that has kept the play from being produced there.

The score, Laird suggests, may be another factor; it is among Schwartz's most musically ambitious and can be fully realized only with a larger orchestra than most Broadway pits can accommodate.[105] By comparison to Schwartz's earlier hit, *Children of Eden* is simpler in tone and intent, but lacks the simplicity (of casting, of staging requirements, of music) that allowed *Godspell* to capture the critical and public imagination. As Matthew Palm wrote of a 2012 Orlando production, "This is a story that screams for simplicity; it's really just a meditation on the idea of parents letting children lead their own lives. So the large chorus, flashing lights and background animal sounds serve more as a distraction than an enhancement to the tale's sentiments."[106] *Children of Eden* is also a more serious work. While it has a couple of comic numbers and some light moments, it is primarily a serious treatment of family dynamics, using God as the ultimate father figure. In short, Schwartz and Caird were not able to find the same precarious balance of spectacle, irony, sincerity, and authenticity that animated *Godspell*. Without sufficient irony or authenticity to ground the play in a kind of reality, *Children of Eden* remains a pageant, an expression of faith that never quite succeeds as a work of theater.

As these "encores" show, there is no one-size-fits-all approach that guarantees success in adapting the Bible for Broadway. Err too far in one direction, you may find commercial success but sacrifice a meaningful exploration of the source (*Joseph*). Err too far in the other, you may find yourself with a work that stays faithful to the source at the expense of playability (*Children of Eden*). Yet both *Joseph* and *Children of Eden* have been more "successful" than many late twentieth-century attempts to stage the Bible. In the next chapter, we will consider two examples of shows that missed the mark by significantly larger margin.

Epilogue: Lambs of God

The Times Square Church was neither the first nor the only religious group that sought to clean up the Broadway neighborhood with its pastoral mission. It wasn't even the first group to do so in a building with a rich theatrical history. In 1975, the Manhattan Church of the Nazarene took over the Lambs Club building at 130

West Forty-Fourth Street. Founded in 1874, the Lambs Club was a fraternal organization for members of the theatrical profession.[107] The clubhouse on Forty-Fourth street, designed by Stanford White and opened in 1905, included a private theater space with a seating capacity of approximately 350. Members of the club often used the theater (located on the third floor) for rehearsals, backers' auditions, and private galas, but the space was rarely if ever used for regular productions open to the public. Ironically, it would take the departure of the theater club[108] and the arrival of the Church of the Nazarene before general audiences could attend performances in this space.

Motivated by the belief that "we are called to God to resurrect the arts by the power of the resurrection," the first regularly offered Equity theater production at what would become known as the Lamb's Theatre was a 1977 revival of *Godspell*.[109] The production was a critical and commercial success, but as playwright, pastor, and Lamb's Theatre chronicler Joey Condon reports, "The literal interpretation of portraying Jesus as a clown in a superman t-shirt was too much for a district pastor who brought his congregation to the Lamb's and took back shock, shame, anger, and accusations of blasphemy."[110] The pastor complained to the church's parent organization, the General Church of the Nazarene in Kansas City, and *Godspell* was forced to closed after just five weeks. Undaunted, Pastor Paul Moore created an independent foundation, the Friends of the Lamb's, to provide financial support for the church and its theatrical activity.[111] Theater productions continued at the church, and in 1979 Carolyn Rossi Copeland—who had performed in the 1977 *Godspell*—launched the Lamb's Theatre Company.[112] Over the next thirty years, the Lamb's Theatre would produce or play host to more than fifty off-Broadway productions, including *Godspell* (1988),[113] as well as several lesser known biblical adaptations such as Harry Chapin's *Cotton Patch Gospel* (1981) and Alec McCowen's solo recitation of *St. Mark's Gospel* (1990). Throughout this time, the third-floor stage also served as the church's primary worship space.

In 2006, the Manhattan Church of the Nazarene sold its building to a developer. The final public performance at the Lamb's Theatre was given on September 17, 2006.[114] The interior of the building was renovated, eliminating the theater space. The upscale Chatwal Hotel now occupies 130 West Forty-Fourth Street. The exterior facade and a ground-floor restaurant called the Lambs Club are all that remains of the building's rich history. For a brief period, however, theater and worship coexisted as joint tenants in Times Square, offering a vision of a peaceable kingdom, where the wolf shall dwell with the lamb.[115]

CHAPTER SEVEN

Hard Job Being God

Based on the Bible—the world's oldest and newest bestseller in
all languages and dialects of humanity—the musical has a
built-in success formula.

—King Solomon Productions Company, brochure for
prospective investors, 1966[1]

God, as the saying goes, answers all our prayers. Sometimes, however, the answer is no. When we look only at the *Superstars* and
Godspells, we might wonder why more playwrights and producers
have *not* tried to build on the foundation laid by *Ben-Hur, The Green
Pastures,* and *The Flowering Peach.* Because nothing that has *already*
happened can truly surprise, analyzing only successful adaptations of
the Bible may lead us to underestimate the difficulty (if not outright
peril) of trying to balance spectacle, sincerity, authenticity, and irony
in a constellation that successfully captures the imagination and approval of audiences and critics, secular theatergoers and spectators of
faith. So rather than a conventional conclusion, in which we recap
the productions examined thus far, this chapter briefly recounts two
of the least remembered attempts in the history of biblical adaptation on Broadway: *I'm Solomon* (1968) and *Hard Job Being God*
(1972). Just as apocryphal texts offer comparison points that can inform our understanding of canonical scripture, the alternative history
offered by these "lost scrolls" highlights some of the key characteris-
tics of more successful adaptations. They also illustrate the degree to
which the very idea of staging the Bible on Broadway remains simultaneously appealing and absurd.

When our subject is religion, it is tempting to interpret commercial and critical success as evidence of divine intervention (or at least approval). Conversely, like those who opposed Salmi Morse's *The Passion*, we may wish to ascribe failure to divine retribution. But as Job learned, the ways of the Lord are dark and mysterious. The Bible recounts the stories of many people whose great faith was justly rewarded. It also recounts stories of those unfortunates who, "though well attested by their faith, did not receive what was promised."[2]

In theater history, we similarly seek to use the success or failure of a given play as clearly indicative of a broader cultural or artistic paradigm shift. Certainly changing social attitudes toward religion can partly account for the rise and fall of certain biblical dramas. Changing attitudes toward race explain why a show like *The Green Pastures* has fallen out of the repertoire. The spectacular fan fiction of *Ben-Hur* has found a home on the silver screen, where questions of presence resonate differently. Yet pop cultural phenomena like *Ben-Hur* and *The Green Pastures* shared their cultural moments with less-remembered works like *The Sign of the Cross* and *Noah*. Relative failures such as *The Creation of the World and Other Business* and *God's Favorite* and catastrophes such as *Hard Job Being God* and *I'm Solomon* trod Broadway's boards in close company with *Jesus Christ Superstar* and *Godspell*. The zeitgeist, in other words, is a necessary but not sufficient condition for success. While the relationship between religion and popular culture does wax and wane over time, even in the same generation some biblical adaptations flourish like a palm tree and grow like a cedar in Lebanon, while others are destroyed forever.[3]

In Someone Else's Sandals

Jesus Christ Superstar was not the first biblical musical to grace the stage of the Mark Hellinger Theatre. In April 1968, the theater played host to an ill-fated musical comedy called *I'm Solomon* that closed after sixteen performances (one week of previews and one week of regular performances) at a reported loss of $800,000—a staggering sum for the era.[4] "For, lo, the winter is past, the rain is over and gone, the flowers appear on the earth," reported the *New Yorker* in May 1968 in mock biblical verbiage. "And in the city of John, at the Theatre of Mark the Hellinger, a musical called 'I'm Solomon' opened like a sunburst and then quickly closed, done to death by an icy blast of critical disapproval."[5] Other reviews said more explicitly what the *New Yorker* had playfully implied: whatever the play's faults (many) or virtues (few), a biblical epic is out of place on Broadway. "'I'm Solomon' is certainly no ordinary musical," suggested Clive Barnes.[6] "If 'I'm Solomon' makes it on Broadway, it probably will be the first major musical ever to have its last act end with prayers," offered out-of-town critic R. P. Hariss.[7] Martin Gottfried summed up the general mood, assessing *I'm Solomon* as "something else—a Broadway attempt at actually being a Hollywood spectacular. I would say you'd have to see it to believe it only seeing it isn't worth the trouble."[8] Placed against the history laid out in the previous chapters, we recognize the now familiar quality of such declarations that the biblical adaptation is somehow alien to the legitimate stage, inconsistent with Broadway's style, values, and means of production. Nearly every biblical adaptation to reach the Great White Way has been treated, at least initially, as a dubious experiment, offering little more than novelty value. The Broadway establishment—critics, producers, and investors—is, if anything, more skeptical about biblical theater than religious leaders are.

This observation may help explain why some (though not all) of New York's most successful adaptations of the Bible (including *Ben-Hur*, *The Book of Job*, *The Green Pastures*, *Godspell*, and *Jesus Christ Superstar*) have been produced by relative outsiders. Israeli journalist and filmmaker turned stage producer Zvi Kolitz (1912–2002) was one such outsider when he set out to bring the story of King Solomon to the stage in the middle of the 1960s. Sammy Gronemann's light comedy, *King Solomon and the Cobbler*, was first produced in Israel in 1942. A Hebrew-language version translated by Nathan Alterman enjoyed an extended run of more than three hundred performances at Tel Aviv's Cameri Theater. There was also a brief New York run at Pargod Studio, an experimental Hebrew theater, directed by R. Ben Ami and Erwin Piscator. A later musical adaptation (also in Hebrew) proved even more popular, running for over six hundred performances in Tel Aviv and touring to Paris, London, and Expo 67 in Montreal, Quebec. The plot echoes that of *The Prince and the Pauper*, revolving around King Solomon and a cobbler named Shamgar who looks exactly like him. Allegedly inspired by a midrashic narrative in which Solomon is forced to wander through Jerusalem as a beggar,[9] *King Solomon and the Cobbler* is a clear example of the fan fictional approach to biblical adaptation. It takes a scriptural character, King Solomon, and builds a story around an episode not contained in the biblical text.[10]

In February 1965, the *New York Times* reported that Kolitz had purchased the American rights to the play, with the goal of producing *King Solomon and the Cobbler* as a Broadway musical.[11] In a letter to *New York Times* theater writer Sam Zolotow, Kolitz—who was not a total neophyte, having scored a modest success as the third-billed producer of *The Deputy* (1964)—urged the *Times* to cover *King Solomon* as a major event. "I'd like to draw your kind attention," he wrote, "to the fact that this will be Broadway's FIRST BIBLICAL MUSICAL COMEDY."[12] A brochure printed by Kolitz's King Solomon Productions for the purpose of enticing potential investors touted the play, now called *In Someone Else's Sandals*, as "a natural for benefits. A synagogue or a church, a sisterhood or a men's club, a school or a hospital, or any charity of any kind, any creed, any group—what could be a more ideal means for fundraising-purposes than a Biblical musical comedy?"[13]

Yet if Kolitz overestimated the marketability of a "Biblical musical comedy," he underestimated the difficulty in adapting King Solomon's story for the stage.[14] The Hebrew version had been scored using folk-style melodies and staged by the Cameri Theatre as possibly the first native Israeli musical.[15] The Cameri was known for its modern performance style, sometimes called "native realism" to distinguish it from its European-influenced rival, the Habima company.[16] Believing that such an approach would not suit the tastes of a Broadway audience, Kolitz decided not to commission a direct translation, but instead asked his creative team to rewrite the show from the ground up. In the process, director Michael Benthall looked for ways to scale up the production's spectacular elements to meet American expectations of biblical epics based on films such as *The Ten Commandments* (1956) and *Ben-Hur* (1959). Among the strategies Kolitz and Benthall hoped to use to enhance the dramatic spectacle was the titillation of a potential interracial romance. As Charles McHarry reported in the *Daily News* in early 1968:

> The producers of Broadway's forthcoming "In Someone Else's Sandals" have so far been unsuccessful in their search for a beautiful Negro girl to

play the role of the Queen of Sheba. Although the show is a musical, the girl doesn't have to sing. Beauty is main qualification. Candidates may send pictures and resumes to King Solomon productions, 400 Madison Ave.[17]

The potential presence of this exotic female body as a spectacle ("Beauty is main qualification") may have given the production a problematic but real aura of authenticity, much in the way that racially "other" bodies have done in other biblical adaptations. Apparently unable to find a suitable "girl," however, the production began out-of-town tryouts a few weeks later—the title by this time had been changed to *I'm Solomon*, underscoring the biblical theme— with white actress Salome Jens in the role.

Kolitz made another attempt to secure an authentic body that might attract publicity to the production. In January, he wrote to the Ethiopian Mission to the United Nations seeking their assistance in importing a live lion that would appear in the queen's entourage.[18] Less central to the plot than the horses of *Ben-Hur*, the presence of a real lion on the stage might nevertheless have raised the ontological stakes of *I'm Solomon*. Despite several letters back and forth and an optimistic press release declaring, "His Majesty, Haile Selassie, King of Ethiopia, has approved the request of producer Zvi Kolitz for the sending of a lion to the opening of 'I'm Solomon,'" the lion never made it to the stage.[19]

I'm Solomon's use of spectacle, then, was reduced to more traditional theatrical means: lavish sets, costumes, and a "Cast of 60," as advertisements touted. As William Goldman in his acerbic chronicle of the 1967–1968 Broadway season asked, "When movies have made 'a cast of thousands' a cliché, what's a 'cast of 60' supposed to do your pulse?"[20] Meanwhile, the development of *I'm Solomon* had been bumpy in other ways. Book writer Erich Segal left the show during tryouts in Baltimore over creative differences with lyricist Anne Croswell and director Benthall. Segal was replaced by Israeli satirist Dan Almagor, who had the advantage of familiarity with the material but little time to do more than play script doctor. When *I'm Solomon* opened, critics universally panned the show's book, complaining of a confusing storyline, an uneven tone, and trite jokes that diminished the epic grandeur of the biblical setting.

Hard Job Being God

Thanks to the arrival of *Godspell* and *Superstar*, the biblical musical was less of a novelty by May 15, 1972, when *Hard Job Being God*, a rock musical with music and lyrics by Tom Martel, opened at the Edison Theatre.[21] But if the Bible was no longer a novelty to Broadway critics, neither was it entirely welcome. Radio critic Richard J. Scholem, for example, used the occasion for a short discourse on the subject:

> I must admit I have a bias toward this type of show . . . the story is known, the ending is known, the only new thing is the contemporary vernacular used by the author to get there. And that goes for "Jesus Christ Superstar," HARD JOB BEING GOD, and all the rest. We said HARD JOB BEING GOD is far from the worst of this religious brew. The rock music has pleasing overtones of country, blues, spiritual, and even ragtime.[22]

Even in what amounts to a positive review, the critic's tone is grudging ("far from the worst"), making very clear that he considers the biblical genre lacking in originality. A similarly double-edged assessment was offered by William Glover of the Associated Press: "As in all those versions of Christ's life which have previously dominated youthful biblical stage interest, the treatment is hippie yet reverential, unawed but sincere."[23] Drawing obvious comparisons to *Superstar*, the sung-through musical included a five-person ensemble (three men and two women) backed by a four-piece onstage rock band (keyboard, bass, drums, and guitar). All the actors played multiple roles except the twenty-four-year-old Martel, who played the role of God, making him the youngest person in Broadway history to embody the God of the Old Testament.

A young singer-songwriter with a degree in world religions from United States International University in San Diego, a nonsectarian college known at the time for its emphasis on humanistic psychology, Martel imagined God in exceedingly human terms. "If you saw me on the street," he sings at the top of the show, "you'd pass me by / Never knowing I / Am really you."[24] As in *The Green Pastures*, God's presence provides a narrative frame encompassing a series of biblical vignettes. Martel's God, however, has minimal character development as the company, clad according to one critic, "in current shaggy garb,"[25] plays out a series of episodes drawn from the Old Testament. *Hard Job Being God* had a minimal book, functioning more as a kind of song cycle, an impression furthered by a stripped-down production that used almost no scenery.[26] The minimalist staging may have offset, in part, the fragmented nature of the plot by putting the focus on the ensemble as a site of continuity, but it is clear that unlike *Superstar*, the production offered little in the way of spectacle. The first and last scenes, according to the program, take place "Anytime, Anywhere," and feature God singing about his troubles using the same refrain both times:

> Yes, it's a hard road
> And it's a long road
> And it's a hard job being God.[27]

In between these bookends are a dozen other episodes, each with its own musical number, and each listed in the program with its time and place, from "Canaan c. 1935 B.C." (Abraham and Sara, Genesis 15) to "Court of Ramses II, Pharaoh of Egypt, c. 1240 B.C." (Exodus 7) to "Royal Shrine of Bethel in Israel, 749 B.C." (Amos 1–9). During these episodes, God appears in only two numbers, once to explain to the Hebrews that they will have to get by without his direct intervention ("You're On Your Own") and once to give instructions to the prophet Amos ("I'm Counting on You"):

> Well, Amos, prayin' is good
> Prayin's essential
> But it don't always get things done
> Sometimes you've got to raise a little hell
> If you want to see the next day's sun.[28]

Martel's approach as a lyricist was similar to that taken by Tim Rice in *Superstar* and *Joseph and the Amazing Technicolor Dreamcoat*, restating the biblical narrative in contemporary vernacular language. The irony created by this device is further emphasized by having God himself use phrases like "raise a little hell," echoes of Miller's *Creation of the World*. Yet Martel's lyrics lack the humor and self-awareness of other biblical musicals, tending instead toward lines that rephrase biblical dialogue in literal and earnest terms.[29]

This lack of self-awareness may have contributed to the musical's "hippie but reverential" affect of sincerity. Yet where *Godspell* used a similarly sincere approach to establish a communion with its audience, *Hard Job Being God* failed to do so. Some of this was doubtless due to the staging, but many spectators may have been alienated by the play's eschatological subtext: though the episodes in *Hard Job Being God* are all drawn from the Old Testament, the musical is clearly both Christian and apocalyptic in its overall theology. God's opening and closing numbers make oblique reference to Jesus.[30] The traditional Jewish patriarchs Abraham, Isaac, and Jacob have less stage time than King David (whom Christian tradition claims as a direct ancestor of Jesus); King Solomon, by contrast, appears not at all. In the last fifteen minutes of the show, where the audience would expect a narrative climax, the score offers three numbers built on the apocalyptic book of Amos, evoking the specter of Judgment Day.

The Final Trump came early for *Hard Job Being God*, which closed after seven previews and seven regular performances at a loss of its entire $85,000 capitalization.[31] In the end, Tom Martel's legacy may have been reminding the world that it takes more than God and guitars to do business on Broadway. On May 16, 1972, five days after the Feast of the Ascension, Clive Barnes used his review of *Hard Job Being God* as an occasion to offer a eulogy of sorts for the biblical rock musical:

> I find all these musicals devoted to showing that Christ or God or—wait for the raga-rock musical to end them all—Buddha were really regular guys in their private life are coy and self-seeking. Even the title "Hard Job Being God" sends a shudder of revulsion through what is left of my central nervous system. If religion has come to this, I weep for the Judeo-Christian philosophy that has sustained us in the past.[32]

A large percentage of all Broadway shows bomb. From what I've been able to determine, the success-to-failure rate of biblical adaptations is not significantly different from the same rate for all productions. Yet the critical response to *I'm Solomon* and *Hard Job Being God* highlights the degree to which Broadway continues to regard even successful adaptations of the Bible as aberrations. Such judgments may accurately reflect the historical enmity between theater and religion, but they overlook the even more ancient link between performance and faith.

Epilogue: A Reading from *The Book of Mormon*

In March 2011, not long after I began researching this book in earnest, *The Book of Mormon* opened at the Eugene O'Neill Theatre, where it is still running as of this writing, having reached over 1,500 performances. The notoriously foul-mouthed musical from the creators of the cartoon series *South Park*, Matt Stone and Trey Parker (with *Avenue Q* cocreator Robert Lopez), won nine Tony Awards, including Best Musical, and has spawned a popular London production and two national touring companies. As a consequence, when I tell people that I am writing about Broadway adaptations of the Bible, the most common question I hear is, "Are you going to cover *The Book of Mormon?*" And in all that time (if it is all that time), I've been explaining to friends, colleagues, and students, that my study does *not* cover *The Book of Mormon*, but my reasons are dramaturgical, not religious. As I told a group of Mormon students during a lecture at Brigham Young University, I am perfectly willing to accept that the Book of Mormon is part of the Bible, on equal footing with the Old and New Testaments, but *The Book of Mormon* the Broadway musical is *not* an adaptation of the sacred scripture of the Church of Jesus Christ of Latter Day Saints, and therefore falls outside the scope of my investigation.

On further reflection, however, Parker, Stone, and Lopez's musical *does* have a bearing on the present study, because a key dimension of its humor is the satirizing of biblical drama. As with *Jesus Christ Superstar*, the very idea of *The Book of Mormon* the Broadway musical is simultaneously presumptuous and absurd. The double-edged joke depends in part on the audience's assumption that the Church-sponsored pageants with which it will inevitably be associated are themselves Bad Art, and in part on the audience's assumption that the Broadway stage is far too irreverent a space for the treatment of religion. We arrive, in other words, expecting a double blasphemy, a profaning of both the sacred text and the pretentions of the stage.

It is to the credit of *The Book of Mormon*'s creators that the musical both acknowledges these assumptions and subverts them. This is accomplished through a pair of pageant-within-a-play sequences. The first-act number "All American Prophet" is a send-up of the traditional religious pageant, sincere to the point of absurdity. The audience is encouraged to laugh at the melodramatic production, a simplified version of Joseph Smith and the LDS origin narrative that emphasizes the most outlandish elements of the story. It is presented with naive simplicity by Elder Price (Andrew Rannells) and filled with cheesy special effects, wooden dialogue, and grotesque overacting. The Ugandan "natives" who are the onstage audience respond with derision and disbelief. If the medium is the message, the pageant is the punchline.

"All American Prophet" is bookended by the second act's "Joseph Smith American Moses," which is positioned as the show's climactic revelation scene. This elaborate production number, staged as a pageant performed by the Ugandans as a demonstration of their faith, is a spectacular travesty: the Ugandans' version of the Mormon origin narrative is grotesquely distorted by the "embellishments" that Elder Cunningham (Josh Gad) has devised in an attempt to capture their imagination: Joseph Smith is explained to have had sex with a frog, the angel Moroni (now transformed into a "wizard") arrives from the starship *Enterprise*, Salt Lake City is peopled by Ewoks.[33]

Performed in a "native" idiom that includes chanting and masks, "Joseph Smith American Moses" owes more than a little to "The Small House of Uncle Thomas" (*Uncle Tom's Cabin*) number from Rodgers and Hammerstein's *The King and I* (1951).[34] In both scenes, a narrative that was imparted by a white missionary is refracted comically through the "innocent" understanding of "colorful" and "primitive" people. In both, the innocence and enthusiasm of the distorted rendition is presented to the audience as more sincere than, and hence superior to, the authorized original. Yet though the framing device may be an homage to Rodgers and Hammerstein, the scene (and, in many ways, the story arc of the entire show) recalls *The Green Pastures*. The childlike Negroes help the disillusioned white men to reconnect with their faith.[35]

Viewed in this perspective, *The Book of Mormon*'s liberal use of four-letter words and toilet humor, which appears at first to be a gratuitous and irreverent mockery of religion, may also be a sign of authenticity. For the person of faith, blasphemy is real, not representational, the one sin that cannot be accurately described without committing it. This authentic blasphemy provokes an affective response, laughter, that connects spectators to something larger than themselves. Thus even as the musical ironically uses profanity to highlight the sacred, it leavens its apparent irreverence with a kind of communal sincerity that points in the direction of transcendence. Like the ragged clowns of *Godspell*, the company members of the *Book of Mormon* bring both greasepaint and halo to the stage. Through joyous comic numbers from the opening "Hello" to Elder Price's anthem "I Believe," the musical celebrates religious belief as much as it satirizes it. In *The Book of Mormon*'s potent combination of the scatological and the eschatological, there is a sincere expression of faith: both in God and in the soul-cleansing powers of the theater.

Conclusion: Acts of Faith

Like God, the theater artist creates a world. Yet the world of the theater is always an imperfect copy. Thus getting a show up at all requires a significant act of faith. Though we know that a performance will not and, in a very real sense, cannot transcend the limitations of the medium, we continue *as if* it were possible, believing that in the failure to perfectly capture the original, we can catch a glimpse of something larger than ourselves. Theater based on the Bible offers special challenges, because the original is both powerful and unknowable. Why then does the Broadway theater continually return to the sacred text? Why do we continue to shout into the whirlwind?

Perhaps we do so because, as we have seen throughout the preceding chapters, the unique challenges of staging the Bible in a way that will satisfy religious audiences have often led to aesthetic innovations that later were used in nonbiblical shows. The need to tell the story of *Ben-Hur* without representing the Christ in human form led to innovations in lighting and scenography, many of which would become standard Broadway practice. *The Green Pastures* proved that an all-black company could attract audiences beyond the black community, enjoying a critically and commercially successful run on Broadway and on tour. *Noah*'s use of animal masks and nonrealistic scenography anticipated later successes such as *The Lion King. The Flowering Peach* showed that Broadway audiences and critics could find universal meaning in the story of an ironic yet faithful Jewish family ten years before *Fiddler on the Roof*. Walker's *Book of Job* and MacLeish's *J.B.* showed that the "legitimate aids of the theatre" could engage the thorniest of theological dilemmas. *Jesus Christ Superstar* heralded the way for a wave of megamusicals that transformed Broadway as an industry, while at the same time *Godspell* demonstrated that small, intimate musicals that drew on the aesthetics of the downtown theater also had a place in Times Square.

Of course, simply turning to the Bible as a source for a Broadway play does not guarantee originality or innovation, nor does it guarantee box-office success. Yet as we have seen, the need to balance spectacle, authenticity, sincerity, and irony has often spurred producers and directors, playwrights and performers, designers and marketers to new heights of creativity. Given the right circumstances, the right blend of performance strategies, and, maybe, a dash of divine inspiration, the unique challenges of staging the Bible can produce miracles.

Notes

Chapter 1

1. Salmi Morse, *The Passion: A Miracle Play in Ten Acts* (San Francisco: E. Bosqui, 1879).

2. For a detailed history of Morse's production and the opposition it faced, see Norton B. Stern and William Kramer, "The Strange Passion of Salmi Morse," *Western States Jewish History* 16, no. 4 (July 1984): 336–347; Alan Nielsen, "Salmi Morse's Passion, 1879–1884: The History and Consequences of a Theatrical Obsession," diss., City University of New York, 1989; Charles Musser, "Passions and the Passion Play: Theatre, Film, and Religion in America, 1880–1900," *Film History* 5 (1993): 419–456; and Edna Nahshon, "Going Against the Grain: Jews and Passion Plays on the Mainstream American Stage," in Edna Nahshon, ed., *Jews and Theater in an Intercultural Context* (Boston: Brill, 2012), 67–100. David Belasco also devotes several pages to Morse's play in his memoir, *The Life of David Belasco* (New York: Moffat, Yard, 1918), 114–124.

3. Musser, "Passions," 425.

4. Belasco, *Life of David Belasco*, 116.

5. Musser, "Passions," 425.

6. Musser, "Passions," 426.

7. As qtd. in Musser, "Passions," 427.

8. "Aldermanic Virtue Aroused," *New York Times*, November 24, 1880, 8.

9. "The Passion Play Read," *New York Times*, December 4, 1880, 2.

10. "The Passion Play Read," 2.

11. "Salmi Morse Determined: The Mayor Refuses a License and a Mandamus Threatened," *New York Times*, December 30, 1882, 2.

12. "A (*writ of*) *mandamus* is an order from a court to an inferior government official ordering the government official to properly fulfill their official duties or correct an abuse of discretion." Cornell University Legal Information Institute, December 2, 2014, www.law.cornell.edu/wex/mandamus.

13. "Salmi Morse Discharged," *New York Times*, March 14, 1883.

14. "The Passion Play Given," *New York Times*, March 31, 1883, 1.

15. "Salmi Morse's Surrender," *New York Times*, April 17, 1883, 8. Gerald Bordman and Thomas S. Hischak in *The Oxford Companion to American Theatre* (New York: Oxford University Press, 2004 [1984]) include an entry on *The Passion Play*, which states that the play "was produced in New York" (491). While technically true (a production was built and rehearsed in New York with the intent to perform it), the play never officially opened.

16. Shimon Levy, *The Bible as Theatre* (Brighton: Sussex Academic Press, 2000), ix. See also Levy's prior work, *Theatre and Holy Script* (Brighton: Sussex Academic Press, 1999).

17. See Seokhun Choi, "Performing the Passion of the Christ in Postmodernity: American Passion/Passion Plays as Ritual and Postmodern Theatre," diss., University of Kansas, 2012.

18. John Fletcher, *Preaching to Convert: Evangelical Outreach and Performance Activism in a Secular Age* (Ann Arbor: University of Michigan Press, 2013).

19. Claire Sponsler, *Ritual Imports: Performing Medieval Drama in America* (Ithaca: Cornell University Press, 2004).

20. Peter Brook, *The Empty Space* (New York: Macmillan, 1968), 42.

21. Lee Breuer, *Sister Suzie Cinema: The Collected Poems and Performances* (New York: Theatre Communications Group, 1987), 124.

22. Cf. Exodus 3:5.

23. New International Version.

24. The African American vaudeville team of Williams and Walker performed a limited run at the Star Theatre in 1900 under the title *Sons of Ham*, a euphemism for "black people" drawn from the story of Noah.

25. It is not easy to pinpoint the origins of "Broadway theater." Though playhouses were built on or near Broadway (the avenue) as early as 1798, it was not until the middle of the nineteenth century that a distinct theater district emerged, centered around Union Square. The term "Broadway" to refer to professional theater in New York appears to have come into vogue in the latter half of the nineteenth century. The current theater district, centered around Times Square, began to emerge in the 1890s, and the establishment of the Tony Awards in 1947 occasioned a clearer distinction between "Broadway" and "off-Broadway" houses. As of this writing, forty-one venues are considered Tony Award–eligible "Broadway theaters" by the Broadway League and the American Theatre Wing. This designation is based on both location and seating capacity. For more information, see inter alia Arthur Hornblow, *A History of the Theatre in America from Its Beginnings to the Present Time* (New York: B. Blom, 1919) and Martin Banham, ed., *The Cambridge Guide to Theatre* (Cambridge: Cambridge University Press, 1995).

26. "The Sign of the Cross" (review), *New York Times*, November 10, 1896, 5.

27. Unsigned feature story, "Religious Subjects as Matter for Dramatic Treatment," *New York Times*, December 16, 1906, X2.

28. "Religious Subjects."

29. "Dramatic and Musical," *New York Times*, April 10, 1900, 7.

30. "Religious Subjects."

31. "Religious Subjects."

32. "Religious Subjects."

33. Certainly, Broadway producers' references to the centuries-old

Oberammergau Passion Play (common in the early part of the twentieth century) fell out of fashion after two wars with Germany.

34. David Savran, "Toward a Historiography of the Popular," *Theatre Survey*, November 2004, 214–215.

35. See Jody Enders, *Rhetoric and the Origins of Medieval Drama* (Ithaca: Cornell University Press, 1992); Michal Kobialka, *This Is My Body: Representational Practices in the Early Middle Ages* (Ann Arbor: University of Michigan Press, 1999); and many others.

36. See, for example, Barbara Kirshenblatt-Gimblett, "'Contraband': Performance, Text and Analysis of a 'Purim-Shpil,'" *TDR* 24, no. 3 (September 1980): 5–16.

37. For an interesting take on this from a performance studies perspective, see Wayne Ashley, "The Stations of the Cross: Christ, Politics, and Processions on New York City's Lower East Side," in Robert A. Orsi, ed., *Gods of the City: Religion and the American Urban Landscape* (Bloomington: Indiana University Press, 1999), 341–366.

38. See Megan Sanborn Jones, "Performing Mormon History," *Journal of Mormon History* 35, no. 3 (Summer 2009): 204–208 and "(Re)living the Pioneer Past: Mormon Youth Handcart Trek Re-enactments," *Theatre Topics* 16, no. 2 (September 2006): 112–130.

39. See, for example, Andrea Most, *Making Americans: Jews and the Broadway Musical* (Cambridge: Harvard University Press, 2004); Sarah Blacher Cohen, *From Hester Street to Hollywood: The Jewish-American Stage and Screen* (Bloomington: Indiana University Press, 1983); Henry Bial, *Acting Jewish: Negotiating Ethnicity on the American Stage and Screen* (Ann Arbor: University of Michigan Press, 2005).

40. See Andrea Most, *Theatrical Liberalism: Jews and Popular Entertainment in America* (New York: New York University Press, 2013).

41. See, for example, S. E. Wilmer, *Theatre, Society and the Nation: Staging American Identities* (Cambridge: Cambridge University Press, 2002).

42. This usually means leaving religious faith offstage, or keeping it as simple and neutral and inoffensive as possible.

43. Until the advent of the five-day workweek, this was the only day that many audience members did not have to work.

44. Josiah W. Leeds, *The Theatre: An Essay upon the Non-accordancy of Stage-Plays with the Christian Profession*, 3rd ed. (Philadelphia: "published for the author," 1886), 8–9.

45. Margot Heinemann, *Puritanism and Theatre* (Cambridge: Cambridge University Press, 1982).

46. John Houchin, *Censorship of the American Theatre in the Twentieth Century* (Cambridge: Cambridge University Press, 2003).

47. Martin Puchner, *Stage Fright: Modernism Anti-theatricality and Drama* (Baltimore: Johns Hopkins University Press, 2002).

48. Donalee Dox, *The Idea of the Theater in Latin Christian Thought*

(Ann Arbor: University of Michigan Press, 2009); Kevin Wetmore, *Catholic Theatre and Drama: Critical Essays* (Jefferson, N.C.: McFarland, 2010).

49. A Yiddish phrase (literally, "shame in front of the non-Jews") that indicates an embarrassment for the entire community.

50. See, for example, Most, *Theatrical Liberalism*. For a discussion of Ernst Bloch's concept of secular utopia and its influence on twentieth-century theater, see Kelly J. G. Bremner, "Total Theatre Re-envisioned: The Means and Ends of Appia, Kandinsky and Wagner," diss., University of Wisconsin–Madison, 2008.

51. Janet R. Jakobsen and Ann Pellegrini, eds., *Secularisms* (Durham: Duke University Press, 2008), 2.

52. WFA, "Ben-Hur (review)," *Boston Herald*, December 21, 1900, *Ben-Hur* clipping file, New York Public Library for the Performing Arts.

53. Charles Isherwood, "A Vision of Spirituality Returns to Broadway," *New York Times*, November 7, 2011, C1.

54. See Sponsler, *Ritual Imports*, 123–155 and elsewhere.

55. "The Sign of the Cross" (review), *New York Times*, November 10, 1896, 5.

56. Charles Isherwood, "A Glitzy Execution in a Religious Revival: 'Jesus Christ Superstar' at the Neil Simon Theater," *New York Times*, March 22, 2012, C1.

57. Hebrews 4:12, New Revised Standard Version. Church tradition once held that the book was authored by the apostle Paul, though this has since been challenged.

58. James Huneker, "Mary of Magdala" (review), *New York Sun*, November 20, 1902, *Mary of Magdala* clipping file, New York Public Library for the Performing Arts.

59. Cf. Matthew 6:24 and Luke 16:13, "Ye cannot serve God and mammon."

60. Levy, *The Bible as Theatre*, 6.

61. Linda Hutcheon, *A Theory of Adaptation*, 2nd ed. (London: Routledge, 2013 [2006]), 7.

62. Hutcheon, *A Theory of Adaptation*.

63. Hutcheon, *A Theory of Adaptation*.

64. The Wooster Group, for example, is commonly identified with this practice, in works such as *Brace Up* (adapted from Chekhov's *Three Sisters*) and *L.S.D.* (adapted from Miller's *The Crucible*). See Susie Mee, "Chekhov's 'Three Sisters' and the Wooster Group's 'Brace Up!'" *TDR* 36, no. 4 (Winter 1992): 143–153.

65. Cf. Thomas Leitch, "Adaptation Studies at a Crossroads," *Adaptation* 1, no. 1 (March 1998): 64.

66. This abstract schematization is a Platonic one, devised to help highlight the various attitudes and decision points that one encounters when cre-

ating theatrical adaptations or when trying to compare issues between and among multiple adaptations. My terms are independent of, though perhaps in some way shaped by, legal, contractual, and conventional definitions. Recent theater history is littered with stories real and apocryphal of the wrangling between theater companies (or directors) and playwrights (or their estates) over what aspects of a play a subsequent production should be allowed to change. Contemporary licensing agreements tend to insist on retaining the spoken words of the play, but not necessarily the stage directions. Musicals also tend to insist on the melody but not necessarily the orchestrations. Choreography is a vast gray area still being litigated. Often the task of sorting out competing imperatives falls on the shoulders of a dramaturg, especially as such scholar-artists become increasingly important to the collaborative process. Noting the similarity between the task of the dramaturg and that of the adapter, Jane Barnette argues that "dramaturgy is the very lifeblood of adaptation." Barnette, "Literary Adaptation for the Stage: A Primer for Dramaturgs," in Magda Romanska, ed., *The Routledge Companion to Dramaturgy* (London: Routledge, 2014), 294–299.

67. Some biblical adaptations may overshadow the original in the sense that audiences may not recognize where authorial liberties have been taken with the source—but the Bible retains the position of the Original against which the adaptation must be measured.

68. Roland Barthes, "The Death of the Author," in *Image, Music, Text*, trans. Stephen Heath (New York: Hill and Wang, 1977), 145.

69. Michael Bloom, *Thinking Like a Director: A Practical Handbook* (New York: Macmillan, 2011), 14.

70. The counterargument—that the playwright is just one source of raw material for a more collective creative process—has been articulated by many directors and theorists, especially so-called auteur directors such as Peter Brook and Richard Foreman. But while the auteur theory of directing has become mainstream in the world of film, live theater that does not begin and end with the playwright's vision still tends to be considered "avant-garde," a term that—after the collapse of history, or in a revaluing of the primacy of the original—has exchanged some of its positive connotation of cutting edge for a negative connotation of marginality.

71. Because without a copy, the concept of the Original has no meaning. See "The Work of Art in the Age of Mechanical Reproduction," in Walter Benjamin, *Illuminations: Essays and Reflections*, ed. Hannah Arendt, trans. Harry Zohn (New York: Schocken, 1968).

72. For the purposes of this project I have chosen to consider all adaptations of books that a significant group of people consider part of the Bible to fall within my definition of "biblical." So, even though I am Jewish, this book will consider Broadway adaptations of the New Testament as well as the Old. The reason *The Book of Mormon* is treated only tangentially (see chapter 7)

is that the award-winning musical is not actually an adaptation of The Book of Mormon, and *not* because I regard the Church of Jesus Christ of Latter-day Saints as somehow outside the Judeo-Christian tradition.

73. W. B. Gallee, "Essentially Contested Concepts," *Proceedings of the Aristotelian Society* 56 (1956): 169.

74. Gallee, "Essentially Contested Concepts," 180.

75. "Three Opinions on 'J.B.,'" *Life* 46, no. 20 (May 18, 1959): 135–138.

76. See Most, *Theatrical Liberalism.*

77. See, for example, Nathan O. Hatch and Mark A. Noll, eds., *The Bible in America: Essays in Cultural History* (New York: Oxford University Press, 1982).

78. Amy Hughes, *Spectacles of Reform* (Ann Arbor: University of Michigan Press, 2012), 6–8.

79. Hughes, *Spectacles of Reform,* 4.

80. Henry Jenkins, *The Wow Climax: Tracing the Emotional Impact of Popular Culture* (New York: New York University Press, 2007), 3.

81. Jill Stevenson, *Sensational Devotion: Evangelical Performance in Twenty-First-Century America* (Ann Arbor: University of Michigan Press, 2013), 24.

82. Stevenson, *Sensational Devotion,* 29.

83. Stevenson, *Sensational Devotion,* 38.

84. Rebecca Schneider, *Performing Remains: Art and War in Times of Theatrical Reenactment* (London: Taylor and Francis, 2011), 15.

85. Lionel Trilling, *Sincerity and Authenticity* (Cambridge: Harvard University Press, 1971), 2.

86. This shift in emphasis is critical because, in the words of sociologist Orlando Patterson, "Sincerity, [Trilling] said, requires us to act and really be the way that we present ourselves to others. Authenticity involves finding and expressing the true inner self and judging all relationships in terms of it." Orlando Patterson, "Our Overrated Inner Self," *New York Times*, December 26, 2006, A35.

87. Matthew Stratton, *The Politics of Irony in American Modernism* (New York: Fordham University Press, 2014), 14.

88. Stratton, *Politics of Irony,* 12–22.

89. Cf. Genesis 6:9, King James Version.

90. This is the traditional rabbinical formulation of one of the central theological problems in Judaism. Cf. *Babylonian Talmud*, Tractate *Berakhot*, 7a.

Chapter 2

1. "Religious Subjects as Matter for Dramatic Treatment," *New York Times*, December 16, 1906, X2.

2. David Mayer, ed., *Playing Out the Empire: Ben-Hur and Other Toga Plays and Films, 1883–1908. A Critical Anthology* (Oxford: Clarendon Press, 1994).

3. Amy Lifson, "Ben-Hur," *Humanities* 30, no. 6 (November–December 2009), December 1, 2014, www.neh.gov/humanities/2009/novemberdecember/feature/ben-hur.

4. Lifson, "Ben-Hur."

5. Marc Klaw and A. L. Erlanger, both American-born children of German Jewish immigrants, helped found the Theatrical Syndicate, a powerful alliance of theater owners and booking agents established in 1896.

6. "How General Lew Wallace's Famous Novel Was Turned Into a Religio-Historic Spectacle," *New York Herald*, November 5, 1899, *Ben-Hur* clipping file, New York Public Library for the Performing Arts (emphasis added).

7. Exodus 20:4–5 and Deuteronomy 5:8–9 (New International Version).

8. Bronwen Thomas, "What Is Fanfiction and Why Are People Saying Such Nice Things about It?," *StoryWorlds* 3 (2001): 1.

9. See Abigail Derecho, "Archontic Literature: A Definition, a History, and Several Theories of Fan Fiction," in Karen Hellekson and Kristina Busse, eds., *Fan Fiction and Fan Communities in the Age of the Internet* (Jefferson, N.C.: McFarland, 2006), 61–78; and Rachel Barenblat, "Transformative Work: Midrash and Fan Fiction," *Journal of Religion and Literature* 43, no. 2 (Summer 2011): 171–177.

10. Daniel Boyarin, *Intertextuality and the Reading of Midrash* (Bloomington: Indiana University Press, 1994), 41. Many such commentaries may take the form of exegesis of passages pertaining to the law (*halakha*) and are sometimes referred to, therefore, as *Halakhic midrash*. These commentaries tend to be analytical rather than narrative in form, though the work sometimes takes the form of imagining an extended dialogue that happens in between verses of the Bible. *Halakhic midrashim* (plural), many of which have themselves been transcribed and annotated over the centuries, occupy a curious status in Judaic religious practice. They are not considered to be divinely authored; many, in fact, are attributed to specific rabbis. Nor are they considered to be divinely inspired, though the rabbis whose commentaries have been preserved through the centuries are, unsurprisingly, those who were considered particularly holy, wise, and learned.

To the degree that the Torah functions as the Law for the Jewish nation, American readers might find it helpful (though imprecise) to think of it this way: The Torah is the Constitution—the fundamental legal document against which all else must be measured—while the Talmud is the record of Supreme Court decisions—the authoritative (though sometimes conflicting) interpretations of the law that inform subsequent legal decisions. In this analogy, the midrashic commentaries (or *midrashim*) are akin to lower-court decisions. Such commentaries were often generated to resolve a situation for which there was no clear precedent in either the written or oral law. However, midrashim are generally considered informative—rather than binding—on subsequent decisions.

In addition to halachic midrash, there exists a tradition of narrative, or *Aggadic*, midrash. Though often associated specifically with the Passover Seder (cf. *Haggadah*), the term *Aggadah* refers to all classical rabbinical literature that is not explicitly concerned with the law. Because these commentaries were not tied to specific legal problems, the rabbis who authored them were free to expand and invent in more creative ways. Often, these took the form of inventing stories about biblical characters that filled in gaps in the scriptural narrative. In contemporary practice, *halachic midrashim* are most relevant to orthodox Jews, because many orthodox communities still regard the Torah as the Law (which is to say, as a legal document as well as a religious one). Aggadic midrashim, however, have often captured the imagination of less observant or secular Jews because they help explain gaps in the biblical narrative.

11. Genesis 12:2, Revised Standard Version.

12. David Stern and Mark Jay Mirsky, eds., *Rabbinic Fantasies: Imaginative Narratives from Hebrew Classical Literature* (New Haven: Yale University Press, 1998), 4.

13. Arthur Miller, *Timebends: A Life* (New York: Grove Press, 1987), 559.

14. On the tradition of dissent, see Sergei Dolgopolski, *What Is Talmud? The Art of Disagreement* (New York: Fordham University Press, 2009).

15. Henry Jenkins, *Textual Poachers: Television Fans and Participatory Culture* (London: Routledge, 2003).

16. Rabbi Rachel Barenblat writes, "Whereas Jenkins's analogy positions fans as serfs poaching game from the lord's estate in order to make meaning and to reclaim ownership of the storytelling that fans see as their birthright, the midrash analogy positions fans as respected interpreters, analogous both to the classical rabbis who for centuries interpreted scripture and to the modern midrashists who continue that work today." Rachel Barenblat, "Fan Fiction and Midrash: Making Meaning," *Transformative Works and Cultures* 17 (2014), journal.transformativeworks.org/index.php/twc/article/view/596.

17. Lifson, "Ben-Hur."

18. Mayer, *Playing Out the Empire*, xii.

19. Mayer, *Playing Out the Empire*, xii.

20. Hughes, *Spectacles of Reform*, 37.

21. Matthew 2:1.

22. Lew Wallace, *Ben-Hur: A Tale of the Christ*, ed. David Mayer (New York: Oxford University Press, 1998 [1880]), 9.

23. Hughes, *Spectacles of Reform*, 37.

24. Hughes, *Spectacles of Reform*, 44.

25. Wallace, *Ben-Hur*, 121.

26. Wallace, *Ben-Hur*, 336–350. These thirteen pages follow nine pages describing the arena and the crowds on the day of the race.

27. Hughes, *Spectacles of Reform*, 32.

28. Wallace, *Ben-Hur*, 499–500.

29. Critics noted in passing that this was not the first known incident of a live horse and treadmill, but also noted that *Ben-Hur* used the device on an unprecedented scale.

30. "Elaborate Production of Lew Wallace's Dramatized Story," *New York Globe-Democrat*, December 2, 1899, *Ben-Hur* clipping file, New York Public Library for the Performing Arts.

31. "At the Play and with the Players," *New York Times*, December 3, 1899, 18.

32. Clement Scott, "Clement Scott Sees the Wallace Drama" (review of *Ben-Hur*), *New York Herald*, November 30, 1899, *Ben-Hur* clipping file, New York Public Library for the Performing Arts.

33. WFA, "Ben-Hur" (review), *Boston Herald*, December 21, 1900, *Ben-Hur* clipping file, New York Public Library for the Performing Arts.

34. Hughes, *Spectacles of Reform*, 41.

35. Stevenson, *Sensational Devotion*, 24–49 and elsewhere.

36. Such an embodied confrontation with the unknown may also be experienced as an encounter with "the numinous, that quality defined by Rudolf Otto as the paradoxical combination of fear and fascination experienced in the non-rational perception of the mysterious and sacred." Jane Barnette, "Staging the Numinous," *Text and Performance Quarterly* 29, no. 4 (October 2009): 416.

37. Stevenson, *Sensational Devotion*, 233.

38. Schneider, *Performance Remains*, 41.

39. Schneider, *Performance Remains*, 41.

40. Stevenson, *Sensational Devotion*, 38.

41. Billy Sunday, "'Ben-Hur' Appeals to Billy Sunday," *Morning Telegraph*, November 6, 1916, *Ben-Hur* clipping file, New York Public Library for the Performing Arts.

42. Wilson Barrett, *The Sign of the Cross*, in Mayer, *Playing Out the Empire*, 187.

43. Untitled editorial, *New York Times*, May 24, 1896, 4.

44. "The Sign of the Cross" (review), *Memphis Commercial Appeal*, April 16, 1895, *The Sign of the Cross* clipping file, New York Public Library.

45. Clement Scott, "The Playhouses," *Illustrated London News*, January 26, 1896, 92.

46. As quoted in "The Sign of the Cross" (review), *Memphis Commercial Appeal*, April 16, 1895.

47. Unsigned review, *Illustrated American*, November 28, 1896, *The Sign of the Cross* clipping file, New York Public Library.

48. "The Sign of the Cross" (review), *New York Times*, November 10, 1896, 5.

49. Unidentified clipping, *The Sign of the Cross* clipping file, New York Public Library for the Performing Arts.

50. "The Sign of the Cross" (review), *Boston Transcript*, October 27, 1897, *The Sign of the Cross* clipping file, New York Public Library for the Performing Arts.

51. In *American Women Stage Directors of the Twentieth Century* (Champaign: University of Illinois Press, 2008), Anne E. Fliotsos and Wendy Vierow note that Harrison Fiske was his wife's de facto co-manager during this period, and that they were notably opposed to the Theatrical Syndicate; this meant that they did not always have access to the most desirable new play-scripts, which may account for the bold choice of *Mary of Magdala*.

52. For a detailed account of the censorship of *Maria von Magdala*, see Gary D. Stark, *Banned in Berlin: Literary Censorship in Imperial Germany, 1871–1918* (New York: Berghahn Books, 2009), 176–180.

53. Paul Heyse, *Mary of Magdala*, trans. William Winter (New York: Macmillan, 1903).

54. Fliotsos and Vierow, *American Women Stage Directors*, 170.

55. Colm Tóibín's *The Testament of Mary* (2013) is the story of Mary, mother of Jesus.

56. Unsigned review of *Mary of Magdala*, *Brooklyn Daily Eagle*, October 26, 1902, clipping file, New York Public Library for the Performing Arts.

57. Minnie Maddern Fiske, "Mrs. Fiske Promises a Dignified Production," *Brooklyn Daily Eagle*, October 26, 1902, *Mary of Magdala* clipping file, New York Public Library for the Performing Arts.

58. Unsigned review of *Mary of Magdala*, "Mary of Magdala" (review), *Boston Herald*, March 31, 1903, clipping file, New York Public Library for the Performing Arts.

59. Unsigned review of *Mary of Magdala*, "'Mary of Magdala' A Great Drama" (review), *Brooklyn Eagle*, November 20, 1902, clipping file, New York Public Library for the Performing Arts

60. Clayton Hamilton, "News of the Theatres" (review), *Brooklyn Eagle*, November 23, 1902, 40.

61. Clayton Hamilton, *The Theory of the Theatre* (New York: Henry Holt, 1910), 117.

62. Andrew Sofer, *Dark Matter: Invisibility in Drama, Theater, and Performance* (Ann Arbor: University of Michigan Press, 2013), 2.

63. Sofer, *Dark Matter*, 3.

64. Sofer, *Dark Matter*, 4–15.

65. "Mrs. Fiske in 'Mary of Magdala'" (review), *New York Times*, November 20, 1902, 9.

66. Rev. Percy Stickney Grant, "Mrs. Fiske's 'Mary of Magdala'" (review), *Critic* 41 (July–December 1902): 533.

67. Unsigned editorial, *New York Times*, May 24, 1896, 4. If the insinuation is true, it is worth noting that "various interested persons" (presumably, Jewish or atheist theater producers) had followed an admittedly commercial path to an intersection of theater and ritual that would soon be legitimized by classical scholars such as Gilbert Murray and Jane Harrison (who first met in 1900). Though the so-called Cambridge School anthropologists did not comment on contemporary religious drama, they helped advance the theory that classical tragedy must be understood in the context of myth and ritual, i.e., religion. Of course, for a Christian audience, especially an American one, the fact that the ancients may have used drama in the service of their "pagan" religion did not quite allay fears about the potential blasphemy of representing Jesus on stage.

68. Charles Ramm Kennedy, *The Terrible Meek: A One-Act Stage Play for Three Voices. To Be Played in Darkness* (New York: Harper and Brothers, 1912), 44.

69. Brooks Atkinson's review in the *New York Times* indicates that, with regard to the representation of the divinity at least, the *Freiburg Passion Play* is the exception that proves the rule. "On coming into the theatre," writes Atkinson, 'The Passion Play' . . . inevitably becomes theatricalized . . . here the pageant and the trappings of the theatre do not give the sacred story an aura, but reduce it to a colorful, stately spectacle." J. Brooks Atkinson, "The Passion Play a Colorful Pageant: Freiburg Players Give a Highly Theatricalized Performance of Sacred Story," *New York Times*, April 30, 1929, 27.

Chapter 3

1. Genesis 1:27, King James Version.

2. Joseph B. Soloveitchik, *The Lonely Man of Faith* (New York: Doubleday, 2006), 17–18.

3. Genesis 1:26, King James Version.

4. Genesis 2:7, King James Version.

5. Genesis 2:15, King James Version.

6. Soloveitchik, *Lonely Man of Faith*, 20.

7. Genesis 1:3, King James Version.

8. Genesis 2:18, King James Version.

9. Marc Connelly, *Voices Offstage: A Book of Memoirs* (New York: Holt, Rinehart and Winston, 1968), 148.

10. Mary Austin, "'Green Pastures' Reveals New Field for Dramatist," *New York World*, March 9, 1930, *The Green Pastures* clipping file, New York Public Library for the Performing Arts.

11. Even some religious authorities felt that our understanding of the scriptures would benefit from being updated to reflect modern scholarship and attitudes: in 1930 the International Council of Religious Education set

up a committee to develop what would become the Revised Standard Version. Derek Wilson, *The People's Bible: The Remarkable History of the King James Version* (London: Lion Books, 2013), 172.

12. Roark Bradford, *Ol' Man Adam and His Chillun': Being the Tales They Tell about the Time When the Lord Walked the Earth Like a Natural Man* (New York: Harper and Brothers, 1928).

13. Connelly, *Voices Offstage*, 145.

14. "'Green Pastures' Reaches 500th Showing Friday," *New York Herald Tribune*, April 26, 1931, *The Green Pastures* clipping file, New York Public Library for the Performing Arts.

15. Connelly, *Voices Offstage*, 145.

16. Connelly, *Voices Offstage*, 7.

17. Marc Connelly, *The Green Pastures* (New York: Holt, Rinehart and Winston, 1930), 7. The use of this stylized "Negro" dialect throughout the text is perhaps one reason why *The Green Pastures* has fallen out of the general repertoire.

18. Connelly, *The Green Pastures*, 8.

19. Connelly, *The Green Pastures*, 44.

20. Hosea is a prophet who brings the children of Israel the message that they have strayed from God's message, but that they nevertheless have his unconditional love. Hosea 1–14.

21. Connelly, *Voices Offstage*, 154.

22. Connelly, *Voices Offstage*, 165–166.

23. Connelly, *Voices Offstage*, 168.

24. Biographical details drawn from Walter C. Daniel, *"De Lawd": Richard B. Harrison and "The Green Pastures"* (New York: Greenwood Press, 1986).

25. Daniel, *De Lawd*, 54.

26. Andrea Nouryeh, "When the Lord Was a Black Man: A Fresh Look at the Life of Richard Berry Harrison," *Black American Literature Forum* 16, no. 4 (Winter 1982): 142–146.

27. At least one other actor had previously played God as an offstage voice (see chapter 4), but Harrison was the first to embody the role in full view of the audience.

28. J. Brooks Atkinson, "New Negro Drama of Sublime Beauty," *New York Times*, February 27, 1930, 26.

29. Robert Garland, "Green Pastures" (review), *New York Telegram*, February 27, 1930, 12.

30. Walter Winchell, "'Green Pastures' Artistic Triumph at the Mansfield," *New York Daily Mirror*, February 27, 1930, *The Green Pastures* clipping file, New York Public Library for the Performing Arts.

31. J. Brooks Atkinson, "The Play: 'The Green Pastures' and Mr. Harrison Return to Celebrate a Fifth Anniversary," *New York Times*, February 27, 1935, 16.

32. "Heaven on Earth," *Time* 25, no. 9 (March 4, 1935): 43–48.

33. William Warner Lundell, "Marc Connelly Speaks His Mind: The Author of the Green Pastures Discusses the Art of Playwriting," *New York World*, September 7, 1930, *The Green Pastures* clipping file, New York Public Library for the Performing Arts.

34. Lundell, "Marc Connelly Speaks," emphasis added.

35. Lundell, "Marc Connelly Speaks."

36. John Mason Brown, "The Play: The Green Pastures" (review), *New York Evening Post*, February 27, 1930, 12.

37. Burns Mantle, "Darkey Lord Takes Kindly to Fried Fish," *New York Herald Tribune*, March 9, 1930, *The Green Pastures* clipping file, New York Public Library for the Performing Arts.

38. Arthur Ruhl, "The Green Pastures" (review), *New York Herald Tribune*, February 27, 1930, *The Green Pastures* clipping file, New York Public Library for the Performing Arts.

39. Curtis J. Evans, *The Burden of Black Religion* (Oxford: Oxford University Press, 2008), 206.

40. Gilbert Seldes, "The New Play: The Green Pastures" (review), *Evening Graphic*, February 27, 1930, 22.

41. Connelly, *The Green Pastures*, 167.

42. Doris B. Garey, "The Green Pastures Again," *Phylon Quarterly* 20, no. 2 (1959): 194.

43. Evans, *Burden of Black Religion*, 208.

44. Richard Watts Jr., "Sight and Sound," *New York Herald Tribune*, March 12, 1930, 16.

45. Austin, "Reveals New Field."

46. "Churches Ask Lord of 'Green Pastures' to Be Their Guest," *New York Herald Tribune*, undated, circa October 1930, *The Green Pastures* clipping file, New York Public Library for the Performing Arts.

47. See Hughes, *Spectacles of Reform*, 18–25 and elsewhere.

48. Langston Hughes, *The Big Sea: An Autobiography* (Columbia: University of Missouri Press, 2002 [1940]), 176.

49. Winchell, "'Green Pastures' Artistic Triumph."

50. We might also recognize in Harrison the trope of the "magic negro." See, for example, Cerise L. Glenn, "The Power of Black Magic: The Magical Negro and White Salvation in Film," *Journal of Black Studies* 40, no. 2 (November 2009): 135–152.

51. Evans, *Burden of Black Religion*, 213.

52. Bosley Crowther, "Pastures Green for All," *New York Times*, April 28, 1935, X2. Among the financial data provided by accountants Laurence Rivers, Inc., the article estimates that the show's original production costs were approximately $70,000, including $9,500 for each of two large treadmills that spanned the width of the stage.

53. "The Green Pastures" Souvenir Program, 1932 National Tour, Billy Rose Theatre Collection, New York Public Library for the Performing Arts.

54. Unsigned, "'Green Pastures' Reaches 500th Showing Friday," *New York Herald Tribune*, April 26, 1931, *The Green Pastures* clipping file, New York Public Library for the Performing Arts.

55. J. J. Van. N., "The Green Pastures" (review), undated, circa 1932, *The Green Pastures* clipping file, New York Public Library for the Performing Arts.

56. Aberjhani and Sandra L. West, eds., *Encyclopedia of the Harlem Renaissance* (New York: Facts on File, 2000), 132.

57. Austin, "Reveals New Field."

58. Evans, *Burden of Black Religion*.

59. Evans, *Burden of Black Religion*, 213.

60. This proposition cannot be reversed. That is, an African American audience would not have seen a white God as exotic, but as a holdover of the hated theology of the plantation.

61. Bock and Harnick also wrote the book, although Jerome Coopersmith (*Baker Street*) was credited for "Additional book material."

62. In 1990, actor David Birney would write his own adaptation of the same material, *The Diaries of Adam and Eve*. Though there have been several regional and touring productions (several of which featured Birney as Adam), it has never been produced on Broadway.

63. Mark Twain, *Extracts from Adam's Diary* (New York: Harper and Brothers, 1904).

64. Walter Kerr, "Theater: 'The Apple Tree,' Three Playlets, Opens," *New York Times*, October 19, 1966, *New York Theatre Critics' Reviews* 27, no. 13 (October 24, 1966): 262.

65. Nichols's staging and Tony Walton's set and costume design emphasized this, eschewing a naturalistic garden for a nearly bare stage, and the traditional fig leaves for modern dress: Adam in brown slacks and a button-down shirt, Eve in a simple shift dress, and the Snake in a tuxedo. Martin Gottfried, writing in *Women's Wear Daily*, suggested that the play "broadens the outlines of Genesis to fit an everyday-urban couple of the sort usually found at Second City." The recurrence of Alda and Harris as the lovers in the second and third parts of the triple bill only confirms this reading of the Adam and Eve characters as symbols not of religion but of humanity writ large.

66. Harris was the true star of *The Apple Tree*, the three separate plays offering her a chance to demonstrate her comedic range across three divergent roles, while Alda served as her straight man. Her performance would win a Tony Award for Best Actress and lead the producers of *The Creation of the World and Other Business* to identify her as a likely choice for the role of Eve in yet another Adam and Eve comedy.

67. *Variety*, December 20, 1972, *The Creation of the World* clipping file, New York Public Library for the Performing Arts.

68. Richard Watts, "Arthur Miller's 'Creation' Opens at Shubert The-

ater" (review), *New York Post*, December 1, 1972, in *New York Theatre Critics' Reviews* 33, no. 24 (December 11, 1972): 150.

69. T. E. Kalem, "The Theater: Adam and Evil" (review), *Time*, December 11, 1972; Douglas Watt, "Miller's 'Creation of the World' Is a Plodding Comedy-Drama" (review), *Daily News*, December 1, 1972, in *New York Theatre Critics' Reviews* 33, no. 24 (December 11, 1972): 153.

70. The play is also one of only two in Broadway history to explicitly depict Adam and Eve in the Garden of Eden (*The Apple Tree*).

71. William Glover, "Arthur Miller Deplores 'Heroic' Letdown," Associated Press wire story, September 12, 1972, *The Creation of the World* clipping file, New York Public Library for the Performing Arts.

72. For extended discussion of Jewishness in *Death of a Salesman*, see Bial, *Acting Jewish*, 49–58.

73. Miller, as quoted in Leo Seligsohn, "Arthur Miller on the Eve of Creation," *Newsday*, November 26, 1972, 5, brackets in original.

74. As quoted in Seligson, "Arthur Miller," 4.

75. Cf. Ezekiel 28:13–16.

76. Isaiah 14:12 refers to the fall from heaven of a character called *helel* in Hebrew, and translated as "Lucifer" in the King James Version. In Luke 10:18, Jesus says, "I beheld Satan as lightning falling from heaven" (King James Version), leading many to equate Lucifer with Satan.

77. Cf. Genesis 3:24.

78. David Richards, "God Serves Scrambled Eggs" (review), *Washington Evening Star*, October 23, 1972, D6.

79. Richard L. Coe, "Confusion in Eden" (review), *Washington Post*, October 23, 1972, *The Creation of the World* clipping file, New York Public Library for the Performing Arts.

80. From Alan Alda.

81. William Inge's *Where's Daddy* (1966). With Clurman's departure from *Creation*, this turned out to be his last Broadway credit.

82. Batson's only prior Broadway credit was as a swing in *George M!* (1968).

83. Tom Buckley, "In the Beginning, Miller's 'Creation' . . . ," *New York Times*, December 5, 1972, 67. Brackets in original.

84. Buckley, "In the Beginning," 67.

85. Martin Bookspan, "The Creation of the World and Other Business" (review), WPIX–Channel 11 television, transcript in *The Creation of the World* clipping file, New York Public Library for the Performing Arts.

86. Miller scholars such as Christopher Bigsby and Terry Otten note that by this point in his career, the New York critics were generally unsympathetic to Miller's new work, but the response to *Creation* was especially negative.

87. Dennis Welland, *Miller: A Study of His Plays* (London: Eyre Methuen, 1979), 127.

88. Watt, "Miller's Creation," 151.

89. Edwin Wilson, "Adam and Eve in the Garden" (review), *Wall Street Journal*, December 4, 1972, in *New York Theatre Critics' Reviews* 33, no. 24 (December 11, 1972): 152.

90. Terry Otten, *The Temptation of Innocence in the Plays of Arthur Miller* (Columbia: University of Missouri Press, 2002), 159.

91. Welland, *Miller*, 127.

92. Welland, *Miller*, 126.

93. Otten, *Temptation of Innocence*, 161.

94. Arthur Miller, *The Creation of the World and Other Business* (New York: Dramatists Play Service, 1998 [1972]), 26.

95. Miller, *Creation*, 7.

96. Miller, *Creation*, 29.

97. Miller, *Creation*, 66.

98. Wilson, "Adam and Eve."

99. Miller, *Creation*, 11.

100. Wilson, "Adam and Eve"; Jack Kroll, "Theater" (review), Newsweek, December 11, 1972, in New York Theatre Critics' Reviews 33, no. 24 (December 11, 1972): 151.

101. Kevin Sanders, "The Creation of the World and Other Business" (review), WABC-TV, November 30, 1972, in *New York Theatre Critics' Reviews* 33, no. 24 (December 11, 1972): 153.

102. Biographical details for Elliott drawn from his obituary in the *Los Angeles Times*, May 24, 2005.

103. Watt, "Miller's Creation," 151.

104. Watt, "Miller's Creation," 151.

105. Kalem, "The Theater," 152.

106. Martin Gottfried, "The Creation of the World and Other Business" (review), *Women's Wear Daily*, December 4, 1972, in *New York Theatre Critics' Reviews* 33, no. 24 (December 11, 1972): 152.

107. Miller, *Creation*, 18.

108. Richards, "God Serves Scrambled Eggs," D6.

109. Watts, "Arthur Miller's 'Creation.'"

Chapter 4

1. See Sponsler, *Ritual Imports*, 163–183.

2. Genesis 6:17, King James Version.

3. Genesis 6:8, King James Version.

4. Genesis 7:12, King James Version.

5. "And the bow shall be in the cloud; and I will look upon it, that I may remember the everlasting covenant between God and every living creature of all flesh that is upon the earth." Genesis 9:16, King James Version.

6. Heinz-Dietrich Fischer, *The Pulitzer Prize Archive*, vol. 22: *Chronicle of the Pulitzer Prizes for Drama* (Munich: K.G. Saur Verlag, 2008), 15.

7. Robert Garland, "'Noah,' a Unique Play, Opens at Longacre," *New York Herald-Tribune*, February 14, 1935, 24.

8. Garland, "'Noah,' a Unique Play."

9. André Obey, *Noah*, trans. Arthur Wilmurt (New York: Samuel French, 1935), 9.

10. Obey, *Noah*, 9.

11. "Noah" (review), *Time*, February 25, 1935, *Noah* clipping file, New York Public Library for the Performing Arts.

12. The original program credits Ludwig Bemelmans, creator of the *Madeline* series of children's books, with "personal supervision" of "costumes animals and scenery." Noah program file, New York Public Library for the Performing Arts.

13. J. Brooks Atkinson, "Noah" (review), *New York Times*, February 14, 1935, 25.

14. Though the Bible is clear on the names of Noah's sons, their wives (and Noah's wife) are not named.

15. Obey, *Noah*, 68–69.

16. Obey, *Noah*, 71, emphasis in original.

17. Robert Garland, "'Noah' a New Picture of Flood Patriarch," *New York World-Telegraph*, February 28, 1935, 24.

18. Arthur Ruhl, "Second Nights," *New York Herald Tribune*, February 17, 1935, *Noah* clipping file, New York Public Library for the Performing Arts.

19. Atkinson, "Noah," 25.

20. "Noah" (review), *Time*, February 25, 1935, *Noah* clipping file, New York Public Library for the Performing Arts.

21. Arthur Wilmurt, "On 'Noah' and 'The Green Pastures,'" *New York Times*, March 3, 1935, X2.

22. Wilmurt, "On 'Noah,'" X2.

23. Wilmurt, "On 'Noah,'" X2.

24. "New Deal on Ararat," *Stage*, April 1935, 16; Garland, "'Noah,' a Unique Play," 16.

25. Garland, "'Noah,' a Unique Play," 24.

26. Atkinson, "Noah," 25.

27. See, for example, "Lafayette Opens Fall Season with Noah," *New York Amsterdam News*, September 19, 1936, 8.

28. Gilbert Seldes, "'Noah'—from the French" (review), *New York American*, February 14, 1935, 16.

29. Francis Fergusson, *The Idea of a Theater* (Garden City, N.Y.: Doubleday Anchor Books, 1958 [1949]), 222.

30. Wilmurt, "On 'Noah,'" X2.

31. Garland, "'Noah,' a Unique Play," 24.

32. Federal Theatre Project Harlem Unit program file, New York Public Library for the Performing Arts.

33. Biographical information for Carlton Moss drawn from his obituary, *New York Times*, August 15, 1997, written by Robert McG. Thomas Jr.

34. "Lafayette Opens Fall Season with 'Noah,'" 8.

35. "First Play Produced under All-Negro WPA Administration Due This Month," *Norfolk Journal and Guide*, September 19, 1936, 4.

36. I have been unable to locate a copy of Moss's script, and therefore this discussion of the play is based exclusively on reviews and other descriptive accounts.

37. Ralph Matthews, "Noah Has Hard Time; So Does the Audience," *Afro American*, October 17, 1936, 13.

38. Biographical information for Jean Stor drawn from the Black Metropolis Research Consortium Survey, hosted online by the University of Chicago. Retrieved May 2, 2014, from http://bmrcsurvey.uchicago.edu/collections/2544.

39. Matthews, "Noah Has Hard Time," 13.

40. Billy Rowe, "Presentation of 'Noah' Ineffective Says Billy Rowe," *Pittsburgh Courier*, October 17, 1936, A10.

41. Roi Ottley, "Negro Theatre 'Noah' Seems at Sea, Says Reviewer in Account" (review), *New York Amsterdam News*, October 10, 1936, 10.

42. "Thomas Mosely Praised for Role in 'Noah,'" *Norfolk Journal and Guide*, October 24, 1936, 4.

43. Ottley, "Negro Theatre," 10.

44. Ottley, "Negro Theatre," 10.

45. Matthews, "Noah Has Hard Time," 13.

46. Barry Witham, *The Federal Theatre Project: A Case Study* (Cambridge: Cambridge University Press, 2003), 70.

47. Genesis 7:24, King James Version.

48. Euphemia Van Rensselaer Wyatt, "The Flowering Peach" (review), *Catholic World*, February 1955, *The Flowering Peach* clipping file, New York Public Library for the Performing Arts.

49. Though it is not a biblical play, the title of *Awake and Sing!* is drawn from the King James Version of Isaiah 26:19 ("Awake and sing, ye that dwell in the dust").

50. Herbert Mitgang, "Odets Goes to Genesis," *New York Times*, December 26, 1954, X1.

51. Clifford Odets, *The Flowering Peach* (New York: Dramatists Play Service, 1954), 5.

52. Robert Whitehead, press release, *The Flowering Peach* clipping file, New York Public Library for the Performing Arts.

53. Whitehead, press release.

54. Odets, *The Flowering Peach*, 10.

55. An Odets invention—there is no such animal—the *gitka* apparently derives its name from a Yiddish variation on the Sanskrit and German *gita*, meaning "song of God."

56. In a press release, publicist Barry Hyams claimed that Odets got his title from the name of the eighteenth hole at Augusta National Golf Club—home of the Masters tournament. Odets, the release explains, was reading the sports page on a break from writing the play in summer of 1953 when the phrase captured his imagination ("Press Release from Barry Hyams, NYC Exclusive to Lewis Funke," *The Flowering Peach* clipping file, New York Public Library for the Performing Arts).

57. Cf. Genesis 9:12–15, "And God said, This is the token of the covenant which I make between me and you and every living creature that is with you, for perpetual generations / I do set my bow in the cloud, and it shall be for a token of a covenant between me and the earth / And it shall come to pass, when I bring a cloud over the earth, that the bow shall be seen in the cloud / And I will remember my covenant, which is between me and you and every living creature of all flesh; and the waters shall no more become a flood to destroy all flesh."

58. Odets, *The Flowering Peach*, 85.

59. Odets, *The Flowering Peach*, 26.

60. Yiddish for "daughter."

61. Thomas R. Dash, "The Flowering Peach" (review), *Women's Wear Daily*, December 30, 1954, 27.

62. *The Flowering Peach* Photo File "B," New York Public Library for the Performing Arts.

63. Louis Sheaffer, "Odets Retells Noah Story with Fresh, Warm Humor," *Brooklyn Eagle*, December 29, 1954, *The Flowering Peach* clipping file, New York Public Library for the Performing Arts.

64. J. Brooks Atkinson, "The Flowering Peach" (review), *New York Times*, January 9, 1955, XI.

65. Tom Donnelly, "You Were Expecting Maybe Bernard Shaw?," *Washington Times*, November 23, 1954, *The Flowering Peach* clipping file, New York Public Library for the Performing Arts.

66. Virginia Lambert, "Odets's Noah Lands the Ark in the Bronx," *Bergen County Record*, December 23, 1974, *The Flowering Peach* clipping file, New York Public Library for the Performing Arts.

67. Harold Stern, "Showtime" (review), *American Hebrew*, undated, circa January 1955, *The Flowering Peach* clipping file, New York Public Library for the Performing Arts.

68. Wyatt, "The Flowering Peach."

69. Alice Hughes, "A Woman's New York," King Features Syndicate, January 7, 1955, *The Flowering Peach* clipping file, New York Public Library for the Performing Arts.

70. "The Flowering Peach" (review), *New Yorker*, January 8, 1955, *The Flowering Peach* clipping file, New York Public Library for the Performing Arts.

71. Richard Cooke, "Skulnik as Noah" (review), *Wall Street Journal*, December 30, 1954, *The Flowering Peach* clipping file, New York Public Library for the Performing Arts.

72. Dash, "The Flowering Peach."

73. George Oppenheimer, "On Stage," *Newsday*, February 4, 1955, *The Flowering Peach* clipping file, New York Public Library for the Performing Arts.

74. Hal Eaton, "Skulnik Magnificent in Flowering Peach" (review), *Long Island Daily Press*, December 29, 1954, *The Flowering Peach* clipping file, New York Public Library for the Performing Arts.

75. Atkinson, "Flowering Peach," X1.

76. "The Flowering Peach" (review), *New Yorker*.

77. David Daiches, "Is This Jewish Humor?" *Commentary*, January 1952, 87.

78. Ellen Schiff, *From Stereotype to Metaphor: The Jew in Contemporary Drama* (Albany: SUNY Press, 1983), 42.

79. A light comedy of the same title played the Selwyn Theatre for two weeks in 1925; despite the biblical allusion in the title, however, this play was not an adaptation of the Bible.

80. Tom Burke, "Just a Guy Who Can't Say Noah," *New York Times*, November 8, 1970, Arts 3.

81. Charnin may be best known to casual fans as the lyricist for *Annie* (1976).

82. Goz was also Kaye's understudy, and went on as Noah for two weeks in February 1971 when Kaye was unable to perform due to injury.

83. Though he appeared on a Broadway in two "Danny Kaye on Broadway" reviews (1953, 1963), his previous appearance in an actual play was as Jerry Walker in *Let's Face It* (1941).

84. Burke, "Just a Guy," 1.

85. Burke, "Just a Guy," 1.

86. Richard Rodgers and Martin Charnin, *Two by Two: Original Broadway Cast Recording*, Sony Broadway, 1992 (1970), CD.

87. Martin Gottfried, "Two by Two" (review), *Women's Wear Daily*, November 12, 1970, in *New York Theatre Critics' Reviews* 31, no. 22 (November 16, 1970): 161.

88. Clive Barnes, "Stage: 'Two by Two'; Danny's the One," *New York Times*, November 11, 1970, 37.

89. John J. O'Connor, "The Theater," *Wall Street Journal*, November 12, 1970, in *New York Theatre Critics' Reviews* 31, no. 22 (November 16, 1970): 164.

90. This assessment is based on listening to the original cast album. For

extended discussion of how Jewishness does or does not appear in Rodgers's musicals, see Most, *Making Americans.*

91. In addition to Kaye, Jewish performers in the original cast included Goz, Kahn, and Joan Copeland (younger sister of Arthur Miller) as Esther. Walter Willison (Japheth) and Marilyn Cooper (Leah) did not speak publicly about their religious backgrounds, but both played many Jewish characters over the course of their careers. For extended discussion of how audiences do and do not perceive Jewishness in performance, see my *Acting Jewish.*

92. Cf. Marvin Carlson, *The Haunted Stage* (Ann Arbor: University of Michigan Press, 2003).

93. Roderick Nordell, "Kaye Opens Season as Noah," *Christian Science Monitor, Two by Two* clipping file, New York Public Library for the Performing Arts.

94. Nordell, "Kaye Opens Season."

95. "What's New in the Theater," *New York Times*, November 15, 1970, D7.

96. Barnes, "Stage."

97. Frank Segers, "'Two by Two' Now an 'Entertainment' and Audiences Love It, Sez Danny," *Variety*, May 26, 1971, *Two by Two* clipping file, New York Public Library for the Performing Arts.

98. *Two by Two* closed in September 1971 after a run of six previews and 343 regular performances. *Variety* initially estimated that the show had lost "about $300,000 on its $600,000 investment," though later reported that Rodgers claimed the show had made a small profit. Source: *Variety*, September 15, 1971, and September 22, 1971, *Two by Two* clipping file, New York Public Library for the Performing Arts

99. Darren Aronofsky, "Art Matters: The Thing about the Ark," *New York Times*, March 19, 2014, M278. Aronofsky's film offers this destruction as a spectacle of its own sort, using technological means not available to the stage.

Chapter 5

1. Rev. Alfred Walls, *The Oldest Drama in the World: The Book of Job Arranged in Dramatic Form with Elucidations* (New York: Hunt & Eaton, 1891), 7.

2. Levy, *The Bible as Theatre*, 11.

3. King James Version.

4. Walls, *Oldest Drama*, 21.

5. Walls, *Oldest Drama*, 9–12.

6. Walls, *Oldest Drama*, 103.

7. Walls, *Oldest Drama*, 65.

8. Walls, *Oldest Drama*, 3.

9. Richard G. Moulton, ed., *The Book of Job* (London: Macmillan, 1896).

10. David Norton, *A History of the English Bible as Literature* (Cambridge: Cambridge University Press, 2000), 371.

11. Moulton, *The Book of Job*, vi.

12. Moulton, *The Book of Job*, 6.

13. See chapter 1.

14. Martin Goodman, ed., *The Oxford Handbook of Jewish Studies* (New York: Oxford University Press, 2002), 871.

15. Leone di Somi, "The Dialogues of Leone di Somi," trans. Allardyce Nicoll, in Allardyce Nicoll, ed., *The Development of the Theatre*, 5th ed. (New York: Harcourt, Brace and World, 1967), 256–257.

16. Genesis 7:5, King James Version.

17. Job 7:21, King James Version.

18. Harold S. Kushner, *The Book of Job: When Bad Things Happened to a Good Person* (New York: Schocken, 2012), 15.

19. Kushner, *The Book of Job*, 15.

20. Kushner, *The Book of Job*, 15.

21. Job 1:8, King James Version.

22. Job 1:12, King James Version.

23. Job 1:22, King James Version.

24. Job 2:6, King James Version.

25. Job 2:9, King James Version.

26. Kushner, *The Book of Job*, 31.

27. Kushner, *The Book of Job*, 41.

28. Job 42:6, King James Version.

29. Lawrence Besserman identifies two other important twentieth-century dramas based on Job. Poet Robert Frost's comic *The Masque of Reason* (1945), which purports to be the missing forty-third chapter of the biblical book, has been staged as a one-act off-off-Broadway (1973); British literary critic I. A. Richards's *Job's Comforting* (1970), as far as I can determine, has never had a New York production or a major professional production elsewhere. See Lawrence Besserman, "Job," in David L. Jeffrey, ed., *A Dictionary of Biblical Tradition in English Literature* (Grand Rapids: William B. Eerdmans, 1992), 404. See also Besserman, "Job in Literature: Characters and Quotations," in Lawrence Boadt, ed., *The Book of Job: Why Do the Innocent Suffer?* (London: Lion, 1997), 31–32.

30. Constance D'Arcy Mackay, *The Little Theatre in the United States* (New York: Henry Holt, 1917), 39.

31. Unless otherwise noted, biographical details on Stuart Walker are drawn from Edward Hale Bierstad's introduction to Stuart Walker, *Portmanteau Plays* (Cincinnati: Stewart & Kidd, 1917), iii–xl.

32. *Stanford University Bulletin*, 3, no. 29 (March 15, 1920): 18.

33. According to Belasco, the first manager of the Play Bureau was Henry Stillman, who resigned in 1910. Source: "Always Being Sued, Sighs David Belasco," *New York Times*, August 1, 1912, 11.

34. Mackay, *Little Theatre*, 39.

35. Mackay, *Little Theatre*, 40.

36. Stange and Mears's play was adapted from Booth Tarkington's 1916 novel of the same name.

37. "A Theatric Version of the Book of Job," *New York Times*, March 8, 1918, 9.

38. Stuart Walker, "'Job' Really Modern," *New York Tribune*, March 3, 1918, D5.

39. Walker, "'Job' Really Modern," D5.

40. "Book of Job to Be Presented at Booth," *New York Tribune*, February 24, 1918, C6.

41. "A Theatric Version of the Book of Job," 9.

42. "Theatric Version," 9.

43. "Theatric Version," 9. Lowry, coincidentally, would go on to play a supporting role in MacLeish's *J.B.*

44. "Theatric Version," 9.

45. Jolo, "Stuart Walker Players," *Variety*, March 7, 1919, 16.

46. Jolo, "Stuart Walker Players," 16.

47. "Theatric Version," 9.

48. John Corbin, "Job and His Adversary's Book," *New York Times*, March 9, 1919, 46.

49. Helmut Kallman, "Os-ke-non-ton," *The Canadian Encyclopedia*, May 25, 2014, www.thecanadianencyclopedia.ca/en/article/os-ke-non-ton/.

50. Jolo, "Stuart Walker Players"; John Corbin, "Drama," *New York Times*, March 4, 1919, 8.

51. As a consequence of the early publication of MacLeish's script, there are several differences between the play as published by Houghton Mifflin and the acting edition published by Samuel French, Inc. Unless otherwise noted, citations of the play in this chapter refer to the acting edition.

52. John Ciardi, "The Birth of a Classic," *Saturday Review*, March 8, 1958, *J.B.* clipping file, New York Public Library for the Performing Arts.

53. Elliott Norton, "J.B." (review), *Boston Record*, April 29, 1958, *J.B.* clipping file, New York Public Library for the Performing Arts.

54. Brooks Atkinson, "Archibald MacLeish's New Play, 'J.B.,'" *New York Times*, April 24, 1958, 37.

55. Robert Downing, "J.B.'s Journeys," *Theatre Arts*, February 1960, 29.

56. Eliza Kazan, *Kazan: A Life* (New York: Random House, 1988), 36. Kazan also reports that James Baldwin, who regularly sat in on rehearsals, hated the play.

57. Kazan, *Kazan*, 36.

58. Sponsler, *Ritual Imports*, 149.

59. Archibald MacLeish, *J.B.: A Play in Verse* (New York: Samuel French, 1958), 17.

60. Masks were also used to represent the supernatural in many medieval plays.

61. MacLeish, *J.B.* (New York: Houghton Mifflin, 1956), 21 (emphasis in original).

62. MacLeish, *J.B.* (1958).

63. MacLeish, *J.B.* (1958), 26 (emphasis in original).

64. MacLeish, "Foreword," in *J.B.* (1958), 8.

65. MacLeish, *J.B.* (1958), 63 (emphasis in original). Cf. Job 2:21.

66. MacLeish, *J.B.* (1958), 64 (italics in original).

67. MacLeish, "Foreword," 7.

68. MacLeish, "Foreword," 7.

69. MacLeish, *J.B.* (1958), 95 (emphasis in original).

70. MacLeish, *J.B.* (1958), 98 (emphasis in original).

71. MacLeish, *J.B.* (1958), 107 (italics in original).

72. Brooks Atkinson, "Theatre: MacLeish's 'J.B.,'" (review), *New York Times*, December 12, 1958, A2.

73. Richard Watts Jr., "Watts Looks at the New Plays," *New York Post*, December 29, 1958, in *New York Theatre Critics' Reviews* 19, no. 25 (December 31, 1958): 168.

74. John McClain, "J.B." (review), *New York Journal-American*, December 29, 1958, in *New York Theatre Critics' Reviews* 19, no. 25 (December 31, 1958): 169.

75. According to a report in the *Herald Tribune* (February 6, 1959), *J.B.* would have been more profitable had the production followed the then-common practice of selling standing room at the back of the orchestra. Unfortunately, because so much of the play took place on a raised platform representing the heavens, the balcony would obstruct standees' view of critical moments. The company therefore elected not to offer standing room tickets.

76. Rathbone actually played Nickles in the touring production, opposite Frederic Worlock as Mr. Zuss.

77. "Religion: J.B. vs Job," *Time* 73, no. 15 (April 13, 1959): 97.

78. As quoted in "Religion: J.B. vs. Job," 97.

79. "Three Opinions on 'J.B.,'" *Life* 46, no. 20 (May 18, 1959): 135.

80. "Three Opinions on 'J.B.,'" 135.

81. MacLeish, "Foreword," 6.

82. Bruce McConachie, *American Theater in the Culture of the Cold War: Producing and Contesting Containment, 1947–1962* (Iowa City: University of Iowa Press, 2003), 212.

83. McConachie, *American Theater*, 212.

84. McConachie, *American Theater*, 213.

85. McConachie, *American Theater*, 51–52.

86. McConachie, *American Theater*, 222.

87. Cf. Manhattan Project leader Robert Oppenheimer's citation of the

Bhagavad Gita, "I am become death, the destroyer of worlds," or Albert Einstein's contention that "God doesn't play dice with the world."

88. Neil Simon, "Notes from the Playwright," in Edythe M. McGovern, *Not-So-Simple Neil Simon: A Critical Study* (Van Nuys, CA: Perviale Press, 1978), 11.

89. James Lipton, "Neil Simon, The Art of Theater No. 10" (interview), *Paris Review* 125 (Winter 1992), May 25, 2014, www.theparisreview.org.

90. James Fisher, "A Reassessment of *God's Favorite*," in Gary Konas, ed., *Neil Simon: A Casebook* (New York: Garland, 1997), 90.

91. Lipton, "Neil Simon."

92. Martin Gottfried, "Neil Simon's Latest," *New York Post*, December 12, 1974, in *New York Theatre Critics' Reviews* 35, no. 22 (December 9, 1974): 148.

93. Howard Kissell, "God's Favorite" (review), *Women's Wear Daily*, December 13, 1974, in *New York Theatre Critics' Reviews* 35, no. 22 (December 9, 1974): 145.

94. Clive Barnes, "'God's Favorite' Is Simon's Job on L.I.," *New York Times*, December 12, 1974, 59.

95. Douglas Watt, "'God's Favorite' Is Awesomely Funny," *New York Daily News*, December 12, 1974, in *New York Theatre Critics' Reviews* 35, no. 22 (December 9, 1974): 145.

96. Neil Simon, *God's Favorite*, in *Collected Plays of Neil Simon*, vol. 2 (New York: Plume, 1986), 484.

97. Simon, *God's Favorite*, 494.

98. Simon, *God's Favorite*, 494.

99. Simon, *God's Favorite*, 504.

100. Simon, *God's Favorite*, 543. Emphasis and ellipsis in original.

101. Simon, *God's Favorite*, 508.

102. Simon, *God's Favorite*, 529.

103. Simon, "Notes from the Playwright," 11.

104. Fisher, "Reassessment of *God's Favorite*," 89.

105. Simon, *God's Favorite*, 520.

106. Fisher, "Reassessment of *God's Favorite*," 85.

107. Jack Kroll, "The Patience of Joe," *Newsweek*, December 23, 1974, in *New York Theatre Critics' Reviews* 35, no. 22 (December 9, 1974): 147.

108. Kushner, *The Book of Job*, 13.

109. Kushner, *The Book of Job*, 14.

110. Kushner, *The Book of Job*, 14.

Chapter 6

1. See, for example, Margaret Croyden, "The Box-Office Boom," *New York Times*, May 10, 1981, via digital archive.

2. Times Square Church, official website, April 18, 2014, www.tsnyc. org/history.

3. Bloomberg served three terms (2002–2013).

4. There is a large body of scholarship on the late twentieth-century transformation of Times Square. See, for example: Stephen Nelson, "Broadway and the Beast," *TDR* 39, no. 2 (Summer 1995): 71–78; Elizabeth L. Wollman, "The Economic Development of the 'New' Times Square and Its Impact on the Broadway Musical," *American Music* 20, no. 4 (Winter 2002): 445–465; and Stephen Adler, *On Broadway: Art and Commerce on the Great White Way* (Carbondale: Southern Illinois University Press, 2004).

5. For an extended discussion of the Times Square Church, see Hans E. Tokke, "Disneyfication and Religion in Times Square," in Richard Cimino, Nadia A. Mian, and Weishan Huang, eds., *Ecologies of Faith in New York City: The Evolution of Religious Institutions* (Bloomington: Indiana University Press, 2012), 25–54.

6. Tokke, "Disneyfication," 38.

7. See Stevenson, *Sensational Devotion,* 55–60.

8. David Wilkerson, "God's House Turned into a Den of Thieves," World Challenge Pulpit Series, May 31, 2014, sermons.worldchallenge.org/ en/devotions/2010/gods-house-turned-into-a-den-of-thieves.

9. As mentioned in chapter 1, Samuel Morse's theater on Twenty-Third Street, the site of his never-opened production of *The Passion*, was later transformed into a church.

10. As noted in chapter 2, producer David Belasco staged the *Freiburg Passion Play* at New York's Hippodrome in 1929. This production of the traditional Passion play was imported from Germany and featured Adolf Fassnacht in the role of "The Christus." Some historians suggest that the Hippodrome was not a "legit" Broadway theater, given its enormous size (over five thousand seats) and the fact that it hosted circuses, animal acts, boxing matches, and films as well as stage productions. In any case, the *Freiburg Passion Play* is the only recorded case of an actor playing the role of Jesus on Broadway prior to 1971.

11. Jessica Sternfeld, *The Megamusical* (Bloomington: Indiana University Press, 2006), 10, 8–9.

12. Sternfeld, *The Megamusical,* 9.

13. Ethan Mordden, *One More Kiss: The Broadway Musical in the 1970s* (New York: Palgrave, 2003), 15.

14. Though *Les Misérables* originated in France, the Trevor Nunn–directed production brought to New York in 1987 had originated in London.

15. Michael Walsh, *Andrew Lloyd Webber: His Life and Works,* updated ed. (New York: Harry N. Abrams, 1997), 32–35.

16. Walsh, *Andrew Lloyd Webber,* 37.

17. Walsh, *Andrew Lloyd Webber,* 37.

18. As quoted in Walsh, *Andrew Lloyd Webber,* 37.

19. Walsh, *Andrew Lloyd Webber*, 37.

20. The Joseph Consortium consisted of an undistinguished rock group called the Mixed Bag, plus Lloyd Webber's father Bill on Hammond organ, and Rice singing the role of Pharaoh (Walsh, *Andrew Lloyd Webber*, 39).

21. The B-side was "John 19:41," an instrumental that comes near the end of the show.

22. Walsh, *Andrew Lloyd Webber*, 74.

23. Mel Gussow, "'Superstar' a Hit Before Opening," *New York Times*, October 12, 1971, 48.

24. Andrew Lloyd Webber, *Jesus Christ Superstar* (sound recording), MCA/Decca Records, 1970, CD.

25. An "eleven o'clock number" is a major song that appears shortly before the end of a musical. The phrase dates to an era when Broadway shows typically began at 8:30 p.m. and ran about two hours and forty-five minutes.

26. Elizabeth Wollman, *The Theater Will Rock* (Ann Arbor: University of Michigan Press, 2006), 96.

27. Wollman, *The Theater Will Rock*, 97.

28. Jack Kroll, "Theater" (review), *Newsweek*, October 25, 1971, in *New York Theatre Critics' Reviews* 32, no. 15 (October 31, 1971): 243.

29. John Simon, as quoted in John Gruen, "'Do You Mind Critics Calling You Cheap, Decadent, Sensationalistic, Gimmicky, Vulgar, Overinflated, Megalomaniacal?' 'I Don't Read Reviews Very Much' Answers Tom O'Horgan," *New York Times Magazine*, January, 2, 1972, 68.

30. Kroll, "Theater," 243.

31. As quoted in Gruen, "Do You Mind," 68.

32. David Chidester, *Authentic Fakes: Religion and American Popular Culture* (Berkeley: University of California Press, 2005), 31.

33. Cf. Christopher Moreman, "Devil Music and the Great Beast: Ozzy Osbourne, Aleister Crowley, and the Christian Right," *Journal of Religion and Popular Culture* 5, no. 1 (Fall 2003), http://utpjournals.metapress.com.

34. Cf. Marcus Breen, "A Stairway to Heaven or a Highway to Hell? Heavy Metal Rock Music in the 1990s," *Cultural Studies* 5, no. 2 (1991): 191–203.

35. Chidester, *Authentic Fakes*, 32–33.

36. Jean L. Bosch, "Bridging the Musical and Scriptural Generation Gap: The Jesus People Movement and *Jesus Christ Superstar*," master's thesis, University of Kansas, 2011, 11–18. Bosch writes, "The Jesus People Movement is typically classified as a religious movement, but part of what made it distinct was its unique approach to culture. While preachers raged in pulpits about the evils of long hair on men, the Jesus People let their hair grow out, put on fringed jackets and beads, and swayed to the rhythms of popular music. Furthermore, the Jesus People began copying the language, music, and structures of the counterculture for their own purposes. They spoke the street argot, but they talked about Jesus. They formed rock bands, but substi-

tuted evangelistic or worshipful lyrics. They opened nightclubs, but they used them to preach the gospel."

37. Chidester, *Authentic Fakes*, 31.

38. See Mark Sullivan, "'More Popular Than Jesus': The Beatles and the Religious Far Right," *Popular Music* 6, no. 3 (October 1987): 313–326.

39. David Morgan, *Visual Piety* (Berkeley: University of California Press, 1998), 1.

40. Gruen, "Do You Mind," 68.

41. Guy Flatley, "They Wrote It and They're Glad," *New York Times*, October 31, 1971, D1.

42. Douglas Watt, "'Jesus Christ Superstar' Is Full of Life, Vibrant with Reverence" (review), *New York Daily News*, October 13, 1971, in *New York Theatre Critics' Reviews* 32, no. 15 (October 31, 1971): 242.

43. John 8:3, Revised Standard Version.

44. Bosch, "Bridging," 56. In more recent times, other adaptations of the Passion, including Mel Gibson's 2004 film *The Passion of the Christ*, have conflated two or three of these women.

45. Wollman, *The Theater Will Rock*, 99.

46. Bosch, "Bridging," 51–52.

47. As Sponsler, Chansky, and others have noted, concerns about anti-Semitism have arisen in regard to nearly all American Passion plays and films. *Superstar* is unusual, however, in that it premiered in New York City at a critical time for Jewish-Catholic relations in that region.

48. Gerald K. Strober, as quoted in "Jesus Christ Superstar Opera Hit," *Jewish Transcript*, October 28, 1971, 5.

49. Arnold Forster and Benjamin Epstein, *The New Anti-Semitism* (New York: McGraw-Hill, 1974), 93.

50. For more on Asian American representation on Broadway, see Karen Shimakawa, *National Abjection: The Asian American Body Onstage* (Durham: Duke University Press, 2002).

51. See Stephen Prothero, *American Jesus: How the Son of God Became a National Icon* (New York: Farrar, Straus and Giroux, 2003).

52. Jeff Fenholt official website, June 1, 2014, www.jefffenholt.com.

53. Unless otherwise noted, this early history of the play is drawn from Carol de Giere, *Defying Gravity: The Creative Career of Stephen Schwartz from "Godspell" to "Wicked"* (New York: Applause Books, 2008), 43–68.

54. Sonia Manzano, as quoted in de Giere, *Defying Gravity*, 47.

55. Though the company neither imitated nor mocked the ceremony of communion as practiced by Christian churches, the formal similarities are clear.

56. As quoted in Paul R. Laird, *The Musical Theater of Stephen Schwartz: From "Godspell" to "Wicked"* (Lanham, Md.: Rowman and Littlefield, 2014), 33.

57. Clive Barnes, "The Theater: Godspell" (review), *New York Times*, May 18, 1971, 45.

58. Barnes, "The Theater."

59. Walter Kerr, "Why Make St. Matthew Dance? Just for the Fun of It," *New York Times*, May 30, 1971, 2:9.

60. Daniel L. Migliore, "Godspell" (review), *Theology Today* 28, no. 3 (October 1971): 390.

61. Migliore, "Godspell," 390.

62. Migliore, "Godspell," 390.

63. Cf. Stacy Wolf, *Changed for Good: A Feminist History of the Broadway Musical* (New York: Oxford University Press, 2011), 106.

64. Wolf, *Changed for Good*, 105–111.

65. John Bush Jones, *Our Musicals, Ourselves: A Social History of the American Musical Theatre* (Hanover: Brandeis University Press, 2003), 269–304.

66. Jones, *Our Musicals, Ourselves*, 283.

67. Wollman, *The Theater Will Rock*, 86.

68. Sternfeld, *The Megamusical*, 9.

69. See, among others, de Giere, *Defying Gravity*; and Paul R. Laird, *"Wicked": A Musical Biography* (Lanham, Md.: Scarecrow Press, 2011).

70. Laird, *Stephen Schwartz*, 44.

71. *Godspell* was almost certainly influenced by other collectively created ritualistic performances of the "downtown theater" such as the Performance Group's *Dionysus in 69* (1968) and the Living Theatre's *Paradise Now* (1968). Yet where these productions included overt antiauthoritarian politics and nudity that were considered shocking even by off-off-Broadway standards, *Godspell*'s overt Christianity and family-friendly staging made it a more palatable candidate for a transfer uptown.

72. The 2011 production, which I attended shortly after it opened, added some scenic extravagance through creative use of trapdoors in the stage floor and the use of a flying harness for the crucifixion scene.

73. Harvey Cox, *The Feast of Fools: A Theological Essay on Festivity and Fantasy* (Cambridge: Harvard University Press, 1969), 140–141.

74. See Paul Baker, *Contemporary Christian Music: Where It Came From, What It Is, Where It's Going* (Westchester, Ill.: Crossway Books, 1985), 50.

75. Cf. Matthew 3:1–3 and Mark 1:3–4, King James Version.

76. Wolf, *Changed for Good*, 110.

77. Migliore, "Godspell," 389.

78. Migliore, "Godspell," 389.

79. As quoted in Laird, *Stephen Schwartz*, 33.

80. Schwartz, in "Godspell—Notes for Performers," writes: "The main thing to remember is that the story of the show is that Jesus comes into a

group of disparate and desperate individuals and leads them into becoming a community." StephenSchwartz.com, 2010, December 25, 2014, www.stephenschwartz.com.

81. Laird provides a thorough survey of critical responses to *Godspell* in *Stephen Schwartz*, 24–27.

82. As quoted in Laird, *Stephen Schwartz*, 25.

83. Kerr, "St. Matthew Dance," 9.

84. Barnes, "The Theater," 45.

85. John blows a shofar to start the number. This traditional Jewish ritual instrument—made from a ram's horn—offers its own kind of nonmimetic authenticity. Even more than other musical instruments, the call of the shofar does not *represent*; it simply *is*.

86. "God Spell Songs: Stephen Schwartz Answers Questions about the *Godspell* Score," StephenSchwartz.com, 2010, December 25, 2014, www.stephenschwartz.com.

87. Today, many churches have adopted songs from *Godspell* as part of their choral repertoire. Based on Internet searches of church bulletins, "Prepare Ye the Way of the Lord" and "Day by Day" appear to be the most popular choices.

88. Associated Press, "'Godspell' Has Some Parents Upset in Ogden, Utah," wire service report, September 18, 2000.

89. Douglas Watt, "*Godspell* Reaches Broadway," *New York Daily News*, June 23, 1976, in *New York Theatre Critics' Reviews* 37, no. 14 (June 21, 1976): 218.

90. Leonard Probst, "Godspell" (review), NBC radio, in *New York Theatre Critics' Reviews* 37, no. 14 (June 21, 1976): 220.

91. *Joseph and the Amazing Technicolor Dreamcoat* (1982) would surpass *Godspell*, which remains the fourth-longest running biblical Broadway production.

92. Walsh, *Andrew Lloyd Webber*, 58.

93. I saw a performance of this production in the spring of 1982.

94. Revised Standard Version.

95. Andrew Lloyd Webber, *Joseph and the Amazing Technicolor Dreamcoat* (Original Broadway Cast), Chrysalis Records, 1982, LP.

96. Sternfeld, *The Megamusical*, 108.

97. As quoted in Sternfeld, *The Megamusical*, 108.

98. Mel Gussow, "A Biblical Twist," *New York Times*, November 19, 1981, C21.

99. Sternfeld, *The Megamusical*, 110.

100. Sternfeld, *The Megamusical*, 110.

101. Lloyd Webber, *Joseph*.

102. Unless otherwise noted, historical information about *Children of Eden* is drawn from Laird, *Stephen Schwartz*, 173–229.

103. Laird, *Stephen Schwartz*, 173.

104. Laird, *Stephen Schwartz*, 173.

105. Laird, *Stephen Schwartz*, 228–229.

106. Matthew Palm, "Children of Eden" (review), *Orlando Sentinel* August 9, 2012, via digital archive.

107. The New York club was an offshoot of a London club (also called The Lambs) founded in 1869.

108. In 1974, unable to meet its mortgage obligations on what is still called the Lambs' Building, the club moved to less palatial quarters.

109. Joey A. Condon, "An Examination into the History and Present Interrelationship between the Church and the Theatre Exemplified by the Manhattan Church of the Nazarene, the Lambs Club, and the Lamb's Theatre Company as a Possible Paradigm," master's thesis, University of Missouri–Kansas City, 2007, 137.

110. Condon, "Examination," 125.

111. Condon, "Examination," 137.

112. Condon, "Examination," 119.

113. I attended a performance of this production.

114. Jake Ehrenreich's solo show, *A Jew Grows in Brooklyn.*

115. Cf. Isaiah 11:6, Revised Standard Version.

Chapter 7

1. *I'm Solomon* clipping file, New York Public Library for the Performing Arts.

2. Hebrews 11:39, Revised Standard Version.

3. Cf. Psalms 92:12, King James Version.

4. *New York Daily News*, April 30, 1968, *I'm Solomon* clipping file, New York Public Library for the Performing Arts.

5. "The Theatre: Thinking Big, Thinking Little," *New Yorker*, May 4, 1968, 129.

6. Clive Barnes, "Theater: 'Musical Fable'" (review), *New York Times*, April 24, 1968, 51.

7. R. P. Hariss, "I'm Solomon" (review), *Baltimore New American*, March 21, 1968, *I'm Solomon* clipping file, New York Public Library for the Performing Arts.

8. Martin Gottfried, "I'm Solomon" (review), *Women's Wear Daily*, April 24, 1968, in *New York Theater Critics' Reviews* 29, no. 11 (April 29, 1968): 297.

9. Sam Zolotow, "Israeli Musical Due Here in Fall," *New York Times*, February 5, 1965, 37.

10. In this story, which does not contradict anything in the biblical account of Solomon's life, the King trades places with Shamgar and learns a powerful lesson: the ersatz King's every pronouncement is treated as great

wisdom, while everything Solomon says in the guise of the cobbler is dismissed as foolishness. For added dramatic interest, the moralistic fable is intertwined in a fairly elaborate sex farce involving Solomon's legendary harem, the cobbler's wife, and the Queen of Sheba.

11. *Jerusalem Post*, November 2, 1965, *I'm Solomon* clipping file, New York Public Library for the Performing Arts.

12. Unpublished letter from Zvi Kolitz to Sam Zolotow, February 1, 1965, *I'm Solomon* clipping file, New York Public Library for the Performing Arts. Kolitz's letter hinted optimistically that both Christopher Plummer and Marlon Brando were under consideration for the title role. After the news item appeared in the *Times*, however, it was revealed that Kolitz had not, in fact, secured the American rights from the play's representatives, Moadim Play Publishers and Literary Agents of Tel Aviv. Still, after some additional legal wrangling, Kolitz pressed forward; by the end of 1965, the rights had been secured and Laurence Harvey was rumored to be in line for the role of King Solomon, which would ultimately go to comedian Dick Shawn.

13. Undated brochure circa 1965, *I'm Solomon* clipping file, New York Public Library for the Performing Arts.

14. Kolitz assembled a reasonably accomplished creative team (also Broadway outsiders), including British director Michael Benthall (a former artistic director of London's Old Vic), Oscar-winning composer Ernest Gold (*Exodus*), lyricist Anne Croswell (*Tovarisch*), and book-writer Erich Segal (who would later write *Love Story*, but was then an assistant professor of classics at Yale University with two off-Broadway musicals to his credit).

15. To hear selections from the Israeli score, see Israel Broadcast Service, *Vistas of Israel: Program # 243, Songs from "The King and the Cobbler" at the Cameri Theatre* (sound recording), circa 1965, Judaica Sound Archives, Florida Atlantic University, June 1, 2014, faujsa.fau.edu/jsa.

16. Gabrielle Cody and Evert Sprinchorn, eds., *Columbia Encyclopedia of Modern Drama*, vol. 1 (New York: Columbia University Press, 2007), 96.

17. Charles McHarry, untitled notice, *New York Daily News*, January 6, 1968, *I'm Solomon* clipping file, New York Public Library for the Performing Arts.

18. Zvi Kolitz, letter to Ethiopian Mission to UN, January 17, 1968, *I'm Solomon* clipping file, New York Public Library for the Performing Arts.

19. Max Eisen, "Hailie Selassie Approves Sending of Lion for Premiere of 'I'm Solomon'" (press release), April 18, 1968, *I'm Solomon* clipping file, New York Public Library for the Performing Arts.

20. William Goldman, *The Season: A Candid Look at Broadway* (New York: Harcourt, Brace and World, 1969), 376.

21. The approximately five-hundred-seat Edison Theatre was sometimes referred to as an off-Broadway venue, but throughout most of the 1970s and 1980s it operated as a Broadway house in terms of contracts, publicity, and Tony Award eligibility. Based on the way *Hard Job Being God* was marketed

and reviewed in the New York press, I have chosen to consider it a Broadway (rather than off-Broadway) production. Interestingly, the same production is listed in *both* Thomas Hischak's encyclopedia *Broadway Plays and Musicals* (Jefferson, N.C.: McFarland, 2009) and Dan Dietz's companion volume, *Off Broadway Musicals, 1910–2007* (Jefferson, N.C.: McFarland, 2010).

22. Richard J. Scholem, "I'm Solomon" (review), Greater New York Radio, May 16, 1972, *I'm Solomon* clipping file, New York Public Library for the Performing Arts (emphasis in original).

23. William Glover, "Hard Job Being God" (review), Associated Press, May 15, 1972, *Hard Job Being God* clipping file, New York Public Library for the Performing Arts.

24. Liner notes, *Hard Job Being God, Original Cast Album*, GWP Records, 1971.

25. Glover, "Hard Job Being God."

26. Glover, "Hard Job Being God."

27. Liner notes, *Hard Job Being God.*

28. Liner notes, *Hard Job Being God.*

29. Moses, for example, sings:

Hey, Pharaoh, how would you like to see
My stick turn into a snake?
When the darkness falls
And the plagues begin
Well then you'll know you made a big mistake
I'm telling you all this, Pharaoh
I'm warning you so you'll know
You'd better let my people go!
Liner notes, *Hard Job Being God.* Cf. Exodus 7:8–13.

30. E.g., "If you saw me dying on a hill somewhere / you wouldn't care." Liner notes, *Hard Job Being God.*

31. Unsigned archivist's note, *Hard Job Being God* program file, New York Public Library for the Performing Arts.

32. Clive Barnes, "The Program" (review), *New York Times*, May 16, 1972, 49.

33. The fictional teddy bear-like creatures made popular by *Star Wars Episode III: Return of the Jedi.*

34. Parker and Stone have frequently acknowledged the American musical theater canon as an influence in their work.

35. That the faith, in this instance, is that of the Church of Jesus Christ of Latter-day Saints adds a layer of irony because the vast majority of the Broadway audience is likely to be unfamiliar with the specific theology and history *The Book of Mormon* burlesques. Gentiles, that is, may recognize the irreverence of the musical without a clear understanding of the stakes involved.

Bibliography

Aberjhani and Sandra L. West, eds. *Encyclopedia of the Harlem Renaissance.* New York: Facts on File, 2000.

Adler, Stephen. *On Broadway: Art and Commerce on the Great White Way.* Carbondale: Southern Illinois University Press, 2004.

"Aldermanic Virtue Aroused." *New York Times*, November 24, 1880, 8.

"Always Being Sued, Sighs David Belasco." *New York Times*, August 1, 1912, 11.

[Archivist's note]. *Hard Job Being God* program file, New York Public Library for the Performing Arts.

Aronofsky, Darren. "Art Matters: The Thing about the Ark." *New York Times*, March 19, 2014, M278.

Ashley, Wayne. "The Stations of the Cross: Christ, Politics, and Processions on New York City's Lower East Side." In Robert A. Orsi, ed., *Gods of the City: Religion and the American Urban Landscape*, 341–366. Bloomington: Indiana University Press, 1999.

Associated Press. "'Godspell' Has Some Parents Upset in Ogden, Utah." Wire service report, September 18, 2000.

"At the Play and with the Players." *New York Times*, December 3, 1899, 18.

Atkinson, [J.] Brooks. "Archibald MacLeish's New Play, 'J.B.'" *New York Times*, April 24, 1958, 37.

Atkinson, J. Brooks. "The Flowering Peach" (review). *New York Times*, January 9, 1955, X1.

Atkinson, J. Brooks. "New Negro Drama of Sublime Beauty." *New York Times*, February 27, 1930, 26.

Atkinson, J. Brooks. "Noah" (review). *New York Times*, February 14, 1935, 25.

Atkinson, J. Brooks. "The Passion Play a Colorful Pageant: Freiburg Players Give a Highly Theatricalized Performance of Sacred Story." *New York Times*, April 30, 1929, 27.

Atkinson, J. Brooks. "The Play: 'The Green Pastures' and Mr. Harrison Return to Celebrate a Fifth Anniversary." *New York Times*, February 27, 1935, 16.

Atkinson, [J.] Brooks. "Theatre: MacLeish's 'J.B.'" (review). *New York Times*, December 12, 1958, A2.

Austin, Mary. "'Green Pastures' Reveals New Field for Dramatist." *New York World*, March 9, 1930. *The Green Pastures* clipping file, New York Public Library for the Performing Arts.

Baker, Paul. *Contemporary Christian Music: Where It Came From, What It Is, Where It's Going.* Westchester, Ill.: Crossway Books, 1985.

Barenblat, Rachel. "Fan Fiction and Midrash: Making Meaning." *Transformative Works and Cultures* 17 (2014). journal.transformativeworks.org/index.php/twc/article/view/596.

Barenblat, Rachel. "Transformative Work: Midrash and Fan Fiction." *Journal of Religion and Literature* 43, no. 2 (Summer 2011): 171–177.

Barnes, Clive. "'God's Favorite' Is Simon's Job on L.I." *New York Times*, December 12, 1974, 59.

Barnes, Clive. "The Program." *New York Times*, May 16, 1972, 49.

Barnes, Clive. "Stage: 'Two by Two'; Danny's the One." *New York Times*, November 11, 1970, 37.

Barnes, Clive. "The Theater: Godspell" (review). *New York Times*, May 18, 1971, 45.

Barnes, Clive. "Theater: 'Musical Fable'" (review). *New York Times*, April 24, 1968, 51.

Barnette, Jane. "Literary Adaptation for the Stage: A Primer for Dramaturgs." In Magda Romanska, ed., *The Routledge Companion to Dramaturgy*, 294–299. London: Routledge, 2014.

Barnette, Jane. "Staging the Numinous." *Text and Performance Quarterly* 29, no. 4 (October 2009): 415–417.

Barthes, Roland. "The Death of the Author." In *Image, Music, Text*, trans. Stephen Heath. New York: Hill and Wang, 1977.

Belasco, David. *The Life of David Belasco.* New York: Moffat, Yard, 1918.

Benjamin, Walter. *Illuminations: Essays and Reflections.* Ed. Hannah Arendt. Trans. Harry Zohn. New York: Schocken, 1968.

Bial, Henry. *Acting Jewish: Negotiating Ethnicity on the American Stage and Screen.* Ann Arbor: University of Michigan Press, 2005.

The Bible. King James Version. BibleGateway. BibleGateway.com.

The Bible. New International Version. BibleGateway. BibleGateway.com.

The Bible. Revised Standard Version. BibleGateway. BibleGateway.com.

"The Black Metropolis Research Consortium Survey." May 2, 2014. bmrcsurvey.uchicago.edu/collections/2544.

Bloom, Michael. *Thinking Like a Director: A Practical Handbook.* New York: Macmillan, 2011.

Boadt, Lawrence, ed. *The Book of Job: Why Do the Innocent Suffer?* London: Lion, 1997.

"Book of Job to be Presented at Booth." *New York Tribune*, February 24, 1918, C6.

Bookspan, Martin. "The Creation of the World and Other Business" (review). WPIX-Channel 11 television. Transcript in *The Creation of the World* clipping file, New York Public Library for the Performing Arts.

Bordman, Gerald, and Thomas S. Hischak. *The Oxford Companion to American Theatre.* 3rd ed. New York: Oxford University Press, 2004 [1984].

Bosch, Jean L. "Bridging the Musical and Scriptural Generation Gap: The Jesus People Movement and *Jesus Christ Superstar*." Master's thesis, University of Kansas, 2011.

Boyarin, Daniel. *Intertextuality and the Reading of Midrash*. Bloomington: Indiana University Press, 1994.

Bradford, Roark. *Ol' Man Adam and His Chillun': Being the Tales They Tell about the Time When the Lord Walked the Earth Like a Natural Man*. New York: Harper and Brothers, 1928.

Breen, Marcus. "A Stairway to Heaven or a Highway to Hell? Heavy Metal Rock Music in the 1990s." *Cultural Studies* 5, no. 2 (1991): 191–203.

Bremner, Kelly J. G. "Total Theatre Re-envisioned: The Means and Ends of Appia, Kandinsky and Wagner." Diss., University of Wisconsin-Madison, 2008.

Breuer, Lee. *Sister Suzie Cinema: The Collected Poems and Performances*. New York: Theatre Communications Group, 1987.

Brockett, Oscar G., and Frank Hildy. *History of the Theatre*. 9th ed. Boston: Pearson, 2003.

Brook, Peter. *The Empty Space*. New York: Macmillan, 1968.

Brown, John Mason. "The Play: The Green Pastures" (review). *New York Evening Post*, February 27, 1930, 12.

Buckley, Tom. "In the Beginning, Miller's 'Creation'. . . ." *New York Times*, December 5, 1972, 67.

Burke, Tom. "Just a Guy Who Can't Say Noah." *New York Times*, November 8, 1970, Arts 1, 3.

Carlson, Marvin. *The Haunted Stage*. Ann Arbor: University of Michigan Press, 2003.

Chansky, Dorothy. "North American Passion Plays: 'The Greatest Story Ever Told' in the New Millennium." TDR 50, no. 4 (2006): 120–45.

Chidester, David. *Authentic Fakes: Religion and American Popular Culture*. Berkeley: University of California Press, 2005.

Choi, Seokhun. "Performing the Passion of the Christ in Postmodernity: American Passion/Passion Plays as Ritual and Postmodern Theatre." Diss., University of Kansas, 2012.

"Churches Ask Lord of 'Green Pastures' to Be Their Guest." *New York Herald Tribune*, undated, circa October 1930. *The Green Pastures* clipping file, New York Public Library for the Performing Arts.

Ciardi, John. "The Birth of A Classic." *Saturday Review*, March 8, 1958. *J.B.* clipping file, New York Public Library for the Performing Arts.

Cimino, Richard, Nadia A. Mian, and Weishan Huang, eds. *Ecologies of Faith in New York City: The Evolution of Religious Institutions*. Bloomington: Indiana University Press, 2012.

Cody, Gabrielle, and Evert Sprinchorn, eds. *Columbia Encyclopedia of Modern Drama*. Vol. 1. New York: Columbia University Press, 2007.

Coe, Richard L. "Confusion in Eden" (review). *Washington Post*, October 23, 1972. *The Creation of the World* clipping file, New York Public Library for the Performing Arts.

Cohen, Robert. *Theatre*. 7th edition. New York: McGraw-Hill, 2006.

Cohen, Sarah Blacher. *From Hester Street to Hollywood: The Jewish-American Stage and Screen*. Bloomington: Indiana University Press, 1983.

Condon, Joey A. "An Examination into the History and Present Interrelationship between the Church and the Theatre Exemplified by the Manhattan Church of the Nazarene, the Lambs Club, and the Lamb's Theatre Company as a Possible Paradigm." Master's thesis, University of Missouri–Kansas City, 2007.

Connelly, Marc. *The Green Pastures*. New York: Holt, Rinehart and Winston, 1930.

Connelly, Marc. *Voices Offstage: A Book of Memoirs*. New York: Holt, Rinehart and Winston, 1968.

Cooke, Richard. "Skulnik as Noah." *Wall Street Journal*, December 30, 1954. *The Flowering Peach* clipping file, New York Public Library for the Performing Arts.

Corbin, John. "Drama." *New York Times*, March 4, 1919, 8.

Corbin, John. "Job and His Adversary's Book." *New York Times*, March 9, 1919, 46.

Cornell University Legal Information Institute. "Mandamus." December 2, 2014. www.law.cornell.edu/wex/mandamus.

Cox, Harvey. *The Feast of Fools: A Theological Essay on Festivity and Fantasy*. Cambridge: Harvard University Press, 1969.

Crowther, Bosley. "Pastures Green for All." *New York Times*, April 28, 1935, X2.

Croyden, Margaret. "The Box-Office Boom." *New York Times*, May 10, 1981, magazine.

Csapo, Eric C., and Margaret C. Miller, eds. *The Origins of Theatre in Ancient Greece and Beyond: From Ritual to Drama*. New York: Cambridge University Press, 2007.

Daiches, David. "Is This Jewish Humor?" *Commentary*, January.

Daniel, Walter C. *"De Lawd": Richard B. Harrison and "The Green Pastures."* New York: Greenwood Press, 1986.

Dash, Thomas R. "The Flowering Peach" (review). *Women's Wear Daily*, December 30, 1954, 27.

de Giere, Carol. *Defying Gravity: The Creative Career of Stephen Schwartz from Godspell to Wicked*. New York: Applause Books, 2008.

Derecho, Abigail. "Archontic Literature: A Definition, a History, and Several Theories of Fan Fiction." In Karen Hellekson and Kristina Busse, eds., *Fan Fiction and Fan Communities in the Age of the Internet*, 61–78. Jefferson, N.C.: McFarland, 2006.

Dietz, Dan. *Off Broadway Musicals, 1910–2007.* Jefferson, N.C.: McFarland, 2010.

Dolgopolski, Sergei. *What Is Talmud? The Art of Disagreement.* New York: Fordham University Press, 2009.

Donnelly, Tom. "You Were Expecting Maybe Bernard Shaw?" *Washington Times,* November 23, 1954. *The Flowering Peach* clipping file, New York Public Library for the Performing Arts.

Downing, Robert. "J.B.'s Journeys." *Theatre Arts,* February 1960, 29.

Dox, Donalee. *The Idea of the Theater in Latin Christian Thought.* Ann Arbor: University of Michigan Press, 2009.

"Dramatic and Musical." *New York Times,* April 10, 1900, 7.

Eaton, Hal. "Skulnik Magnificent In Flowering Peach." *Long Island Daily Press,* December 29, 1954. *The Flowering Peach* clipping file, New York Public Library for the Performing Arts.

[Editorial]. *New York Times,* May 24, 1896, 4.

Eisen, Max. "Hailie Selassie Approves Sending of Lion for Premiere of 'I'm Solomon.'" Press release, April 18, 1968. *I'm Solomon* clipping file, New York Public Library for the Performing Arts.

"Elaborate Production of Lew Wallace's Dramatized Story." *New York Globe-Democrat,* December 2, 1899. *Ben-Hur* clipping file, New York Public Library for the Performing Arts.

Enders, Jody. *Rhetoric and the Origins of Medieval Drama.* Ithaca: Cornell University Press, 1992.

Evans, Curtis J. *The Burden of Black Religion.* Oxford: Oxford University Press, 2008.

Fergusson, Francis. *The Idea of a Theater.* Garden City, N.Y.: Doubleday Anchor Books, 1958 [1949].

"First Play Produced under All-Negro WPA Administration Due This Month." *Norfolk Journal and Guide,* September 19, 1936, 4.

Fischer, Heinz-Dietrich. *The Pulitzer Prize Archive.* Vol. 22: *Chronicle of the Pulitzer Prizes for Drama.* Munich: K.G. Saur Verlag, 2008.

Fiske, Minnie Maddern. "Mrs. Fiske Promises a Dignified Production." *Brooklyn Daily Eagle,* October 26, 1902. *Mary of Magdala* clipping file, New York Public Library for the Performing Arts.

Flatley, Guy. "They Wrote It and They're Glad." *New York Times,* October 31, 1971, D1.

Fletcher, John. *Preaching to Convert.* Ann Arbor: University of Michigan Press, 2013.

Fliotsos, Anne E., and Wendy Vierow. *American Women Stage Directors of the Twentieth Century.* Champaign: University of Illinois Press, 2008.

"The Flowering Peach" (review). *New Yorker,* January 8, 1955. *The Flowering Peach* clipping file, New York Public Library for the Performing Arts.

Forster, Arnold, and Benjamin Epstein. *The New Anti-Semitism.* New York: McGraw-Hill, 1974.

Gallee, W. B. "Essentially Contested Concepts." *Proceedings of the Aristotelian Society* 56 (1956): 169.

Garey, Doris B. "The Green Pastures Again." *Phylon Quarterly* 20, no. 2 (1959): 193–194.

Garland, Robert. "'Noah' a New Picture of Flood Patriarch." *New York World-Telegraph*, February 28, 1935, 24.

Garland, Robert. "'Noah,' a Unique Play, Opens at Longacre.'" *New York Herald-Tribune*, February 14, 1935, 24.

Garland, Robert. "Green Pastures" (review). *New York Telegram*, February 27, 1930, 12.

Geisler, Norman L. *Decide for Yourself: How History Views the Bible.* Eugene, Ore.: Wipf and Stock, 1982.

Glenn, Cerise L. "The Power of Black Magic: The Magical Negro and White Salvation in Film." *Journal of Black Studies* 40, no. 2 (November 2009): 135–152.

Glover, William. "Arthur Miller Deplores 'Heroic' Letdown." Associated Press wire story, September 12, 1972. *The Creation of the World* clipping file, New York Public Library for the Performing Arts.

Glover, William. "Hard Job Being God" (review). Associated Press, May 15, 1972, *Hard Job Being God* clipping file, New York Public Library for the Performing Arts.

Goldman, William. *The Season: A Candid Look at Broadway.* New York: Harcourt, Brace and World, 1969.

Goodman, Martin, ed. *The Oxford Handbook of Jewish Studies.* New York: Oxford University Press, 2002.

Gottfried, Martin. "The Apple Tree" (review). *Women's Wear Daily*, October 19, 1966. In *New York Theatre Critics' Reviews* 27, no. 13 (October 24, 1966): 265.

Gottfried, Martin. "The Creation of the World and Other Business" (review). *Women's Wear Daily*, December 4, 1972. In *New York Theatre Critics' Reviews* 33, no. 24 (December 11, 1972): 152.

Gottfried, Martin. "I'm Solomon" (review). *Women's Wear Daily*, April 24, 1968. In *New York Theatre Critics' Reviews* 29, no. 11 (April 29, 1968): 297.

Gottfried, Martin. "Neil Simon's Latest." *New York Post*, December 12, 1974. In *New York Theatre Critics' Reviews* 35, no. 22 (December 9, 1974): 148.

Gottfried, Martin. "Two by Two" (review). *Women's Wear Daily*, November 12, 1970. In *New York Theatre Critics' Reviews* 31, no. 22 (November 16, 1970): 161.

Gottfried, Martin. "Will the 'Godspell' Work on Broadway?" *New York Post*, June 23, 1976. In *New York Theatre Critics' Reviews* 37, no. 14 (June 21, 1976): 219.

Grant, Rev. Percy Stickney. "Mrs. Fiske's 'Mary of Magdala'" (review). *Critic* 41 (July–December 1902): 533.

"'Green Pastures' Reaches 500th Showing Friday." *New York Herald Tribune*, April 26, 1931. *The Green Pastures* clipping file, New York Public Library for the Performing Arts.

"The Green Pastures" Souvenir Program, 1932 National Tour. Billy Rose Theatre Collection, New York Public Library for the Performing Arts.

Gruen, John. "'Do You Mind Critics Calling You Cheap, Decadent, Sensationalistic, Gimmicky, Vulgar, Overinflated, Megalomaniacal?' 'I Don't Read Reviews Very Much' Answers Tom O'Horgan." *New York Times Magazine*, January 2, 1972, 68.

Gussow, Mel. "A Biblical Twist." *New York Times*, November 19, 1981, C21.

Gussow, Mel. "'Superstar' a Hit before Opening." *New York Times*, October 12, 1971, 48.

Hamilton, Clayton. "News of the Theatres" (review). *Brooklyn Eagle*, November 23, 1902, 40.

Hamilton, Clayton. *The Theory of the Theatre.* New York: Henry Holt, 1910.

Hariss, R. P. "I'm Solomon" (review). *Baltimore New American*, March 21, 1968. *I'm Solomon* clipping file, New York Public Library for the Performing Arts.

Hatch, Nathan O., and Mark A. Noll, eds. *The Bible in America: Essays in Cultural History.* New York: Oxford University Press, 1982.

"Heaven on Earth." *Time* 25, no. 9 (March 4, 1935): 43–48.

Heinemann, Margot. *Puritanism and Theatre.* Cambridge: Cambridge University Press, 1982.

Heyse, Paul. *Mary of Magdala: An Historical and Romantic Drama in Five Acts, the Original in German Prose by Paul Heyse, the Translation Freely Adapted and Written in English verse by William Winter.* New York, Macmillan, 1903.

Hischak, Thomas. *Broadway Plays and Musicals.* Jefferson, N.C.: McFarland, 2009.

Hornblow, Arthur. *A History of the Theatre in America from its Beginnings to the Present Time.* New York: B. Blom, 1919.

Houchin, John. *Censorship of the American Theatre in the Twentieth Century.* Cambridge: Cambridge University Press, 2003.

"How General Lew Wallace's Famous Novel Was Turned into a Religio-Historic Spectacle." *New York Herald*, November 5, 1899. *Ben-Hur* clipping file, New York Public Library for the Performing Arts.

Huffman, James R. "Jesus Christ Superstar—Popular Art and Unpopular Criticism." *Journal of Popular Culture* 6, no. 2 (1972): 259–269.

Hughes, Alice. "A Woman's New York." King Features Syndicate, January 7, 1955. *The Flowering Peach* clipping file, New York Public Library for the Performing Arts.

Hughes, Amy. *Spectacles of Reform*. Ann Arbor: University of Michigan Press, 2012.

Hughes, Langston. *The Big Sea: An Autobiography*. Columbia: University of Missouri Press, 2002 [1940].

Huneker, James. "Mary of Magdala" (review). *New York Sun*, November 20, 1902. *Mary of Magdala* clipping file, New York Public Library for the Performing Arts.

Hutcheon, Linda. *A Theory of Adaptation*. 2nd ed. London: Routledge, 2013 [2006].

Hyams, Barry. "NYC Exclusive to Lewis Funke." Press release. *The Flowering Peach* clipping file, New York Public Library for the Performing Arts.

Isherwood, Charles. "A Glitzy Execution in a Religious Revival: 'Jesus Christ Superstar' at the Neil Simon Theater." *New York Times*, March 22, 2012, C1.

Isherwood, Charles. "A Vision of Spirituality Returns to Broadway." *New York Times*, November 7, 2011, C1.

Israel Broadcast Service. *Vistas of Israel: Program # 243, Songs from "The King and the Cobbler" at the Cameri Theatre*. Sound recording, circa 1965. Judaica Sound Archives, Florida Atlantic University. June 1, 2014. faujsa.fau.edu/jsa.

Jakobsen, Janet R., and Ann Pellegrini, eds. *Secularisms*. Durham: Duke University Press, 2008.

Jeff Fenholt official website. June 1, 2014. www.jefffenholt.com.

Jeffrey, David L., ed. *A Dictionary of Biblical Tradition in English Literature*. Grand Rapids: William B. Eerdmans, 1992.

Jenkins, Henry. *Textual Poachers: Television Fans and Participatory Culture*. London: Routledge, 2003.

Jenkins, Henry. *The Wow Climax: Tracing the Emotional Impact of Popular Culture*. New York: New York University Press, 2007.

"Jesus Christ Superstar Opera Hit." *Jewish Transcript*, October 28, 1971, 5.

Jolo. "Stuart Walker Players." *Variety*, March 7, 1919, 16.

Jones, John Bush. *Our Musicals, Ourselves: A Social History of the American Musical Theatre*. Hanover: Brandeis University Press, 2003.

Jones, Megan Sanborn. "Performing Mormon History." *Journal of Mormon History* 35, no. 3 (Summer 2009): 204–208.

Jones, Megan Sanborn. "(Re)living the Pioneer Past: Mormon Youth Handcart Trek Re-enactments." *Theatre Topics* 16, no. 2 (September 2006): 112–130.

Kalem, T. E. "The Theater: Adam and Evil" (review). *Time*, December 11, 1972. In *New York Theatre Critics' Reviews* 33, no. 24 (December 11, 1972): 152.

Kallman, Helmut. "Os-ke-non-ton." *The Canadian Encyclopedia*. May 25, 2014. www.thecanadianencyclopedia.ca/en/article/os-ke-non-ton/.

Kazan, Elia. *Kazan: A Life*. New York: Random House, 1988.

Kennedy, Charles Ramm. *The Terrible Meek: A One-Act Stage Play for Three Voices: To Be Played in Darkness*. New York: Harper and Brothers, 1912.

Kerr, Walter. "A Critic Likes the Opera, Loathes the Production" (review). *New York Times*, October 24, 1971, D1.

Kerr, Walter. "Theater: 'The Apple Tree,' Three Playlets, Opens." *New York Times*, October 19, 1966. In *New York Theatre Critics' Reviews* 27, no. 13 (October 24, 1966): 262.

Kerr, Walter. "Why Make St. Matthew Dance? Just for the Fun of It." *New York Times*, May 30, 1971, 2:9.

Kirshenblatt-Gimblett, Barbara. "'Contraband': Performance, Text and Analysis of a 'Purim-Shpil.'" *TDR* 24, no. 3 (September 1980): 5–16.

Kirshenblatt-Gimblett, Barbara. *Destination Culture: Tourism, Museums, and Heritage*. Berkeley: University of California Press, 1998.

Kissell, Howard. "God's Favorite" (review). *Women's Wear Daily*, December 13, 1974. In *New York Theatre Critics' Reviews* 35, no. 22 (December 9, 1974): 145.

Kobialka, Michal. *This Is My Body: Representational Practices in the Early Middle Ages*. Ann Arbor: University of Michigan Press, 1999.

Kolitz, Zvi. Letter to Ethiopian Mission to UN, January 17, 1968. *I'm Solomon* clipping file, New York Public Library for the Performing Arts.

Kolitz, Zvi. Letter to Sam Zolotow, February 1, 1965. *I'm Solomon* clipping file, New York Public Library for the Performing Arts.

Konas, Gary, ed. *Neil Simon: A Casebook*. New York: Garland, 1997.

Kroll, Jack. "The Patience of Joe." *Newsweek*, December 23, 1974. In *New York Theatre Critics' Reviews* 35, no. 22 (December 9, 1974): 147.

Kroll, Jack. "Theater" (review). *Newsweek*, October 25, 1971. In *New York Theatre Critics' Reviews* 32, no. 15 (October 31, 1971): 243.

Kroll, Jack. "Theater" (review). *Newsweek*, December 11, 1972. In *New York Theatre Critics' Reviews* 33, no. 24 (December 11, 1972): 151.

Kushner, Harold S. *The Book of Job: When Bad Things Happened to a Good Person*. New York: Schocken, 2012.

"Lafayette Opens Fall Season with Noah." *New York Amsterdam News*, September 19, 1936, 8.

Laird, Paul R. *The Musical Theater of Stephen Schwartz: From "Godspell" to "Wicked"*. Lanham, Md.: Rowman and Littlefield, 2014.

Laird, Paul R. *"Wicked": A Musical Biography*. Lanham, Md.: Scarecrow Press, 2011.

Lambert, Virginia. "Odets's Noah Lands the Ark in the Bronx." *Bergen County Record*, December 23, 1974. *The Flowering Peach* clipping file, New York Public Library for the Performing Arts.

Leeds, Josiah W. *The Theatre: An Essay upon the Non-accordancy of Stage-Plays with the Christian Profession*. 3rd ed. Philadelphia: "published for the author," 1886.

Leitch, Thomas. "Adaptation Studies at a Crossroads." *Adaptation* 1, no. 1 (March 2008): 63-77.

Levy, Shimon. *The Bible as Theatre*. Brighton: Sussex Academic Press, 2000.

Levy, Shimon. *Theatre and Holy Script*. Brighton: Sussex Academic Press, 1999.

Lifson, Amy. "Ben-Hur." *Humanities* 30, no. 6 (November–December 2009). December 1, 2014. www.neh.gov/humanities/2009/novemberdecember/feature/ben-hur.

Lipton, James. "Neil Simon, The Art of Theater No. 10" (interview). *Paris Review* 125 (Winter 1992). May 25, 2014. www.theparisreview.org.

Lloyd Webber, Andrew. *Jesus Christ Superstar* (sound recording). MCA / Decca Records, 1970. CD.

Lloyd Webber, Andrew. *Joseph and the Amazing Technicolor Dreamcoat* (cantata). Recorded by the Joseph Consortium. Originally released 1969 by Scepter Records. Rereleased by Gusto Records, 2010. MP3.

Lloyd Webber, Andrew. *Joseph and the Amazing Technicolor Dreamcoat* (Original Broadway Cast). Chrysalis Records, 1982. LP.

Lundell, William Warner. "Marc Connelly Speaks His Mind: The Author of the Green Pastures Discusses the Art of Playwriting." *New York World*, September 7, 1930. *The Green Pastures* clipping file, New York Public Library for the Performing Arts.

Mackay, Constance D'Arcy. *The Little Theatre in the United States*. New York: Henry Holt, 1917.

MacLeish, Archibald. *J.B.* New York: Houghton Mifflin, 1956.

MacLeish, Archibald. *J.B.: A Play in Verse*. New York: Samuel French, 1958.

Mantle, Burns. "Darkey Lord Takes Kindly to Fried Fish." *New York Herald Tribune*, March 9, 1930. *The Green Pastures* clipping file, New York Public Library for the Performing Arts.

Martel, Tom. *Hard Job Being God, Original Cast Album*. GWP Records, 1971. LP.

"Mary of Magdala" (review). *Boston Herald*, March 31, 1903. *Mary of Magdala* clipping file, New York Public Library for the Performing Arts.

"'Mary of Magdala' a Great Drama" (review). *Brooklyn Eagle*, November 20, 1902. *Mary of Magdala* clipping file, New York Public Library for the Performing Arts.

Matthews, Ralph. "Noah Has Hard Time; So Does the Audience." *Afro American*, October 17, 1936, 13.

Mayer, David, ed. *Playing Out the Empire: Ben-Hur and Other Toga Plays and Films, 1883–1908. A Critical Anthology*. Oxford: Clarendon Press, 1994.

McClain, John. "J.B." (review). *New York Journal-American*, December 29, 1958. In *New York Theatre Critics' Reviews* 19, no. 25 (December 31, 1958): 169.

McConachie, Bruce. *American Theater in the Culture of the Cold War: Pro-*

ducing and Contesting Containment, 1947–1962. Iowa City: University of Iowa Press, 2003.

McGovern, Edythe M. *Not-So-Simple Neil Simon: A Critical Study.* Van Nuys, CA: Perviale Press, 1978.

McHarry, Charles. Untitled notice. *New York Daily News,* January 6, 1968. *I'm Solomon* clipping file, New York Public Library for the Performing Arts.

Mee, Susie. "Chekhov's 'Three Sisters' and the Wooster Group's 'Brace Up!'" *TDR* 36, 4 (Winter 1992): 143–153.

Migliore, Daniel L. "Godspell" (review). *Theology Today* 28, no. 3 (October 1971): 389–390.

Miller, Arthur. *The Creation of the World and Other Business.* New York: Dramatists Play Service, 1998 [1972].

Miller, Arthur. *Timebends: A Life.* New York: Grove Press, 1987.

Mitgang, Herbert. "Odets Goes to Genesis." *New York Times,* December 26, 1954, X1.

Mordden, Ethan. *One More Kiss: The Broadway Musical in the 1970s.* New York: Palgrave, 2003.

Moreman, Christopher. "Devil Music and the Great Beast: Ozzy Osbourne, Aleister Crowley, and the Christian Right." *Journal of Religion and Popular Culture* 5, no. 1 (Fall 2003). http://utpjournals.metapress.com.

Morgan, David. *Visual Piety.* Berkeley: University of California Press, 1998.

Morse, Salmi. *The Passion: A Miracle Play in Ten Acts.* San Francisco: E. Bosqui, 1879.

Most, Andrea. *Making Americans: Jews and the Broadway Musical.* Cambridge: Harvard University Press, 2004.

Most, Andrea. *Theatrical Liberalism: Jews and Popular Entertainment in America.* New York: New York University Press, 2013.

Moulton, Richard G., ed. *The Book of Job.* London: Macmillan, 1896.

"Mrs. Fiske in 'Mary of Magdala'" (review). *New York Times,* November 20, 1902, 9.

Musser, Charles. "Passions and the Passion Play: Theatre, Film, and Religion in America, 1880–1900." *Film History* 5 (1993): 419–456.

Nahshon, Edna. "Going against the Grain: Jews and Passion Plays on the Mainstream American Stage." In Edna Nahshon, ed., *Jews and Theater in an Intercultural Context,* 67–100. Boston: Brill, 2012.

Nelson, Stephen. "Broadway and the Beast." *TDR* 39, no. 2 (Summer 1995): 71–78.

"New Deal on Ararat." *Stage,* April 1935, 16.

Nicoll, Allardyce. *The Development of the Theatre.* 5th ed. New York: Harcourt, Brace and World, 1967.

Nielsen, Alan. "Salmi Morse's Passion, 1879–1884: The History and Consequences of a Theatrical Obsession." Diss., City University of New York, 1989.

"Noah" (review). *Time*, February 25, 1935. *Noah* clipping file, New York Public Library for the Performing Arts.

Nordell, Roderick. "Kaye Opens Season as Noah." *Christian Science Monitor*. *Two by Two* clipping file, New York Public Library for the Performing Arts.

Norton, David. *A History of the English Bible as Literature*. Cambridge: Cambridge University Press, 2000.

Norton, Elliott. "J.B." (review). *Boston Record*, April 29, 1958. *J.B.* clipping file, New York Public Library for the Performing Arts.

Nouryeh, Andrea. "When the Lord Was a Black Man: A Fresh Look at the Life of Richard Berry Harrison." *Black American Literature Forum* 16, no. 4 (Winter 1982): 142–146.

Obey, André. *Noah*. Trans. Arthur Wilmurt. New York: Samuel French, 1935.

O'Connor, John J. "The Theater." *Wall Street Journal*, November 12, 1970. In *New York Theatre Critics' Reviews* 31, no. 22 (November 16, 1970): 164.

Odets, Clifford. *The Flowering Peach*. New York: Dramatists Play Service, 1954.

Oppenheimer, George. "On Stage." *Newsday*, February 4, 1955. *The Flowering Peach* clipping file, New York Public Library for the Performing Arts.

Otten, Terry. *The Temptation of Innocence in the Plays of Arthur Miller*. Columbia: University of Missouri Press, 2002.

Ottley, Roi. "Negro Theatre 'Noah' Seems at Sea, Says Reviewer in Account." *New York Amsterdam News*, October 10, 1936, 10.

Palm, Matthew. "Children of Eden" (review). *Orlando Sentinel*, August 9, 2012. Via digital archive.

"The Passion Play Given." *New York Times*, March 31, 1883, 1.

"The Passion Play Read." *New York Times*, December 4, 1880, 2.

Patterson, Orlando. "Our Overrated Inner Self." *New York Times*, December 26, 2006, A35.

Probst, Leonard. "Godspell" (review). NBC radio. In *New York Theatre Critics' Reviews* 37, no. 14 (June 21, 1976): 220.

Prothero, Stephen. *American Jesus: How the Son of God Became a National Icon*. New York: Farrar, Straus and Giroux, 2003.

Puchner, Marin. *Stage Fright: Modernism Anti-theatricality and Drama*. Baltimore: Johns Hopkins University Press, 2002.

"Religion: J.B. vs Job." *Time* 73, no. 15 (April 13, 1959): 97.

"Religious Subjects as Matter for Dramatic Treatment." *New York Times*, December 16, 1906, X2.

Richards, David. "God Serves Scrambled Eggs" (review). *Washington Evening Star*, October 23, 1972, D6.

Rice, Tim, and Andrew Lloyd Webber. *Jesus Christ Superstar: The Authorized Version*. Compiled by Michael Braun with Richard Eckford and Peter Simpson. London: Pan Books, 1972.

Rodgers, Richard, and Martin Charnin. *Two by Two: Original Broadway Cast Recording*. Sony Broadway, 1992 [1970], CD.

Rozik, Eli. *The Roots of Theatre: Rethinking Ritual and Other Theories of Origin*. Iowa City: University of Iowa Press, 2002.

Rowe, Billy. "Presentation of 'Noah' Ineffective Says Billy Rowe." *Pittsburgh Courier*, October 17, 1936, A10.

Rudnick, Paul. *The Most Fabulous Story Ever Told*. New York: Dramatists Play Service, 1999.

Ruhl, Arthur. "Second Nights." *New York Herald Tribune*, February 17, 1935. *Noah* clipping file, New York Public Library for the Performing Arts.

Ruhl, Arthur. "The Green Pastures" (review). *New York Herald Tribune*, February 27, 1930. *The Green Pastures* clipping file, New York Public Library for the Performing Arts.

"Salmi Morse Determined: The Mayor Refuses a License and a Mandamus Threatened." *New York Times*, December 30, 1882, 2.

"Salmi Morse Discharged." *New York Times*, March 14, 1883, 3.

"Salmi Morse's Surrender." *New York Times*, April 17, 1883, 8.

Sanders, Kevin. "The Creation of the World and Other Business" (review). WABC-TV, November 30, 1972. In *New York Theatre Critics' Reviews* 33, no. 24 (December 11, 1972): 153.

Savran, David. "Toward a Historiography of the Popular." *Theatre Survey*, November 2004, 211–217.

Schiff, Ellen. *From Stereotype to Metaphor: The Jew in Contemporary Drama*. Albany: SUNY Press, 1983.

Schneider, Rebecca. *Performance Remains*. London: Routledge, 2011.

Scholem, Richard J. "I'm Solomon" (review). Greater New York Radio, May 16, 1968. *I'm Solomon* clipping file, New York Public Library for the Performing Arts.

Schwartz, Stephen. *Godspell: A Musical Based on the Gospel according to Saint Matthew*. Original Off-Broadway Cast Recording. Arista Records, 1974. CD.

Schwartz, Stephen. *Godspell: A Musical Based on the Gospel According to Saint Matthew*. Vocal score. New York: Hansen, 1973.

Schwartz, Stephen. "Godspell Songs: Stephen Schwartz Answers Questions about the *Godspell* Score." StephenSchwartz.com. 2010. December 25, 2014. www.stephenschwartz.com.

Scott, Clement. "Clement Scott Sees the Wallace Drama" (review of *Ben-Hur*). *New York Herald*, November 30, 1899. *Ben-Hur* clipping file, New York Public Library for the Performing Arts.

Scott, Clement. "The Playhouses." *Illustrated London News*, January 26, 1896, 92.

Segers, Frank. "'Two by Two' Now an 'Entertainment' and Audiences Love It, Sez Danny." *Variety*, May 26, 1971. *Two by Two* clipping file, New York Public Library for the Performing Arts.

Seldes, Gilbert. "The New Play: The Green Pastures" (review). *Evening Graphic*, February 27, 1930, 22.

Seldes, Gilbert. "'Noah'—from the French" (review). *New York American*, February 14, 1935, 16.

Seligsohn, Leo. "Arthur Miller on the Eve of Creation." *Newsday*, November 26, 1972, 4–5.

Sheaffer, Louis. "Odets Retells Noah Story with Fresh, Warm Humor." *Brooklyn Eagle*, December 29, 1954. *The Flowering Peach* clipping file, New York Public Library for the Performing Arts.

Shimakawa, Karen. *National Abjection: The Asian American Body Onstage.* Durham: Duke University Press, 2002.

"The Sign of the Cross" (review). *Boston Transcript*, October 27, 1897. *The Sign of the Cross* clipping file, New York Public Library for the Performing Arts.

"The Sign of the Cross" (review). *Illustrated American*, November 28, 1896. *The Sign of the Cross* clipping file, New York Public Library.

"The Sign of the Cross" (review). *Memphis Commercial Appeal*, April 16, 1895. *The Sign of the Cross* clipping file, New York Public Library.

"The Sign of the Cross" (review). *New York Times*, November 10, 1896, 5.

Simon, Neil. *Collected Plays of Neil Simon.* Vol. 2. New York: Plume, 1986.

Sofer, Andrew. *Dark Matter: Invisibility in Drama, Theater, and Performance.* Ann Arbor: University of Michigan Press, 2013.

Soloveitchik, Joseph B. *The Lonely Man of Faith.* New York: Doubleday, 2006.

Sponsler, Claire. *Ritual Imports: Performing Medieval Drama in America.* Ithaca: Cornell University Press, 2004.

Stanford University Bulletin 3, no. 29 (March 15, 1920).

Stark, Gary D. *Banned in Berlin: Literary Censorship in Imperial Germany, 1871–1918.* New York: Berghahn Books, 2009.

Stern, David, and Mark Jay Mirsky, eds. *Rabbinic Fantasies: Imaginative Narratives from Hebrew Classical Literature.* New Haven: Yale University Press, 1998.

Stern, Harold. "Showtime." *The American Hebrew*, undated, circa January 1955. *The Flowering Peach* clipping file, New York Public Library for the Performing Arts.

Stern, Norton B., and William Kramer. "The Strange Passion of Salmi Morse." *Western States Jewish History* 16, no. 4 (July 1984): 336–347.

Sternfeld, Jessica. *The Megamusical.* Bloomington: Indiana University Press, 2006.

Stevenson, Jill. *Sensational Devotion: Evangelical Performance in Twenty-First-Century America.* Ann Arbor: University of Michigan Press, 2013.

Stratton, Matthew. *The Politics of Irony in American Modernism.* New York: Fordham University Press, 2014.

Sullivan, Mark. "'More Popular Than Jesus': The Beatles and the Religious Far Right." *Popular Music* 6, no. 3 (October 1987): 313–326.

Sunday, Billy. "'Ben-Hur' Appeals to Billy Sunday." *Morning Telegraph*, November 6, 1916. *Ben-Hur* clipping file, New York Public Library for the Performing Arts.

"The Theatre: Thinking Big, Thinking Little." *New Yorker*, May 4, 1968, 129.

"A Theatric Version of the Book of Job." *New York Times*, March 8, 1918, 9.

"Thomas Mosely Praised for Role in 'Noah.'" *Norfolk Journal and Guide*, October 24, 1936, 4.

Thomas, Bronwen. "What Is Fanfiction and Why Are People Saying Such Nice Things about It?" *StoryWorlds* 3 (2001): 1–24.

Thomas, Robert Mc.G., Jr. "Carlton Moss, 88, Who Filmed the Black Experience, Dies." *New York Times*, August 15, 1997.

"Three Opinions on 'J.B.'" *Life* 46, no. 20 (May 18, 1959): 135–138.

Times Square Church official website. April 18, 2014. www.tsnyc.org.

Trilling, Lionel. *Sincerity and Authenticity*. Cambridge: Harvard University Press, 1971.

Twain, Mark. *Eve's Diary*. London: Harper and Brothers, 1906.

Twain, Mark. *Extracts from Adam's Diary*. New York: Harper and Brothers, 1904.

Van. N., J. J. "The Green Pastures" (review). Undated, circa 1932. *The Green Pastures* clipping file, New York Public Library for the Performing Arts.

Variety, December 20, 1972. *The Creation of the World* clipping file, New York Public Library for the Performing Arts.

Walker, Stuart. "'Job' Really Modern." *New York Tribune*, March 3, 1918, D5.

Walker, Stuart. *Portmanteau Plays*. Cincinnati: Stewart & Kidd, 1917.

Wallace, Lew. *Ben-Hur: A Tale of the Christ*. Ed. David Mayer. New York: Oxford University Press, 1998 [1880].

Walls, Rev. Alfred. *The Oldest Drama in the World: The Book of Job Arranged in Dramatic Form with Elucidations*. New York: Hunt & Eaton, 1891.

Walsh, Michael. *Andrew Lloyd Webber: His Life and Works*. Updated ed. New York: Harry N. Abrams, 1997.

Watt, Douglas. "'God's Favorite' Is Awesomely Funny." *New York Daily News*, December 12, 1974. In *New York Theatre Critics' Reviews* 35, no. 22 (December 9, 1974): 145.

Watt, Douglas. "*Godspell* Reaches Broadway." *New York Daily News*, June 23, 1976. In *New York Theatre Critics' Reviews* 37, no. 14 (June 21, 1976): 218.

Watt, Douglas. "'Jesus Christ Superstar' Is Full of Life, Vibrant with Reverence" (review). *New York Daily News*, October 13, 1971. In *New York Theatre Critics' Reviews* 32, no. 15 (October 31, 1971): 242.

Watt, Douglas. "Miller's 'Creation of the World' Is a Plodding Comedy-Drama" (review). *Daily News*, December 1, 1972. In *New York Theatre Critics' Reviews* 33, no. 24 (December 11, 1972): 151.

Watts, Richard, Jr. "Sight and Sound." *New York Herald Tribune*, March 12, 1930, 16.

Watts, Richard, Jr. "Arthur Miller's 'Creation' Opens at Shubert Theater" (review). *New York Post*, December 1, 1972. In *New York Theatre Critics' Reviews* 33, no. 24 (December 11, 1972): 150

Watts, Richard, Jr. "Watts Looks at the New Plays." *New York Post*, December 29, 1958. In *New York Theatre Critics' Reviews* 19, no. 25 (December 31, 1958): 168.

Welland, Dennis. *Miller: A Study of His Plays*. London: Eyre Methuen, 1979.

Wetmore, Kevin. *Catholic Theatre and Drama: Critical Essays*. Jefferson, NC: McFarland, 2010.

WFA. "Ben-Hur" (review). *Boston Herald*, December 21, 1900. *Ben-Hur* clipping file, New York Public Library for the Performing Arts.

"What's New in the Theater." *New York Times*, November 15, 1970, D7.

Wilkerson, David. "God's House Turned Into a Den of Thieves." World Challenge Pulpit Series. May 31, 2014. sermons.worldchallenge.org/en/devotions/2010/gods-house-turned-into-a-den-of-thieves.

Wilmer, S. E. *Theatre, Society and the Nation: Staging American Identities*. Cambridge: Cambridge University Press, 2002.

Wilmurt, Arthur. "On 'Noah' and 'The Green Pastures.'" *New York Times*, March 3, 1935, X2.

Wilson, Derek. *The People's Bible: The Remarkable History of the King James Version*. London: Lion Books, 2013.

Wilson, Edwin. "Adam and Eve in the Garden" (review). *Wall Street Journal*, December 4, 1972. In *New York Theatre Critics' Reviews* 33, no. 24 (December 11, 1972): 152.

Winchell, Walter. "'Green Pastures' Artistic Triumph at the Mansfield." *New York Daily Mirror*, February 27, 1930. *The Green Pastures* clipping file, New York Public Library for the Performing Arts.

Witham, Barry. *The Federal Theatre Project: A Case Study*. Cambridge: Cambridge University Press, 2003.

Woledge, Elizabeth. "Decoding Desire: From Kirk and Spock to K/S." *Social Semiotics* 15, no. 2 (2005): 235–250.

Wolf, Stacy. *Changed for Good: A Feminist History of the Broadway Musical*. New York: Oxford University Press, 2011.

Wollman, Elizabeth L. "The Economic Development of the 'New' Times Square and Its Impact on the Broadway Musical." *American Music* 20, no. 4 (Winter 2002): 445–465.

Wollman, Elizabeth L. *The Theater Will Rock: A History of the Rock Musical, from "Hair" to "Hedwig."* Ann Arbor: University of Michigan Press, 2006.

Wyatt, Euphemia Van Rensselaer. "The Flowering Peach" (review). *Catholic World*, February 1955. *The Flowering Peach* clipping file, New York Public Library for the Performing Arts.

Zolotow, Sam. "Israeli Musical Due Here in Fall." *New York Times*, February 5, 1965, 37.

Index

Abbey, Henry, 1–2
Abel (biblical figure), 6, 66, 68, 84, 89, 92. *See also* Cain
Abraham (biblical figure), 24, 40–41, 67–68, 105, 108, 180–81
Abyssinian Baptist Church (New York), 69
Adam (biblical figure), 7, 41, 62–66, 68–69, 79–80, 83–84, 87–89, 170. *See also* Eve
adaptation, 3–4, 7–9, 14–16, 18–22, 24–26, 30–33, 35, 37–38, 40, 53, 60, 66, 73, 80, 88, 92–94, 102, 111–14, 125, 137, 144–45, 149–50, 160, 163, 174–77, 181–82; faithful adaptation, 20–21, 30, 57, 93, 114, 127, 154, 165, 171; unfaithful adaptation, 82–82, 114. *See also* fidelity criticism
affective response, 28, 44, 46, 79–50, 53, 59, 64, 150, 163, 167, 170, 181, 183
African-American performers, 6n24, 32, 64, 68–79, 85, 99–102, 136, 152, 156
After the Fall, 82
Ainsley, Paul, 150
Alda, Alan, 79, 80n65, 81n66
Alemany, (Most Reverend) Joseph S., 1
Almagor, Dan, 178
Alterman, Nathan, 176
amateur theater, 33, 110, 127, 159, 167–68
American Jewish Committee, 155
Amos (biblical figure), 180–81
Anderson, Carl, 147
Androcles and the Lion, 60
Angels in America, 11
angels, 67, 87, 107, 142, 149; Angel Gabriel, 68; Angel Moroni, 183. *See also* Lucifer
Annas (biblical figure), 148, 255
ANTA Theatre (52nd St), 125
Anti-Defamation League, 155–56

antitheatricalism, 12–13
apocalyptic literature, 114, 133, 181
apocrypha, 8–10, 174
apostles (biblical figures), 41, 52, 148–49, 151–52, 164
Apple Tree, The, 9, 64, 79–82, 84
Ararat (mountain), 92, 96, 102, 104, 106
Aronovsky, Darren, 114–15
Aronson, Boris, 132
Arrow, Margaret, 96
Atkinson, J. Brooks, 61n69, 70, 91, 96–98, 105, 107–8, 132
Austin, Mary, 65, 76, 78
authenticity, 26–30, 32–33, 38, 47, 50, 52–53, 56–59, 64, 66, 73–77, 81–82, 86–89, 94, 98–100, 102, 112–14, 123–24, 131, 138–40, 144, 150–51, 154, 157, 160, 163, 165–66, 170–71, 174, 178, 183, 185
Avenue Q, 182
Awake and Sing!, 94, 103, 105

Back to Methuselah, 60
Baker, Paul, 162
Baptists, 24, 69, 77, 162
Barcelo, Randy, 149
Barefoot in the Park, 135
Barish, Jonas, 13
Barnardo, Thomas John, 146
Barnes, Clive, 110, 112, 136, 158, 165, 176, 181
Barnette, Jane, 21n6, 49n36
Barrett, Wilson, 6–7, 51–53
Barrymore, John, 68
Barthes, Roland, 22
Batson, Ruth, 85
Batson, Susan, 84–85
Beggar on Horseback, 66
Belasco Theatre, 94, 105, 107, 109
Belasco, David, 1, 6, 39, 60, 120, 144n10, 166
Bellaver, Harry, 96

Ben Ami, R., 176

Ben-Hur, novel, 36–38, 42–47; stage play; 1, 6, 8, 10, 15, 28, 31, 33, 35–42, 47–51, 53, 55–60, 73

Benjamin, Walter, 22

Benthall, Michael, 177–78

Bernhardt, Sarah, 8

Bernstein, Leonard, 9

Beruh, Joe, 158

Biloxi Blues, 138

Bird, Robert Montgomery, 36

Bishpam, David, 123

Black Hills Passion Play, 127

blasphemy, 17–18, 23–25, 31, 38–39, 47, 50, 59, 60n67, 72–73, 127, 155, 163, 172, 182–33

Bloom, Michael, 22

Bloomberg, Michael, 141

Blyden, Larry, 79

Bock, Jerry, 9, 79–80

Bolick, Duane, 157

Book of Job, The (play), 32, 120–25, 130, 139, 176, 184

Book of Mormon, The (musical), 182–84

Booth Theatre (45th St), 121, 124

Booth's Theatre (23rd St), 1

Bosch, Jean L., 151n36, 154–55

Boyarin, Daniel, 40

Bradford, Roark, 66–67, 75, 77

Brecht, Bertolt, 21, 131

Brighton Beach Memoirs, 138

Broadhurst Theatre, 144, 159, 167

Broadhurst, Thomas, 55

Broadway Theatre (41st St), 37

Broken Glass, 82

Brook, Peter, 5, 19, 22n70

Brooklyn Academy of Music, 168

Brown, John Mason, 73

Brukenfeld, Dirk, 165

Buckler, Henry, 123

Bufano, Remo, 96

Bufman, Zev, 168

Burlar, Cora, 96

burning bush, 59, 68

Buttz, Henry A., 117

Caiaphas (biblical figure), 148, 255

Cain (biblical figure), 6, 66, 68, 83–84, 89, 92. *See also* Abel

Caine, Hall, 59

Caird, John, 170–71

Caldwell, Zoe, 83–85, 88 ill.

Cameri Theater (Tel Aviv), 176–77

Canaan, 40, 180

Canfield, F. Curtis, 126

Case of Philip Lawrence, The, 102

Cassidy, David, 169

Cat on a Hot Tin Roof, 93

Catholics, 1, 11–12, 23–24, 39–40, 107, 133, 152, 154, 170

Cats, 146

Chansky, Dorothy, 4, 155n47

Chapin, Harry, 172

Chautauqua circuits, 45, 70

Chayefsky, Paddy, 9

Cherry Lane Theatre, 144, 158, 160

Chidester, David, 150–52

childlike Negroes, 74–75, 78, 99, 183

Children of Eden, 33, 167, 170–71

A Chorus Line, 159

Christ, *see* Jesus Christ

Christian rock, 151, 157

Church of Jesus Christ of Latter-Day Saints, The, *see* Mormons

Church of the Ascension (New York), 58

Church, Catholic, *see* Catholics

churches, 4–5, 11, 56, 58–60, 67–70, 74, 77–78, 100–2, 141–45, 165, 169–72, 177; theater spaces turned into, 34, 141–44, 171–73

Ciardi, John, 125

Circle in the Square Theatre, 9, 160

Claudel, Paul, 75

Clurman, Harold, 84

Colonial Theatre (Boston), 49, 84

communion, 157, 163

communitas, 26

community, 3–5, 12–13, 14n49, 29, 83, 91, 159, 162–63, 165, 170, 181, 184; community-building, 41; community theater, 169–70

Company, 159

Condon, Joey, 172

Connelly, Marc, 8, 32, 62–78, 86, 97

Conway, Bert, 130

Cooke, Richard, 107

Copeau, Jacques, 94

Copeland, Carolyn Rossi, 172

Corbin, John, 123–24

Cotton Patch Gospel, 172

Cox, Harvey, 162

Creation of the World and Other Business, The, 32, 63, 81–90, 180

crisis of representation, 5, 22, 24, 27

Croswell, Anne, 177n14, 178
Crucible, The, 82
Crucifixion (biblical event), 18, 45, 51, 57, 60, 149, 157, 160n72, 163, 166
cycle plays, 91, 108. *See also* mystery plays

Daiches, David, 108
Dalton, Charles, 7, 52
Dash, Thomas R., 105, 107
Davis, Thurston N., SJ, 133
De Liagre, Alfred Jr., 126
Death of a Salesman, 11, 81–82
DeKay, John, 6, 8
di Somi, Leone, 118
Dishy, Bob, 83, 88 ill.
Dithmar, Edward A., 47
Do I Hear a Waltz?, 109
Doggett, Alan, 146
Don't Get God Started, 9
Donnelly, Tom, 105
Downing, Robert, 126
Dox, Donalee, 13
Driver, (Reverend) Tom T., 132
Du Bois, W. E.B., 69–70
Dulcy, 66
Dunbar, Paul Laurence
Dunsany, Lord, *see* Plunkett, Edward
Durkheim, Emile, 152

Eaton, Hal, 107
Eden, Garden of, 63–64, 75, 79, 81, 83–84, 88 ill., 89, 170
Edison Theatre, 179
Edward, Harry F. V., 100
Elliman, Yvonne, 147, 153 ill., 154–56
Elliott, Stephen, 81, 83, 88–90
Empire Theatre, 53
Enemy of the People, 81, 88
Entermedia Theatre, 168
Episcopalians, 58, 67, 70, 116, 158, 165
Epstein, Benjamin, 155–56
Erlanger, A. L., 37
Essman, Manuel, 100
Esther (biblical figure), 9, 11
Eternal Magdalene, The, 6
Eternal Road, The, 79
Eugene O'Neill Theatre, 182
Evangelicalism, 4, 27–28, 36, 151–52; evangelical dramaturgy, 27, 50
Evangelists, 50, 157
Evans, Curtis J., 73, 75, 77–79
Eve (biblical figure), 7, 41, 64, 68, 79–

81, 83–5, 87–89, 170. *See also* Adam
Exodus (1960 feature film), 177n14
Exodus, Book of, 6, 9, 38n7, 68, 79, 180

faith, 5, 11–12, 16, 21–26, 38, 42, 49–51, 58, 62–64, 73, 82, 86–87, 97–99, 104, 107–8, 113–14, 118–19, 122, 127, 132, 135, 138, 155, 162–63, 166, 171, 174–75, 181, 183–84
fan fiction, 40–42; fan fictional approach to staging the Bible, 6, 31, 35–61, 64, 93, 147, 149–50, 154, 175, 177
Farnum, Hilda, 100
Feiffer, Jules, 80
Fenderson, Alonzo, 71 ill.
Fenholt, Jeff, 147, 153 ill., 154–55, 157
Fergusson, Francis, 98
Ferris, Walter, 6
Fiddler on the Roof, 79, 109–10, 184
fidelity criticism, 18–19. *See also* adaptation
Fifth Season, The, 105
Finkelstein, Louis, 133
Firstborn, The, 9
Fisher, James, 135, 138
Fiske, Harrison Grey, 1–2, 39, 55–57, 82
Fiske, Minnie Maddern ("Mrs. Fiske"), 53–57
Fletcher, John, 4
Fliotsos, Anne L, 55
Flood, *see* Noah
Flowering Peach, The, 5, 9, 32, 93, 103–11, 114, 132–33, 137, 163, 167, 174, 184. See also *Two by Two*
Flynn, Gertrude, 96
Ford's Theatre (Washington, D. C.), 168
Forster, Arnold, 155–56
14th Street Theatre, 53
Francis, Ivor, 130
Freedman, Gerald, 84
Freiburg Passion Play, The, 6, 60, 61n69, 144n10, 166
Fresnay, Pierre, 94, 95 ill., 97–98
Friedkin, David, 96
Frohman, Charles, 7
Funny Thing Happened on the Way to the Forum, A, 142
Fry, Christopher, 9

Gad, Josh, 183
Gallie, W. B., 23
Gardenia, Vincent, 136, 138–39
Garey, Doris B., 74
Garland, Robert, 70, 94, 96–99
Gaul, George, 122
General Church of the Nazarene (Kansas City), 172
Genesis, Book of, 7, 9, 23, 32–33, 40, 61, 62–115, 118, 146, 168–71, 180
Gersten, Berta, 104–5, 106 ill.
Gideon (play), 9, 10
Gilbert, Fraye, 96
Gilder, Jeannette, 8
Gladiator, The, 36
Glover, William, 82, 179
God (biblical figure), 16–18, 22–25, 32, 38–40, 45–46, 59–81, 83–84, 86–94, 96–99, 102–5, 106 ill., 107–10, 113–16, 118–20, 123–24, 126–28, 131–41, 144, 152, 155, 163, 169–72, 174, 179–81, 184
God's Favorite, 7, 33, 120, 135–40, 175
Godspell, 9, 15, 33, 144–45, 157–67, 169–72, 174–76, 179, 181, 184–85
Goldbergs, The, 105
Golden Boy, 103
Goldman, William, 178
Goldstein, Daniel, 9
Gone with the Wind (novel), 37
Gospel Trumpet Company, 152
Gottfried, Martin, 80n65, 89, 110, 176
Goz, Harry, 109, 112n91
Grace, Edward, 2
Graham, Billy, 137, 158
Graham, Martha, 134
Grand Opera House (St. Louis), 51
Grant, Rev. Percy Stickney, 58–59
graven images, see Second Commandment
Green Grow the Lilacs, 21
Green Pastures, The, 8, 10–11, 25, 28, 32–33, 60–61, 63–82, 85–87, 90–91, 94, 96–99, 102–3, 107–8, 114, 124, 137, 165, 167, 174–76, 179, 183–84; film adaptation, 65
Greenbaum, Norman, 151
Grizzard, George, 83–84, 88 ill.
Gronemann, Sammy, 176
Gruen, John, 154
Guiliani, Rudy, 141
Gussow, Mel, 148, 169

Habima theater company, 177
Hair, 156, 160
Hall Johnson Chorus, 75–76
Ham (biblical figure), 6n24, 92, 96, 102, 104
Hamilton, Clayton, 57
Hamlet, 68, 122
Hammerstein, Oscar II, 21, 183
Hampden, Walter, 122
Hannaman, Ross, 146
Hard Job Being God, 33, 174–75, 179–81,
Hariss, R. P., 176
Harnick, Sheldon, 9, 79–80
Harris, Barbara, 79, 81, 84–85
Harris, Jed, 68
Harrison, Richard B., 69–72, 76–77, 82, 89–90
Hauptmann, Richard Bruno, 94
Hebrews (ancient people), 117–18, 180
Hebrews, Book of, 16, 175n2
Heinemann, Margot, 13
Henry Sienkiewicz, 6, 8
Here Comes Mr. Jordan, 136
heresy, 22–25, 77, 149, 152, 155, 163
Herod (biblical figure), 44, 148, 150
Heyse, Paul [Paul Johann Ludwig von Heyse], 6, 36, 55–8, 154
Hingle, Pat, 128
Hippodrome, 61, 166
Holbrook, Hal, 84
Holy City, The, 55
Hopkins, Arthur, 68
horses, 28, 47–48, 50–51, 53, 178
Horst, Louis, 92
Hosea (biblical figure), 68, 74
Houchin, John, 13
Houseman, John, 100
Howard, Jay R., 151
Huckleberry Finn, 75
Hughes, Alice, 107
Hughes, Amy, 27, 43–44, 46, 49, 76
Hughes, Langston, 76
Huneker, James, 17
Hutcheon, Linda, 18–19, 25

I'm Solomon, 9, 33, 174–81
Incident at Vichy, 82
irony, 14, 22, 26–27, 29–30, 32–33, 39, 64, 78, 82, 87, 90, 94, 108, 113–14, 120, 128, 130–31, 134, 138–40, 144,

147, 149, 160–63, 171–72, 174, 180, 183–85
irreverence, 59, 150, 184. *See also* reverence
Isaac (biblical figure), 67, 181
Isherwood, Charles, 16
Israel (biblical figure), *see* Jacob
Israel, land of (*eretz Israel*), 42, 149, 157, 176–77, 180; America-Israel Cultural Foundation, 9

J. B., 9–10, 33, 81, 120, 125–36, 138–39, 149, 163, 184
Jacob (biblical figure), 59, 169, 181
Jakobsen, Janet R., 14
Japhet (biblical figure), 96, 104–5
Jenkins, Henry, 27, 41
Jens, Salome, 178
Jerome, Jerome K, 6
Jesus Christ (biblical figure), 1–2, 4, 6, 7, 9, 14, 16–17, 37–47, 49, 51–53, 55–61, 83n, 76, 144–45, 147–67, 172, 179, 181, 184
Jesus Christ Superstar, 9–10, 29, 33, 65, 142, 144–60, 162, 165–69, 174–76, 179–80, 182
Jesus People movement, 151, 164
Jewison, Norman, 157
Jews, 9, 11–12, 15, 23, 32, 37, 39–40, 43–5, 59–60, 62, 78, 82, 88–89, 92–93, 105–8, 110–12, 114, 118, 132, 135, 140, 148, 152, 155–56, 158, 164, 169, 181, 184; Hassidism, 98
Job (biblical figure), 7, 9, 32, 115–40, 175–76
John the Baptist (biblical figure), 43, 45, 53, 162
John, Gospel according to, 10, 149, 154n43
Johnson, Hall, *see* Hall Johnson Chorus
Johnson, James Weldon, 9
Jones, Henry Arthur, 52
Jones, John Bush, 159–60
Jones, Megan Sanborn, 11
Jones, Robert Edmond, 69
Joseph and His Brethren, 59
Joseph and the Amazing Technicolor Dreamcoat, 9–10, 59, 65, 144–48, 167–71, 180
Joseph, son of Israel (biblical figure), 59, 168–70

Judas (1910, John DeKay), 6, 8
Judas (1929, Walter Ferris and Basil Rathbone), 6
Judas (biblical figure), 6, 45, 55, 147–50, 152, 155–57, 162, 164

Kahn, Madeline, 109, 112n91
Kalem, T. E., 81
Katz, (Rabbi) Jacob, 78
Kaufman, George S., 66, 68
Kazan, Elia, 126–27, 132, 134
Keighley, William, 65
Kelley, Edgar Stillman, 8, 37
Kennedy, Charles O'Brien, 77
Kennedy, Charles Ramm, 60
Kerr, Walter, 80, 158, 165
King and I, The, 183
King David (biblical figure), 181
King David (musical), 9
King James Version, 17, 86, 92, 165
King Solomon and the Cobbler, 176
Kirshenblatt-Gimblett, Barbara, 28
Kissell, Howard, 135–36
Klaw, Marc, 37
Knickerbocker Theatre, 7, 52
Kolitz, Zvi, 176–78
Kroll, Jack, 87n100, 138
Kushner, (Rabbi) Harold, 118–99, 137, 139

La MaMa (Café La MaMa), 158
Lafayette Theatre, 92, 99–100, 102
Laird, Paul, 160, 170–71
Lamb's Theatre Company, 172
Lambert, Virginia, 106
Lambs Club, 171–73
Lamos, Mark, 84
Lansbury, Edgar, 158
Last Days of Pompeii, The, 36, 52
Leeds, Rev. Josiah W., 13
Lennon, John, 152
Les Misérables, 146
Levy, Shimon, 4, 18, 116
Life Magazine, 25, 126, 132–33
Lifson, Amy, 42
Lindbergh, Charles, 94
Lion King, The, 184
lions, 94, 95 ill., 178
Lippmann, Walter, 75
Lisanby, Charles, 170
Living Theatre, 157, 160n71

Lloyd Webber, Andrew, 10, 16, 33, 144–57, 167–70
Lloyd, Norman, 96
Lopez, Robert, 182
Lowry, Judith, 123, 130
Lucifer, 83–84, 87–89
Lucrece, 94
Lundell, William Warner, 72–73
Lutherans, 24
Lyric Theatre (London), 7

Mackay, Constance D'Arcy, 120
Macleish, Archibald, 9, 81, 116, 120, 125–36, 138–39, 184
Maeterlinck, Maurice, 55
Magic Show, The, 167
Man of La Mancha, 142
Manhattan Church of the Nazarene, 171–72
Manhattan Theatre (33rd St), 53–54
Mansfield Theatre, 70, 72
Mantle, Burns, 73
Marat/Sade, 88
Mark Hellinger Theatre, 142–44, 159, 175
Mark, Gospel according to, 10, 165, 172
Marquis Theatre, 141
Marshall, Logan, 146
Martel, Tom, 33, 179–81
Martin, Nan, 130, 132
Mary Magdalen (novel), 55–56
Mary Magdalene (biblical figure), 6, 29, 147, 153 ill., 154
Mary Magdalene (play), 55
Mary of Bethany (biblical figure), 154
Mary of Magdala, 6, 36, 42, 53–60, 149, 154
Mary, mother of Jesus (biblical figure), 9, 44, 58, 75
Masks, 96, 100, 127–28, 129 ill., 130–31, 134, 183–84
Massey, Raymond, 126–27, 129 ill.
Matthew, Gospel according to, 17n59, 43n21, 44, 165
Matthews, Ralph, 100, 102
Mayer, David, 35–36, 42
McClain, John, 132
McConachie, Bruce, 133–34
McCowen, Alex, 172
McHarry, Charles, 177–78
McLaughlin, Robert, 6

Me and My Girl, 146
Mears, Stannard, 121
Medina, Louis, 36
Meisner, Sanford, 88
Merton of the Movies, 66
Michael and His Lost Angel, 52
Midrash, 40–44, 107, 147, 176
Midsummer Night's Dream, A, 19
Mighty Nimrod, The, 79
Migliore, Daniel L., 158–59, 163–64
Miller, Arthur, 32, 41, 63, 81–90, 180
Milton, John, 83
Miracle, The, 75
Mirsky, Mark, 41
Modern Reader's Bible, The, 117
Monroe, Marilyn, 81
Moore, (Pastor) Paul, 172
Mordden, Ethan, 145–46
Morgan, David, 152
Morgan, William Astor, see Stor, Jean
Mormons, 11, 23–24, 166, 182–84. See also Book of Mormon, The
Morrison, Priestly, 52
Morse, Salmi, 1–3, 7, 18, 34–35, 38–40, 60, 118, 144n9
Mosely, Thomas, 101
Moses (biblical figure), 6, 23–4, 71 ill., 108, 180n29
Moss, Carlton, 92, 99–102, 113
Moulton, Richard G., 117–18, 120–21, 123, 126
Mower, Margaret, 130
music, 8, 32, 37, 47, 49, 53, 59, 68, 75–76, 92, 99, 100, 123, 130, 143, 146–52, 157, 160, 162, 164, 166, 168, 170–71, 179–85; musicals, 9–10, 21, 33, 64, 79–80, 93, 102, 109–12, 142–70, 174–85; rock and roll, 33, 144–52, 156–58, 160, 179–81. See also Christian rock
Muslims, 23–24, 92, 140
Musser, Charles, 1
My Fair Lady, 142
mystery plays., 4, 39, 58, 91, 98. See also cycle plays

Nathan, Stephen, 161 ill.
nativity, holy, 39, 44–45; nativity pageants, 11, 18
Negro Theatre (Federal Theatre Project Negro Unit), 92, 99–102, 113
Nero (Emperor of Rome), 7, 51

Nichols, Anne, 12
Nichols, Mike, 80
Niebuhr, Reinhold, 132–33
Night Journey, 134
Nixon, Richard, 135
Noah (2014 feature film), 114
Noah (Andre Obey), 5, 29, 32, 79, 92, 94–99, 175, 184; adaptation by Carlton Moss, 92, 99–102
Noah (biblical figure), 6n24, 24, 32, 68, 91–115, 118, 135, 138, 140
Noah, M[ordecai] M[anuel], 12
Nordell, Roderick, 112
Norton, Elliott, 126
nudity, 87, 160n71

O'Connor, John J., 110
O'Horgan, Tom, 150, 154, 156
O'Neill, Eugene, 1
O'Neill, James, 1, 59
Oberammergau Passionspiel, 39, 126–27
Obey, André, 29, 32, 79, 92, 94–105, 113
Ocean (musical group), 151
Odd Couple, The, 135
Odets, Clifford, 9, 32, 93–94, 103–12, 114, 138
offstage voice, 18, 57, 60, 67, 123–24, 131, 134, 136, 138, 140
Oklahoma!, 21, 109
Oppenheimer, George, 107
Oppenheimer, J. Robert, 134n87
Os-ke-non-ton, 124–25
Osmond, Donny, 169
Otten, Terry, 86–87
Ottley, Roi, 101–2

Pacino, Al, 9
pageants, 4, 11, 18, 39, 49, 61, 74, 91, 113, 170–71, 182; pageant wagons, 15, 91
Palm, Matthew, 171
Paper Mill Playhouse, 170
Paradise Lost, 83
Pargod Studio, 176
Parker, Louis, 59
Parker, Trey, 182, 183n34
Passing of the Third Floor Back, The, 6
Passion narrative (Biblical), 38, 45, 47, 55–56, 157

Passion of the Christ, The (film), 154n44
Passion play, 4, 7, 9, 11, 15, 33, 37–39, 159
Passion, The (play by Salmi Morse), 1–3, 7, 18, 34–36, 38, 40, 55–56, 118, 144n9, 175
Passover Seder, *see* Seder
Pellegrini, Ann, 14
Pentecostalism, 143–4
Phantom of the Opera, 146
Pharaoh (biblical figure), 6, 59, 147n20, 180
Pippin, 160, 167
Piscator, Erwin, 176
Plato, 21
Play of the Resurrection of the Lord, 58
Plummer, Christopher, 127, 129 ill., 132
Plunkett, Edward, 18th Baron of Dunsany (Lord Dunsany), 124
Pontius Pilate (biblical figure), 45, 148
Pope Gregory, 154
Powell, Adam Clayton Sr., 69
Price, The, 82
Prime of Miss Jean Brodie, The, 85
Primus, Barry, 84
Prince Edward Theatre (London), 170
Prisoner of Second Avenue, The, 135
Probst, Leonard, 167
Prodigal Son, The, 59
Promenade Theatre, 158–60
Protestants, 1, 12–13, 23, 39, 132, 152
Pslams, Book of, 175n3
Puchner, Martin, 13
Pulitzer Prize, 10–11, 65, 76, 93, 125, 127, 132
Pulitzer, Joseph, Jr., 93
Punch and Judy Theatre, 124
Purimspiel (Purim play), 4, 11, 13

Quakers, 13
Quem quaeritis, 11, 57–58, 166
Quo Vadis, 6, 8, 10

rabbis, 40n10, 55, 62, 78, 118; rabbinic tradition, 40–41
Ramses II, *see* Pharaoh
Rannells, Andrew, 183
Rathbone, Basil, 132
Rathbone, Basil, 6, 132

Raven, Charles E., 78
Redford, Robert, 136
Regan, Sylvia, 105
Reilly, Charles Nelson, 136, 138
Reinhardt, Max, 75, 79
reverence, 23, 25–29, 38, 42, 49–50, 57,
    72, 82, 93, 107, 112, 123, 127, 134,
    139–40, 163, 165. *See also* irrever-
    ence
Revised Standard Version, 17, 65n11
Rice, Tim, 10, 33, 144–57, 167–70, 180
Richards, David, 89
Riggs, Lynn, 21
Ritual, 5, 11, 15, 18, 24, 28, 72, 74,
    105, 127, 144, 152, 160, 163
Rivers, Laurence, *see* Stebbins, Row-
    land
rock and roll, *see* music
Rodgers, Richard, 21, 93, 109, 11, 183
Rose, Susan, 168
Rothschilds, The, 110
Roundabout Theatre Company, 9, 80
Rowe, Billy, 91, 100–1
Royale Theatre, 168
Ruhl, Arthur, 73, 97

Sallman, Warner, 152
Salome (play), 9, 59
Saltus, Edgar, 55–56
Sanders, Kevin, 87
Sanger, Frank W., 7
Sara (biblical figure), 180
Satan (biblical figure), 83, 116, 119,
    123, 127–31, 136–37. *See also* Luci-
    fer
Savran, David, 10
Schenck, Elliott, 123
Schiff, Ellen, 108
Schneider, Rebecca, 50
Schwartz, Stephen, 33, 158, 160, 164–
    65, 167, 170–71
Scientific American, 47–48
Scott, Clement, 49
Second City, 157
Second Commandment, 18, 38–40
Second Vatican Council, 151, 155
seder, 40n10, 74
Segal, Erich, 177n14, 178
Selassie, Haile, 178
Seldes, Gilbert, 73–74, 98
Seventeen, 121–22
Shakespeare, William, 19, 21, 136

Shaw, Fiona, 9
Shaw, George Bernard, 60, 105
Sheaffer, Louis, 105
Sheen, (Bishop) Fulton, 154
Shem (biblical figure), 96, 104–5, 109
Shipman, Herbert, 70
Shubert Theatre, 80–81
Sign of the Cross, The, 6–8, 16, 31, 36,
    41, 51–53, 58, 60, 175
Simon, Joan Baim, 135
Simon, John, 150, 169
Simon, Neil, 7, 33, 120, 135–39
sincerity, 26–27, 29–30, 32–33, 38, 42,
    64, 72–5, 77, 82, 86, 88–90, 93, 97–
    99, 112–14, 120, 122–27, 131–32,
    134, 139–40, 144, 152, 154, 157, 160,
    162–67, 170–71, 174, 179–85
Skin of Our Teeth, The, 7, 80, 126
Skulnik, Menasha, 104–8, 112
Smith, Gerald L. K., 4
Smith, J. A. ("Gus"), 100
Smith, Joseph, 182–83
Society of Friends, *see* Quakers
Sofer, Andrew, 57–58
Sokolow, Anna, 92, 98
Solomon (biblical figure), 176–78,
    181
Soloveitchik, Joseph, 62–63
Sommo, Yehuda, *see* di Somi, Leone
Sound of Music, The, 142
South Park, 182
spectacle, 2, 8, 17, 26–28, 30–33, 35–
    38, 43–53, 57, 59, 64, 66, 72, 76–77,
    79, 85–87, 93, 98–99, 102, 112–13,
    120, 122–23, 126, 128, 134, 138, 140,
    144, 149–50, 160–63, 170–71, 175–
    78, 180, 183
Sponsler, Claire, 4, 127, 155n47
St. Augustine of Hippo, 154
Stange, Hugh Stanislaus, 121
Star Spangled Girl, The, 138
Star Trek, 40, 183
Stebbins, Rowland, aka Laurence Riv-
    ers, 68–70
Stehli, Edgar, 123
Stern, David, 41
Stern, Harold, 106–7
Stern, Norton B., 1n2
Sternfeld, Jessica, 145, 160, 169
Stevenson, Jill, 27–28, 49–50, 59
Stewart, Ellen, 158
Stigwood, Robert, 147–48, 156

Stitzel, Elliott Pershing, *see* Elliott, Stephen
Stockdale, Eugene, 123
Stockton, Frank R., 80
Stone, Matt, 182, 183n34
Stone, Peter, 93, 109, 11
Stor, Jean, aka William Astor Morgan, 100
Stowe, Harriet Beecher, 36
Stratton, Matthew, 30
Streck, John M., 151
Strober, Gerald S., 155
Stuart Walker Portmanteau Theatre Company, *see* Walker, Stuart
Sunday, Billy, 50

tablet theory, 24
Tebelak, John Michael, 157–58, 162, 164–65
Tempest, The, 88
Tents of the Arabs, The, 124
Terrible Meek, The, 60
Testament of Mary, The (play), 9, 55n55
Throckmorton, Cleon, 96
ticket sales, 10, 14–15, 53, 81, 109, 112; advance sales, 148, 156
Tidings Brought to Mary, The, 75
Times Square Church, 141–44, 171
Times Square, 141–44, 171–73, 185
toga plays, 35–36, 64
Tóibín, Colm, 9, 55n55
Tokke, Hans, 142–33
Tomei, Marisa, 9
Tony (Antoinette Perry) Awards, 7n25, 10, 88, 132, 182
Torah, 23, 40n10
transcendence, 3, 5, 26–28, 30, 49–51, 53, 58, 66, 134, 163, 170, 184; transcendental signifier, 22
Trilling, Lionel, 29
Trumpets of the Lord, 9
Twain, Mark, 79–80
Two by Two, 9, 32, 93, 109–14; *see also Flowering Peach, The*

Uncle Remus, 75
Uncle Tom's Cabin, 36, 75, 183

Vatican II, *see* Second Vatican Council
Vereen, Ben, 152, 156
vernacular language, 66, 97, 100, 105, 165, 168, 179–80
Vierow, Wendy, 55
Vincent, Tony, 156
Voodoo Macbeth, 100
Voutsinas, Eliphaz, 130

Wagner, Robin, 149
Waiting for Lefty, 103
Walker, Stuart, 32, 120–25, 127, 130, 139, 184
Wallace, [General] Lew, 8, 35–38, 40, 42–45, 51–52
Walls, (Revered) Alfred, 116–18
Walsh, Michael, 146–47
Walters, Grover C., 77
Watt, Douglas, 86, 136, 167
Watts, Richard, 75, 81, 90, 132
Weill, Kurt, 79
Welland, Dennis, 86
Welles, Orson, 100
Werfel, Franz, 79
Wetmore, Kevin, 14
White, Stanford, 172
Whitehead, Robert, 84–85, 104
Wicked, 160
The Wife with the Smile, 94
Wilde, Oscar, 9, 59
Wilder, Thornton, 7, 80, 94, 126
Wilkerson, (Pastor) David, 141–44
Williams, Tennessee, 93
Wilmurt, Arthur, 92, 94, 97–100
Wilson, Edwin, 86–87
Winchell, Walter, 70–71
Winter, William, 55
Witham, Barry, 102
Wolf, Stacy, 159, 163, 167
Wollman, Elizabeth, 149–50, 160
Wonder Book of Bible Stories, 146
Wooster Group, The, 19n64
"wow" moment, 27–8, 51
Wyatt, Euphemia Van Rensselaer, 103, 107

Yiddish language, 14n49, 89, 105; dialect, 103, 106–7, 111–12
Yiddish theater, 95, 105, 168

Young, Josh, 156
Young, William, 6, 8, 37

Zimmerer, Frank, 123, 124 ill.
Zolotow, Sam, 177